I0700020

PAPERBOY

A Dylan Tomassi Novel

Dan Romanello

Paperboy (A Dylan Tomassi Novel)
Copyright © 2022 by Daniel J. Romanello, Sanitas Publishing, Inc.

For more about this author please visit authordanromanello.com

This is a work of fiction. Names, characters, businesses, places, events, locales, and incidents are either the products of the author's imagination or used in a fictitious manner. Any resemblance to actual persons, living or dead, or actual events is purely coincidental.

All rights reserved. No part of this publication may be reproduced, distributed, or transmitted in any form or by any means, including photocopying, recording, or other electronic or mechanical methods, without the prior written permission of the publisher, except in the case of brief quotations embodied in critical reviews and certain other noncommercial uses permitted by copyright law. Please do not participate in or encourage piracy of copyrighted materials in violation of the author's rights.

For permission requests, write to:
authordanromanello@gmail.com

Editing by The Pro Book Editor
Cover Design by Matthew Watson
Interior Design by IAPS.rocks

paperback ISBN: 979-8-9863151-0-2

    1. Main category—FICTION / Literary
    2. Other category—FICTION / Coming of Age

First Edition

PROLOGUE

D YLAN MCDIRT FURIOUSLY PUMPED THE pedals of his Peugeot ten-speed bicycle as he raced along Stillwater Drive. His eyes teared from the combination of a chilling autumn wind and the anger seething inside his body. It had happened again for the third time in the past two weeks. As he neared the end of his paper route delivering the afternoon edition of the *Stamford Advocate*, he discovered he was short three newspapers. By the time he got the replacement papers to his customers, it would be dark outside and well past the dinner hour. This was not good.

Dylan had been working the paper route for a little over two months. A neighborhood kid had retired at the end of the summer, following his middle school graduation, and bequeathed it to him. The boy had wanted to sell Dylan the route. The going rate at the time was two dollars per unit, and the boy had twenty-two customers. However, the boy's father would have none of it. James Burns had a soft spot for Dylan. He admired the young boy's chutzpah. The elder Burns had proudly stated as much while overseeing the transition of the route and secretly financing the sale to placate his son, Jimmy.

Privately, James Burns's true motivation for the benevolent act had been his habit of sneaking lustful glances at Dylan's mother, Cheryl McDirt. She was raising her son alone in a small house on Cold Springs Road in Stamford, Connecticut. The Burns family lived nearby on Windsor Street. It was the highlight of Mr. Burns's day when he could steal a glimpse of Cheryl with her curly black hair, olive skin, and curvaceously taut body.

Cheryl McDirt was the only child of Anthony and Isabella Tomassi. The Tomassis still lived in Norwalk where Cheryl had grown up. Her father was tall and broad-shouldered with proportionately strong legs and a head of thick, white hair. He maintained defined musculature for a man in his early sixties, owing his physique to a good gene pool and a career as a self-employed mason. Anthony had begun plying his trade of laying bricks and concrete blocks not long after emigrating to the United States from Italy as a young teen and continued until his semi-retirement a year earlier. Anthony was known for his meticulous work, honesty, and easy-going personality. Accordingly, side jobs from word-of-mouth referrals had him out of the house most weekday mornings. Isabella, possessing classic dark, southern Italian features, was a homemaker who took exquisite care of her family. Among her fine qualities, she was an outstanding cook who specialized in cuisine from her native country.

Cheryl had graduated from Norwalk High School and received a degree in elementary education from Western Connecticut State College in Danbury. Her parents were proud of her for obtaining a college degree and hopeful she would escape the deteriorating conditions of their South Norwalk neighborhood and its loathsome characters. Unfortunately, things hadn't all gone as planned. However, the Tomassis showered their daughter with love and support and doted over their only grandchild.

Cheryl, a devout Roman Catholic, taught fourth grade at St. Mary School and moonlighted on weekends as a waitress at the Rockrimmon Country Club. Money had been tight in the McDirt household since Cheryl's husband and Dylan's father, Colin, left home when Dylan was two.

Colin McDirt had been Cheryl's classmate at Norwalk High School. The son of Irish immigrants, he had been a standout athlete. He'd achieved the rare distinction of being named to the Fairfield County All Region teams in football, basketball, and baseball in both his junior and senior years. He was handsome and charming and cut a dashing figure at six foot four. He was also gifted with tremendous speed and athleticism.

Colin went hard in everything he did. His highly aggressive style on the field and on the court earned him the moniker 'McDirty.' His high school career ended abruptly in the final game of his senior year after he initiated a bench clearing brawl during a baseball game against rival Brien McMahon High. Colin was ejected, suspended from school, and never graduated.

Colin began his post-high school career working the assembly line in a textile factory on the Norwalk waterfront. His shift ran from eight in the morning until four in the afternoon. He got a half hour for lunch and regularly spent it at Donovan's Bar on Washington Street, a short walk from the factory. He also stopped by daily after work before heading home. On Fridays, Colin cashed his paycheck at Donavan's, paid his tab, and brought home the difference.

In the summer of 1974, Cheryl had returned home to Norwalk after graduating from West Conn. One night she went out to Donavon's with some girlfriends and ran into Colin. A brief romance ensued, and Cheryl found herself pregnant. Given her devout Catholic beliefs, there was only one option. Against her parents' wishes, Cheryl and Colin were married in a quiet ceremony and settled in a small guest house on the Tomassi property.

Dylan Anthony McDirt was born the following year. Cheryl wanted to name the baby Anthony, but Colin would not hear of it. Shortly after Dylan's second birthday, Colin left for work one morning and never returned home. Neither Cheryl nor Dylan had heard from him since.

When Dylan first obtained the paper route, he'd set out an aggressive expansion plan for his fledgling business. He'd gone to the library, obtained a Xerox copy of a map of the surrounding neighborhoods, and sectioned off an area bounded by Stillwater Road to the west, Bridge Street to the south, and Route 137 to the east. He'd then knocked on every door and offered a subscription to the *Advocate*.

Aside from the usual negative reception resulting from door-to-door solicitations, additional unforeseen consequences had arisen. First, many of the households already received the *Advocate*. A small number had called the newspaper to complain, and Dylan had received a reprimand from his new corporate partner. Second, word had reached his fellow carriers and a few of those young entrepreneurs had been even less enthused with Dylan's practices. One competitor, an eleven-year-old named TJ Marin, had voiced his displeasure to Dylan, threatening that if he saw him around town, he could expect to receive a beating.

Dylan had repeated the same routine each day after school since he started the route. He went home each afternoon and changed out of his Catholic school uniform. At the appointed time, he rode his bike down to the end of Cold Springs Road to pick up the papers. He was required to pay the *Advocate* in advance and collect the subscription fees from his customers. The difference between the wholesale price and the retail subscription fee, plus tips, represented his profits.

The papers were delivered to the carriers in bundles of twenty-five. Because Dylan had only twenty-two customers, he'd received a single, partial bundle each day. Although he'd stopped his door-to-door sales campaign, unexpected fallout had continued. On occasion, toward the end of his route, Dylan discovered he did not have all twenty-two papers. This required him to ride home, call the newspaper circulation department, and wait for the extras to be delivered. Five of the six customers at the end of his route who had received the tardy papers had canceled their subscriptions. The one who'd remained loyal lived in the large gray house at the end of Travis Avenue.

Frustrated with the experience, Dylan had taken up the issue with the *Advocate*. A cursory investigation concluded that all twenty-two papers were dropped at the end of the road each day. Beyond that point, it was Dylan's responsibility. Consequently, each time the shortage occurred, he was billed for the original papers plus the replacements. Unfortunately, the problem persisted sporadically.

It became a simple matter of economics. Increased business expenses were cutting into his profits. The *Advocate* charged each carrier eighty-five cents for a week's worth of papers. The carriers billed their customers weekly for the standard $1.35 home-delivery subscription rate. The customers obtained a discount off the newsstand prices of twenty-five cents daily and fifty cents on Sunday. Dylan had initially figured to make about fifteen dollars a week. However, he was billed fifteen cents for each replacement paper, which included an additional delivery charge. It would have cost him more on Sundays, but fortunately, the papers were never missing on Sunday mornings. Between the cost of replacement papers and the five lost accounts, Dylan's profits had plummeted to about eleven dollars a week.

Dylan also had to cover an expansive area because his accounts were spread out geographically. They overlapped with other routes, including a significantly larger route operated by TJ. Marin. Consequently, it took him about an hour each day to deliver the papers. Accordingly, he was making about a $1.50 an hour, less than half the $3.35 minimum wage and well below what other neighborhood boys earned raking leaves or shoveling snow. Frustrated and losing money, he had been determined to take matters into his own hands but unsure how to proceed.

As an eight-year-old, Dylan was naturally apprehensive about dealing with adults. On Fridays, customers were expected to pay him the weekly subscription fee. After initially knocking on every customer's door and introducing himself, predictable patterns emerged. Some customers routinely left the money in a predetermined spot. Others answered the door and handed him payment in exchange for the paper. A few required several weeks to track down, compelling him to employ the dreaded practice of rousting the delinquent customers out of bed when he delivered the *Advocate* on Sunday mornings. On each occasion, Dylan promptly recorded payment in his notebook ledger, which included the address, full names of each household member, and any specific delivery requests. Likewise, in terms of gratuities, a consistent pattern developed. About half paid with a single dollar bill, a quarter, and a dime. A good number gave him a dollar bill and two quarters, and some a little more. Dylan had met all his customers, with a single exception—the one who lived in the old, gray Victorian house at 216 Travis Avenue.

On his first Friday on the route, Dylan had approached the old gray Victorian and noticed a note taped to its massive oak front door. It was folded in half, addressed simply to Paperboy and instructed him to leave the paper in the cedar box on the side of the porch. It further stated that payment would be inside the box each Friday. Henceforth, an old tobacco tin appeared on the fifth day of each week with an assortment of coins totaling exactly $1.35. The ritual had continued with remarkable consistency for the first two months.

The weather was miserable on the Friday following Dylan's most recent encounter with the missing papers, another chilly, early-autumn day with intermittent drizzle. He shivered from the cold and wet as he came to the end of his route. As he approached the Victorian house, he dropped his bike, leaned forward, and ran onto the covered porch seeking a brief respite from the elements. As he walked over to the cedar box, he noticed a note attached to the front door. It appeared to be unaddressed. When he opened the box, the familiar tobacco tin was missing. Instinctively, he glanced around the porch, walked back to the door, and reached for the note. It read, "Please come in."

Upon reading it, Dylan paced up and down the porch uncertainly as he pondered whether the note was meant for him. He took a moment to look around the property and focused on its details for the first time. It was clearly the largest house in the working-class neighborhood and situated at the end of the road on a deep, sprawling lot. In the distance, he heard the flowing waters of the Rippowam River. He stared up at the oversized front door. Dylan was big for his age, measuring just under five-and-a-half-feet tall, and the imposing door seemed almost twice his height.

Dylan stood there apprehensively a moment longer. He finally took a deep breath and pressed down on the brass handle. The door opened inward and he stepped into a large marble foyer with vaulted ceilings. The foyer opened to the second level, accessible by a spiral staircase with wrought iron railings. A large crystal chandelier hung from the ceiling, illuminating the foyer and a large sitting room off to the right.

Dylan looked over and saw a thin, old woman with coiffed, gray hair dressed in a powder-blue pants suit and black orthopedic shoes. She sat on a couch opposite two matching upholstered chairs. A large, antique coffee table separated the furnishings and a fire blazed in the stone fireplace. A heavy, expensive-looking oil painting, framed in ornate wood, hung above the stone mantel.

Dylan felt a wave of relief wash through his body. He wasn't sure what he had expected but it definitely was not a frail and indolent-looking old woman. She appeared able to pass for his own grandmother's mother.

The woman spoke in a clear voice with a hint of old New England accent, "Please come in, young man, and sit for a moment."

Dylan dutifully wiped his feet on the large mat in the foyer entrance and hung up his slicker on the corner coatrack. He paid careful attention to avoid shedding any excess rainwater on the foyer's limestone floor before making his way to the sitting room. He took a seat in one of the chairs opposite the woman, sat up straight with his hands folded in his lap, and looked her in the eye. "Good afternoon ma'am. My name is Dylan McDirt. I hope I'm not intruding. I'm your new paperboy. I didn't see this week's payment in the box and I read the note on the door. His eyes left her for a brief moment to scan the room. "By the way, you have a lovely home."

"Why, thank you, my dear. My name is Esther Lott. What is it about the house that you admire most?"

"Well, I don't know much about fancy homes. My mom and I live in a small house. It's very comfortable, but nothing like this. I would have to say, though, that I admire the fireplace. My grandfather's a mason."

"How nice. What does your mother do?"

"She teaches fourth grade at St. Mary's."

"Are you in her class?"

"No, ma'am. I'm in third grade. I'll be in her class next year though."

"My, young man, you're big for a third grader. Were you held back?"

"No, ma'am. I do well in school. My mother sees to that. My grandfather is very tall, and I'm told my father is tall also."

"Where is your father?"

"I don't know. He left us when I was a baby. I don't remember him."

"Oh , that's very sad. A boy needs a father."

"Yes, ma'am, but I'm very fortunate. My mother is a special person. And my grandmother and grandfather are around. We all take care of each other."

"You seem like a remarkable young man. But I sense something is troubling you."

Since taking on the job, Dylan had become remarkably well versed in focusing on his customers' interests and concerns when interacting with them. However, on this occasion, Dylan inexplicably found himself opening up to

Esther Lott. He told her all about his saga with the missing newspapers and the resulting financial repercussions.

Esther Lott sat back in silence and listened patiently, seemingly in deep thought. Finally, she spoke. "It appears to me that some investigation is required on your part. What's been done so far?"

Dylan summarized the response from the *Advocate*. "I was told their investigation showed they delivered the correct number of papers to me each time. And once they're dropped at the end of the road, it's my responsibility."

"What if you were to arrive at the drop-off point early each day, meet the delivery driver, and count the papers together."

"That's a good idea. I usually go home after the bus drops me off. But I could go straight to the delivery spot and get there in time to meet him."

"Well then. Why don't you do that and let me know how it works out."

"I'll do that, Mrs. Lott. Thanks for the advice. It was a pleasure meeting you. Again, you have a beautiful home."

Dylan left, somewhat relieved and excited about the new plan to address his problem. As he pedaled home that day, he realized he hadn't collected from Esther Lott for the week.

Following his meeting with Esther Lott, Dylan formulated his plan. In the morning he packed a duffel bag with a change of clothes and an afternoon snack. After the final school bell, he quickly changed out of his uniform and ran to make the afternoon bus. He got off at the end of Cold Springs Road where the papers were delivered.

The initial meeting did not go well. Dylan waited along the side of the road for just a few minutes before an old, brown cab-over-van slowed down and briefly pulled over. The driver was an acne-pocked teen hippie with a trace of stubble around his mouth and chin. He reminded Dylan of the Shaggy character from the *Scooby-Doo* cartoon series. The driver stopped just long enough to throw a bundle of papers out of the van's passenger side window. As the van started to pull away, Dylan ran alongside and waved his arms frantically. "Hold up."

"Yo, li'l dude, what's up?" the Shaggy look-alike replied.

"I need your help. I keep getting shorted on my papers."

"Yeah, I heard something about that. You trying to get *me* in trouble? I don't have anything to do with counting out the papers. They come prepackaged from the printing plant. I'm just the delivery guy, and I got a lot more stops to make."

Dylan saw this was going nowhere fast. "Man, that's a cool flat nose. You got a custom interior in there?"

"What'd you know about vans? You're not old enough to drive."

"No, but I'm huge into cars. I read all the magazines while I'm at the store. *Car and Driver*, *Motor Trend*, even *Van World*."

"Whoa, *Van World* is the bomb. I just finished carpeting the interior and putting in a turntable with new speakers. Wanna check it out?"

"Sure. By the way, I'm Dylan. What's your name?"

"I'm Ralph Johnson, but everyone calls me RJ."

"Nice to meet you, RJ. Are those Jensen speakers?"

A half hour later, after discussing custom vans, Jethro Tull, and the Kiss stage show, RJ agreed to stop and count papers with Dylan each day, provided he was there waiting when RJ arrived.

"If I pull up and you're not here, li'l dude, I'm gone."

"No problem, RJ. I'll be here."

"Cool, anything for a fellow rock 'n' roll gear head."

The new routine worked smoothly for a couple of weeks. RJ usually arrived within ten minutes after the bus dropped Dylan off. RJ stopped, quickly counted the papers, and after a friendly exchange, the two went their separate ways. Each time Dylan then lugged the bundle of papers back to the house, dropped off his books, and grabbed his bike.

One day, RJ showed up, counted out seventeen papers, and handed them to Dylan. He then motioned to the back of the van. "Hey, I just got these new struts installed. The van's all jacked up with the front end dropped down. A real badass ride. How 'bout we go for a spin?"

"Sure," Dylan stated as he subconsciously dropped the papers on the side of the road and hopped into the front passenger seat.

Dylan strapped himself in with the lap belt and RJ peeled out with Twisted Sister's "I Wanna Rock" blaring from the speakers.

RJ shouted above the music. "I just saw them live this past weekend at the Fore and Aft in Brewster. Dee Snider really puts on a show."

"Cool," Dylan yelled back.

RJ had driven down Route 104, turned around, and headed back to Dylan's drop-off point. Only gone about ten minutes, what they saw upon returning surprised them both.

"Would you look at that. That's that Marin punk," RJ said. "I caught him throwing eggs at my van one time. No one messes with my ride."

Dylan thought fast. "Hey, RJ, pull over here and wait a minute. Let's see what he does."

RJ pulled over behind another parked car, about fifty yards from where TJ Marin stood over Dylan's paper bundle, and turned down the music. Marin was older than Dylan but slightly shorter. He was stocky and built like a fire plug. He had long, black hair that reached below his shoulders and concealed his short thick neck. It almost appeared as if Marin's head rested directly on his shoulders. His hair was tucked behind the ears and a cigarette protruded from the right ear. The balance of the smokes in the Marlboro Red box was folded into the left sleeve of his T-shirt, unseasonable attire for that time of year. RJ and Dylan watched as Marin removed three newspapers from Dylan's bundle, got on his bike, and rode off in the opposite direction.

Dylan was visibly shaken. "What should we do about this?" he asked.

"Let me handle it," RJ replied. "I've known this thug for a couple years, and he's nothing but a loudmouth bully." He drove up to the remaining papers, and Dylan jumped out of the van. RJ continued, "Grab your bundle and get back in. I'll give you a ride back to your house. I've got some extra papers in the back. Go ahead and take what you need."

Dylan was quiet on the short ride to his house, but internally he was a mess. When they arrived, he'd gathered up his papers, thanked RJ, and departed the van.

"Don't you worry, I got this," RJ said as he sped off.

Dylan seethed with anger as he thought about all the trouble TJ Marin had caused him and the money he'd lost. However, he felt equally helpless and frustrated as he was unsure what to do about it. He finally decided to let RJ handle the matter. RJ appeared to fit the classic hippy profile he'd often heard about, part of the establishment's message that today's youth was going to hell in the proverbial handbasket. Still, he'd trusted him and figured he had no other options at the moment so he'd wait and see what happened.

Dylan had found out a week later when he was summoned to the *Advocate* offices in downtown Stamford. It was too far for him to travel on his own, so his grandfather picked him up early from school and drove him to the appointment. They were quiet on the trip as Anthony's old green Ford pickup truck rambled down the road. Upon their arrival, they met with Bill Pullian, the *Advocate*'s circulation director.

Dylan had heard of Bill Pullian but they had never met. He was a slightly built man with a bald pate and thin hair on the sides. He wore wire rimmed glasses and dressed in khaki pants, plaid shirt, and Spot-Bilt athletic shoes.

Pullian met Dylan and Anthony in the lobby and led them to a small conference room on the first floor.

After introductions were made and everyone was seated, Pullian began. "First, Dylan, I want to thank you for your dedication and service to our customers. It's a tough job and a big responsibility delivering the *Advocate* to our subscribers' homes each day. You've done an excellent job, particularly for someone your age. Most of our carriers are in middle school, some are even high school students."

"Thank you, sir," Dylan replied.

Pullian continued. "I also owe you an apology. Perhaps my department was a little harsh when the matter of the missing papers first arose. As the head of the circulation department, any omissions in the work we do here fall under my responsibility. We reopened our investigation, and it has now been brought to a final conclusion. TJ Marin has been expelled. Consequently, he has forfeited his route. The next issue we must address is the continued servicing of his former accounts. My department has been covering the deliveries, but, of course, that's just a temporary fix. I've made a decision as to the permanent solution and am offering the route to you."

Dylan was initially speechless. He was flooded with a mix of emotions before they quickly subsided. Then questions arose to the forefront. Pullian sat patiently across the table, a slight smile pursed his lips.

Dylan composed himself, gathered his thoughts and replied. "Well, sir, I appreciate the apology and the additional work the paper did to get to the bottom of things. However, I don't have the means to purchase the route, especially one that size."

Pullian's smile expanded, revealing coffee-stained teeth. "I think you can handle the price. There's no charge. We're giving you the route. As part of our investigation, we talked with some of your customers, including ones who received their papers late through no fault of your own. Each one expressed glowing reviews of your service and the way you've conducted yourself. You're the type of young man we want as the first line of contact with our subscribers. My office will be in touch with you to discuss the details and assist with the transition." He stood, indicating the meeting had come to a conclusion.

Hands were shaken all around, and Dylan thanked him for the opportunity. On the drive home, he looked at Anthony and said, "I noticed you didn't say anything in the meeting, Grandpa."

"I didn't need to," Anthony replied. "You taught me something today."

The balance of the week was a whirlwind. Dylan received the new customer list and, for the first two days, the circulation department drove him around in one of their vans. Once Dylan began delivering his new route by bicycle, it took over three hours. He had inherited fifty-eight new accounts. A few were even outside of the boundaries Dylan had drawn as part of his original expansion plan.

One Friday, the new business problems were weighing on Dylan's mind as he arrived at Esther Lott's house. He'd opened the cedar box, finding it devoid of the venerable tobacco tin as it had been for the past several weeks since their initial meeting. He checked his ledger and confirmed that she now owed for five weeks. Instinctively, he rang the doorbell, something he had been doing every Friday without success. He wondered if something had happened to the old woman.

As Dylan waited, he could hear the cadence of footsteps moving toward the other side of the heavy front door. It certainly didn't sound like Esther Lott. A fit-looking man with a military-style crew cut answered the door, sporting tailored black pants and an open-collared white shirt. He appeared close in age, if not appearance, to Dylan's grandfather. "Mr. Dylan, Mrs. Lott has been expecting you. Please follow me." The man led Dylan into the sitting room where Esther Lott was seated on the same couch as their first encounter. "Mr. Dylan here to see you, ma'am."

"Thank you, Franklin. That will be all."

And with that, the man had disappeared into the bowels of the house.

Esther Lott took a moment to observe Dylan. "I sense some resolution has come to the problem we discussed on your last visit."

"Yes, ma'am." Dylan then provided a summary of what had transpired over the past several weeks.

"Well, it sounds like you have a new problem, but a good one. Have you given any thought as to how to streamline your operation?"

"Streamline?"

"Take steps to adjust your business so that you work more efficiently. Work smarter, not harder, as the saying goes."

"That sounds like good advice, but I'm not sure where to begin."

"Well, your problem sounds like a logistical one." Dylan stared back at Esther Lott with a blank look on his face.

Esther Lott smiled. "What I mean is you need to reduce the physical size of your territory without sacrificing the number of customers you serve."

"But how could I do that? I suppose I could tell some of the new customers that they're too far for me to travel. But then I would lose business and could even harm the paper's reputation."

"You're a very mindful young man. I see you've put some thought into this, but you're still young, nonetheless. I'm going to make a suggestion. It appears that this RJ fellow might be willing to assist you further. He must know the other carriers in the area. Ask him to set up a meeting to discuss a plan that would make everyone's job easier and more profitable. Then, prior to the meeting, get a list of the addresses for each account and suggest tradeoffs. Each carrier takes a smaller geographic area and trades customers so that everyone stays in their territory with the same number of accounts. Everyone will make the same money working less time. You might even reach an agreement with the others whereby you agree to only solicitate new business in your designated areas. That could help avoid future problems like the one with TJ Marin. Perhaps, Mr. Pullian can assist if need be."

Dylan listened intently and thought for a moment before responding enthusiastically, "That's a great idea, Mrs. Lott! You sure are smart. Did you run a business when you were younger?"

Mrs. Lott laughed. "No, dear, I never worked outside the home, but I went to college and did a great deal of work from the house. My late husband, Hendrick, worked as a custodian at Westover Elementary School and taught swimming lessons at the local YMCA for many years. Someday I'll tell you more about that."

Dylan reflected further. It was Mrs. Lott who had made the initial suggestion to elicit help from RJ. That had worked out splendidly, and now she was providing more advice on how to manage the substantial increase in his business. Dylan, against his standard business practices, did not raise the subject of her past-due bill.

Dylan was no longer concerned about the integrity of his newspaper count. He'd even picked up a few new customers by word of mouth from their neighbors. He went back to his original schedule of going home after school, picking up his bike, and riding to the drop-off spot. His profits had increased fourfold, but the extra work meant getting home late each evening, often after dark during the fall and winter months. Each night Cheryl would have dinner waiting and, despite Dylan's hectic schedule, mother and son always made time to talk about their day and catch up on things.

They continued to ride to St. Mary together each morning in Cheryl's yellow 1978 VW Bug. Once they arrived at school and the first bell rang, they rarely saw each other. He took the bus home in the afternoon because Cheryl was always busy with after school activities. She regularly worked on lesson plans and assisted students after classes. She also coached the girls' junior varsity basketball team and worked with the theater students on their annual production.

One night over dinner, Cheryl had asked about the new paper route. "How's it going with all the new customers? I miss seeing you when I get home from work."

"It takes me longer, but I'm making a lot more money. Maybe I can start helping with some of the bills."

Cheryl giggled. "That's very generous of you, Dylan. Before too long, you'll be paying bills for the rest of your life. While we're on the subject, we should probably come up with a plan on how to handle your earnings. What have you been doing with them?"

"I haven't spent anything since I started. Of course, I wasn't making much at first with all the problems I had. I put everything I made into the shoebox in my closet."

"Well, I think it's time to open a savings account for you at the Fairfield County Teachers' Credit Union."

Dylan chewed a bite of his minute steak thoughtfully for a moment. "I've been thinking about talking to the other carriers about trading some customers so we can all streamline our routes and be more efficient. Mr. Pullian set up a meeting with the other kids for the day after tomorrow. Do you think Grandpa can give me a ride down to the *Advocate* office after school?"

"Wow. Streamline and efficient. Those are big words for a third grader, even for a budding entrepreneur. I'm sure he'll be happy to."

The meeting with the other carriers went well. It didn't hurt that Bill Pullian had already worked out a plan and pre-drafted new geographical territories. He had carefully worked out the numbers in an equitable manner, and then encouraged everyone to call on those households within their territory who were not currently receiving the paper about purchasing a subscription.

Dylan had spent a week meeting his new customers and getting his ledger revised and organized to reflect his new customer list. His conversations with Esther Lott continued intermittently. His redrawn delivery route still concluded at the end of Travis Avenue. Since Esther Lott wasn't paying anyway, their conversations were no longer being held on Fridays. Besides, he was busy with collections for all his other accounts on that day.

One midweek afternoon, Dylan knocked on Esther Lott's door.

Franklin answered. "Good afternoon, Mr. Dylan. What can I do for you?"

"I'm here to see Mrs. Lott. Is she available?"

"Mrs. Lott is out in the greenhouse. Please follow me." Franklin turned and headed down the main hallway toward the back of the house with Dylan in tow.

As they'd passed the sitting room, it occurred to Dylan that it was the first time he had seen any other part of the spacious home. Beyond the sitting room was an open door to an office paneled floor-to-ceiling in mahogany. An entire wall with built-in shelves was stocked with books. Beyond the office/library was a large dining room and a kitchen that sparkled clean and smelled fresh but was otherwise outdated with avocado-colored appliances and yellow cabinetry with Formica countertops. They passed through a sunroom and out a set of French double doors, into the back yard. Farther down the property sat a greenhouse enclosed in framed plastic windows. Dylan entered and the considerably warmer temperature was a welcome relief. The interior walls were lined with planting boxes set on top of elevated metal framing. There were vegetables, flowers, and other assorted landscaping plants. Esther Lott had been tending to yellow roses with pruning clippers. She wore a denim dress covered with a dark-blue apron. Her head and face were somewhat concealed in a floppy straw hat and oversized sunglasses. She'd looked much younger and more energetic than in her previous position on the sitting room couch.

Mrs. Lott turned and greeted, "Hello, Dylan. So nice to see you."

"Nice to see you, Mrs. Lott. I came by to tell you that I took your advice and my territory has been redrawn. I now have seventy-five accounts, and it takes me a little over two hours. Plus, I'm making more than four times what I did with my original route."

"That's great, Dylan. How many houses along your route don't subscribe to the paper?"

Dylan considered thoughtfully for a moment. "I'm not sure. Maybe about a half as many."

"So you're riding past forty or so houses every day and not delivering a paper?"

"I suppose that's about right."

"And the paper provides and installs one of those blue plastic *Advocate* boxes next to the mailbox for each new customer free of charge?"

"Yes."

"And most of the papers are delivered to the boxes, correct?"

Dylan nodded in agreement.

Esther Lott continued. "So, if you were to sell subscriptions to all or most of these forty homes, you would increase your profits by as much as fifty percent without traveling any farther on your new route?"

"Yes, I believe so. But how do I convince all those people to buy a subscription?"

"Well, it seems to me that you need a good marketing plan. You know what I discovered? The Sunday paper costs fifty cents at the newsstand. Each Sunday edition contains advertising flyers that include coupons and sales for items people purchase every week. Things like groceries, pet food, and household goods and supplies. Plus, there's always seasonal item sales and features on do-it-yourself projects to save even more money. Not to mention articles on travel and entertainment ideas. The savings on coupons alone from the Sunday paper more than pays for a weekly subscription. And everybody needs to keep up with the news."

Dylan felt a surge of excitement. "I pass right by those houses every day. It would only take me a few seconds to stop and put a paper in the box. I'm gonna start knocking on doors tomorrow." Another thought entered his mind. "I know I've told you before that you have a very nice home. I saw even more of it today. I also remember you telling me that Mr. Lott was a custodian and gave swimming lessons. My mother teaches school, and we could never afford a house like this. You also told me you used to work from home. What type of work did you do?"

"The same type of work I still do every day. You see, Hendrick was a world-class swimmer in his native Germany. He was an Olympic alternate for the West German national team, even though he was much older than the other swimmers. When he came to the United States, he didn't speak English very well and took the job as a custodian. Even after he mastered the language, he loved the teachers and kids at the school and stayed until his retirement." Esther Lott took off her hat, wiped her brow with a handkerchief concealed in her apron and continued. "But swimming was his true passion. He swam at the YMCA from the first day he came to Stamford. That's where we met. Eventually, he began helping with the younger kids, teaching them to swim. He always volunteered and refused to take a salary from the Y. As the kids grew older, many of them swam competitively. Hank, that's what I called him, started giving private lessons. Most of the kids came from wealthy homes, and the parents paid Hank to help them improve their times. The manager at the Y let Hank use the pool for his lessons, free of charge. He did this for over twenty years. He was in great demand because of the results he helped the kids achieve. Often times he was so booked up he had to turn people away."

"I see."

Esther Lott's eyes narrowed. She smiled and her gaze momentarily shifted off into the distance. She appeared briefly-transposed back in time. "Actually, Hank made considerably more money giving private lessons than he did working at the school. And that's where I came in. Hank was a bright man and a generous and loving husband, but he didn't have much formal education. I attended college at Endicott in Massachusetts and majored in finance. I was always interested in investing and still am. It's always been a passion of mine. We never had children and were able to save and live comfortably on Hank's school salary and later his pension. He gave me the money he earned giving swimming lessons, and I invested it."

"What does that mean?"

"Investing means buying things that will earn you even more money."

"I think I understand."

"Let me give you an example. Say you go to a deli and buy a sandwich. You pay the person behind the counter for the sandwich and then you eat it. Once you've eaten the sandwich, both it and the money you paid are gone forever. But if you buy a share of stock, you purchase a piece of ownership in that company. The company, in turn, periodically pays you a portion of its profits. Eventually you could even sell the stock for considerably more than you paid."

"I think I follow you. It's kind of like a paper route. You typically buy the route from the seller. Then you get the profits from working the route. Someday you could sell the route to someone for more than you paid."

"That's right. You certainly are a bright boy! But there's still a difference between the two. After you purchase your paper route, you're still required to do the physical work each day to earn the profits. When you purchase stock, if you do your research and choose wisely, there's no further work involved on your part. You're paid as an owner but not involved in working for the company."

"Wow, that sounds interesting. I've never heard of anything like that before."

"Well, you have plenty of time to learn about things like that. The important lesson is to treat money with respect. The first rule is to always spend less than you earn and save and invest the difference."

"It's funny you say that. I was talking with my mom the other night about that very thing. She asked me what I've done with the money I earned so far. I told her I haven't spent anything, and I offered to help her pay the bills. My mom won't let me do that, but she's going to open up an account at her bank for me so I can put my money there."

"You're mother sounds like a smart lady. Did you know that once you put your money in the bank, they pay you an additional amount on top of your deposit?"

"I didn't know that."

"It's called interest."

Dylan giggled. "That's very *interesting*."

They both busted out laughing.

CHAPTER ONE

As DYLAN McDIRT PEDALED HIS old Peugeot bicycle on the final leg of his newspaper route, several thoughts raced through his mind. Among those on his frontal lobe were his blind date the following night at a gala being held at the Stanwich Club, next week's football district playoff game, and his imminent meeting with Esther Lott.

The newspapers in the bike's rear saddlebags were gone, leaving only those in Dylan's oversized shoulder satchel left to distribute. With a hundred customers spread out over a concentrated section of primarily working-class, single-family homes, it was a tedious daily task, particularly for a high school junior with a number of extracurricular activities and other part-time jobs. Mostly, the *Advocate* was delivered by boys and girls of middle school age, but Dylan needed the money.

As he completed his deliveries, Dylan reflected back on his first meeting with Esther Lott eight years ago, reminiscing about the evolution of their relationship and everything he'd learned from her. He was a good student and a star athlete at Stamford High School. He was popular among his classmates, if not considered a bit eccentric. He had many friends but privately cherished his relationship with the old widow, one that had grown strikingly similar to that of his close-knit family. Despite Dylan's busy high school schedule, he always looked forward to his conversations with Esther Lott. He often reflected fondly at random times about their unconventional relationship. An initial encounter between a widow and young boy had developed into a mutually-respectful friendship with a mentor-protégé component.

Dylan's initial conversations with Esther Lott had profoundly influenced him over the past eight years. Since that time he had grown his paper route and maximized sales and profits with remarkable efficiency. He was an avid saver, with a well-earned reputation for frugality, in stark contrast to the attitudes of his friends and high school classmates, the majority of whom came from wealthier homes with parents who were doctors, lawyers, business owners, stockbrokers, and financiers.

At sixteen, Dylan was at the age when his peers were obsessed with fashion and the latest trends, actively dated, and most had obtained their driver's licenses. The student parking lot at Stamford High was full of late model Nissan 300s, Camaros, Mustangs, and other exotic muscle cars. Dylan did not have his driver's license and either walked, rode his bike, or hitched a ride from friends or family.

He had grown to six feet, two inches tall. His frame had filled out, and he was built like his father and grandfather. He had also developed into a fine athlete, making the varsity football and baseball teams his sophomore year. Now, as a junior, he'd earned a spot as a starting safety on the football team. Come springtime, he was a projected starting outfielder and pitcher on the baseball team.

While continuing his paper route, he still managed to stop and talk with Esther Lott on occasion. The subjects they discussed varied widely, often initiated by whatever was on Dylan's mind. He felt like he could talk to his mother and grandparents about anything, but he also valued Esther Lott's opinion and often confided in her.

Dylan and Cheryl remained close even as he reached the age when most teenagers began to seek independence from their parents. He also started working weekends with Cheryl at the Rockrimmon Country Club. They enjoyed working together, Cheryl waiting tables in the restaurant while Dylan worked as a bus boy and dishwasher. Although they no longer rode to school together in the mornings, mother and son made it a point to continue their tradition of sitting down to dinner together on most nights. They also spent weekends with Anthony and Isabella when their schedules allowed. Isabella always did the cooking, usually Italian. His grandparents were proud of him, and Anthony would tell anyone who cared to listen that Dylan was going to play for both the New York Giants and the Yankees someday.

Once Dylan had entered high school and begun playing sports, practice and game schedules sometimes conflicted with his paper route duties. He insisted on keeping it though, despite Cheryl's pleas to sell and pass it on to a younger kid. Convinced that he was firm in his decision, she relented and even helped on days when his schedule required assistance. Even Anthony would drive up from Norwalk in a pinch to cover the route. But mostly it was covered by another neighborhood boy.

The fact that a popular high school athlete still had a paper route was not lost on some. A few of his high school teammates referred to him as Paperboy. Dylan handled the ribbing from his friends and teammates good naturedly. The moniker spread among his classmates at large, although few who did not know him well were willing to say it to his face. Eventually, rival teams began to hear about the Stamford star athlete's job. It wasn't unusual to occasionally hear opposing fans taunt, "Hey, Paperboy, your guy beat you on that play. When are you gonna *deliver!*" Or "Breaking news: the Paperboy just struck out."

Dylan's meeting with Esther Lott had been initiated by a telephone call from Franklin one night earlier in the week, requesting that he come by the house on Friday. As Dylan had hung up the phone, two things occurred to him. None of his customers had ever called his house, and his meetings with Mrs. Lott had always been impromptu, initiated by one of them as he was delivering her paper.

On the other hand, Esther Lott was not just any client. Dylan always took time for friendly chats and exchanged pleasantries when he saw his other customers, particularly on Fridays. But his days were packed with the busy schedule of a high school student athlete. There was homework, practices and games, and a social life, plus the paper route, along with his part-time job working weekends with his mom.

Dylan had discovered girls about the same time as his rise in popularity, brought on by his status as an underclass member of the varsity football team. He was a starter midway through his sophomore year, the only member of the starting team who was not a junior or senior. The role brought him some notoriety, particularly among his classmates. There was a well-defined social hierarchy at Stamford High School. However, Dylan did not fit squarely into any particular group. Rather, he got along with most of the other students.

After completing his paper route, Dylan continued down Travis Avenue and steered his bicycle toward Mrs. Lott's house for their meeting. Dylan's upcoming blind date weighed on his mind as he approached the house. Despite his popularity he simply did not have much experience with girls. As the large house came into view he attempted to redirect his focus. *I have no idea what this is about, but I have a feeling it's gonna be different.*

Dylan arrived at the house, parked his bike in the driveway next to the garage, walked up onto the porch, and rang the bell.

Franklin answered the door. "Ah, Mr. Dylan, please come in. Mrs. Lott is expecting you. She's in the sitting room." He then turned and disappeared through a side door off to the left, leaving Dylan standing in the foyer.

Dylan turned into the sitting room and took his usual place in a chair facing

Mrs. Lott. A large, plain-white envelope rested on the coffee table between them.

"Good afternoon, Dylan. How are you?"

"I'm doing well, Mrs. Lott. How are you today?"

She studied his expression for a moment. "I'm fine, thank you, but it appears something is weighing on your mind."

He nervously scratched the side of his head, unable to suppress an embarrassing grin. "I have a blind date tomorrow night, I guess I'm a little nervous."

Esther Lott looked back at him disarmingly. "Do you remember what made you successful with your business?" She often referred to the paper route as a business.

"I would have to say a combination of good client relations and consistent reliable service."

"Which would you say is more important?"

"I would say good service."

"Well, I would respectfully agree and disagree."

"Huh?" Dylan muttered, obviously confused.

Mrs. Lott smiled. "I agree with you that both customer service and client relations are important. I disagree that one is more important than the other. Do you recall some of the problems you ran into early on with your business?"

"Of course I do. In the early days I wasn't sure I'd have any customers left."

"Well problems certainly arose, just like they always do in business. The key is how you handle them. During difficult times it's advantageous to have good client relationships to rely upon when resolving issues."

"Okay, I get that, but what does it have to do with girls?"

"Let's say you see a girl around school you think is pretty. You want to ask her out but don't really know her beyond maybe saying hello in the hallways or exchanging a few occasional words while in a class you share together."

"Okay, I can think of a few girls like that."

"Now let's say you get up the courage to ask her out. Since you really don't know her it could be like your old cold-calling days, knocking on doors selling newspaper subscriptions. A lot of rejection."

"Yeah, I see your point."

"And what if she says yes, you go out on a date, and it doesn't go well. You'll still see that girl around school and, trust me, girls talk to each other."

"So what do I do?"

"You take the same approach as you do with your business, but on a social level. Get to know the girl first. Talk with her like you would with any other person. Find common ground, be your charming self and most important, make her laugh."

"Okay." he found himself repeating that word frequently.

"Let me explain. By getting to know this hypothetical girl you'll become friendly. Maybe you find you don't have much in common and decide not to ask her out. So now you have an acquaintance who you know casually that you didn't know at all beforehand. Conversely, maybe you hit it off, go out a few times and decide she's not the right one. Either way you formed a relationship, treated the young lady with respect and don't have someone out there poisoning the dating well."

"Yeah, that sounds better than getting rejected and having to avoid her for the next year and a half."

"Exactly. You get the picture. Rejection from sales cold calling is one thing. Getting turned down for a date by a high school classmate is a whole different bunch of bananas." The same principles apply to this blind date.

Dylan allowed the advice to sink in. "Thank you so much. I really feel better now."

Good. Now, we have some business to discuss."

"Business, ma'am?"

"Yes, do you know what today is?"

"It's Friday."

"Yes, it is Friday, but it's also the eight-year anniversary of our first meeting."

"Really?"

"Yes, it is. We first met on a Friday in October exactly eight years ago today. Do you remember that meeting?"

"I sure do."

"What do you remember about it?"

"I remember it well. I had just started my paper route and was having problems, and you helped me."

"Is there anything else you remember about that day?"

"Not really."

"Well, there was something else. I didn't pay you for that week. And I haven't paid you since then. I owe you for eight years' worth of newspapers. That's 416 weeks at a $1.35 a week. It's time I settle up with you." And with that she reached over and handed Dylan the envelope from the table.

He took the envelope in his hands and sat there speechless, staring down at the bulky packet.

Mrs. Lott waited. "Please open it," she finally said.

He opened the envelope, pulled out a stack of heavy stock papers, and carefully examined the top sheet. It was framed with a gray-brown border and labeled Apple Computer, Inc. "What are these?" he asked.

"They're stock certificates. I'm paying you in Apple stock."

"I don't understand."

"Are you familiar with Apple, the computer company?"

"I don't think so. We have a few computers in the library at school. I think they're IBM though."

"IBM is a good company, but I've been researching Apple. They've been making computers for a few years and are developing some exciting technology. Have you seen those portable phones?"

"Yeah, I've seen some businessmen carrying around those big bags with the phone receiver and I've even seen a few of the ones that look like the bricks my grandfather uses. But I hear it costs like a dollar-a-minute to use them. Why would anyone do that when a pay phone costs ten cents?"

"Apple is one of the companies I've purchased stock in, and I think it's a good investment. Do you trust my opinion on that?"

"Yes, I do. If there's one thing I learned from you, it's that you're smart with money and investments."

"Thank you, Dylan, but do you really, really trust me?"

"Yes."

"Then I want you to make me a promise. Will you do that?"

"What's the promise?"

"I want you to agree to hold the stock and not sell it or do anything else with it."

"How much is it worth?"

"I owe you $561.60 for the papers you delivered over the past eight years. I purchased the Apple stock at about twenty-seven cents a share. There are stock certificates in the envelope for a little over two thousand shares. We've talked about buying ownership in a company, and that is what I've purchased for you. I've evaluated this stock as a buy-and-hold investment. That means it's something to hold onto for the long term. There may be periodic dividends, and those will be used to purchase more stock. I believe the real value here is in the potential appreciation. Will you agree to hold on to it and not sell no matter what happens?"

Dylan considered the request for a moment. He was making about seventy-five dollars a week from his route, plus the money he earned working with Cheryl. He was saving most of his money and hadn't planned on ever getting paid by Mrs. Lott. He was holding an unexpected windfall, and as, he'd been taught, his first instinct was to save it for the future. "Yes, thank you. I'll agree to hold on to the stock."

"Make sure you keep those certificates in a safe place." Mrs. Lott then changed the subject and they talked for another thirty minutes about subjects ranging from his family to the recent turmoil in the financial markets.

Dylan left Mrs. Lott's house and headed home. When he arrived Cheryl was cooking dinner. She looked up at him as he entered the kitchen. "Hi, honey, how was your day?"

"Great, Mom. I just came back from a meeting with Mrs. Lott." As they sat down for dinner, he told Cheryl about the meeting and showed her the stock certificates.

When Dylan had finished, she did some quick math in her head. Roughly five hundred and sixty dollars was involved, or about four mortgage payments on the small two-bedroom, one-bath house they shared. "I don't know what to think about this, but I guess there's not much to say. You promised Mrs. Lott you'd hold on to the stock and not sell it under any condition, so you should stick to your word."

"I plan to. Is there a safe place I can keep the stock?"

"I get a safe deposit box at the credit union. That would probably be best."

"Ok, thanks. Remember, I'm not working at the club with you tomorrow night. I'll be staying at Alex's."

"I remember. I already told the kitchen manager you weren't available this weekend. And I'm taking next Saturday off to come and watch your football game. What are you boys up to this weekend?"

"We're going to an event at one of Alex's clubs. I'm not even sure which one. He's bringing this girl he's been seeing, and they're bringing a date for me."

"Have you met this girl yet?"

"Nope, it's a blind date."

"Uh oh."

"Uh oh, what?"

"I've seen Alex operate with the ladies. He probably took the best one for himself."

"He's been dating this girl, Liz, for a while. He hasn't told me much about my date. Just said leave it to him and I'd be pleased."

Cheryl shook her head and smiled. "If you say so."

"Hey, Mom, how come you never go out? I can't even remember a time when you had a date?"

Cheryl looked at her son askance. "What are you getting at?"

"Nothing, I just thought it might be time for you to go out and have some fun. You're still young and attractive."

Cheryl laughed. "Thanks a lot, but I don't need a boyfriend right now. I have you."

"Huh?"

"What I mean is, I have you to take care of. And I work weekends and summers at the Rockrimmon. You'll be off to college soon. Maybe I'll find time then."

"You know, I've noticed how men look at you, especially at the club."

"You have no idea. I've had a least half a dozen ask me out. Each time I point out they're married, the response is almost always the same. 'I'm looking for a girlfriend, not another wife.' "

"Don't worry, Mom. After I graduate from college, I'm going to make lots of money. Then it'll be my turn to take care of you and Grandma and Grandpa."

"That's very sweet. Have I told you recently what a good son you are?"

"All the time."

CHAPTER TWO

J ACKSON ALEXANDER MALLOY III LIVED with his parents, Jackson Jr. and Lillian, in a gated mansion in an exclusive section of Old Greenwich. His older sister, Kari, was a sophomore at Radcliffe College. Alex, as he was known, attended Fairfield College Preparatory School, the same all-boys prep school from which his father had graduated. It was axiomatic that Alex would matriculate at his father's alma mater, Yale University in New Haven, in a couple years where he would be a legacy to the Wolf's Head Society.

Jackson Malloy Jr. was the president and chief executive officer of Malloy Williamson & Associates, a venerable New York brokerage house with a seat on the New York Stock Exchange. Malloy Williamson was founded in 1903 by Jackson's great grandfather. Lillian Malloy, formerly Lillian Williamson, had attended Holyoke College in Massachusetts and was the granddaughter of the firm's co-founder, Lawrence Williamson. The Malloys were well connected with all the right people in Manhattan and Fairfield County and members of Greenwich's Stanwich and Round Hill Country Clubs and the Riverside Yacht Club.

Alex was a member of the football and baseball teams at Fairfield Prep, but to say he played those sports was a stretch. He was an outgoing, young man and a gifted orator. That skill set served him well. He was just under six foot tall, with a thin build and wide, bony shoulders. His face was accented with piercing blue eyes and a square jaw line. He loved all sports but was not gifted athletically. He was slow-footed and not particularly coordinated. He had tried soccer, lacrosse, and rugby but was drawn to the more mainstream sports. He had an amazing grasp of the intricacies of those games and could recite the statistics of Major League Baseball and NFL players with the best. Alex made the football and baseball teams at Prep, in large part due to his father's generous donations to the Booster Club. However, the head coaches of both teams thought of Alex as another assistant coach because he was constantly asking pointed questions and making astute observations and productive suggestions on game strategy.

Alex had met Dylan at a summer baseball camp in Pawling, New York following their eighth-grade school year. Alex had been enrolled for a month while his parents entertained friends and business associates at their summer home in Newport, Rhode Island. Dylan had attended the camp for a week on a financial aid scholarship for promising young players. Having taken quick notice of Dylan's smooth, powerful swing, strong throwing arm, and superior presence on the field, Alex had introduced himself to Dylan at the camp cafeteria and they'd become instant friends.

At first glance, the two young men appeared to be an odd couple. Both lived in separate towns and at opposite ends of the socioeconomic scale. Although Alex's personality was the antithesis of the prototypical high societal progeny snob, he possessed all the material trappings of wealth but in a surprisingly disarming fashion. He was a clothes horse, sporting the latest sartorial styles and boasting an impressive wristwatch collection. Alternatively, Dylan's wardrobe was limited to shorts, T-shirts, and Puma tennis shoes in summer and blue jeans, sweatshirts, and Timberland boots during the cold weather months. Alex drove a BMW 325E while Dylan lacked a driver's license and rode around town on his old bike.

Although Alex was extremely outgoing, his social circle in Greenwich revolved around the country club scene simply because he did not attend local schools. Before he began driving himself, he had commuted to school in Fairfield by private car and driver. The two friends spoke regularly on the phone about the requisite subjects, particularly sports and girls. On weekends, they often spent time at each other's homes, alternating in no particular order between Stamford and Greenwich. Occasionally they took the train into New York to explore the city and attend Yankee games.

Cheryl approved of Alex and welcomed him into her home. When the boys spent the weekend in Stamford, Alex slept on the living room couch and got up early on Sunday morning to help Dylan with his paper route. It was not lost on Cheryl that he readily embraced the conditions, notwithstanding his privileged background.

Anthony and Isabella were also fond of Alex. Isabella often made dinner for the boys before they headed out for the evening. Alex loved her lasagna and Rigatoni Bolognese. He never failed to express his gratitude and talk with her about subjects ranging from cooking to her native Italy.

Similarly, Dylan was accepted and comfortable visiting the Malloy compound. Mr. and Mrs. Malloy took an instant liking to him, and he was at ease discussing finance and investments with Jackson Malloy. They found him to be smart, articulate, and socially graceful. Alex's parents were aware of their son's mischievous streak and found Dylan to be a positive influence.

CHAPTER THREE

DYLAN WOKE UP EARLY THE following morning and did some homework and a few chores around the house. As with most days, his Saturday schedule was packed tightly. Alex would be there by ten thirty to pick him up, and they would head over to the Raymond Crowe Athletic Complex where Dylan had to umpire two fall league youth baseball games. The games were scheduled for 11:15 a.m. and 12:45 p.m. with one-hour-and-fifteen-minute time limits. Afterwards, they would head directly to Alex's house in Old Greenwich with plenty of time to get ready for their double date.

The evening's event was the Harvest Moon Youth Gala at the Round Hill Club. It was one of three annual events held at the club that catered to the memberships' teenage and young-adult offspring. The affair was semiformal and featured a four-course, sit-down dinner, followed by entertainment provided by a live band that played a combination of contemporary hits and traditional dance numbers. Alcohol would be served and wrist bands issued at the door for members and their guests, orange for those over twenty-one and black for those underage. Dylan had been to the Round Hill Club with Alex and his family on a few prior occasions, but this would be the first time he and Alex attended an evening event together without them.

Alex's parents were out of town for the weekend so the boys would have the house to themselves. Mr. and Mrs. Malloy trusted them alone for the weekend, primarily because of Dylan. He did not own a suit, which was required for the event, so Mr. Malloy had his tailor come to the house a few weeks earlier and fit Dylan with a rental for the occasion.

While Dylan was being measured and fitted, Mrs. Malloy had given Dylan a reminder. "No parties while we're gone, Dylan. You're in charge."

Alex arrived at the McDirt house on time, came inside, and said hello to Cheryl while Dylan finished packing his umpire gear and overnight duffel bag into the BMW. Then they headed off to the ball fields.

Stamford was a wealthy town with large swatches of opulent neighborhoods. The Raymond Crowe Athletic Complex was a showplace funded with city property taxes. The beautifully landscaped and manicured park covered more than ten acres and included two Little League and two regulation-size baseball fields. All four resembled mini stadiums with built-in dugouts, shaded stands, padded outfield walls, and electronic scoreboards. The complex also included softball fields, a soccer/lacrosse field, a roller hockey rink, outdoor basketball courts, and a state-of-the-art playground. All the athletic venues were equipped with modern lighting systems so games could be played in the evenings. Paved trails for walking, jogging, and cycling surrounded the park's perimeter.

It was an unseasonably warm late-October day, and the complex was already crowded when the boys arrived. Alex dropped Dylan at the baseball fields and he proceeded directly to the large building near the fields. As he walked along the building, he passed a concession stand with an impressive menu, restrooms, and administrative office. A separate outbuilding housed a fleet of maintenance equipment used to manicure the fields and keep the complex in pristine condition. Adjacent to the administrative office was a locker room for employees and game officials. Dylan entered the locker room. He was already dressed in his umpire uniform but had to disrobe to strap on his shin guards and chest protector, which fit underneath his clothing. After redressing, he grabbed his mask and umpire indicator and headed to the field. The teams were still warming up. Dylan immediately took charge, summoning the managers to home plate for a brief pregame meeting.

Alex drove on to park his car in the remote lot. As he pulled in, a black pickup truck with Johnny Paycheck's country song, "Take This Job and Shove It," blared from its speakers. Besides the driver and passenger, there were three other young men seated in the bed. As Alex drove by, windows down, the truck's driver turned down the radio. "Nice car, Biff," he yelled. Alex ignored the comment and found a space on the opposite side of the lot.

Alex walked back to the ball field and took a seat at the top of the stands behind the third base dugout just as the first game was underway. At the conclusion of the game, he went to the concession stand and grabbed a soft pretzel and a Coke. The second game began and proceeded along uneventfully for the first couple of innings.

In the top of the third inning, a group of five loud, rough-looking hoodlums settled in the stands directly behind home plate. Four of the five had unfashionably long, unkept hair. The fifth was overweight and sported a crew cut. He reminded Alex of a cross between Curly from *The Three Stooges* and a wanna-be skin head. All five were dressed in rudimentary uniforms of denim and leather and looked to be in their late teens or early twenties. The group clearly stood out among the other adults and children at the park.

After the next break between innings, Alex focused back on the game. His attention was suddenly drawn to the stands behind Dylan, where one member of the unruly group pointed at Dylan, arms flailing while the other four gathered around him. Alex moved in closer to listen in on the conversation. As he repositioned his vantage point, it suddenly occurred to him that they were the same group from the pickup truck in the parking lot. He watched and listened intently.

The one doing all the talking had long black hair. His build reminded Alex of a fire hydrant. He listened as the hydrant continued to point in Dylan's direction. "That's the kid who stole my paper route. He cost me a fortune. I told that twerp if I ever saw him around, I was gonna beat his ass. Well, today's the day."

Dressed in dirty denim jeans, greasy work boots, and a black leather vest over a black T-shirt, the biggest guy in the group finally spoke up and addressed the hydrant. "Give it a rest, TJ. That was years ago."

TJ replied, "I don't give a shit, Tiny, and you just made my point. I hear that loser still works the route. He's stolen from me for eight years now. Today's payday. If you don't like it, you can walk home."

"Whatever," replied Tiny.

Uh oh, Alex thought, as he instinctively got up and headed back in the direction of his car. A short time later as he returned to the field, he checked his stainless-steel Rolex Submariner. The hands read one fifty-five. The game was about to end. He drifted over in the direction of the concession stand to wait for Dylan.

As soon as the game was called, Dylan made a beeline for the locker room, nodding to Alex standing on the side of the building near the entrance. Before Dylan could reach the locker room, TJ, Tiny, and company intercepted him, flanking him on all sides.

"Well, well. If it isn't the infamous paperboy," TJ Marin said.

Dylan quickly evaluated the situation and stood tall as he replied, "Whadda *you* want?"

"I want the money you owe me for stealing my paper route, plus compensation for the last eight years."

"Compensation. That's a big word for a high school dropout,"

The comeback elicited a chorus of loud groans from the hoodlum group. One of them shouted above the chorus, "You gonna take that from him?"

TJ Marin took a few steps toward Dylan and pointed an index finger in his direction. "How much money you got on you?"

Dylan maintained eye contact with Marin, thoughts racing through his mind. *Why this and why now? This isn't a good time. Big date tonight and huge game next week.* Finally, he replied, "I'm not giving you a dime."

"Then you choose option B. We're going back behind the building, away from all these people, so I can kick your ass."

Dylan glanced in Alex's direction. They made eye contact, and Alex nodded in the affirmative. Alex slipped around the corner unnoticed by the posse of hoodlums.

Dylan locked in on Marin again. "Fine. Your boys wait here."

Marin snickered. "You don't make the rules, Paperboy." He turned and headed toward the side of the building.

Dylan followed as the others fell in line along either side of him with Tiny bringing up the rear. When they reached the back of the building, Dylan said, "How we gonna do this?"

Marin became more animated and cocky, balling up his fists and taking warm-up punches like a boxer eagerly waiting the opening bell. "You're gonna go in that locker room and take off all that protective gear. You wouldn't want an unfair advantage, would you?"

Marin's posse waved their fists in the air and grunted whooping sounds.

Dylan slowly backed up, facing the group as disappeared around the corner and into the locker room.

As he entered, Marin called out, "We'll be waiting here for you."

Dylan changed into street clothes and stored his umpire uniform and gear in his locker, then took a deep breath and walked outside. Marin and company were there waiting as promised. They went around back, and Dylan and Marin squared off surrounded by the other four.

Dylan and Marin sized each other up, fists raised. Although Marin was three years older, Dylan was considerably taller and had a reach advantage.

Marin was no pushover, however. He was stocky and street smart with plenty of fighting experience.

Suddenly, yelling came from around the corner as Alex appeared brandishing a twenty-eight inch wooden Louisville Slugger in his left hand.

The entire group turned to look at him.

Standing a few yards shy of the group he gripped the bat with both hands and rested it on his right shoulder. Alex said in a deep, authoritative voice, "Listen, you Neanderthals, this is between those two. You all are staying out of it."

Tiny looked at Alex and smirked. "Whadda you gonna do, preppy? I'll shove that bat up your ass."

Tiny was clearly the biggest guy in the group, taller even than Dylan and outweighed him by at least thirty pounds. Alex, although thin and not overly athletic in the conventional sense, was nonetheless wiry. He walked straight up to Tiny, took a step past him, and elbowed him in the throat. Tiny hit the ground like a sack of rocks. The others started toward Alex, and he kicked the skin head hard on the side of his right knee. He instantly joined Tiny on the ground, both simultaneously writhing in pain.

Alex then took a fierce, conventional practice swing with the bat before he began swinging it above his head in a circular motion. "Anyone else wanna get nuts?" He shot glances at each member of the group. "Didn't think so. We all gonna behave now and watch the fight?"

The remaining two upright degenerates backed off slightly.

Dylan and Marin squared off again. Marin lunged toward Dylan, swinging wildly. Dylan side stepped him, and Marin regrouped. Dylan then threw a couple left jabs toward Marin's face. Marin instinctively raised his fists up in self-defense, and Dylan threw a right haymaker that landed squarely in the solar plexus. Marin doubled over in severe respiratory distress, gasping for air.

Dylan and Alex looked at each other and headed for the parking lot. As they were leaving, Alex raised the bat and took a full swing at the two remaining, unmolested guys, intentionally missing them by a good foot-and-a-half.

They both flinched.

"Real tough guys," Alex smirked.

Alex and Dylan were quiet as they walked calmly but briskly toward the parking lot. As they reached the car, Alex threw the bat in the rear seat. Dylan looked back at the fields and saw all five running in their direction. Two were out in front, followed by Marin, Tiny, and Curly. The last three were wobbly on their feet and gradually trailed behind.

"You know they're gonna come after us," he said to Alex.

"I already took care of that," Alex replied, motioning to the black pickup truck as they passed by.

Dylan observed two flat tires on the passenger side of the truck. "You didn't?"

"I sort of anticipated what might happen, so I took some pre-emptive measures. Don't worry, no permanent damage. I just let the air out."

They both screamed loud hoots and hollers and high fived each other, then hopped into the car and Alex steered the BMW toward Greenwich.

CHAPTER FOUR

DUE TO THE DETOUR, COURTESY of TJ Marin and company, it was late afternoon when Alex and Dylan arrived at the house. The Malloy's lived in a six-thousand-square-foot colonial-style home situated on three acres in Hillcrest Park Estates. Two twenty-four-hour manned security gates were the only means of ingress and egress for the exclusive development. The Malloy mansion itself was surrounded by a six-foot-high concrete wall with its own remote-controlled entry gate. A keypad and phone with a direct link to the house were used for guests, servants, and maintenance workers. Dylan had embarrassingly got lost in the house on his first visit. As a frequent visitor, he now had his own designated guest bedroom.

The boys had a few hours left before they had to leave to pick up Elizabeth Finn. Liz, as she was known to her friends, was the daughter of two anesthesiologists, Drs. Warren and Donna Finn. Liz attended Sacred Heart Greenwich, an all-girls Catholic prep school and was a year older than Alex and Dylan. She was heading to Haverford College the following year.

Dylan's date had arranged to meet the others at the Round Hill Club at seven-thirty. Liz and Alex dated occasionally but were not serious. Dylan thought Liz was attractive in an upper-class sort of way. She had a thin, athletic body, and her long, brown hair and glowing skin accented her hazel eyes and soft features. Her smile revealed perfect white teeth, the manifestation of excellent orthodontic work.

Alex and Liz made a handsome, albeit convenient, couple. She was ambitious and looking forward to leaving for college next fall. Consequently, she was not interested in a serious relationship, and Alex was too much of a playboy to be boyfriend material anyway. Neither attended a co-educational high school, and both families belonged to the same clubs. They enjoyed each other's company and so the arrangement worked well for them.

After they arrived at the house the boys made their way into the kitchen.

Dylan hadn't eaten anything since breakfast, so he heated up some leftover chicken Marsala the Malloy's chef had prepared the day before. Alex retreated upstairs to get ready. He always took longer. Alex showered and went into his large walk-in closet, where an entire section was filled with neatly-lined suits, dress pants and blazers, all displayed on cedar hangers. The closet itself was larger than Dylan's bedroom. He selected a custom-tailored navy Calvin Klein suit with subtle gray pinstripes, and a blue dress shirt with a white collar and French cuffs. He got dressed and meticulously completed the ensemble with a silk, maroon and navy paisley necktie, a contrasting pocket square, gold tiepin, and matching gold and black cuff links. He admired himself in the mirror, and then selected a rose gold Patek Philippe with a brown alligator band from the motorized watch winder and strapped it to his left wrist.

Dylan finished eating and went upstairs to his own ensuite bedroom and shaved and showered. His evening wear was waiting for him in the closet. The black rental suit was paired with a white dress shirt and maize pin dot tie. No attention to detail had been spared. Johnston & Murphy black, calfskin dress shoes and black wool herringbone socks completed his outfit. He got dressed and checked himself in the mirror. The suit draped perfectly, following the lines of his athletic body, courtesy of Jackson Malloy's tailor.

By the time the boys met downstairs it was time to leave. It was a short drive to the Finn residence, an impressive waterfront home located on an inlet in Old Greenwich that led to Long Island Sound. Since sunset, the weather had cooled considerably from the mild afternoon. The young men were met at the front door by Dr. Warren Finn.

Dr. Finn greeted Alex, who then introduced Dylan. "Welcome to our home, Dylan. Please, won't you both come in."

The group entered the home from the covered front porch that led directly into a formal living room. Sitting on the living room sofa, Dr. Donna Finn stood to greet the young men. Everyone was then seated and made small talk while they awaited Liz's entrance.

A short time later, Liz descended the staircase looking elegant in a black silk dress with a matching chiffon wrap. The outfit was completed with sensible high heels and diamond stud earrings. A strand of pearls hung from her delicate neck. Alex stood to greet her. They held hands while he kissed her on the cheek, careful not to smudge her lightly applied makeup. Dylan waited his turn and at the appropriate moment gave Liz a warm but brief hug.

After a few more minutes of discussion about the gala, Liz took advantage of a pause in the conversation. "Well, I guess we'll be off." With that she went to the front coat closet and produced a black clutch purse and an Armani leather overnight bag.

"Remember, Mom, I'm spending the night at Mary Lou's." Mary Lou Hansen was Liz's classmate. "We're meeting her at the Round Hill Club. She's Dylan's date for the night."

"Okay, dear," Dr. Donna Finn replied. "Will you need a ride home in the morning?"

"No, I'll get a ride from Mary Lou or her parents. And if for some reason they're unavailable, I can always get Alex to come and pick me up."

"No problem," Alex replied. "Dylan's staying the night at my house, and we don't have anything going on tomorrow."

Dr. Warren Finn addressed his daughter, "All right, honey. Please call us when you get to Mary Lou's house. The gala ends at eleven. We should still be up. If we fall asleep, just leave a message on the machine."

"Of course, Daddy." Liz kissed both parents.

Alex hugged Liz's mother and shook hands with her father. Dylan shook both Drs. Finns' hands and the group headed outside to the car. Liz's parents stood on the porch to see them off.

Alex opened the BMW's trunk and stowed Liz's bag, then said loud enough for her parents to hear, "Don't let me forget to transfer your bag to Mary Lou's car when we get to the club. I don't want to forget and have to drive all the way to her house afterward." He held the passenger door for Liz, and she took the front seat.

Dylan went to the driver's side and climbed into the back. The BMW was a two door and a tight fit for him, so he settled into the middle. As they left the driveway and headed down the road, Alex and Liz started laughing.

"We're so bad," Liz finally said.

Alex produced a flask from his jacket pocket, unscrewed the cap, and offered it to Liz.

She took a sip, turned, and offered it to Dylan. "Blackberry brandy," she said.

Dylan declined, and Alex chimed in, "Come on, pal, have some. Usually, I have no problem sneaking drinks at the club, but management is strict at these youth events. Kat is twenty-one, but the three of us will be sporting those dreaded black bracelets."

Dylan thought for a moment and was perplexed. Alex hadn't said much about his blind date. He knew she was older and thought she attended college.

Now he was sure Mary Lou was not her name. "What are you two up to?" he finally said.

"Nothing, buddy," Alex replied. "Liz and I are spending the night together at my house. We just needed an alibi. Mary Lou and Liz use each other all the time. If things go well, Kat will be your overnight guest."

Alex and Liz both suppressed another giggle.

"So my date's name is Kat? You never told me…"

"I'm not sure. It's Katherine or Katrina or something, but everyone calls her Kat. I met her at the club. I've known her for a while."

"Whatever," Dylan replied, not overly optimistic about the entire ordeal. He grabbed the flask, took a generous hit of brandy, and handed it back to Liz.

The Round Hill was a very private and exclusive golf and country club catering to Greenwich's affluent establishment. The BMW pulled up to the clubhouse entrance, and two red-jacketed valets rushed to either side of the car. One opened and held the door for Liz while she alighted the vehicle. Alex and Dylan exited the driver's side. Alex handed the other valet two single dollar bills. He, in turn, handed Alex a ticket, thanked him, hopped in the car, and sped off in the direction of the remote parking lot.

Alex and Liz walked hand in hand and made their way to the main entrance. People were milling about outside on the large porch. Dylan stood alone for a moment and admired the stately building. The old stone masonry clubhouse was built in 1921. The porch was covered in a series of awnings. The interior was regularly updated with the latest amenities, having last undergone a major renovation in 1988.

Just as Dylan made his way over to join them, Alex disappeared into the crowd. A moment later, he returned with a strikingly tall, shapely female in tow. Introductions were made. Dylan struggled to maintain eye contact, desiring to take in more of the young woman.

"Kat Jones, nice to meet you," she said with a seductive smile.

"The pleasure is all mine," Dylan replied.

Kat snuggled close to Dylan as they walked toward the reception area.

Alex checked in all members of their party, and a staff member fastened plastic bracelets to each persons' left wrist, orange for Kat and black for the rest of the group. They made their way into the main ballroom, walking beneath a large banner at the entrance that read, Welcome to the Harvest Moon Youth Gala. The banquet hall was decorated in shades of yellow, red, orange, and brown. The band played light instrumental jazz on a stage set up in the front of the room while members and their guests were escorted to their assigned seats. Each table was set with four place settings consisting of fine bone china, crystal glasses, and sterling silverware. A cornucopia centerpiece was placed in the middle of the tables. Two portable bars were set up on either side of the room. No cash ever changed hands inside the club. All purchases, including gratuities, were handled through members' accounts and billed monthly.

As they followed the maître de toward their table, an older male member of about sixty walked past the group in the opposite direction and greeted Kat with a mischievous smile. The man was overweight and balding with considerably large jowls and a red complexion. Kat smiled politely and returned the greeting without breaking stride. Dylan looked at Alex, who shrugged without notice by either woman. The group continued toward their table, stopping occasionally so Alex and Liz could greet other members. Dylan was comfortable in the setting, if only because of his experience working at the Rockrimmon. Secretly pleased the Malloys were not members there, he thought for a moment about how awkward it would be if he showed up as a guest. He wasn't even sure it would have been allowed.

Another older, distinguished-looking gentleman stopped and spoke briefly with Kat. The conversation was limited to an extended innocuous greeting. However, it gave Dylan an opportunity to observe her further.

She wore a tight-fitting camel-colored knit dress that gathered and ended well above the knee, paired with black lace stockings and stiletto heels. She was slim in her overall appearance with disproportionately large breasts and a round backside that was well accentuated by the dress. She had long, thick blonde hair, but Dylan wasn't sure if it was all her own. He thought her face was attractive enough, but she wore considerable makeup in an apparent attempt to deemphasize hard features. Conspicuously, she wore no jewelry and carried no purse. Much to Dylan's delectation, Kat presented an overtly sexy appearance. He ruminated that her attire was a bit tawdry for the occasion, clearly in stark contrast to Liz and the other members who portrayed a more classy, conservative appearance.

They were finally seated at a table toward the front of the room, to the left of the stage and past the bars. A waitress promptly appeared, observed their bracelets, and asked if they wanted anything to drink. Kat ordered a Tanqueray and tonic. The others indicated the water already on the table would be fine. Shortly, an Italian wedding soup was served followed by a garden salad with gorgonzola dressing. A basket of crusty, fresh-baked bread was placed on the table along with the salads.

"So what do you do, Kat?" Dylan asked.

"I'm a student at Southern Connecticut."

"Really? What year are you in?"

"I'm a sophomore."

"That's up in New Haven, isn't it? Are you from around here?"

"Yes and no."

"Excuse me?"

"Yes, Southern Connecticut is in New Haven, but no, I'm not from around here."

"Where are you from?"

"My family is originally from Woonsocket, Rhode Island."

Dylan felt like the conversation was forced but continued. "So where do you stay when you're down here?"

"I have some friends who keep apartments in Greenwich. I stay with them."

Dylan was getting a weird vibe from the conversation. In his experience, girls typically liked to talk about themselves. Kat's short and direct answers indicated otherwise. He decided to focus the conversation on a more group dynamic. She was clearly the quietest of the four, although she laughed politely whenever Dylan or Alex said something clever.

Dinner was beef medallions served over garlic mashed potatoes with a side of roasted green beans and carrots. Dessert was apple pie à la mode. During dinner, Kat ordered a second gin and tonic, never offering to share her drink with Dylan or the others.

After dinner, the band switched from instrumental jazz to dance music featuring numbers from Kool and the Gang, Michael Jackson, and Prince to Donna Summer and Cyndi Lauper. The upbeat music was accompanied by a light show. Kat excused herself from the table a couple of times and disappeared into the crowd. Alex and Liz just looked at Dylan and smiled. Dylan danced with Kat once, and she appeared to enjoy herself. He and Alex switched off another time, and Dylan danced with Liz.

Occasionally, the lights dimmed and the band played a slow number. They began to play "I Can Love You Like That" by All-4-One, and Dylan asked Kat to dance a second time. She enthusiastically agreed and led him by the hand. They merged into the center of the dance floor, completely engulfed by other couples. They each had their arms around the other's neck and waist. Kat pulled Dylan closer and seductively grinded against his crotch. "You have a very hard body."

Dylan leaned his head back, looked her in the eye, and smiled. When the song ended, they worked their way back to the table where Alex and Liz were standing as if ready to go.

"What do you say we take this party back to my house?" Alex asked.

Before Dylan could reply, the girls said in unison, "Heck yeah."

The four of them headed for the exit. The temperature had dropped further, and once outside, Liz shivered. Alex rearranged the wrap around her shoulders. Dylan looked at Kat in the moon light, musing about how sexy she looked in that tight dress. The valet retrieved the BMW, and Dylan contemporaneously held the passenger door open and front seat forward while Kat climbed into the back seat. He then reset the front seat and held the door for Liz.

"Ever the gentleman," remarked Alex from outside the driver's door.

"Always," replied Dylan as he ran around the car and hopped in the back seat behind Alex.

Everyone was quiet on the ride home. Kat leaned into Dylan and placed her head on his shoulder. As they approached the main entrance to Hillcrest Park Estates, the guard recognized Alex's BMW, lifted the gate, and waived them in. As they pulled up to the house, Alex pressed a clunky remote-control device clipped to his sun visor and the front gate opened. The house's exterior and surrounding landscaping were brightly illuminated.

Alex dropped Dylan and the girls off at the front door and pulled the BMW into the adjacent six-car garage. He joined them shortly, opened the door, and let everyone inside, then promptly took charge. "Let's all go to the theater room. There's a bar in there, and no one's checking the bracelets."

Everyone laughed and followed Alex through the house. They made their way past formal living and dining rooms and down a hallway to the theater room. It contained a large projection TV and a state-of-the-art, videocassette recorder system. The room was equipped with two love seats and four matching recliners. The individual chairs were closest to the screen on the floor level. The two couches were situated directly behind the chairs on an elevated platform. Alex took drink orders. Kat asked for a brandy, and Liz concurred. Alex served the ladies' drinks and brought Dylan and him beers. The couples occupied the couches and sipped their drinks in silence.

Alex stood up, went over to the video equipment, and loaded a VHS tape into the player. He looked at Liz, and as if on cue, she arose from the couch. "Well, we're heading upstairs. I put in a movie I think you two might enjoy. The remote control is on the end table. It's all set up, just hit Play." And with that the pair exited the room with their arms around each other's waists.

Dylan took a healthy gulp of his beer and looked at Kat. "What do you want to do?" he asked.

She displayed a seductive smile. "Anything you want," she said.

"What time do you have to leave?" Dylan wasn't sure why he asked the question as soon as the words left his mouth.

"I have until midnight."

Thoroughly confused and eager to move past yet another awkward moment, Dylan said, "Why don't we just watch the movie."

"Sure, honey, anything you want."

Why does she keep saying that? Dylan thought.

The McDirts didn't have a VCR, nor did Dylan's grandparents. He had watched VHS movies at the Malloys before but was otherwise intimidated by the technology. Dylan got up and walked over to the video equipment, looking down at two empty movie boxes atop the VCR. *Atlantic City*, starring Susan Sarandon and Bert Lancaster and *Educating Rita*, an English romantic comedy. Dylan had seen both movies and figured Alex had selected one for the occasion. *Not bad choices*, he decided.

Dylan walked back over to the table, picked up the remote, pointed it at the equipment, and pressed the Play button. The screen started to light up, and Dylan went back and sat down on the couch with Kat. The picture came into view, featuring a platinum blonde wearing nothing but a garter belt, stockings, and high heels. The movie's title flashed across the screen, *Blonde Heat* starring Seka and John Leslie. Dylan sat frozen in stunned silence. Before he could recover, the scene cut to Seka orally arousing her male costar.

Seated to Dylan's left, Kat stared at the screen with an amused look on her face and placed her right hand between his legs. "It's okay, honey. I like these movies. Guys ask me to watch with them all the time." She gazed intently for a moment as the well-endowed, male costar became fully erect. "I've seen them bigger than that."

Suddenly, the proverbial light bulb went on and Dylan exited the dim-witted state that had hijacked his brain all evening. *Good grief, she's a hooker*, he said to himself. He clicked the VCR remote again and the television's screen went blank.

As if Kat could read his mind, she looked over at him. "You didn't know, did you?"

Dylan usually came across pretty smooth when talking with girls, but this was a novel experience, particularly for a sixteen-year-old. "Honestly, no, not until just now."

She smiled. "It's no big deal. I come from a broken family. I figured out early on that I was going to have to survive on my own. During high school, I went to class, then to the library afterwards to study so I could stay out of my family's way. I left home right after graduation. I moved to New Haven with no money and no place to stay." Kat slid back away from Dylan, then turned and faced him before she continued. "I was admitted to Southern Connecticut, looked into financial aid, and applied on my own. I received a grant and partial tuition scholarship, but it wasn't enough. When I got to campus, guys my age kept asking me out, but they were so clumsy. One night during my freshman year, I met a businessman in a hotel bar. He was in town once a week and offered me an arrangement. I did that for a short time, then met another girl from school who was doing the same thing. I came down to Greenwich with her one weekend and realized this was a better set up. More money, safer, the men are smarter and don't expect anything beyond an enthusiastic evening to-gether. My clients are wealthy and generous. They buy me clothes and pay for spa treatments. It doesn't hurt that I love sex."

"So how does this story end?"

"I'm a good student. I study hard, and I don't do drugs or spend my money on other vices." She smiled again. "Of course, it's different if someone else is buying." Her expression returned serious. "I plan on going to law school and doing this until I graduate. After that, I'm done. I save a lot of my money, and I'll have a big nest egg to start my new life as an attorney."

They both sat in silence and looked around the room awkwardly for a moment. Then Dylan gathered himself and turned back toward Kat. "Well, it's getting late, and I understand you turn into a pumpkin at midnight. I'd give you a ride home, but I don't drive."

"You're sweet. I'll call a cab." Kat got up and went into another room to use the phone.

Dylan stared at the floor, as he attempted to sort through the flood of con-voluted thoughts swirling through his mind.

She returned to the theater room a moment later. "Cab will be here in fifteen minutes. Security will call Alex and disturb whatever he's doing so he can let them in."

Tired and flummoxed, Dylan thought about excusing himself and going upstairs. Then he remembered what Mrs. Malloy had said to him. He waited until the cab arrived and Kat left. He would deal with Alex in the morning.

CHAPTER FIVE

THE NEXT MORNING, DYLAN HEARD the sounds of Alex and Liz leaving the house. He immediately fell back to sleep, waking an hour later when Alex returned. Dylan stormed downstairs and confronted him in the kitchen. "What the hell, Alex?"

"Whatta you mean, what the hell? I expect a thank you is in order?"

"Thank you, for what? Making a fool out of me?"

"So, what happened?"

"Nothing happened. I figured out what she did for a living, and she left a little while later."

Alex grimaced. "What a waste. Look, pal, you got a lot going on, and I haven't seen you with a girl in a good while. I thought a sure thing before your big game next weekend was just what you needed."

"You're a real piece of work, you know that? What did that cost you anyway?"

"Believe me, you don't want to know."

"Don't tell me you've been with her?"

"Heck no. I don't pay for sex. I heard about her through the grapevine."

"Great, so you don't pay for it, but I'm the pathetic schmuck who has to?"

"First of all, you didn't pay. Second, you didn't have sex with her, so no harm, no foul. Besides, I got something important to show you."

Dylan regarded him skeptically. "Let's get something to eat first."

"We can go get lunch later. Grab an instant breakfast bar from the cupboard and wait here for a minute."

Dylan grabbed two chocolate Carnation Instant Breakfast bars while Alex ran upstairs and returned with a black, unmarked box in his hand.

Dylan narrowed his eyes. "What is that?"

"Follow me."

"Where are we going?"

"To the theater room."

"Oh no. I'm not watching porn with *you*."

Alex laughed. "I was just trying to help you out. Give it a break."

"I'm not going in there until you tell me what this is about."

"Fine. Southington beat Danbury yesterday, so you'll play Southington on Saturday. We played them this season. They hammered us, but I got a copy of the game film and broke down their passing game."

"How'd you get the game film? And when did you do this?"

"The coaches let me sit in on film sessions sometimes. Even though I don't play, I know the game and they appreciate my input on strategy. Because I'm a student, I obviously can't coach, but I probably know as much as any of the assistants. Coach Matheson, the head coach, trusts my opinion and lets me participate. I knew Stamford had a bye week and was waiting to play the winner. I also knew Southington was heavily favored, so I asked Coach for the tape from our game and broke it down."

Dylan followed Alex into the theater room, plopped down in a chair in the front row, and sat back waiting as Alex cued up the film. Alex sat down next to him, remote control in hand. They went over the film together for almost two hours, teacher and student.

As they were wrapping up, Alex made a point to emphasize, "Okay, now here's one more important thing. Most of the time when they're in a passing formation, their wide receiver, Cantwell, is going to be lined up on the right side. You'll be responsible for deep cover on the weak side. Cantwell is by far their best receiver. I heard he's about to sign with Michigan. Anyway, watch this."

Alex played back four separate clips of Southington wide receiver Derrick Cantwell running pass patterns. Twice he ran intermediate out routes. The other two times he ran stop-and-go fly patterns. On each play, he caught the ball. One of the fly patterns went for a touchdown.

"What did you see there?" Alex asked after the clips were played.

Dylan had been watching intently, but the clips were in full speed and he hadn't picked up on any tendencies. "I'm not sure except that guy's big and tall and looks damn fast."

"Why the heck do you think he's going to Michigan. Let me play it back in slow motion and show you what I see." Alex played the two out routes again, then the two stop-and-go patterns. "Okay, first, Cantwell wears number 81. On all the routes he goes eight yards down field. Notice how on the stop-and-go, Cantwell always uses an out move. On all patterns, he plants his inside foot and rotates his hips. But when he makes his fake move on the go-pattern, he only rotates his hips about forty-five degrees. Of course, on the out pattern he fully rotates his hips a full ninety degrees and cuts directly to the sideline. If you take a slight outside position in coverage and he's going to fake, you'll be able to see the 1 on the front of his jersey the whole time. If the 1 disappears, he's taking the out pattern. Don't bite on the move until the 1 disappears. If you jump the route at that moment, you'll have a clear path to the end zone."

Dylan stared off in deep concentration for a moment and then focused back on the screen. "Play those again at full speed."

Alex obliged, and Dylan leaned forward, laser focused on the screen. When the video finished, he remarked, "Okay, so I see the pattern on those four clips, but how do I know he's gonna do that every time?"

Alex broke into his cocksure smile. "I just pulled those four plays to show you. I watched an isolation of Cantwell on every offensive play of the game. He makes that same move every time. Plus, I was there watching on the sidelines. Cantwell only runs six routes. Those two, plus a straight fly and deep post. He also goes across the middle straight off the line, and they run a screen to him. It's not a complicated offense. They just take advantage of Cantwell's superior speed and athletic ability." He stood and gestured with his hands. "In case it's not apparent, Cantwell's gotten lazy and predictable. That'll change when he gets to college. And here's the other thing. Their quarterback, number ten, has a so-so arm. When he throws that out pattern, the ball has some air under it. Even if you hesitate a second, you can still jump the route."

Dylan knew Alex was a sports geek savant. He knew this stuff inside and out and trusted his judgment. Why shouldn't he, if the Fairfield Prep coaches did? He turned to his friend and said, "We won't even watch film and start preparing until Monday's practice. You did good, Alex. Almost makes up for humiliating me last night."

"Humiliate? I did you a favor. You messed up."

"I'm not you. But just thinking about what you spent on that girl somehow makes it all worthwhile. Now you can buy me lunch, and if this scouting report works out, we'll call it even."

CHAPTER SIX

T HE FOLLOWING WEEK FLEW BY. Dylan managed to concentrate in class, but his primary focus was football practice and preparation for Saturday's playoff game against Southington. Cheryl and Anthony pitched in during the week to help with the paper route, but a neighborhood kid did the bulk of the work.

Tommy Peck and his little brother, Ricky, lived three houses down from the McDirts on Cold Springs Road. Tommy had helped Dylan with the route since he'd entered high school on those occasions when Dylan's other activities conflicted with his newspaper deliveries. However, Tommy recently landed a job pumping gas after school and informed Dylan he was no longer available. A sixth grader at Dolan Middle School, Ricky loved sports and idolized Dylan. He sometimes followed along on his bike while Dylan delivered papers. He took a liking to Ricky and trained him to deliver the papers after Tommy moved on. Ricky handled the job perfectly each time he substituted for Dylan. Privately, he decided Ricky would be the heir apparent when it was time for him to give up the route.

The Stamford Black Knights were Fairfield County Conference champions. Based upon their record and first-place finish, Saturday's game would be held at Stamford's iconic Boyle Stadium. In 1942, the football stadium had been named for Michael A. Boyle, the school's longtime coach and athletic director who presided over the program from 1907 until 1938, compiling 229 victories and a remarkable .809 winning percentage.

On Friday, the school held a pep rally in the stadium. Students, teachers, and staff filled the stands. The school marching band played fight songs and the cheerleaders and pep squad entertained the crowd. Each player wore his game jersey to school, Dylan sporting his number 31.

The game kicked off at one o'clock on Saturday to a sold-out crowd, with both teams well represented. Also present were coaches from several college programs. Those in attendance included University of Connecticut head coach, Terry Stafford. The Huskies were on a bye week, and Coach Stafford was heavily recruiting two juniors from Stamford High and one from Southington. Stamford offensive tackle, Mike Marinelli, and linebacker, Levon Jones, had verbally committed to UConn. Southington cornerback, Victor Whitehead, had offers from several schools including Boston College, West Virginia, and William and Mary. Stafford wanted him badly.

The game started out uneventfully. Neither team scored in the first quarter with both teams punting twice and playing for field position. Early in the second quarter, Stamford broke the scoreless tie when running back Darius Douglas ran nineteen yards for a touchdown. Southington tied the game late in the second half when quarterback Donald Flood hit Derrick Cantwell for a forty-eight yard touchdown pass. Cantwell had originally lined up on Dylan's side but went in motion before the snap, so the touchdown took place on the opposite side of the field.

Dylan had a good first half. Only one short pass was caught in front of him on third and long, and Southington was forced to punt on the next play. He also had four first-half tackles and a highlight-reel jarring hit on a slot receiver who attempted to catch a pass over the middle. The hit caused the receiver to drop the ball and remain motionless on the turf for several seconds before getting up and returning to the huddle.

A defensive battle continued in the second half until Southington kicked a field goal to start the fourth quarter and was up 10-7. With less than three minutes remaining and Stamford moving down the field, quarterback Keith Lucheski threw an interception, giving Southington the ball on the Stamford forty-two yard line. All Southington had to do was run out the clock. But Stamford's defense dug in and held Southington to one yard on first down and no gain on second.

On third and nine, Derrick Cantwell lined up on the right side. Stamford's cornerback attempted to jam him on the line, but Cantwell juked him and released quickly. Dylan picked him up, and eight yards down field, Cantwell made his cut to the outside. Dylan back pedaled directly in front of him and focused on his midsection as the receiver made his move. Cantwell fully rotated his hips and the 1 on his jersey disappeared. Dylan looked up and read the quarterback's eyes, locked in on number 81. Dylan jumped the route, snatched the ball out of the air, and ran untouched into the end zone.

The stadium erupted in cheers while Dylan was mobbed by his teammates in a wild, end-zone celebration. He scanned the stands as he jogged back to the bench. Cheryl, Anthony, and Isabella stood screaming wildly. Alex was standing next to Cheryl, and the two friends made eye contact. Dylan pointed at Alex and he replied with a thumbs up.

With Stamford leading 14-10 and less than a minute remaining, the Knights went into their prevent defense. Dylan and five other defensive backs kept everything in front of them. Dylan broke up a last-ditch Hail Mary pass to end the game.

A raucous celebration followed in the Stamford locker room. Their head coach, Gino DaSilva, addressed the team and handed out game balls. Dylan was named defensive player of the game and awarded the actual ball he intercepted for the game-winning touchdown. Afterward, he was interviewed by sports reporter Mark Shepard from the *Advocate*.

Dylan knew his family would be waiting outside for him and he also wanted to thank Alex for his help with game preparation and go over his big play. He showered and changed as quickly as he could.

As he was departing the locker room, Coach DaSilva intercepted him. "McDirt, there's someone here who wants to meet you. Come with me."

Dylan followed Coach DaSilva to his office, where came face to face with UConn Coach Stafford standing in front of the coach's desk. Coach DaSilva introduced the two. They shook hands, and everyone sat down.

Coach Stafford said, "You played a great game out there today, Dylan. I've got to admit, I came here today to see some of my recruits, but the way you played caught my attention. And that was well before your game-winning play."

"Thank you, Coach," Dylan promptly replied.

"Have you thought about going to school at UConn?"

"Oh, yes, sir. UConn is a good school. That's my first choice. I have excellent grades and just scored in the eighty-fourth percentile on the SATs. I want to major in economics or finance."

"That's good to hear, son. But have you given any thought to playing college football?"

"To be honest, sir, I haven't received any attention. I also play baseball and do pretty well at both sports, but I had planned on concentrating on my education."

"Well, it sounds like a bright boy like you could handle football and schoolwork. Student athletes at UConn receive all types of tutoring and other assistance. Not to mention athletic aid to pay for school."

Dylan sat there in stunned silence for a moment, reflecting that UConn was his best option for college. His family didn't have much money, so he was destined for a state school. UConn was the state's flagship university with an excellent academic reputation.

Coach Stafford gestured with his hand. "I'm going to speak with Coach DaSilva some more about your play and look at some game film. I'd like to keep in touch."

"I'd like that, sir," Dylan replied.

"Great, then I'll get your contact information from Coach and we'll be in contact."

Dylan took that as the cue that the impromptu meeting was about to conclude.

They both stood and shook hands again.

"Thank you. It was nice meeting you, Coach Stafford. I look forward to speaking with you again," Dylan said.

He left the office and headed for the locker room exit. When he got outside, a large crowd of parents, students, and fans still gathered around greeted him with a loud round of applause. He smiled and waved, then looked through the mob for his family. He found his mother and gave her a big hug as tears of pride flowed down her cheeks.

Next he hugged both of his grandparents, who'd been standing behind Cheryl and eagerly waited to congratulate him as well. His grandfather exclaimed with a lump in his throat, "Great game, Dylan. Your grandmother and I are so proud of you."

Dylan smiled modestly and looked around. "Where's Alex?"

Cheryl grinned and shook her head. "He was out here with us waiting for you and met a cheerleader. They took off together somewhere."

Dylan laughed. "That sounds like Alex."

CHAPTER SEVEN

STAMFORD'S SEASON ENDED THE FOLLOWING Friday night with a quarter final loss to eventual state champion, New Britain High School. Suddenly, without football practice, weightlifting sessions, and games, Dylan's schedule was considerably less hectic. It would remain that way until early March when baseball practice started.

Dylan was back to his regular afternoon routine delivering papers, much to the chagrin of Ricky Peck. One afternoon as he approached Mrs. Lott's house, he saw Franklin out in the front yard.

"Ah, Dylan how are you?"

"Fine, Franklin. How are you?"

"Very well."

"How is Mrs. Lott?"

"She's doing well. Today would be a good day for a visit if you have time."

"Sure."

"Mrs. Lott is in the sitting room. Please go right in and bring the paper with you."

Dylan entered the house and found her seated in the usual position on the couch. "Good afternoon, Mrs. Lott."

"Dylan, it's nice to see you. You haven't been around much lately. I understand you've been receiving some help with your paper route."

"Yeah. With football practice and all, my family was pitching in and I think I found my eventual replacement. He's been helping me out too."

"Well, it's wise of you to plan ahead. After all, you'll be heading off to college before too long. Any more thought about where you'll be going?"

"I really want to go to the University of Connecticut. It's a good school, and I may even get a scholarship."

"Really? Tell me about this scholarship opportunity."

Dylan relayed the story of his meeting the UConn football coach.

"That's great, Dylan. I'm very proud of you. I'm not much of a sports fan, but I do follow Stamford High School sports. I read you had a good game a couple weeks ago. Too bad about the loss to New Britain."

Dylan looked at her with raised eyebrows. Despite all their past conversations, neither sports nor his playing career had ever come up. "Thanks. I didn't know you followed sports."

"I follow your career. The *Advocate* does a good job covering high school sports."

Dylan looked around and saw copies of the *Wall Street Journal* and *New York Times* on the coffee table between them. "Do you get those papers delivered too?"

"Oh yes. They're delivered by a Dow Jones van. The driver throws them in the front yard. They arrive around midmorning."

"You sure are well read."

Mrs. Lott smiled. "It's all part of my investment research. I'm a fairly conservative investor. I own treasury bills, municipal bonds, and blue-chip stocks. But a portion of my portfolio is invested in growth stocks. I seek out fledgling innovative companies and invest in them early on. I thoroughly research a company and their management team. When I find something I like, I buy and hold the stock for the long term. Historically, my best investments have been in growth stocks."

"But how do you know which companies to invest in?"

"That's where the research comes in. *The Journal* regularly covers start-up companies and initial public offerings."

She took a moment to explain the concepts, then said, "First, I sift through the daily barrage of business news. Then I do further research on companies that appear promising. I send for annual reports and read everything I can find on a prospective company's principals and its industry. The public library is also an excellent source of information. The pace of technological change is quickening, and there are ample opportunities for savvy investors who do their homework. I believe future technology will have a profound effect on how we live. However, I'm afraid some of the changes will have adverse consequences on society."

Dylan took it all in. "Do you ever miss on a stock?"

She smiled again. "Once in a great while an investment doesn't turn out well. But you must appreciate the concept of diversification. My investments are spread out over a variety of stocks and bonds. Purchases of the start-up growth stocks we're discussing can be somewhat riskier than other investments, but the potential reward is greater. I can afford an occasional mistake on a purchase because all my other investments balance it out."

"My friend's father runs a brokerage house. Do you ever use a broker to advise you on where to invest?"

This time she laughed out loud. "At the expense of coming across as insolent, not particularly. I find stockbrokers a necessary evil. Investing used to be very expensive and out of reach for many people. Laws changed some years ago, which made it easier for people to buy and sell securities. I use a discount broker simply to conduct transactions on decisions I make." She hesitated for a moment, then continued in a softer tone. "Tell me about this football scholarship opportunity."

"I don't know much else. Coach Stafford—he's the football coach at UConn—said he would be back in touch with me."

"Have you thought about what you'll do if the football scholarship doesn't come through?"

"I've saved up most of the money I made from my paper route and other jobs. Plus, my mom and grandparents will help me out as best they can. I really want to go to UConn, but it's more expensive than the other state schools. If the scholarship doesn't come through, I'm not sure. I could always go to West Conn. That's where my mother went. Or possibly Southern Connecticut. I just met a girl who's a student there."

The old woman's face brightened. "Oh, a college girl. Is this older woman a potential girlfriend?"

"No, nothing like that." Dylan replied sheepishly.

"Well, I better let you get back to your paper route. It's good to see you back on the job."

CHAPTER EIGHT

A LEX HAD A DAILY COMMUTE of about forty minutes to and from school each day, so he and Dylan usually talked at night after both returned home. Alex was fervent about the prospect of Dylan playing college football and constantly badgered him over the weeks following his impromptu meeting with the UConn coach. He was beginning to wear Dylan down with his annoying fanboy routine. The conversations were always the same. "That'll be great," he'd say. "I could come up to Storrs on weekends and watch you play. And UConn plays Yale every year. It'll be awesome!"

"Easy, big fella, I just met the coach. Let's wait and see what happens."

"When do you expect to hear from UConn again?"

"I told you a dozen times, I'm not sure. I wrote Coach Stafford a note thanking him for meeting with me and looked forward to speaking again. All I can do now is wait."

UConn completed their season at the end of November, finishing with a 5-6 record. One evening in early December, Cheryl and Dylan had retired to their rooms after dinner. The phone rang, and Cheryl ran into the kitchen to answer it. She shouted to Dylan, who was mired in trigonometry homework.

"Phone for you, Dylan."

As Dylan got up and walked into the kitchen, his mother held her hand over the mouthpiece and whispered, "I think it's UConn."

Dylan took the phone and turned his back to her. "Hello."

"Dylan, this is Coach Bo Fuller. I'm the defensive backs coach at UConn."

"Yes, sir, hello. I know who you are."

"I understand that you and Coach Stafford spoke in Stamford following your playoff game in October. He asked me to follow up with you. Our season just ended, and we're back to recruiting full-time. I wanted to call and introduce myself. We have a short window to contact recruits before the dead period. We're not permitted to speak with prospects for about a month during the holiday season, until school's back in session in January. Do you have some time to talk?"

"Yes, sir."

They spoke for about fifteen minutes, discussed football, what the UConn program had to offer, and briefly touched on academics.

Coach Fuller explained that he had received and reviewed tape from Dylan's high school coach, then went on to say, "I like what I see in your game, Dylan. You're a good athlete, aggressive and have a nose for the ball. You'll need to bulk up and work on your technique, but we have the resources here to develop those things. However, we do have a limited number of scholarships available, and quite frankly, you weren't on our radar until recently."

Dylan shut his eyes as he processed the critique

Fuller continued. "I've spoken with Coach DaSilva, and he tells me you play baseball as well. I've investigated that further and talked with our baseball coaches. I understand you play the outfield and also pitch. We have a good baseball team here. The program has made it to the College World Series five times and produced plenty of professional players. UConn doesn't normally recruit dual sport athletes, but I understand you'll need financial assistance to attend school here. Playing both sports may be a way to get you athletic aid. Does that sound like something you'd be interested in?"

Dylan began pacing around the small kitchen, restrained only by the length of the phone cord, awash in a sudden wave of overwhelming excitement. Not only was he delighted to hear back from UConn, but now the prospect of playing college football *and* baseball blew him away. He took a deep breath in an effort to reduce his heart rate as he simultaneously labored to gather his thoughts. "Oh yes, sir," he finally jabbered.

"Great. Let me ask you, what other schools are recruiting you for football?"

His lucidity returning, Dylan cleared his throat and replied, "I'm looking at number of schools, but none of them have discussed the opportunity to play baseball too. And UConn is my number one choice."

"That's great to hear. I'll get back with our football and baseball coaching staffs and let them know of your interest. I'm sure the baseball coaches will be in touch with you personally. I'll be your primary contact person for football." Coach Fuller gave Dylan his office phone number. "Feel free to contact me at any time. If I'm unavailable, leave a message and I'll get back to you."

"Yes, sir, and thanks for calling, Coach Fuller. It was a pleasure speaking with you, and I look forward to pursuing this opportunity further."

His mother had been standing in the adjacent living room and heard the entire conversation from Dylan's side. Since he hadn't said much, she pounced on him the second he hung up the phone. "Well?"

"Well, what?"

"How'd the conversation go?"

"It went well. That was Coach Fuller, the defensive backs coach. Apparently, UConn is interested in me playing football and baseball for them."

She gave him a huge hug. "That's great, honey. You should call your grandfather and tell him. He'll be so excited. We should all go out and celebrate."

"You sound like Alex. Nothing's definite yet."

"You should be more optimistic. A scholarship will pay for school, and you won't be that far away. We can come and watch you play. This is so exciting. We really should all go out and celebrate."

"I guess you didn't hear me," Dylan said as he headed back to his room.

CHAPTER NINE

BRAD DAVIES WAS BORN AND raised outside of Boston. He had one sister, Coral, six years his senior. After high school, Coral attended Bridgewater State University. She started dating a history professor, got married, and dropped out of school to have a baby. Consequently, Brad had ostensibly lived with his parents as an only child since he was in middle school.

His parents divorced when he was a teenager. The primary reason for the split was financial. Brad's father, Kenneth, owned a small chain of dry cleaning stores and made a decent living. However, the Davies' were spendthrifts and their extravagant lifestyle led to a series of financial disasters that nearly cost Kenneth his business.

As the family's financial condition deteriorated, both parents looked elsewhere for solace. Kenneth came home one evening and announced to his wife that he had taken a girlfriend eighteen years his junior. To his chagrin, his wife took the opportunity to break the news that she was having an affair with the vice president of a local bank and leaving her husband for him. Brad quickly learned that the banker was divorced, his children were out of the house and his interest in Brad's mother did not extend to a package deal for him.

He ended up living with Kenneth and his girlfriend, who resembled a sister more than his father's new companion. Actually, she was significantly closer in age to Brad, so the concept was not farfetched. All parties endured the arrangement for a year and a half until Brad left home for college.

Not a particularly good student, he settled for Western New England University. After graduation, he held a series of jobs in large Boston-based companies with the objective of climbing the corporate ladder. Unfortunately, his myriad character flaws foiled his career plans. First, Brad had inherited his parents' reckless financial habits. He craved status in material possessions and lived well beyond his means. Additionally, his personality turned off his coworkers. He was condescending to subordinates, and his obnoxiousness and poor work habits resulted in unsatisfactory evaluations from management. Consequently, he was assigned to inferior projects and overlooked for promotions. Most significantly, he was a misogynist who sexually objectified women. His final job in corporate America ended when he was fired for unremitting sexual harassment of a supervisor's secretary.

Humiliated and essentially ostracized from the Boston business community, Brad packed up and moved to Connecticut. He settled in Darien and took a job working as a telemarketer, offering people credit cards from department stores and oil companies. As usual, he alienated his coworkers, but the job duties minimized his interaction with others.

Furnished with a script and printout of phone numbers from across the country, Brad sat in a cubicle with a headset strapped to his noggin and made cold calls in the afternoon and evenings when it was the best time of day to reach a decision-maker. Despite his repugnant personality, he quickly found success. His narcissism and lack of self-awareness proved to be a positive combination in the world of direct phone sales.

Brad quickly realized that his sales increased proportionately to his deviation from the script. He regularly dispensed with the required disclaimers and legal notifications. Initially, this brought reprimands from his supervisor. However, his tactics were eventually overlooked as the job paid straight commission and his manager's bonus was based on the number of prospects that received credit cards.

Wanda Peeples was the office sales manager. A few years older than Brad, she had been in the top twenty-five percentile when she'd worked in sales. She'd been promoted based upon her tenure and willingness to accept an initial pay cut, which resulted from switching to salary from commission. Most high-performing salespeople eschewed management to remain in sales. She was unattractive by any measure. She was overweight, and the excess poundage settled around her midsection, hips, and thighs. Her frizzy hair was unkept, and she wore thick black rimmed glasses. Her attire consisted of sets of monochromatic chinos and tops in pinks, yellows, and light blues.

Fortunately for Brad, direct sales was a profession where job performance was easily evaluated based upon objectively-quantifiable results. Within a few months, he was the top performer and the number one earner in the office. Wanda was impressed with Brad and gradually became enamored. Her conduct toward him reflected her infatuation. Brad found himself in the rare position as the target of a woman's affections. Although not overly selective about the women he harassed, he had no interest in Wanda but deviously contrived a plan to take advantage of the situation that presented itself.

He began seeing Wanda outside of the office. Not wanting to be seen with her in public, he cited office policy as the excuse to carry on their trysts in private. They typically met at Wanda's apartment. Quite perceptively, he ascertained that Wanda was more than willing to comply with his demands, both in and out of the bedroom. He gave her a list of his food and beverage preferences, and she made sure the house was fully stocked. He requested Johnnie Walker and red wines exclusively from France and imbibed voraciously. He was habitually selfish and demanding in bed. Once again, Wanda had no problem submitting to his demands. He forced Wanda, at her expense, to purchase and dress up in bedroom costumes as a prerequisite to sex. His preferences ranged from French maid and nurse to prostitute. He regularly humiliated her during their sexual encounters, and she accepted the submissive role although she secretly desired an occasional evening of conventional romance.

One night after Chinese takeout and two bottles of Saint Julian Bordeaux, Brad disappeared into the bedroom and came back out a short time later barking orders at Wanda. "Your outfit is laid out on the bed. Go take a shower, get changed, and wait for me. And make sure you shave down there."

"Yes, sir," she replied meekly as she got up and waddled toward the bedroom.

Brad waited patiently in the living room, watching the Red Sox-Tigers game while he enjoyed a snifter of Courvoisier. After two innings, he yelled out in the direction of the bedroom, "Are you ready for me?"

"Ready and willing."

He got up and staggered into the bedroom.

Sprawled out on the bed with her legs spread, Wanda wore a white fishnet bodystocking and black six-inch stripper heels. The bodystocking featured spaghetti straps and connected the bodice to the thigh-high stockings with a garter, allowing for access to her vagina and ass. She was pleasuring herself with a pink vibrator he had set out on the bed alongside her outfit.

Brad watched her for a moment before undressing. After he was naked, he stood in front of the bed. "It looks like you've had some fun without me. Get up and get on your knees."

Wanda complied and took him in her mouth, playing along as he occasionally pulled out and slapped her across the face with his erect penis.

"Get back up on the bed and get on all fours," he finally commanded.

Once again Wanda acquiesced, and he entered her from behind. After a few minutes, he came and rolled over, then uncharacteristically kissed her passionately and snuggled next to her.

Taken by surprise at the sudden act of tenderness, Wanda kissed him on the neck and worked her way down his chest toward his crotch. "Do you want me to blow you again?"

"No, it's okay, honey. You were great," he atypically answered.

Psychologically transcended by Brad's sudden change in behavior, Wanda laid her head on his chest.

He continued. "You know, I've been thinking. We make a pretty good team both at work and at play." He lifted his head and made eye contact with a sincere effort at an affectionate smile. "I think we should leave that place together and start our own telemarketing company. I have some seed money to get us started, but we probably wouldn't be able to take much in the way of salary at the beginning. But in the long run, I think it could be a great partnership." He eyed Wanda, waiting for her response.

"I think that's a great idea. I have some money saved so I could get by for a while."

"That's great, dear." He kissed her again on the mouth. "You were great tonight. Let's get together again tomorrow and discuss our exit plan."

Within two weeks, Brad Davies started his own boiler room operation, but with a twist. He hawked high-interest credit cards to people with substandard credit histories. He also maintained a list of customers who were approved and, upon issuance of a new card, had a separate marketing department promptly call back. The customer was offered time shares, useless household gadgets, and discount vacations to tourist destination areas with accommodations in rundown, roadside hotels. The strategy was designed to run up balances on the newly minted cards before other purchases taxed the spending limits. It worked brilliantly.

When they got started, Brad explained to Wanda that he was putting ownership of the company in his name to personally guarantee the office space, equipment leases, and credit line so she could not be held personally liable. Wanda, blinded by the prospect of a promised future with Brad, concurred.

Brad ran the sales and marketing departments while Wanda handled office management, setting up policies and procedures for legal, accounting, purchasing, and personnel. At Brad's request, she had clandestinely copied and smuggled out confidential documents from their former employer to assist with setting up the new business. Within a year, they had over one hundred employees and Brad moved them from an office warehouse in the industrial district to four full floors in a gleaming glass office tower in downtown Stamford. On the day prior to the move, he fired Wanda and had her escorted from the premises.

He also made an effort to elevate his social standing. He wore tailored suits, rented a five-thousand-square-foot pool home in Stamford's Shippan neighborhood and leased a new Mercedes 400 SEL sedan. He joined the local Chamber of Commerce and Rotary Club.

Despite his efforts, Brad failed to assimilate into the Fairfield County upper crust. He applied for, and was denied, membership in four of the better country clubs. Inevitably when it came to meeting the right people, Brad's character flaws emerged and his personality betrayed him. However, he was tenacious and managed to elicit occasional invites as a country club guest or an exclusive charity event attendee.

Brittany Sturm lived with a divorced businessman in a condominium in Riverside. The man provided food, shelter, and clothing in exchange for companionship. One day the man returned home from a business trip and told Brittany it was time for her to move on. He instructed her to pack up her things, handed her three one-hundred-dollar bills as a parting gift, and told her a cab would arrive in thirty minutes to take her wherever she wanted to go.

Brittany had no education beyond high school, no job experience to speak of, and no marketable skills. She did, however, possess a look that elicited lascivious desires in a significant portion of the male population. While not beautiful in the classic sense, she was blessed with a voluptuous body highlighted by disproportionately large, natural breasts. She died her hair blonde and dressed provocatively

With no place to go, no job, and limited funds, Brittany piled into the cab with her two hastily-packed suitcases in tow. She moved into a cheap motel along Route One. Two days later, she found work as a cocktail waitress at a nightclub called the Dialtone. Her black monochromatic uniform of leather hot pants, low-cut halter top, fishnet stockings, and high heel ankle boots accentuated her physical attributes. She took home cash each night from the tips she earned, allowing her to pay for the motel room but not much else.

One slow, weekday night about a month later, a customer paid extra special attention to her. In addition to a lack of job skills, Brittany had little-to-no work ethic. She was not interested in the guy, in the least, much less from a romantic perspective. However, the man grabbed her attention with a fifty-dollar tip and the promise of a well-paying office job. Britany had no office work skills or experience and told him as much. The man insisted none were necessary. He gave her his business card and told her to meet him at his office at two o'clock the following day to discuss the opportunity.

The next afternoon, Brittany uncharacteristically arrived on time at the offices of OPM Enterprises and asked to see Brad Davies. She wore a tight-fitting skirt that was too short for appropriate office attire, a sleeveless turtleneck sweater, and slingback high heels. She was promptly escorted to Davies's office by a secretary who announced Brittany, turned, and left the office, closing the door behind her.

Brittany looked around. The office was large with panoramic views of downtown Stamford through windows along two sides of the room. A large, cherry desk and matching credenza situated on one wall afforded the downtown view. The other wall contained a bar and full-size couch opposite matching leather chairs. Just beyond the bar was a private restroom. Davies stood and motioned for Brittany to sit in one of the leather chairs in front of his desk.

Davies got right to the point. "I'm looking for a personal assistant. The job pays seven hundred and fifty dollars a week, cash under the table, plus a clothing allowance. There may be a need to work some nights. You'll be paid overtime for working after hours. How does that sound?"

She struggled to conceal her eagerness before gathering herself. "The money sounds good, but what exactly would I be doing? I told you at the Dialtone that I don't have any experience working in an office."

"And I told you that type of experience is unnecessary. I'm going to have a drink. Will you join me?"

Accustomed to acquiescing to men's desires, she replied, "Sure. I'll have whatever you're having."

Davies strolled over to the bar, took two glasses and added a couple ice cubes from the machine hidden behind a wood-paneled door. He poured two generous fingers of Johnnie Walker Black Label from an elegant decanter and sat down on the couch, motioning to her to join him

Brittany complied and sat next to Davies.

He raised his glass. "To the beginning of a mutually-beneficial relationship."

She fought the urge to roll her eyes and instead lifted her glass slightly in his direction. "Tell me what you do here."

"That's not important. All you need to know is that I'm the owner of the company. The job I'm offering you as my personal assistant emphasizes the personal part. You met Carmella. She's my secretary and handles all my business requirements."

Brittany was starting to get the picture. She quickly assessed the situation and, given her current predicament, decided to play along. "And what personal requirements do you desire?"

"I won't require much in the mornings, but I expect each afternoon you'll take dictation."

She was on her own turf here, caught on immediately, and made a split-second decision that would allow her to instantly improve her financial standing as well as her living conditions. She licked her lips seductively before responding, "I love dictation. But before we get there, a little more negotiation is in order. I require a week's pay up front and a new car. A lease through the company will be fine."

Davies felt blood rushing to an area just below his beltline. "You're asking for a lot. I'll require appropriate reciprocation for this arrangement to work."

Brittany put her drink down, unbuckled Davies's pants, and unzipped his fly. "You sit back and enjoy your drink."

She got down on her knees in front of him, freed his throbbing penis, and took him expertly into her mouth. Less than two minutes later, Davies exploded in orgasm. Brittany patiently waited for him to finish before going into the bathroom to freshen up.

When she returned, Davies handed her an envelope full of cash. "I guess you started today. You need to be here each morning by nine o'clock. Tomorrow we'll go and lease you a car. Is a Ford Mustang acceptable?"

"As long as it's red."

"Of course. I'll see you tomorrow."

CHAPTER TEN

D YLAN'S FAMILY PREPARED FOR THE Christmas holidays. Cheryl and Dylan both had two weeks off from school for their respective holiday breaks. Alex came by and the three of them decorated the tree together. Cheryl made cookies for the boys. Alex thoroughly enjoyed the casual and close family atmosphere. He teased Dylan about some of the decorations he had made as a child that Cheryl had kept and hung on the tree each year.

Cheryl bought gifts for Dylan and her parents and picked out a small gift for Alex. She was aware of his extravagant tastes and opted for a book on antique watches. Due to financial constraints, discretionary purchases in the McDirt household were limited to birthdays and Christmas.

Cheryl paid into a Christmas-club savings account all year long and splurged during the holidays. Aside from that, if needed, Dylan got some clothing or a new pair of shoes at the beginning of the school year. There simply wasn't a lot of expendable income after the mortgage, utilities, Fairfield County taxes, food, and other household expenses.

Anthony and Isabella were generous with Dylan throughout the year, as funds permitted. The Tomassi house was paid for, and Anthony continued to work part-time so they had some flexibility in their budget. This may have caused friction in some families, but not in their case. Cheryl was cognizant of their financial situation and grateful for her parents' generosity wherever they were able to assist.

Cheryl stayed busy working holiday parties at the Rockrimmon, and Dylan often worked with her. Members were typically in a festive mood that time of year, and tips increased commensurately. Cheryl was an attentive server with a pleasant personality that mirrored her appearance. A vast majority of the male members found her attractive, but her style was nonthreatening to other women. She came across as genuinely friendly but not flirtatious. Consequently, she was well known and appreciated by most of the membership, and several found a moment to discreetly hand her cash in a plain envelope in appreciation for a year of excellent service.

Cheryl rarely had an issue with men's behavior at the club. The members that had asked her out behaved appropriately toward her, notwithstanding their marital status. However, there was one guy who gave her the creeps. She did not know his name, but he had attended as a guest on a few occasions. Strangely, she noted, he was never with the same member. He was outwardly cordial toward her in front of his guests. However, at opportune times when others were out of earshot, he made crude and suggestive comments.

At a party just before Christmas, Cheryl went over to a table to take drink orders and there he was. The guy placed his hand under the tablecloth and rubbed her leg. She recoiled and gathered herself before the others seated at the table noticed.

Later, as she was leaving the restroom, she saw him again. Clearly inebriated, the guy cornered her in an alcove at the pay-phone bank. He grabbed Cheryl in a bear hug and started licking her face, then groped her on the backside. She kneed him in the crotch and made a hasty exit to the kitchen.

Cheryl did not report the incident. Rather, she told herself to let it go. The guy was not a member, and she was unlikely to encounter him again. Still, the experience weighed on her mind as she prepared to celebrate Christmas with her family.

Dylan and Cheryl spent Christmas Eve at her parents' home in Norwalk. Isabella made the traditional Italian dinner of seven fishes, featuring grilled Oysters Rockefeller, baccala, shrimp scampi, seafood pasta, and baked trout. On Christmas morning, the family gathered at the McDirt home and opened gifts. Afterward, an Italian antipasto including mortadella, capocollo, hard salami, acciuga, sharp provolone, mozzarella, green and black olives, and roasted peppers was served with baskets of Italian bread. Christmas dinner included roasted prime rib, ham, and Isabella's famous baked ziti.

Cheryl had a few days off from the Rockrimmon before the parties geared up again as New Year's approached. Connecting with friends who'd remained in Norwalk where she grew up, she made plans for a girls' night out and let her parents know she was going to stay with them that evening rather than drive back to Stamford.

South Norwalk was situated on Long Island Sound and had several marinas and a public beach. In response to the area declining over the past several years, city planners had started providing tax incentives to redevelop the waterfront and surrounding areas. Washington Street ran through the city, connecting downtown to the beaches. A commercial portion of the street near the waterfront had been blighted and many buildings had been boarded up for years. The city's redevelopment plan focused on this area. Bars, nightclubs, and restaurants opened in the vacant spaces. The area was renamed SoNo and became so popular it attracted throngs of people from the southwestern Connecticut suburbs and New York City.

Cheryl met two of her girlfriends at SoNo Prime, a steak restaurant, located in the heart of the Washington Street entertainment district. Due to the area's popularity, Washington Street vehicular traffic crawled down the road, avoiding pedestrians that spilled out into the streets from the overflowing sidewalks. The scene resembled a typical night on a street in New Orleans' French Quarter.

The three girlfriends had a reservation but arrived early and were told their table wouldn't be ready for fifteen minutes. They decided to go to the bar and have a drink while they waited. In addition to serving excellent food, SoNo Prime's bar was a hotspot and a known pickup joint. Singles packed the bar every evening and, consequently, it was standing room only as usual.

Cheryl's two friends were married with three children each. It was fair to say both expended more time and energy taking care of their families than working on their appearances. They told Cheryl to wait and look for an open table or space for them to stand while they maneuvered their way to the bar to get drinks.

Cheryl wore flared blue jeans over tan boots and a cream-colored turtleneck sweater. Her clothes fit her well and accentuated her curvaceous figure. It was a mild enough winter evening, and the breeze off the waterfront was uncharacteristically calm. The snug-fitting sweater allowed her to dispense with a coat. She stood with her back against a wood-paneled wall, glancing around the crowded bar and smiling to herself. She didn't go out much socially and couldn't even remember the last time she'd had a date.

As she waited for her friends to return, she observed a group of men gathered around a high-top table, talking loudly and leering in her direction. Suddenly one of the men broke away from the table and walked toward her. As he got closer, Cheryl recognized the man and froze. Despite the comfortable room temperature, she felt a shiver run down her spine. It was the guy from the Rockrimmon who had attacked her, approaching as if they were friends.

"It's me, Brad. Damn, you look good tonight. I just can't get enough of that body." He reached over and attempted to put his arm around her.

Cheryl winced and then instinctively screamed, "Get away from me, you creep!"

Suddenly, some of the other patrons stopped and stared at them. The expressions on the faces of the men in his group ranged from incredulous to embarrassment.

Brad, incognizant of the scene he was creating, kept at it. "It's a shame we didn't hook up last time. How about I buy you a drink?" He continued groping at Cheryl.

She pushed him away and slapped him across the face.

The crowd broke out in applause.

"You bitch! You're gonna be sorry for that."

Then two large men wearing tight-fitting, black SoNo Prime polo shirts appeared. The pair could have easily been mistaken for New York Giants linemen. One grabbed him by the shoulder. "Let's go buddy," he said.

"I'm not your buddy. Me and my girl here just have a misunderstanding", he said.

"You're the only one in this place who believes that, and you're leaving," the other behemoth replied.

With that, he was escorted out of the bar and deposited onto Washington Street. As he left the bar, he had turned and looked back at Cheryl. "This isn't over bitch."

Cheryl's two girlfriends had returned in time to see the backs of the two bouncers escorting the man out and hugged her compassionately. "Are you okay?" one of them asked.

Tears streamed down Cheryl's face as she gasped for air. "That guy's been harassing me at the Rockrimmon. He attacked me the last time."

"That guy's a member at your club?" the other friend asked.

"Heck no," Cheryl uttered, as she tried to catch her breath. "The club would never accept a man of his ilk. But he manages to come in occasionally as a guest."

The manager came over and apologized profusely to Cheryl. "Please stay for dinner. Your meals are on the house."

Cheryl thought about the offer. She wasn't up to staying but decided she didn't want that creep to ruin her friends' evening. She further reasoned that staying for dinner would give this Brad person time to cool down and put some distance between them.

The group stayed for dinner and shared a bottle of wine. Halfway through the meal, the mood improved. The friends laughed and reminisced about old times. By the time their plates were cleared, Cheryl had calmed down considerably.

"Let's go down to Donovan's for a nightcap," one of her friends suggested.

"You two go ahead," Cheryl replied. "I'm going to head home. I parked my car in the garage on the other side of South Main Street. I don't want to walk down there alone, so I'm gonna call my dad to come pick me up and drive me over to the car."

"Are you sure, honey?" the other friend asked. "You really need to get out more."

She shot her two friends a blank stare and said with a straight face, "No, I don't. See what happens when I try to have fun."

The two friends regarded her, equally stone-faced as they awaited her reaction. Finally, Cheryl smiled and all three burst into laughter.

Cheryl called Anthony from a pay phone and they left the restaurant. "Do you want us to wait here with you?" one of the friends asked when they were outside.

"No, I'm fine," Cheryl said. "You two go ahead and enjoy the rest of your night. I'll speak with you soon."

They all hugged, and the two women headed in the direction of Donovan's.

The wind had picked up since Cheryl arrived and there was now a chill in the air. The front of the SoNo Prime building opened directly to the sidewalk with no recessed area where she could wait and shield herself from the cold. People still milled about on Washington Street by that time of the night, but the crowd had diminished significantly. She reasoned that Anthony would be there any moment and walked down one building to a darkened office entrance that provided some shelter from the weather. She turned, faced the wall, crossed her arms and shivered against the chill.

Suddenly, she felt someone grab her around the neck and place a hand over her mouth. She struggled and tried to scream, but the assailant had a good hold of her and her cries were muffled.

"If you don't wanna get hurt, do what I say. Nod yes if you agree."

Petrified and in shock, Cheryl instinctively nodded in the affirmative.

The perpetrator moved her deeper into the corner of the recessed entrance. It was dark, and no one could see the two of them unless they looked straight into the area. His hand slowly moved from Cheryl's mouth. She inhaled loudly in an effort to catch her breath, but she did not scream. His other arm moved down across her shoulders.

"Now, you've been very rude to me the last couple times, and that's about to change. Do you understand?"

Cheryl stood motionless and quiet.

"I'll take that as a yes." He jammed his hand underneath Cheryl's sweater and tore at her bra. "You've got some set of tits."

She spun around, temporarily escaping his grasp, and slapped him across the face for the second time that evening. He never flinched as he punched her in the face. Her knees buckled. He bent over her fallen body and began to tear at her jeans.

Suddenly, she heard a sickening sound of metal striking skull and the man dropped to the pavement next to her. Cheryl looked up and saw Anthony standing over the two of them with a large trowel in his right hand. She was hysterical but surprisingly hushed. As she attempted to get to her feet, Anthony began violently kicking the man about the head and body. Blood trickled from underneath the heap.

Cheryl got up and grabbed her father's arm. "Stop. You're going to kill him."

"He's lucky if that's all I do to him."

Cheryl and her father focused on each other. "Are you okay, honey? What did he do to you?"

"I'll be alright. He tore at my clothes and punched me in the face." Cheryl's right eye had begun to swell shut and blacken.

Suddenly, the man grabbed Anthony around the legs and pulled him to the ground. Anthony was the larger of the two men, but the other man had the advantage of youth by at least twenty years and managed to get to his feet. He punched Anthony in the stomach, doubling him over at the waist, then got up and ran in the direction of South Main Street.

As he was fleeing, he called back over his shoulder, "I know who you are. I'm not through with you. Next time I'm gonna finish what I started, and I'm not gonna be so gentle."

Anthony made a move to go after him, but Cheryl grabbed his shoulder. "He's gone."

They watched in silence as the assailant disappeared into the night. They gathered themselves and got into Anthony's truck, which was double-parked in front of SoNo Prime. He dropped the trowel back in the bed of his truck on the way to the driver's side door.

Father and daughter were quiet on the short ride home. When they got in the house, Isabella was already asleep in bed.

Anthony hugged her. "It's alright now, you're safe honey. Get some sleep and we'll talk about this in the morning," he said.

"Yes, Daddy. I love you." Cheryl hugged him back tightly and retired to her old bedroom.

Cheryl slept uncharacteristically late the next morning. It was past nine-thirty when she walked into the kitchen, finding her parents seated at the table drinking coffee both wearing concerned expressions. Isabella gasped when she saw her daughter's face, her eye was swollen and the hue a dark purplish black. She went over and gently examined the eye. "Oh my Lord."

"It's okay, Mama. It looks worse than it feels," Cheryl said as she poured herself a cup of coffee.

Anthony chimed in. "Please tell me what happened last night."

Cheryl described her encounter with the man.

"Have you given any thought on how to deal with this?"

"What can I do, Daddy?"

"We need to contact the police. This man assaulted you twice last night."

"I'm afraid to do that. It may make him angrier. And an investigation could involve the Rockrimmon. I don't want to make trouble for them or risk losing my job. We need the money."

"The Rockrimmon? What does the club have to do with this?"

"That same guy has been a guest at the club on occasion and just before Christmas he harassed me and later attacked me when I was coming out of the restroom."

"Did he hurt you?"

"No, I kicked him in the balls and ran."

"Good girl! What did the club do about it?"

"Nothing. There were no witnesses, and I didn't report it."

"How did this guy harass and attack you with all those people around, without anyone seeing or hearing something? What's his name anyway?"

"I only know his first name is Brad. And he's sneaky and sleezy, like a stalker."

"The club would know his name from the guest list."

"Again, that would cause them to get involved."

"I see your point."

After a prolonged silence, Cheryl said, "I'm just going to let it be. I don't even know who this guy is. It was a freak thing running into him here after the incident at work in Stamford. It's unlikely I'll ever see him again. And if he does show up at the Rockrimmon, I'll deal with it then."

Anthony's expression turned to one of exasperation. "Okay, dear. I don't like it, but I'll respect your wishes."

"One other thing. This stays between us. I don't want anyone else to know, especially Dylan."

"What're you going to say to him when he sees your eye?"

"I'll tell him I tripped and fell." Cheryl wasn't hungry and declined breakfast. "I think I'm going to just head home."

"Please shower and clean yourself up before you go," her mother pleaded.

"Good idea, Momma. Do you have some makeup I can borrow?"

"Sure, honey, it's in the drawer underneath the sink."

Cheryl excused herself, grabbed a fresh set of clothes, and went into the single, small bathroom where she showered and changed. She usually wore little makeup but applied a thick coat of foundation in an effort to conceal her black eye. After she was finished, she checked her face in the mirror and went back into the kitchen. Both of her parents were seated at the table, bearing the same concerned expressions.

"Why don't you stay a little longer?" her mother implored.

"Thanks, Momma, but I just want to get home." She hugged and kissed her goodbye. "I love you."

"I love you too, dear."

Anthony drove Cheryl to where she had left her car the night before. After they arrived, she held her father in a long embrace, then put her bag in the front trunk of the VW beetle. Anthony watched her start the car and drive off before he got back in his truck and headed back home.

Cheryl arrived before noon, finding Dylan and Alex at the house. They had gone out for pizza and watched a movie the night before, and Alex had slept over.

Dylan freaked out when he saw his mother. "Oh my God, what happened to your face?"

Cheryl feigned an attempt at humor. "You should see the other girl."

"Really, Mom, what happened? It looks pretty bad."

"I'm fine. I was walking down Washington Street last night, tripped on the sidewalk, and fell face-first. It was so embarrassing."

She looked at both boys inquisitively, seeking a hint as to whether they were buying the story. Neither of them spoke as they stared at her eye, each deep in his own thoughts.

Finally Alex said in as sincere a tone as he could muster, "Wow, Mrs. McD, that's something. Did you over-imbibe?"

Cheryl giggled. "No, Alex. I was talking with my girlfriends, and I guess I just wasn't looking where I was going."

Alex replied, "I've been out on Washington Street a few times. Where'd you go last night?"

"We had dinner at SoNo Prime. You know the place?"

"Sure, I've eaten there before. Good food. That area has really picked up. A few years ago, you wouldn't have caught me dead in South Norwalk. Now everyone hangs out there. Did you go anywhere else last night?"

"No, Alex. Why the sudden interest in my social life?"

"Just curious, that's all. I think it's a cool area. Just wondering if you went anywhere else that I might wanna check out."

"Nope that was it. Just had dinner and caught up with some friends from high school."

"Well, as always, it was good to see you, Mrs. McD. I should be getting home." Alex grabbed his overnight bag and headed for the front door. "Dylan, I'll check in with you later."

Dylan stood there in silence, taking in the entire scene.

Alex drove home from the McDirts, consumed with thoughts about Cheryl the entire trip. He loved his parents, and they were very generous and supportive. But his father was busy running the brokerage, and both were heavily involved in the social, civic, and charity scenes. Consequently, his relationship with his parents had become more distant as he'd gotten older.

Dylan was his best friend, and the loving bond between him and his mother had been apparent from the outset of their friendship. Alex thought of Dylan as a brother and, by extension, considered Cheryl a second mom. He didn't buy her story about falling and found the thought troubling.

Later that night, Alex called Dylan. "What's up?"

"Not much, I'm just hanging out at home. I'm kind of worried about my mom. She's been real quiet and spent all day in her room sleeping. That's unusual for her."

"Did you talk with her about it?"

"I tried to. I asked her more about last night, but she was short with me. She made it clear she was embarrassed about falling in front of all those people and didn't want to talk about it anymore."

A thought began to formulate in Alex's mind. "I wouldn't worry about it."

"That's easy for you to say."

"Trust me on this." Alex hung up the phone and walked into Jackson's study where father and son engaged in a prolonged conversation.

CHAPTER ELEVEN

MALLOY WILLIAMSON & ASSOCIATES WAS originally headquartered in Lower Manhattan. In 1986 Jackson Malloy II moved the headquarters to Greenwich, but the company continued to maintain its original offices in New York's Financial District. The new headquarters occupied an entire six-story office building in the Greenwich Office Park.

Kurt Nesbitt, Malloy Williamson's chief of security, maintained an office in the opulent edifice. Nesbitt was a retired New York City Police Officer who had run the First Precinct in the Wall Street District. Nesbitt was well-connected in law enforcement throughout New York and Connecticut.

The security department was ostensibly limited to Nesbitt and his uniformed, private-security officers. The officers were stationed at the entrances of both locations. Employees presented identification badges for entry. Clients and visitors presented themselves to the security desk. Clients were promptly admitted while the screening process for visitors took longer.

In reality, the Malloy Williamson Security Department was a large clandestine operation. The department ran out of an anonymous office in a Greenwich industrial park. There was no signage, directory, or any other outward indication of its existence. The department was staffed with fifteen full-time employees. Several others of various specialty skill sets were on retainer. The security department was responsible for protecting the firm's data processing systems, financial records, and client information. It also conducted background checks and investigations on prospective employees and clients. Additionally, it furnished personal security services to company executives and assisted the firm's Compliance Department when necessary. However, the scope of its work was even broader.

Receipt of timely, accurate information was critical to the company's investment results and ultimate profitability. Deep intelligence on such data ranging from a business's evaluation, activities, and management team to prospective IPOs, stock splits, and mergers and acquisitions also fell into security's bailiwick. Additionally, corporate espionage was an ongoing threat from competitors. Security regularly monitored for such activity and once discovered, dealt with the matter accordingly.

Finally, the firm's highest producers were analysts and stockbrokers with wealthy client bases, so these team members operated in highly competitive, stressful environments. Accordingly, many of them played as hard as they worked. Occasionally a top producer would find themself in a difficult personal predicament. Issues such as DUIs or other scrapes with the law, unhappy or, occasionally, pregnant mistresses, and personal safety threats resulting from various transgressions occurred periodically. The firm could not afford to have its top people distracted or functioning at less than full capacity. Hence, the security department stepped in to remedy the problem.

Security played a vital role in assisting management with evaluating and monitoring employee productivity. When an issue was detected, the affected person was summoned to meet with a manager. Employees were encouraged to provide feedback on the source of the trouble. If necessary, a staff psychologist was available to intervene. Once such a problem was identified, the security department went to work and routinely brought the matter to a quick resolution. Employees were typically unaware as to how or who was involved, but it became known within the firm that management was supportive on such matters.

A former army military policeman, Bryan Aranoff, was an investigator in the Malloy Williamson Security Department. He had worked for the New York City Police Department under Kurt Nesbitt when he ran the First Precinct. Aranoff was a good investigator with substantial skills acquired during his military and law enforcement careers. He was adept at conducting high tech surveillance, skip tracing, and witness interrogation. During his tenure with the NYPD, Nesbitt had identified Aranoff as one of his best and brightest young officers and later brought him along when he'd accepted the job with Malloy Williamson.

In the afternoon of the day after New Year's, Nesbitt summoned Aranoff to his office to discuss an assignment. "I've got a job for you. This one's coming down from the top. I need you to look into an incident that occurred last weekend in the SoNo district. We don't have much to go on." Nesbitt handed Aranoff a thin file folder. "This is high priority job one. Find out as much as you can about what happened to this Cheryl McDirt on Saturday night. It may be nothing but see where it goes."

"I'm on it, Boss." Aranoff left the office and returned to his cubicle. He opened the file and reviewed its contents, which consisted of a bio with an accompanying photograph of an attractive brunette, the name and address of a restaurant called SoNo Prime, and family background information with explicit instructions not to contact Dylan McDirt.

Bryan Aranoff drove over to South Norwalk in the early afternoon. SoNo Prime was only open for dinner, so the front door was locked when he arrived. He went around back, finding a small loading dock. The loading dock rolldown door was up for a Tristate Provisions truck making a delivery. Aranoff saw no one in the immediate area so he walked in. He stepped into the kitchen and observed several people in white uniforms milling about, discernibly engaged in various tasks in preparation for that evening. He approached one of them and asked for the manager.

"He's in the dining room."

"Thanks."

Aware he was taking a complete shot in the dark, Aranoff proceeded into the dining room where a single person sat at the bar hunched over paperwork. Approaching the man, he said, "Hey, buddy, can I speak with you for a moment?"

The manager removed his reading glasses and eyed him warily. "What can I do for you?"

"I'm looking into an incident that happened on Saturday night involving this woman." He handed the manager the photo of Cheryl.

The manager looked at the photo. "Who are you, a cop?"

"No, nothing like that. I'm a private investigator."

"What's your interest in this?"

Okay, so maybe something did happen, Aranoff thought. "Were you working on Saturday?"

"Yeah, I was here. I had to get my security guys involved. We handled the matter quickly. Does this have anything to do with SoNo Prime?"

"Not at all. But since you were there, can you give me your version of what you saw."

"Pretty straight forward. The guy appeared to be real obnoxious. Nothing overly serious, but he apparently got a little aggressive with the woman. When he put his hands on her, she slapped him. It got a little loud, but my guys were all over it. We threw him out, and I comped the bill for the woman and her two friends."

Now he was getting somewhere. "That's what I understood. I'm trying to locate the guy who was involved."

"Why?"

"Client confidentiality. What I can tell you is that my client is trying to find this guy on an unrelated matter."

"What's his name? We didn't get that information because no report was made. Quite honestly, it wasn't that big of a deal."

Aranoff sat down on the bar stool next to the manager. "It's not important if you didn't get it. He's been avoiding service on an unrelated lawsuit. I thought maybe he was a regular here."

The manager sat up straight in his chair and regarded Aranoff for a moment. "Not that I recognized. The bar gets pretty crowded, but I don't recall ever having seated that guy in the dining room."

Aranoff thought for a moment. "You mentioned the woman's friends. Did you recognize either of them?"

The manager looked at him askance. "What does that have to do with anything?"

Aranoff got creative. "This guy has cheated a lot of people out of large sums of money, including a significant number of elderly. My client is the lead plaintiff in a class-action lawsuit. One of the other plaintiffs was in the bar on Saturday and recognized the guy when he bothered this woman. We thought he'd fled the jurisdiction, and this was the first sighting of him in some time. Quite honestly, I'm desperate to find him. I'm chasing down any possible lead that will help locate the scumbag so we can serve him and get on with the pursuit of justice."

The manager, persuaded by a combination of conviction that Aranoff's interest didn't involve the restaurant and a pullulating disdain for this lowlife, replied, "Yeah, one of the women comes in regularly. Her last name is Rainford. I've heard her called Gee Gee, but I remember her name on a credit card slip saying Gina, Gina Rainford."

Aranoff made a mental note. "I appreciate your help. Is there anything else you can tell me that could help track this guy down?"

"That's about it. I routinely make rounds in the dining room, and I know most of the regular customers by name. This guy I don't know, and I'm not sure who he came in with or if he was alone."

Aranoff stood and shook the manager's hand. "Well, thank you again for your time."

"My pleasure. This guy sounds like a real miscreant."

Bryan Aranoff headed back to his office. He ran a background on Gina Rainford and produced a dossier complete with driver's license and passport photographs. Married to Harold Rainford. Three children ages ten through fifteen. Lived in Rowayton. Stay-at-home mom. Drove a Volvo station wagon. He made a note of the address and decided to visit Mrs. Rainford in the morning.

The next day he drove out to Rowayton with an estimated arrival time of ten o'clock, planning to catch Gina Rainford while her husband was at work and the kids in school. He figured if she wasn't home, he could wait around for her to return. After all, he had no other options to pursue at the moment.

Aranoff found the address and parked on the street in front of the house next door. The Rainford residence was located in a middle-class neighborhood several notches below Rowayton's exclusive enclaves. It was a two-story, ranch-style home, the exterior's wood shingles painted an almond wisp and the windows accented in cherry-colored shutters.

Bryan Aranoff was five feet, eleven inches tall and outwardly fit. He stood ramrod straight and sported a full head of coiffed, chestnut hair. He was neatly dressed in tan wool slacks, loafers, and an LL Bean jacket.

He rang the doorbell. Predictably, Mrs. Rainford was home. She answered the door in a matching navy sweatshirt and pants and brown fuzzy slippers. Gina Rainford was an inherently attractive woman, but not aging well. She had a puffy exterior, and her face was devoid of any makeup. She was clearly not expecting company.

Gina eyed Aranoff with a roguish smile. "Good morning, sir. What can I do for you today?"

"Good morning. Mrs. Rainford, I was hoping to speak with you about Cheryl McDirt."

"Oh gosh, is everything okay with Cheryl? I was out with her on Saturday night, and I haven't spoken to her since."

"Yes, she's fine. Actually, I was hoping to get more information about what happened on Saturday at SoNo Prime."

"Please call me Gee Gee. All my friends do. Are you a cop?"

"No. I'm a private investigator. Cheryl's family is concerned about her and thought something may have happened on Saturday. They asked me to look into it."

"Hmm, I know Cheryl and neither she nor her family would spend money on a PI, even for something this serious."

Aranoff leaned in closer to Gee Gee and lowered his voice. "I'm doing this as a favor to the family. In fact, they're adamant about not letting Cheryl know. They don't want to upset her any further. Can we speak in confidence?"

"Absolutely, I'm really good at keeping secrets." Again with the mischievous smile.

Aranoff didn't know what to make of that but continued. "What do you know about this guy who bothered her?"

"Not much. I was out with Cheryl and Laurie LaBush. We're all friends from high school. We went to dinner at SoNo Prime. The three of us went to the bar to have a drink while we waited for our table. The bar was crowded, and we left Cheryl alone to find a spot to wait while Laurie and I went to fetch drinks. Some creep was harassing Cheryl, and she slapped him. They threw the guy out, and that was it. The manager came over and apologized and offered to pay for our meals."

"Was Cheryl hurt or upset?"

"Hurt, no. Upset, yes. She told us she'd seen this guy before, but always at the Rockrimmon Club where she works on weekends. Apparently, he's harassed her there and even attacked her once. She was pretty freaked out by seeing him again in Norwalk."

Pay dirt. "I can imagine. What happened after the guy was thrown out?"

"Not much. Cheryl calmed down, and we had a nice dinner. By the end of the night, we were laughing and reminiscing about old times like we always do when we get together." She flashed a full set of teeth and licked her lips. "You know, I was pretty wild back then."

Aranoff looked away briefly before continuing. "Did Cheryl mention the guy's name?"

"No. In fact I don't know if she knew it. I do remember her saying he's not a member at the Rockrimmon."

"Did you go anywhere else after dinner?"

"Laurie and I went to another bar for a nightcap, but Cheryl wanted to go home. We were worried about her. She called her dad to come and meet her. He lives around there."

Feeling he had all the salient information she had to offer, Aranoff concluded, "Thank you, Mrs. Rainford, you've been helpful. And please, not a word about our conversation to Cheryl. The family insists."

Another suggestive grin. "No problem, I'm really good at keeping secrets. You need anything else, you come back and see me. It's best to catch me during the day. No distractions with the kids and all."

"Sure thing." He departed the encounter without ever having been asked his name.

Aranoff's file also contained the names and address of Cheryl's parents with accompanying photographs. Less than ten minutes from the Tomassi home, he headed in that direction. Fortuitously, as he approached the house, Anthony was pulling into the driveway in his green pickup truck.

Aranoff stopped his car in front of the house just as Anthony was exiting the truck. He rolled down his front passenger window. "Excuse me, can I speak with you for a moment."

Anthony walked over to the car. "What can I do for you?"

"Mr. Tomassi, I'm looking into the incident involving your daughter, Cheryl, at SoNo Prime on Saturday night. Can I speak with you for a moment?"

Anthony sized up the guy seated in the nondescript black Ford sedan. "Who the hell are you, and what business is it of yours?" He took a step back and glared at Aranoff. "You better not be a friend of that perverted prick, because if I see him again, I'm gonna finish what I started."

"Trust me, I'm no friend of the guy. I don't even know his name. I was hoping you could help me out with that."

"How the hell should I know? We didn't introduce ourselves as I was kicking the shit outta him. We done here?"

Interesting. Aranoff figured it was time to cut this short. "Yeah, sure, for now. Sounds like you wouldn't mind running into that asshole again. That makes two of us. Good day."

Aranoff drove back to the office while reviewing the day's progress in his mind. He was starting to get the idea that there was more troubling Cheryl McDirt beyond an isolated incident at SoNo Prime with this nefarious unidentified man. He would report his preliminary findings to Kurt Nesbitt and go from there. Otherwise, he felt like he was now at a standstill, unmindful of just how clairvoyant he had been in his conversation with the restaurant manager.

CHAPTER TWELVE

D URING THE WEEK, ALEX CALLED Dylan to make plans for the
weekend. It was important that they included an opportunity for him to
have a word with Dylan's grandfather. Dylan told him there was open gym
at the Stamford YMCA on Saturday night and they could play some pickup
basketball.

Alex took advantage of the opening. "That sounds good. I'll come up to
you on Friday and stay the weekend. Do you think your grandmother would
make us dinner? I really miss her cooking."

"Sure, my grandparents would love to see you, and they get excited when I
visit. I'll set it up for Friday."

"Perfect. Maybe we can go down to Washington Street and look for girls
afterward."

"Now that sounds like a plan. See ya Friday."

On Friday night, Alex picked up Dylan at the house. Cheryl had already
left for work at the Rockrimmon. As they drove over to Norwalk, Alex turned
to his friend. "How's your mom doing?"

"She seems better. Her eye is about back to normal. She wears a little
makeup, and you can't even tell."

"Glad to hear it. Did you ever hear anything more about what happened?"

"Not a word since the day you last saw her."

The boys received an affectionate welcome at Dylan's grandparents. Isa-
bella was busy in the kitchen but came out and hugged and kissed both boys.
The aroma of simmering tomatoes and parmesan wafted through the house.
She brought them each a soda and handed Anthony a beer.

Anthony sat in his recliner and raised his beer to the boys. "A few more
years for you two."

The three of them sat and talked in the living room while they waited for
Isabella to call them to dinner.

"What are you boys up to tonight?"

Alex jumped in. "We just drove down to see you and have dinner. It's been a while, and it's always good to see you."

"So the two of you are gonna go out later and chase girls?"

"Of course. What else does Alex ever wanna do," Dylan added.

Anthony gestured with his beer can. "Christ sakes, the Giants had a terrible year. They really missed Simms after he got hurt. You think they'll bounce back next year?"

Alex the sports geek jumped in. "Oh yeah. With Simms healthy and their draft picks, I guarantee they make the playoffs next year."

"Alex, you sure are optimistic. They just went six and ten," Anthony replied.

"Sure, Mr. Tomassi, but with Simms back next year, I predict they'll win double-digit games and reverse those numbers."

"Ha. You're a heck of a lot more of an optimist than me, but I hope you're right."

When Isabella called everyone for dinner, they sat in the small, comfortable kitchen. She served Beef Braciola stuffed with parmesan cheese, breadcrumbs, and fresh herbs. It was prepared in a wine-infused red sauce and served over rigatoni pasta. Anthony and Isabella shared a bottle of Sangiovese. The boys stuck with soda. Dinner conversation flowed naturally and covered the boys' recent football seasons and upcoming baseball season. Naturally, Anthony and Alex wanted to talk about Dylan's recruiting, but he would have none of it. The boys both had second helpings and were sure to gratefully praise Isabella's culinary skills.

After dinner, Isabella cleared the dishes while sports dominated the discussion at the table. For dessert, she served a homemade mint gelato. Then everyone retired to the living room where the conversation continued for a short time. As the boys were getting ready to leave, they said their goodbyes and thanked Isabella for dinner. She hugged and kissed them both and headed back to the kitchen to finish cleaning up. It was dark outside, so Anthony turned on the exterior lights and stood in the front doorway to see the two young men off.

"Have a good night. Good luck with the ladies and stay safe."

As the boys headed toward the car parked in the driveway, Alex handed Dylan the keys. "You go ahead and open the car. I forgot something." He turned around and headed back to the house.

He approached Anthony as he stood on the porch, Alex palmed him a business card and spoke with his back to Dylan. "The next time this guy contacts you, please talk with him. And please, not a word of this to anyone."

Anthony stood there in silence and stared in the direction of the car. He watched as it backed out of the driveway and took off down the road. After the BMW was out of sight, he finally looked at the card. It was plain, white card stock with black, embossed lettering that simply read Bryan Aranoff, Private Investigator. Printed below that was a single telephone number.

CHAPTER THIRTEEN

P ER HIS INSTRUCTIONS, THE NEXT day, Bryan Aranoff filed his report verbally in a meeting with Kurt Nesbitt. Nesbitt listened attentively as he repeated in detail his interviews with the restaurant manager and Gina Rainford and his interaction with Anthony Tomassi.

Less than a week later he was called back into Nesbitt's office. Nesbitt stood and greeted him, indicating this would be brief. "Arrangements have been made. Mr. Tomassi should be more receptive to a conversation. Go back out and see him."

"Yes, sir. I'm on it."

Aranoff drove back out to Norwalk the same day. He drove by the Tomassi house, but the old green pickup was not in the driveway. He didn't figure the guy would park that type of vehicle in the garage. He peered through a garage-door window anyway and confirmed his deduction. He parked his own black Ford Taurus in the street and waited.

About an hour and a half later Anthony's truck drove up and pulled into the driveway. He got out, looked around, and began walking in the direction of the parked black car. Aranoff watched closely, his gait not betraying his demeanor. Anthony continued directly up to the driver's side front door and motioned for Aranoff to roll down his window.

"Mr. Aranoff, you and me have something to discuss."

"It's pretty cool out there. Hop in the car."

Anthony got into the front passenger seat, and Aranoff started in. "Like I said before, I'm looking into this guy that's bothered Cheryl. I do know you've mixed it up with him yourself. What I don't have yet is a full appreciation of the extent of this guy's actions toward Cheryl or his identity. I was hoping you could fill me in on what else you know."

Anthony repeated in detail the entire incident outside SoNo Prime on the night he had gone to meet Cheryl. He also told Aranoff everything Cheryl had told him about the previous verbal harassment and physical attack at the Rockrimmon.

Aranoff listened unabatedly until Anthony was finished. He never took notes during an interview because he had an ironclad memory. "Do you know who this guy is?"

"No. Cheryl doesn't know his full name. What she did tell me is that his first name's Brad and he's not a member at the Rockrimmon. He's been there a handful of times as a guest, but I don't believe he's a regular guest of any single member."

"Is there anything else?'

"No, I've told you all I know. But I should have said this from the beginning. Don't let Cheryl know I spoke with you. She's made it clear she doesn't want to pursue this further, although I do want another shot at him."

"I was about to tell you the same thing regarding Cheryl. The only other thing I can say is I'll find this guy and he'll be dealt with."

Anthony leaned back in his seat until he hit the headrest, then turned and regarded Aranoff. "I hope so." He got out of the car and walked back toward the house.

As Aranoff drove off, he made a mental note to utilize a contact who would allow him to review the Rockrimmon guest list.

CHAPTER FOURTEEN

Gary Lavoy was a financial advisor with Malloy Williamson's High Net Worth Division. For those fortunate enough to hire Gary, the minimum investment was five million dollars. He had more than half a billion dollars in assets under his management and regularly outperformed the Standard & Poor's 500 index. Gary was a forty-one-year-old divorced father of two with an annual income of more than a million dollars. Thanks to the Malloy Williamson Security Department, his take home pay after deductions, including child support, was considerably more than what it could have been.

Gary had joined the firm directly from Harvard after receiving his undergraduate and MBA degrees. He quickly ascended through the ranks and broke the one-million-dollar-a-year income barrier before his thirtieth birthday. By then he was married with two young children, a boy and a girl. He lived in a mansion in Darien and kept an apartment in New York. The family took regular vacations and had a live-in nanny from Denmark to assist with caring for the children.

Gary had started to pay more attention to the twenty-three-year-old blonde Danish nanny than his wife. Eventually, nature took its course between the two. They became adept at fully satisfying each other to exhaustion and rearranging themselves without a trace of evidence in the time it took his wife, Glenda, to leave the house with the kids for such activities as play dates or doctor appointments.

Ultimately, Gary found he required variety in his extracurricular activities. His insatiable desire for college-age girls had led him to spend more nights in the New York apartment where he entertained a variety of coeds from various universities. He'd been generous with the young women, showering them with gifts, and never failed to come through on a request for financial assistance. His largesse came with a price. He purchased schoolgirl outfits for the women to wear during their trysts and demanded they dress up. Gary had found the excitement level was not quite the same without the uniforms.

Eventually he'd brought home uniforms for the nanny to wear. It required more time for her to leave the room, get dressed, and make her entrance for an eagerly-awaiting Gary. Increased foreplay had also added to the length of their encounters. Imminently, one afternoon Gary lost track of time. Glenda had walked into the house to find Gary standing buck naked in the living room, with the nanny kneeling in front of him wearing only white knee socks. A plaid uniform skirt and white blouse lay on the floor next to her.

Glenda had promptly filed for divorce and sought full custody of the children, child support, and lifetime alimony. Things looked bleak for Gary, and his work performance began to suffer. Hence, the Malloy Williamson Security Department became involved. A blue-ribbon investigative team was assembled, led by Bryon Aranoff.

The team had hit pay dirt when it was discovered that Glenda had her own fetishes. Swingers' clubs were her thing. She particularly enjoyed activities involving three or more participants. But Glenda's ultimate downfall had been her preference for videotaped performances she could relive in private with her battery-operated toys. The security team obtained recordings of both Glenda's group activities and solo performances. The solo acts had been recorded using hidden cameras with angles that captured Glenda in action as well as the movies she was viewing.

In addition to the investigation services, Malloy Williamson had assisted Gary with hiring top New York City divorce lawyers. The team, led by three female attorneys, employed a strategy highlighted by the screening of a feature film starring Glenda and her swinger friends at the first mediation. The session was abruptly continued and rescheduled at the request of Glenda's lawyers. They'd promptly withdrawn from her case.

Glenda's new lawyers, not surprisingly, had adjusted their demands. Glenda's revised offer to settle included weekend custody for Gary and five years of alimony. Gary's lawyers countered with an amended answer and counterclaim for full custody and no alimony along with a motion for an expedited trial. On the courthouse steps, the parties had agreed to fifty-fifty custody, no alimony, and an airtight confidentiality agreement. Each party had further agreed to bear their own costs and attorneys' fees.

Two days after his meeting with Anthony Tomassi, Bryan Aranoff drove over to the Malloy Williamson building in Greenwich. The uniformed guards manning the reception area saluted him. He took the elevator to the fifth floor and walked over to Kurt Nesbitt's office. The door was slightly ajar, so Aranoff knocked lightly and entered.

Nesbitt greeted him and motioned to a chair. "Your man will be here in ten minutes, so bring me up to speed on this meeting."

"I have a first name only on our subject. He's been a guest at the Rockrimmon Club on more than one occasion. He's definitely not a member. Lavoy's on the board of directors at the Rockrimmon, and he'll be able to provide me access to the guest list. I want to review the list for the past six months, looking for a first name Brad. Anthony Tomassi mixed it up with the guy, so he'll be able to make a definite ID once we obtain photos."

"What about confidentiality? Our instructions are Ms. McDirt and her son know nothing about this."

"Remember, Tomassi is Ms. McDirt's father. He demanded our discussions be in confidence and, specifically, that his daughter not be notified or involved under any circumstances. We're all on the same page in that regard."

"Alright, our man should be here any moment. Coffee?"

"No, thanks. I've had mine this morning."

Shortly, Gary Lavoy presented himself to Kurt Nesbitt's office. Aranoff stood and greeted the man. They shook hands warmly, and he observed that Lavoy looked trim and more relaxed since they'd last worked together.

"You look well, Mr. Lavoy. How are you?" Aranoff asked.

"I'm doing fine, thanks to you and your team. Please call me Gary. To what do I owe the pleasure?"

Kurt Nesbitt took over. "Gary, I understand that you're a member at Rockrimmon and that you also sit on the board. We require your assistance."

"Sure, I'm happy to help in any way I can."

"We need to get a look at the Rockrimmon guest list for the past six months."

Lavoy hesitated momentarily, then spoke with an air of authority. "Gentlemen, the Rockrimmon is a very private and exclusive club. I don't know that I can assist in that regard. Members' privacy is sacrosanct."

Nesbitt made eye contact, and the two men engaged in a stare down. Aranoff watched them, feeling as if time had stood still. Finally, Lavoy blinked and looked away. Nesbitt indicated with his chin at Aranoff, who responded to the objection. "Mr. Lavoy, as you will recall the firm, and this department in particular, pulled out all the stops to assist you with your, uh, predicament. I take it you were pleased with the quality of our services."

"You know the answer to that question. I'm eternally grateful. However, my fiduciary duty as a board member is inviolate."

"Perhaps further enlightenment is in order. We currently have a situation that requires identifying a single subject who was a guest on a few occasions. The information is essential to resolving an urgent matter for another of the firm's valued members. I assure you no confidences will be breached beyond determining the identity of this guest. In fact, in identifying the subject, we'll be providing a service to the Rockrimmon."

Lavoy narrowed his eyes and shot him a perplexing look. "How do you figure?"

"Our subject is an irrefutable miscreant. I can assure you the Rockrimmon will be spared future problems through his expulsion from the club."

"If I was to agree, how do you propose we handle it?"

"The less people involved the better. Can you obtain a list of names of the guests? I'd prefer to limit our dealings on this between the two of us."

"I could get that information."

"What information do you obtain from guests?"

"The club requires full name, address, phone number, and verification through a valid form of identification."

"Does the club maintain a copy of the identification?"

"No, it's just visually confirmed by one of the member services team."

"I see. Once I review the list and narrow it down, I would need copies of that information for him, or worst-case scenario, a short list of possible subjects."

"What are you looking for initially?"

"I prefer to review the list first and then let you know. All will be shared at that time."

"Okay. Give me a day. I'll call you tomorrow and arrange a meeting at the Rockrimmon. It's best to meet midafternoon on a weekday, after the lunch crowd."

Nesbitt and Aranoff rose, and Nesbitt spoke. "Mr. Lavoy, we appreciate your cooperation on this."

"Please know there are very few people I would do this for."

"I understand."

Two days later, Lavoy and Aranoff drove over to the Rockrimmon together in Lavoy's Austin Martin Mirage. Lavoy led the way to a small windowless office and produced a fanfolded computer printout. Aranoff studied the list. He mentally noted two Brads and a Bradley. One Brad and Bradley had been guests more than once. He looked across the desk at Lavoy who was staring into space.

"These three, he said, indicating to each with an index finger. I'm recording the addresses and phone numbers for each of them."

"So, you're looking for a Brad or Bradley?"

"Yes. Do you know any of them?"

"No."

"Well, we're done here. I don't expect I'll need anything further."

The two men got up and left. Lavoy drove them back to the Malloy Williamson office. Aranoff thanked him again, got into his black Ford, and drove to his own office. He called a contact at the Connecticut State Police and requested color copies of the Brad/Bradley driver's licenses. Two days later, they arrived in the mail. Aranoff walked them over to technical services. The guy in charge printed out enlarged, quality headshots from the men's license photos.

Aranoff called Anthony Tomassi and reached him at home. After the men hung up, Aranoff drove over to South Norwalk and pulled into the Calf Pasture Beach parking lot. It was deserted except for a familiar green pickup truck. Aranoff parked next to the truck, and Anthony transferred into the Ford's passenger seat. Aranoff handed him three photographs. Anthony quickly flipped through the first two and stopped at the last one. He studied it for a moment and handed it to Aranoff.

"Him."

"Any doubt about it?"

"Negative."

"That's all I need. We'll take it from here."

"What about my shot at him."

"I'll make you this promise. You'll be apprised of the final outcome. If you're dissatisfied in anyway, you'll get your shot."

"Fair enough." Anthony departed the Ford, got back into his truck, and drove off.

Aranoff looked at the photo, then drove back to the office compiling a mental to-do list on the subject of Mr. Brad Davies.

CHAPTER FIFTEEN

After the Christmas holiday break, Cheryl and Dylan settled back into their routines. One evening in early January, Dylan received a phone call from University of Connecticut head baseball coach Mark Lundy. Coach Lundy introduced himself and confirmed the earlier discussion between Dylan and Coach Fuller about the prospect of playing football and baseball for UConn. He had researched Dylan's high school statistics and spoken with the Stamford baseball coach. Coach Lundy wanted to ask Dylan about a few more things.

"Do you play summer ball?"

"Yes, I play American Legion."

"Who's your summer ball coach?"

"I play for a team sponsored by 7UP. Evan Fedorko is the coach."

"Yeah, I'm familiar with Coach Fedorko. He's been a fixture in Legion ball in Fairfield County for decades."

"Yes, sir."

"Do you pitch in Legion ball as well or strictly play outfield?"

"I do both, just like in high school."

"I plan on speaking with Coach Fedorko and coming down to watch you play during the summer. With our schedule, it's tough for me to get down there during season." Coach Lundy hesitated momentarily. "You understand that athletic aid is contingent upon the football coaches. They have considerably more scholarship money available than we do in the baseball program. But the fact that you also play baseball weighs in your favor."

"Yes, sir, that's been explained to me."

"Well, Dylan, it was nice speaking with you. I look forward to watching you play."

After the call, Dylan reflected on the conversation. Coach Lundy's take on things sounded consistent with what the football coaches had told him. He realized that, in his case, the recruiting process had gotten off to a late start. But he did have the advantage of UConn's interest in him as a two-sport athlete.

High school baseball practice began in early March. Due to inclement weather, teams' initial practices and conditioning took place in the school gymnasiums around the basketball teams' schedules.

One evening, Alex called Dylan. "Great news. I've got two tickets to the company's suite at Madison Square Garden on Saturday night to see the Rangers and Flyers. Great seats and all the food we can eat. The suite holds twenty-four, so maybe some of the other guests will bring their daughters. We can take the train to Grand Central. It's less than a thirty-minute walk to the Garden. We have to pass right through Time Square, so maybe we can hang out too."

"Look at you. Always figuring out ways to meet girls. Let me take care of a few things. I gotta get Ricky Peck to cover my route. It shouldn't be a problem. The kid idolizes me, and he can use a few bucks."

"Great. I'll pick you up on Saturday and leave my car at the train station."

On Saturday, Alex picked up Dylan. As always, he took time to stop in and see Cheryl. He gave her a hug. "How are you, Mrs. McD?"

"I'm doing well, Alex. And you?"

"Great as usual." As they all made small talk for a few moments, Alex noted that Cheryl looked and acted like her usual self.

As they started to depart, Cheryl admonished, "Have fun, but please be careful in the city. It can be a little crazy."

Alex considered himself a putative New Yorker. "Don't worry, Mrs. McD. I'll take care of the bright-eyed suburban kid."

Dylan chimed in, "Yeah right. You're the one who needs the babysitter."

The boys took the train from Stamford to Grand Central and then walked to Times Square. They spent time window shopping and people watching. The only store that interested Dylan was Modell's Sporting Goods. Eventually Alex couldn't resist going inside several of the clothing and jewelry retailers. Dylan followed his au courant friend into the stores and paced around impatiently while Alex checked out the latest fashions.

At the appointed time, they walked down Seventh Avenue and turned onto West Thirty-First Street. When they arrived at Madison Square Garden, they presented themselves at the VIP entrance, where a uniformed receptionist led them down a hallway to a bank of elevators. The man sported a burgundy velvet tuxedo with black trim. They took the elevator to a private level, and the receptionist escorted them to the suite. As they walked down the hallway, they saw Howard Stern and Billy Crystal pass in the opposite direction. Fastened to the suite door was an engraved nameplate that read Malloy Williamson & Associates. The receptionist handed them off to a similarly-attired butler and retreated back toward the elevator.

The boys entered the suite and stood and looked around for a moment. The large room was paneled in mahogany and decorated with oil paintings of iconic New York landmarks. Televisions, tuned to the closed-circuit broadcast channel for the game, sat on shelves mounted in each corner. A bar was set up along one wall with a large buffet table on the opposite side. The front of the room had sliding glass windows that could be opened and closed. Single chairs mounted to the floor looked down on center ice. Couches, high-top tables, and chairs were set up throughout the rest of the suite. All the furniture was uphol-stered in matching brown leather, and there was ample room for people to stand and move about. About a dozen people were present when the boys arrived. Most were older men, and a few were accompanied by women.

Alex didn't recognize anyone, so he directed Dylan over to the buffet table. An impressive array of offerings featured shrimp cocktail, breaded chicken filet strips, and skewered teriyaki steak. There was also a sushi platter, Caesar salad, and impressive fruit and cheese trays. A smaller, adjacent table displayed an assortment of desserts. The boys filled their plates and sat down at a table.

About a half hour before the game started, a distinguished-looking gentle-man arrived with two young women. Both were attractive, but Dylan and Alex were immediately drawn to one in particular, as was every other man in the suite. One of the other men received an austere look from his female compan-ion.

The object of everyone's attention was a striking brunette with dark fea-tures and full lips highlighted by bright-red gloss. She was dressed in a black pleated leather miniskirt and a gray low-cut lace top, which revealed a gener-ous amount of cleavage. She wore suede knee-high black boots with four-inch heels. Her female companion was also attractive with light brown hair. She was more conservatively dressed in a tailored houndstooth skirt hemmed just above the knee. Her outfit was completed with a black cashmere sweater and black boots.

Alex put down his fork and pounced while Dylan watched with amusement. He went directly up to the man and introduced himself. "Hello, sir, I'm Alex Malloy. Welcome."

The man regarded Alex for a moment. "Good evening, son. My name is Winston Stanhill. I'm a client of the firm." He put his hand on the shoulder of the more conservatively dressed young woman standing beside him. "This is my daughter Penelope." Then he indicated to the other woman. "This is Lourdes Quinn. She's a friend of Penel's."

Alex looked at both women and smiled, careful to maintain eye contact. "It's nice to meet you all. Are you Ranger fans?"

Mr. Stanhill replied, "I am. I enjoy watching hockey in person. The game really doesn't lend itself to television."

"Yes, sir. I agree. There's no better place to watch a game than from up here. I prefer it to being down close to the ice. You can really follow the puck and watch the plays develop."

The two young women stood by with facial expressions that betrayed a combination of boredom and confusion.

Alex picked up on this and continued, "What about you, ladies? Are you hockey fans?"

Penelope Stanhill stepped forward. "I like hockey, but I don't know much about it."

"Well, you've come to the right place. My friend and I would be happy to give you a short tutorial before the game starts." He motioned toward Dylan who smiled and nodded. "That is, with your permission, Mr. Stanhill."

"That's fine with me. I'm meeting my broker and a couple of the firm's analysts here. What do you think, ladies?"

Penelope replied, "Yes, Daddy."

"Why don't the two of you get some food and a drink and meet us at the table? We're right over there." Alex indicated again in Dylan's direction.

As the young women made their way over to the buffet table, a gregarious man of about fifty came up to Winston Stanhill sporting a huge grin. He put his arm around the man's shoulder. "Winston, welcome. It's great to see you. So glad you could come. Let's grab a drink."

Dylan observed Alex put the charm on Mr. Stanhill and the girls from the table, thinking, *Alex is incorrigible when it comes to the ladies, and Mr. Outgoing is obviously the man's broker.*

Alex came back to the table and sat across from Dylan, subtly moving an empty chair close to his seat. He similarly used his foot and pushed the other chair closer to Dylan. Both sets of chairs were now paired off by distinct gaps on either side of the round table.

Alex whispered, "Let's see where they choose to sit and go from there."

The ladies made their way over, plates and water glasses in hand. Lourdes took the lead and sat down next to Alex. Penelope sat with Dylan.

"Good evening, ladies. I'm Dylan McDirt. It's nice to meet you both."

Lourdes smiled. "Nice to meet you, Dylan." Then she turned to Alex with a bigger smile, lips in full plump mode. "I noticed your last name is on the door. What do you do?"

Dylan looked at Penelope who rolled her eyes and smiled at him, revealing perfect teeth. Dylan smiled back.

"I'm a student at Fairfield Prep. Dylan goes to Stamford High," Alex answered.

Lourdes giggled and placed a hand on Alex's leg. "Uh oh, looks like I'm a cradle robber."

Now Penelope bore a semi-stern look. "Lourdes, behave yourself."

Dylan looked at Penelope. "What do you do?"

"Lourdes and I are freshman at NYU. We're roommates. We live in the Brittany Hall freshman dorm."

"We are you from?"

"Here in the city. My parents have a townhome on the Upper West Side."

Alex turned to Lourdes. "What's your story, morning glory?"

Lourdes giggled, composed herself, and utilized her lips to enunciate, carefully concealing a Boston accent. "My family is from Taunton, Massachusetts."

"What are you studying?" Alex asked.

"Husband hunting."

Everyone was silent. Penelope rolled her eyes again. This time the entire group saw her.

After a moment Lourdes, in a rare instance of self-awareness, realized her faux paus and attempted to recover. She placed a hand over her mouth. "Oops, did I say that out loud? What I meant was I'm in exploratory studies."

"What about you, Penelope?" Alex asked.

"Please call me, Penel. I'm studying global finance."

Dylan chimed in. "Cool, I'm interested in studying economics and finance. How do you like it so far?"

"I'm just in my second semester and mainly taking core courses, but I have a class in money and banking that I find interesting. It's fascinating how the monetary systems work. Where are you planning on attending college?"

"My first choice is UConn."

Alex interrupted. "Okay, Mister and Misses JP Morgan, class is now in session and today's subject is hockey. We only have a few minutes before the puck drops." He indicated to the two young women. "Have either of you ever seen a hockey game?"

"No, I haven't," Penel replied. "We came tonight mainly because Daddy invited us. I think he misses me."

Alex looked at Lourdes who was staring down at the ice as the players were going through their warmups. "I haven't been to a game either. How much money do those guys make?"

Alex ignored the question. "You both know soccer, right?"

The ladies nodded in unison.

"What about lacrosse?"

Penel indicated in the affirmative, Lourdes the negative.

"Well, it's like soccer or lacrosse except played on ice instead of a field. The idea is to score more goals than the opponent. No ball is involved. Instead, they use a hard rubber disk called a puck. They actually keep them frozen in an ice chest to use during the game." He briefly described the significance of the red and blue lines as well as penalties and power plays.

Suddenly the room became quiet and everyone stood for the playing of the national anthem. Dylan eyes darted around the suite. It appeared to be at full capacity with mostly middle-aged and older men and the few women who had accompanied them. *Everyone was well dressed,* he thought, *particularly for a sporting event.*

Dylan glanced over at Penel standing at attention with her right hand on her heart. He noted her perfect posture. *Very classy young lady.* He then looked over at Alex and Lourdes. She was standing uncomfortably close to Alex, her hand occasionally grazing his leg. Dylan wondered what the two young women had in common besides sharing a dorm room.

The anthem ended to thundering applause, and the teams took the ice. The arena went dark, and a laser light show accompanied by Queen's "We Will Rock You" blared from the speakers. After a few moments, the arena lights went on, the seating areas darkened, and the music stopped. The puck was dropped, and the game was underway. At the end of the first period, the house lights came up and the noise in the suite increased.

Penel asked Dylan, "What else do you do besides attend high school?"

"I play football and baseball. I also work a lot.

"What kind of work do you do?"

"I have a paper route, and I bus tables and wash dishes at a country club on weekends."

Penel's expression remained unchanged. "What does your father do?"

"I don't remember my father. He left my mother and me when I was an infant."

"Oh, I'm sorry."

"It's fine. My mother borders on sainthood, so she more than makes up for it."

Alex and Lourdes were playing footsies under the table and engaged in their own whispered conversation, but Alex's ears perked up. "I'll vouch for that last statement. Dylan's mother is the best."

Lourdes chimed in, "What does your mother do?"

"She's a schoolteacher, and we work together at the country club on weekends."

Lourdes immediately refocused on Alex.

Alex leaned away and said, "Hey, Dylan, what do you say we hit the dessert table?"

"Sure. Excuse us, ladies. Can we get you anything?"

Penel replied, "No, thank you."

Lourdes smiled and stared at Alex. "I know what I want for dessert."

The boys headed over to the opposite side of the room and grabbed small dessert plates.

Alex looked at Dylan. "So, what do you think?"

"Penel is very nice."

"Lourdes is all over me like flies on honey. I see a trip to NYU in my near future."

"How near?"

Alex laughed. "Relax, not tonight. Plus, I have to keep the firm in mind. I get the impression that Mr. Stanhill's an important client. I never do anything to mess with the firm's business. Penel is off limits for me. Fortunately, that prohibition does not extend to you, my friend."

"Penel is very nice. I was floored by Lourdes when they first walked in, but I'm pleased with the seating assignments."

The boys filled their plates with a variety of cookies, mini-cupcakes and brownies in case the girls changed their minds. Alex eyed the crowd. "We better get back over there. I've noticed how some of these old guys have been leering at the girls."

As they walked back over to the table, the ladies were engaged in conversation, their voices inadvertently raised to hear each other over the noise in the suite.

Lourdes had her back to them and could clearly be heard. "Why are you even thinking about that guy? He's obviously a pauper, destined for a life among the working class."

"Lourdes, that's terrible."

Penel looked up, startled to see Alex and Dylan standing behind Lourdes. She swung around and looked at Alex, then back at Penel. "Well, it's true."

Dylan stood there dumbfounded.

Alex took charge. "I think it may be time for you to leave, Lourdes. I'll call you a cab. An usher will be up here shortly to escort you down to the VIP exit and make sure you get in safely." He then looked over at Penel. "My apologies to you and your father. You're certainly welcome to stay, but your roommate just insulted my best friend." He then stepped away.

Lourdes barged off in the direction of the suite's private restroom.

Dylan stood there awkwardly.

Penel looked at him with compunction. "Dylan, I'm so sorry. I apologize for Lourdes's boorish behavior. I brought her here, and I'm responsible."

"Nonsense. It's not your fault."

"Still, I feel horrible. Lourdes can be sweet at times. Ironically, she comes from a hardscrabble background and her way of dealing with it can be obnoxious. She's way too obsessed with social status. For what it's worth, you appear very polished and mature for your age. I thought you were in college or maybe a young broker with Malloy Williamson." She reached into her purse, pulled out a business card, and handed it to Dylan.

He looked at it. The printed card included her home and school addresses and phone numbers.

"I'd like to see you again, just the two of us. Call me sometime, and we can meet in the city. Those are both my private lines, so leave a message if I don't answer."

Dylan had substantially recovered. "I'd like that, Penel. And thank you for your kind words."

She smiled and kissed him on the cheek. "I need to say goodbye to my father and take Lourdes home. Until next time."

Dylan sat back down and looked around. The second period was underway.

It didn't appear that any of the other guests had noticed the minor uproar. He focused on the game for a time. During the next break in play, he scanned the room and saw Alex speaking with Winston Stanhill. The two shook hands, and Alex headed back toward the table.

"Well, that was something," Alex said to Dylan as he sat back down. "Mr. Stanhill seemed to grasp a reasonable understanding of the situation. I did notice his broker sweating profusely though."

"Alex, I'm sorry if I caused any problem here. The last thing I want to do is mess with your father's business."

"Relax. You behaved like a boy scout, as usual. Winston Stanhill will be fine. Apparently, this isn't his first exposure to his daughter's roommate. It's a shame because she's quite a looker. I'll never see her again."

"Maybe not, but the lovely Ms. Stanhill gave me her number and invited me to meet her in the city."

"You dog! To borrow a hockey phrase, save and a beauty by McDirt."

The two friends laughed and enjoyed the rest of the game.

CHAPTER SIXTEEN

ONCE THE HIGH SCHOOL BASEBALL season began, the balance of the spring semester flew by. The team finished the season two games above .500 with a 13-11 record and failed to make the state playoffs. Dylan had a good season, hitting .351 with ten home runs. He also pitched twelve innings, all in relief, and his final line was 1-0 with a 2.10 ERA and four saves. He was now a rising senior.

Once school ended, Dylan's schedule lightened considerably. He was beginning his third season on the 7UP summer travel team. Tryouts were held each year and open to all players eighteen years of age and younger. Coach Evan Fedorko was legendary, and membership on the twenty-five-man roster was highly competitive. The team served as a feeder program to universities and junior colleges throughout the northeast.

Alex had literally no chance of making the team. However, for the second year in a row, he secured a spot as the twenty-sixth player. He rarely played, but his deep knowledge of game strategy assisted Coach Fedorko as a de facto assistant. The team traveled to the most competitive invite-only tournaments throughout New England and the tristate area. The bulk of player expenses were covered through sponsorships.

In July the team traveled to Brewster, New York for a weekend tournament. The format included two seeding games on Saturday and a single elimination tournament on Sunday. Attendees at the multifield complex consisted primarily of parents and college scouts. Team 7UP's first game on Saturday was played against a team from Tarrytown. Dylan started in right field and went hitless with two strikeouts in a 6-2 loss. In game two, a pitcher for the Litchfield, Connecticut team threw a three-hit shutout, defeating 7UP 9-0 in a mercy-rule shortened game. Dylan made his second start in right field and again went hitless in three at-bats with another strikeout. He struggled to make good contact in his other plate appearances, popping up to shortstop and grounding out meekly to second base. However, he came in relief and pitched two shutout innings, giving up just one infield single and striking out three with no walks.

Following game two, the team met briefly in the outfield for a debriefing with Coach Fedorko. After the meeting broke up, Dylan gathered up his equipment for the ride back to the Howard Johnson Motor Inn where the team was staying. Dylan and Alex made their way toward the team van in the parking lot and observed Coach Fedorko speaking with UConn's Coach Lundy.

Alex looked over at Dylan. "I knew Coach Lundy was here, but I didn't say anything."

"Great. How long has he been here?" Dylan asked.

"Since the first game, but he did move around the fields some."

"Ideal time to take the collar in back-to-back games."

"Relax, it's a game of failure. Coaches know that as well as anyone."

Recruiting rules prevented college coaches from prolonged discussions with unsigned recruits while at travel ball venues. However, collaboration between college and travel ball coaches was a common occurrence. Coach Fedorko motioned for Dylan to come over and join the conversation. Alex continued toward the van.

Dylan jogged over, his head held high. "Hello, Coach Lundy. Nice to see you."

"Same here, Dylan. Couple of tough games today."

Dylan thought to himself. *That's just great.* "Yes sir, Coach. But tomorrow's another day."

"I like your attitude, son. It's a game of failure, and too many players have a difficult time with that. Well, I just wanted to say hello. I'll be here the rest of the day and then I'm headed to a tournament in Massachusetts tomorrow. Take care, and we'll be in touch."

Coach Fedorko chimed in. "It was nice to see you again, Mark. Come on, Dylan, I'll walk over to the van with you."

Coach Lundy shook hands with player and coach and headed off toward another field.

Coach Fedorko didn't speak at first, so Dylan felt like he should say something. "Not my best day for Coach Lundy to come watch me play."

The coach put an arm across the back of his shoulders. "Don't sweat it, Dylan. Understand, coaches use the opportunity to observe how a player handles himself in adverse situations. Coach liked the way you carried yourself after an obviously rough day at the plate. You continued to hustle, fielded your position flawlessly, and came in and pitched well at the end of game two. I made that move specifically at Coach Lundy's request. How often have the two of you spoken?"

"Really just a couple times since he first contacted me in January."

"Have you ever called him?"

"No, should I?"

"Only if you have a legitimate reason. It might be a good idea to call him next week and let him know how Sunday goes. But still, it's a good sign that he's calling you. When those calls stop and he's no longer taking yours, it's a sure-fire sign he's moved on."

"Yes, Coach."

"You also have to remember that your situation is unique with your being recruited as a two-sport athlete. How often do you speak with the football coaches?"

"At least a couple times a month. I've been invited to a football camp up at Storrs in early July, and we're in the process of finalizing an official weekend visit in the fall."

"Well, I have to say that sounds very encouraging. These coaches don't waste their time on official visits if they're not serious about a recruit."

Suddenly, Dylan felt better. "Thanks, Coach."

"For what it's worth, UConn would be lucky to have you."

Fedorko patted Dylan on the back as they entered the van. Dylan found a seat next to Alex. Coach Fedorko got behind the wheel and drove off in the direction of the Howard Johnson's.

Team 7UP was at the fields early the next morning. Based upon Saturday's games, they were seeded fifteenth and drew the second seeded team in the first game. 7UP, behind Dylan's three-hit, five-RBI performance, won handily 6-1. They won their next three games and took home the first-place tournament trophy.

Dylan continued his bounce-back day, finishing nine for fifteen with a homerun, three doubles, and eight RBI. He also pitched five innings in the third game, yielding just one run and scattering four hits while striking out six with no walks. During the team's post-tournament celebration, Coach Fedorko acknowledged Dylan's comeback performance and reminded Dylan to call and let the UConn coach know how Sunday went. He also made a mental note to call himself on Monday.

CHAPTER SEVENTEEN

DYLAN SPOKE TO PENELOPE STANHILL on occasion, beginning midweek following the hockey game. She was clearly pleased to hear from him. In subsequent phone calls they spoke about various subjects, and Dylan never failed to make her laugh. Their conversations flowed easily. They concluded most calls with plans to get together as their schedules allowed. They had different spring break schedules, and Penel went to Florida on her break followed by a two-week trip to Europe as soon as school let out.

Mid-July was the first opportunity for Dylan to visit Penel in New York, and she was back living at home for the balance of the summer. The Stanhills spent July and August at the family summer compound in the Hamptons, so plans were made to meet there. Arrangements were made for a weekend visit with Dylan regulated to the guest house.

On the appointed Saturday morning, Dylan awoke early and Cheryl drove him to the Stamford train station. From there he traveled to Grand Central and connected to the Long Island Railroad. By late morning he arrived at his destination and departed at the East Hampton stop.

As Dylan exited the train, duffel bag in hand, he saw Penel waiving frantically and exhibiting a warm smile. They hugged, and he stepped back to take her in. Her true, natural beauty was on display. She sported a deep tan and wore no makeup with her hair pulled back in a ponytail. She was dressed in a white halter top and matching tennis shorts with pink sandals.

Penel led Dylan to the parking lot where a topless and doorless Jeep Wrangler awaited. She handed him the keys. "You drive."

Dylan looked inside the Jeep. It had a standard transmission. "Uh, I have a confession to make. I never got my license. You better drive."

Penel smiled broadly. "Not having a license is so unpretentious and so you." She hugged him again, kissed him on the cheek, and jumped into the driver's seat.

Dylan shrugged and hopped in on the passenger side. They both strapped on their seat belts and were soon cruising along Ocean Avenue with the wind in their hair. After a short trip, they came upon a stretch of semi-isolated beach with homes on large lots located directly on the Atlantic Ocean. Penel pulled into a long, winding driveway.

The house was a nine-bedroom, twelve-bath Gambrel-style home situated on two acres in Georgica Beach. There was a pool, gardens, and tennis court, and a two-bedroom guest cottage sat nestled behind the main house just beyond the dunes. They entered the house where Winston Stanhill and his considerably younger wife greeted them.

Mr. Stanhill handled the introductions. "Welcome, Dylan. It's nice to see you again. This is my wife, Candice."

Dylan shook hands firmly with Winston Stanhill. Candice Stanhill extended dainty, well-manicured fingers. Winston Stanhill continued, "Please make yourself at home. Penelope will show you to the guest house. I'm sure you kids have plans, but please be here at eight o'clock. We're having some people over, and I'd like you both to be here."

"Sure, Daddy. I think we'll go into town, have lunch, and then I'll show Dylan around."

She grabbed Dylan by the hand and led him through the house and out the back to the guest cottage. They passed the rectangular pool and surrounding travertine deck where a staff of six was setting up tables and chairs. Large folding tables underneath blue canopies were erected off to one side.

"Daddy's idea of having people over is 200 guests. Candice insists on entertaining. It took me a while, but I learned to accept that she makes Daddy happy and that's what counts. And whatever you do, don't call her Candy."

Dylan did some quick math in his head. Finally, all but convinced there was no way Penel was Candice's offspring, he replied, "Duly noted. I take it Candice isn't your mom."

"Good deduction. My mom and dad split up when I was in high school. It was no surprise really, because it was obvious they'd grown apart. My dad took good care of my mom until she remarried. Her new husband is a retired college professor and was a lifelong bachelor when they met. They live in Pound Ridge. Everyone seems happy so who am I to judge."

Dylan dropped off his duffel, and the couple got back in the Jeep and headed downtown. They lucked out and found a parking spot on Main Street. Walking hand in hand, Penel showed Dylan around as they browsed in the luxury store windows. Dylan recognized Gucci, Tiffany & Company, and Ralph Lauren.

Others such as J. McLaughlin, Elie Tahari, and Magaschoni were foreign to him.

They stopped in Bostwick's Chowder House for lunch, ordering bowls of Lobster Bisque and New England clam chowder and sharing both. Afterwards they headed back to the house, changed into swimsuits, and spent the rest of the afternoon on the beach.

The private beach was otherwise abandoned. After a vigorous swim, they fell asleep in each other's arms for a short time. When they awoke, the sun was beginning to sink toward the horizon.

"We'd better go back to the house and get ready."

"Whatever you say," Dylan replied.

"Casual dress is fine."

"Perfect cause that's all I own."

Penel broke out in laughter. "Of course it is."

"Are you making fun of me?"

"Not at all. Somehow I feel like you dress exactly the way you want and you always look nice. One of the many things I admire about you is that you're comfortable in your own skin."

"It's a good thing because it's the only skin I've got."

Penel smiled again, revealing her perfect white teeth. She gazed into Dylan's eyes and kissed him passionately on the mouth. The two ended up back on the blanket, exploring each other's bodies, an exercise made facile as they were practically naked in their swimsuits. Eventually they came up for air and a brief respite.

Penel spoke in a breathless tone. "I suppose we should really get back now and get ready."

They rearranged themselves, gathered up their belongings, and trudged through the sand and back to the house.

They entered from the rear and walked inside. Penel reached the staircase and turned to Dylan. "The party's out back. I shouldn't be more than an hour. Meet me out there."

"Will do."

Dylan returned to the guest cottage. He had the place to himself, so he took a moment to look around. The kitchen was updated with custom wood cabinets, marble countertops, and modern appliances. Porcelain tile flooring covered the entire cottage. He selected the larger of the two bedrooms, which contained a king-size bed and its own full-size bathroom with walk-in shower and custom closet. He showered and changed into his new ensemble of a navy Lacoste polo shirt, tan tennis shorts, and tan GH Bass deck shoes. After Anthony and Isabella got word Dylan was spending the weekend in the Hamptons, they had insisted on taking him shopping. Isabella's favorite store was Bargain World in downtown Norwalk, featuring designer brands at discount prices. She'd practically picked out the items. "Such a handsome boy needs to dress the part," she had told her grandson." Dylan had acquiesced and thanked his grandparents for taking such good care of him.

Dylan waited until about a quarter past eight before walking over to the main house. As he approached, he could hear an acoustical guitarist playing a familiar Beetles song. The entire back pool area was lit with lanterns strung from the house and extending beyond the pool deck. Tiki torches set on metal poles also provided illumination as nightfall approached. Multiple sets of double pane sliding glass doors at the rear of the house were opened, facilitating a seamless indoor-outdoor party area. There was a warm, summer breeze and large misting fans were set up on either side of the pool deck.

Dylan looked around the crowded outdoor area. Everyone was dressed in elegant resort wear. He thought he recognized a retired pro tennis player and a few celebrities, including an actress from a long-running soap opera that Isabella watched religiously. Captains of industry, finance, and banking were also present along with a select group of politicians, but those persons went unnoticed by Dylan.

After taking in the outdoor scene for a few moments, he made his way toward the rear of the house and went inside. People were seated on couches and chairs while others stood around engaged in conversation. Servers dressed in black and white offered trays of hors d'oeuvres with shrimp, beef, and bruschetta mozzarella. There were two bars set up on either end of the open living space. The bar set up was duplicated on the pool deck.

Dylan walked over to the bar and ordered a Coke. After being served, he turned and saw Penel speaking with an older man. He approached but kept his distance until the discussion waned, taking the moment to observe Penel. Her shoulder-length, brown hair was slightly poofed, and she wore little makeup. She looked stunning in tight-fitting, white pants and a pink, sleeveless shirt.

Dylan could hear enough of the conversation to glean that the man was asking about school. Penel looked over and motioned to Dylan. He handed off his drink to a passing waiter carrying an empty tray and stood next to her. Penel reached for his left hand and intertwined their fingers.

"This is my friend Dylan. This is Edwin Reeves. He's a dear old family friend."

The man smiled and extended a right hand. "Old is the operative word. Dylan, it's nice to meet a friend of Penel's."

Dylan extended his right hand, his left still holding Penel's. He shook firmly. "It's nice to meet you, sir."

"Are you at NYU also?"

"No, sir. I live in Fairfield County. I'm finishing my senior year of high school."

"Ah, I see. Where do you plan on attending university?"

Dylan considered for a moment. "I'm being recruited as a student athlete, and right now my leading choice is the University of Connecticut. They're giving me the opportunity to play both football and baseball."

"Very good. You are a strapping, young lad at that. By the way, you two make a handsome couple. Be sure and treat her well, son. She's a very special young woman."

Dylan looked over at Penel. Their eyes met, and they shared a smile. He looked back at Edwin Reeves. "Yes, sir. I've come to the same conclusion about our mutual friend."

"Well, you two have indulged an old man long enough. I see someone I need to have a word with. If you'll both excuse me."

"Yes, sir. Again, it was a pleasure meeting you."

Penel gave the man a hug. "It was so nice to see you again, Uncle Edwin." Then she led Dylan outside. "Come on. Let's get something to eat. Was that Coke you were drinking?"

Dylan nodded.

"I think we can do better than that." They found a small table on the very edge of the pool deck. "You sit. I'll take care of the refreshments."

Dylan looked around while she was gone. He estimated there were close to 200 people. Suddenly he saw a beautiful, blonde woman with a short, familiar-looking man. They appeared an odd couple, but there was something recognizable about them. Dylan was obviously staring when Penel came back with a tray containing two appetizer plates and two glasses of a yellowish liquid.

"Yeah, that's Billy and Christie. Once in a while, when the mood strikes, he'll go over to the piano and sing a few songs."

"Ouch. It just hit me. That's Billy Joel and Christie Brinkley."

Penel laughed. "You are so funny. I bet you didn't notice John McEnroe or Donald Trump either."

"They're both here too?"

"It's July in the Hamptons. A lot of New Yorkers spend the summer out here."

"Any New York Giants or Yankee players gonna be here tonight?"

"Is that supposed to be a trick question? Even I know it's the middle of baseball season and NFL training camps just started."

"Wow, I'm impressed. I guess you are a sports fan."

"I love sports. I'm not much of a hockey fan if you remember. Baseball and football are my favorite spectator sports and golf and tennis are my passions. I play on the NYU club tennis team."

"We should play tennis sometime. I noticed you have a court on the property."

Penel displayed a cocky smile. "You wouldn't stand a chance."

"You're probably right. You're amazing. Smart, beautiful, athletic, and a genuine good person. If I keep looking, I may eventually find a flaw in there somewhere."

"You left out adventurous. Take a sip of your drink."

Dylan tasted the concoction. "Mmm, it's good. Tastes like spiked lemonade. What's in it?"

"Grey Goose and lemonade, a summer favorite."

They drank, ate, and continued their conversation. Occasionally, someone would come by and say hello to Penel. Each time, she introduced Dylan affectionately as her friend. Penel excused herself for a moment and was gone for about fifteen minutes. She returned with two more vodka and lemonades.

"Sorry for the delay. All these people are Daddy's friends and associates. I had to stop and say hello to some of them."

"I didn't notice anyone else in our age bracket."

"You probably won't tonight. I didn't invite anyone else because I wanted you to myself for the evening." She leaned across the table and kissed Dylan on the lips.

After they finished their drinks, Penel suggested they go for a walk on the beach. They left their shoes at the base of the dunes and walked along the shoreline hand in hand. The moon illuminated their way aided by an occasional well-lit house, music and noise emanating from the backyards set off in the distance. They talked about their plans for the rest of the summer. Dylan tried to steer the conversation toward Penel, but she insisted on a balance, asking Dylan about his college recruiting experience.

"Is anyone mentoring you through the process? It can be quite complex and cutthroat."

Dylan was surprised by her grasp of the recruiting system. He chose his words carefully. "I have some people advising me."

"I hope it's more than just family. They can become excitable and emotional, and that can be a lethal combination."

Dylan was reluctant to reveal that he valued the opinion of a reclusive old widow. "I have people mentoring me outside of family. I've known them all a long time, and they have my best interests at heart."

"I'm glad to hear that because I can tell you're a special person and destined to accomplish great things, Dylan McDirt."

By the time they headed back to the house, it was after midnight and most of the guests had left. The balance were saying their goodbyes and thanking their hosts.

Dylan made it a point to approach Mr. and Mrs. Stanhill. "Thank you both for inviting me to your home this weekend and for allowing me to attend the party. I've thoroughly enjoyed myself."

Candice Stanhill stood by and smiled while her husband replied, "It was our pleasure, Dylan. You're a fine young man, and you're welcome at my home anytime. I didn't have an opportunity to mention this before, but I wish to apologize for the poor behavior of Penelope's former college dormmate. I invited her to the hockey game and felt responsible for the rude conduct she displayed toward you. You handled the situation like a perfect gentleman."

"Thank you for the kind words, sir. But I believe the only person responsible for that young woman's actions was herself."

"Quite right. Well, I'll bid you two young people a good night. Penelope, I'd like a word with you inside after Dylan is settled into the guest house."

Penel walked Dylan to the guest house and kissed him passionately on the mouth. They embraced, came up for air, and kissed a final time. "Good night, Dylan."

"Well, I do require a ride to the train station in the morning."

Penel laughed hysterically. "You are really something." And with that she turned and sauntered in the direction of the main house.

Dylan retired to his bedroom. The digital clock on the nightstand read 1:48 a.m. He undressed down to his underwear, neatly folded his new clothes, and fell asleep the moment his head hit the pillow. A few hours later, he was awakened by a light filtering into his bedroom. He looked up and saw the silhouette of a tall woman standing in the doorway. He adjusted his eyes and recognized Penel, barefoot and wearing only a red, silk tank top and matching panties. She smiled and climbed into bed, an index finger to her lips.

The two embraced and began kissing each other passionately. Penel worked her way slowly down Dylan's chest with her mouth, her hand working its way to his crotch. She felt his erection and moaned with approval. "Mmmm."

Penel removed Dylan's underwear and skillfully stroked his penis while her other hand alternatively massaged and cupped his balls. "Sit back and enjoy."

He obeyed and a short time later he climaxed. Penel allowed him a moment to bask in the glow of the aftermath, then began hugging and kissing again, indicating through passionate body language that it was her turn.

Dylan carefully removed her top and panties and began kissing her small, perky breasts. Her erect nipples confirmed the daintily-suppressed moans. He slowly worked his hand down between her legs, feeling a small patch of hair above her vagina. She was otherwise hairless. He lightly moved his fingers across the lips of her vagina. They were moist and slightly swollen. He alternated hand movements between her inner thighs and the vaginal area, eventually settling on her genitals.

He could sense Penel's deepening breaths as her moaning intensified. He finally inserted two fingers and worked around the vagina while alternately probing the clitoris. She began lightly rocking her pelvis back and forth, eventually increasing the speed and intensity. She kissed him passionately on the mouth as her body shook in orgasmic pleasure.

After Penel collapsed in exhaustion, they both laid there for a moment. She finally snuggled up to Dylan and kissed his neck. "Thank you. That was wonderful."

Dylan brushed her hair away from her face and kissed her cheek and ear. "You weren't so bad yourself."

Penel slapped him playfully in the shoulder. "You really know how to compliment a girl." She kissed him again on the mouth before snuggling back into his arms. Shortly they both fell asleep.

When Dylan awoke, sunlight was entering through the bedroom windows. He jumped up and looked at the bedside clock. It read 7:14 a.m. Frantically, he looked next to him on the bed. Penel was gone. He got up, showered, and dressed. At precisely eight o'clock, Penel knocked on the cottage door and entered. She had bagels, cream cheese, and lox.

"Good morning. I trust you slept well."

"Some of the best sleep ever. It must have been my pre-bedtime routine. A guy could get used to that."

"You should know that routine and similar numbers are reserved for a select few."

"And you should know that I consider it, and your company in general, an honor and privilege."

Penel bowed demurely. "Thank you, kind sir."

They set out plates and silverware at the small dinette in the kitchen alcove. Orange juice from the fridge was served with the bagels. They ate in silence for a moment.

Penal daintily finished chewing a bite of her bagel. "After breakfast, I thought we'd hang out at the beach for a few hours before I have to take you to the train station."

"Sounds good to me. If you don't mind my asking, what did your father want to speak with you about last night?"

"Oh, a bunch of stuff. Daddy likes to pontificate on the ways of the world. Do you really mean did it have anything to do with you?"

"Sure, okay."

Penel laughed. "After reminding me of his fine judgment of character, Daddy said you are a refined young man. He's one of the good ones, Penelope, and I know people."

"And?"

"He reminded me that true gentlemen prefer women who respect themselves and don't appear too aggressive."

"Well, I'll vouch for your virtue."

"Thank you. I expect your kind words shall be rewarded again in the future."

Dylan raised his orange juice glass. "Here's to the future."

The couple hung out on the beach for a few hours. When Penel returned to the house to get ready, Dylan went to the cottage, showered again, packed, and presented himself at the main house. He found Winston Stanhill seated at the kitchen table drinking coffee and reading the Sunday edition of *The New York Times*.

"I want to thank you again, sir, for having me as a guest. You have a beautiful home."

"You're most certainly welcome, Dylan. You're a virtuous young man, and I sincerely mean it when I say you are welcome anytime."

Penel entered the room and cut things short. "Daddy, I'm taking Dylan to the train station and then I'll be back. Do you need me to bring anything from town while I'm out?"

"No, dear. I think we're well situated here."

"Safe travels back to Connecticut, Dylan."

"Thank you again, Mr. Stanhill."

They rode quietly in the topless Jeep with the breeze blowing through the cabin. When they arrived at the train station, Penel jumped out, hugged Dylan, and kissed him. "Until next time."

"Thank you again for a great weekend. I look forward to next time."

Dylan watched as Penel drove off in her Jeep. He already had his return ticket, so he sat on a bench and waited for his train. He reflected on how much he'd enjoyed his time with Penel but found himself dwelling on his glimpse into the extravagant lifestyles of the ultrawealthy.

I could get used to this, he finally concluded.

CHAPTER EIGHTEEN

B RYAN ARANOFF LEFT HIS OFFICE and went down to the basement where the data center for the Malloy Williamson Security Department was housed. The state-of-the-art data center was a large, sterile room full of microcomputers housed in banks of servers that lined the walls. The data center provided backup for all the firm's computer systems in the Manhattan and Greenwich headquarters as well as the outlying offices. A separate office served as the security department research center.

Aranoff approached the research center's large steel door and punched an eight-digit code into the keypad lock. After gaining access, he walked over to a thin man seated at a desk, hunched over a computer screen. The man sported greasy hair and thick glasses. He wore a short-sleeve, yellow dress shirt with a pocket protector. The back of his shirt collar was speckled with dandruff. Aranoff was one of the research center's rare visitors.

"What's up, Joe? How are things coming along?"

"Bryan, good to see you. I'm just about done. I should have a full report to you by the end of the day. Are you interested in a preview?" Joe Smerling was the classic computer geek, equal parts social cripple and information technology genius.

"Sure Joe, what've you got?"

Joe smiled, revealing crooked, yellow teeth. "Sixty second bio. Brad Davies. Age thirty-three. Born and raised outside of Boston. Graduated from Western New England University where he majored in art history. Solid C student. After graduation, worked in the Boston area for several companies over a period of approximately five years. Most notably, John Hancock Financial. Consistently poor job evaluations with several documented complaints of inappropriate conduct. Relocated to Fairfield County approximately four years ago. Worked in telemarketing sales, and three years ago, started his own telemarketing company, OPM Enterprises, where he is sole owner. Single, never married, no children. No criminal record to speak of. He doesn't own real estate, cars, boats, or any other personal property. Has no investment accounts, but approximately two hundred and fifty thousand dollars in cash in the business account and another eight hundred thousand dollars in personal accounts, mostly checking and money markets. He may have more in the safe deposit boxes he's rented. Fits the profile of a guy ready to run on a moment's notice. Leases his house and car. He has a poor credit rating and is in substantial debt."

That's all pretty benign, Aranoff thought. "Joe, you got anything good for me on this guy."

Joe smiled again. "Of course. OPM employs approximately a hundred people. A small administrative staff and mostly telemarketers who work on straight commission. OPM hawks credit cards to people with poor credit ratings, like Mr. Davies. The cards' main features are high interest rates and exorbitant quarterly fees. But that's not the juicy stuff. A separate marketing department using proprietary information from the telemarketing operation follows up with customers who receive the cards. That's where we hit pay dirt. Guess what OPM stands for?"

"What?"

"Other peoples' money. I won't spoil the ending, but suffice it to say, after hacking into their computers, I found some very troubling practices. I also checked OPM's record with the Better Business Bureau as well as complaints with the State of Connecticut Consumer Affairs Department and State Attorney General's Office. Inexplicably, given the high volume of complaints, OPM has no BBB rating. And despite a smaller but not insignificant number of complaints filed with the state, no formal inquiry has been opened by either Consumer Affairs or the AG."

"That's good work, Joe. I look forward to reading your report."

"There's more. I checked with the both the state and federal Equal Employment Opportunity Commissions. There are six open complaints for discrimination. All by female employees, all against Mr. Davies, and all involving claims of sexual harassment. Each of them is pending with no action taken to date."

"Joe, that's really fine work, as usual."

"It's what I do."

"I'll see you later. Please hand deliver the report to me when it's ready."

Aranoff left the data center and looked at his watch. He was five minutes late for a meeting upstairs with the lead field investigator for a presentation on the surveillance results for Brad Davies. He went upstairs to the conference room where Frank Gillespie was waiting. Gillespie had the large, white screen pulled down and the video recorder queued up.

"How goes it, Frank?"

"Great, Bryan." He handed Aranoff a large, padded envelope. "Here's the full written report along with all of the raw surveillance footage. I made a high-light film, which I'm going to show you now. This guy's a piece of work. You may want to grab some popcorn for this."

Gillespie closed the blinds, dimmed the lights, and turned on the recorder. There was video of Davies in his executive office, at three different bars and nightclubs, and in a seedy area of South Norwalk where he picked up a woman of questionable virtue. The video concluded with detailed images of the pair's subsequent meeting at a Super 8 Motel off Route Seven. The video footage inside Davies's office and the motel room was taken through windows but, nonetheless, was of clear, high quality. Aranoff watched in amazement. When the video was finished, he sat there in silence staring at the blank screen.

"Do you have a good handle on this guy's schedule?"

"Very good. He's a creature of habit. Meets with that same woman you saw in his office most every afternoon. Hits the bar scene regularly and sometimes takes the party home, other times on the road as you saw at that Super 8."

"Good work, Frank." Aranoff grabbed the envelope while Gillespie popped the highlight film out of the VCR and handed it to him.

"Stand down on this for now. I'll let you know if I need anything else."

Aranoff went back to his office, returned some phone calls, read Gillespie's surveillance report, and worked on another project. A few hours later, Joe Smerling knocked on his door and handed him a bound notebook. "Here you go, Hoss. As promised."

"Thanks, Joe." It was obvious from Smerling's body language that he wanted to hang around and discuss his work. Aranoff looked at him dismissively. "I'll review the report and let you know if I need anything else."

Smerling turned on his heels and left the office, sporting the mien of a rejected puppy dog.

Aranoff read the lengthy report. When he was finished, he sat there in a state of excited astonishment. *Time to go see Nesbitt and put the final plan into action.*

CHAPTER NINETEEN

D YLAN SPENT THE REST OF the summer working, playing out the balance of the summer baseball season, and hanging out with Alex. He also worked out regularly, getting prepared for football practice, which began in mid-August. He managed to speak with Penel Stanhill at least every couple of weeks, though their schedules did not allow them to get together again. She got an apartment in the city for her sophomore year at NYU, and Dylan received an invitation to visit in the fall.

Just before the start of high school practice, Dylan attended a football prospect camp at the University of Connecticut. The camp was, as required under NCAA rules, open to all boys ages fifteen through eighteen. To ensure participation by active recruits, all prospects' high school coaches were provided information for early registration. The coaches then instructed their players to call the number at a precise time, which, coincidentally, was one hour before the registration time advertised to the public. This was standard practice throughout college athletics and ensured that the majority of attendees were actively-recruited prospects. Any stragglers that managed to sign up before enrollment was capped were subtly placed in a segregated group, apart from the other participants.

The camp took place on the UConn campus over a three-day period. Attendees were housed in a dormitory. Camp activities featured weightlifting and skill drills designed to measure speed, agility, and general athleticism. Campers were also broken into groups for position-specific drills. The camp culminated with a seven-on-seven, all-star scrimmage on the Memorial Stadium field featuring offensive versus defensive prospects.

Dylan fared well at the camp, scoring high on general football and position-specific skill drills. He was also in the upper-tier in overall sprint times and strength and agility exercises. Most significantly, he shined during the scrimmage with an interception and several passes defended. Only a few balls were caught in front of him, and the receiver was quickly touched down, which ended the play. Dylan got in a little work in the slot position at wide receiver, but it was clear he was being recruited to play defensive back.

While Dylan was on campus, Coaches Stafford and Fuller confirmed his official visit, which was scheduled to take place in early October. That weekend the Huskies would be hosting Towson University. The visit was conveniently scheduled for a time when the Stamford High football team had a bye week. The basics were discussed, and Dylan was advised that he would receive a complete itinerary beforehand. It would be an all-expense paid trip, and two family members were permitted to accompany him. They would arrive on Friday midmorning and were required to leave campus by Sunday. Dylan would also have an opportunity to meet with Coach Lundy and tour the baseball facilities.

Classes began the Tuesday after the Labor Day weekend. Dylan had already been at school for football practice the past two-and-a-half weeks, but it was good to see all his classmates. On that first day it was not lost on Dylan that it would be the last time he would enter Stamford High School to begin a new school year.

The UConn coaches had explained to Dylan that it was unnecessary for him to apply through the usual admission department channels. He was sent his application by mail from an administrator who would serve as his academic advisor. After he received the package, the administrator called to walk him through the plethora of forms. A prepaid envelope addressed to the assistant at the SAAC, an acronym for the Student-Athlete Academic Center, was included with the packet. Approximately one week after Dylan submitted his application, he received his acceptance letter in the mail.

Alex began his senior year at Fairfield Prep. He was already admitted to Yale on early admission for the following fall.

The Stamford High School football team got off to a good start. In September, Dylan made plans to meet with Penel in New York the first week in November. It was the only other weekend that fall when Stamford had no football game scheduled. One early-autumn afternoon as Dylan completed his paper route, he pedaled home in a state of bliss, dwelling on his good fortune and bright future prospects. As he arrived home, his thoughts were interrupted by the ominous rumbling of thunder in the distance. He looked up and saw dark clouds on the horizon.

On Monday of the week of Dillon's official visit to the University of Connecticut, an envelope arrived by express mail. The packet included an itinerary of the weekend's events. Early Friday morning, Dylan, Cheryl, and Anthony departed for the three-hour drive to Storrs in Anthony's vintage blue Plymouth Satellite. Upon arrival on campus, they met the other recruits and their families at the team football facility. From there the recruits were separated from family members, who were delegated to rooms at the University Inn. Family members were transported around town in vans for the balance of the weekend. The recruits were paired with player chaperones and housed separately in guest rooms in the dormitory where student athletes were required to reside during their freshmen year.

Recruits and their families were reunited in the afternoon for an orientation and toured the campus together, including the academic buildings, the SAAC, football training facility, locker room, and stadium. In the evening they all attended a social hour and the evening concluded with dinner at Huskies Steakhouse.

The following day featured a private, pregame tailgate reception at the football facility. Afterwards, recruits were escorted to the locker room and issued passes that permitted them to stand on the sidelines during the game. Family members were seated together in the stands. UConn lost to Towson in a close game, and the post-game mood dampened considerably. In the evening, the recruits attended a party with the players while family members attended a dinner hosted by a group of UConn assistant coaches. On Sunday morning, everyone met for a breakfast held at Coach Stafford's home.

Coach Lundy attended the breakfast and spoke briefly with Coach Stafford and his wife. Dylan, his mother and grandfather were motioned over. Coach Stafford advised that Coach Lundy would take Dylan and his family over to the baseball facility for the remaining two hours of the visit. They said their goodbyes to the football staff and their spouses and left with Coach Lundy. He transported the group over to the baseball complex in an extended golf cart. They spent an hour touring JO Christian field and the adjacent baseball facilities and discussed the prospect of Dylan's two-sport career.

"Football will be paying your way, so I expect you'll be obligated to some extent to participate in spring practice. But once football season ends, you can dedicate yourself full-time to baseball training until then. You should be ready to go for the season and available for games as football dictates."

At the appropriate time Coach Lundy loaded the group back into the golf cart and drove them to Anthony's car. They said their goodbyes, and Anthony drove the Plymouth Satellite toward Interstate 395 to make the connection to I-95 back to Stamford.

Anthony turned and looked back at Dylan seated in the rear. "So, what'd you think Dylan?"

"It's a good opportunity, and it's where I want to go to school."

"I didn't feel a whole lotta love, to quote Led Zepplin."

Cheryl chimed in, "Compared to West Conn, this is the big time. If athletics is going to pay for your education and you understand school is as much a priority as sports, you'll be way ahead of the game."

"You know, Mom, you sound an awful lot like Mrs. Lott."

"Smart women have to stick together."

Dylan laughed. "I can't disagree with that."

"How is she doing anyway?"

"Great. I stopped by and saw her a couple weeks ago.".

Following Dylan's official visit, the UConn football team went into a tailspin. They lost their next three games, including a rare loss to Yale much to the delight of Alex. The following day, on a Sunday morning, he showed up at the McDirt house sporting a Yale sweatshirt and baseball cap, a brash smile on his face.

"Good day, one and all. It's great to be a Bulldog."

"Give it a rest, Alex. Check the overall record."

Alex broke into song. "Hey, hey it's okay, you're gonna work for us someday."

Dylan glared at Alex for a second, then bull rushed him and tackled him on the living room floor.

Cheryl intervened. "Boys, enough!"

Dylan stood on top of Alex a moment before relenting, displaying pent up frustration. "Fine, you Ivy League snob. The only way you're getting up is when I let you."

Alex broke the momentary tension between the two friends. "Come on, let me enjoy my rare moment of glory. Who knows how long it's gonna be before we win this game again?"

Dylan relented. "Sorry about that. I'm just worried. I'm feeling a lot of pressure until I sign my letter of intent in February." He was referring to the first Wednesday in February, known as National Signing Day, when high school football players and colleges formally consummated their commitments.

Alex astutely recognized the anomaly in his friend's behavior. "No problem, buddy. Forget about it."

The boys hung out for a few hours. Cheryl made them lunch and they watched the Giants-Eagles game on TV.

As darkness fell, Alex decided to head back to Greenwich. "I better be going. I have some homework and a progress report due on my senior paper."

"No problem. I'll talk to you later."

Shortly after Alex left, Dylan got a call from Penel Stanhill. It took him a moment to think back to the last time they spoke. *It's been a few weeks*, he decided. Nonetheless, his spirits were immediately lifted. Cheryl, recognizing who was on the phone, left the kitchen and retired to her bedroom.

Dylan waited for Cheryl to close her bedroom door. "Hey, it's so nice to hear your voice. It's been kind of a rough week. I'm really looking forward to seeing you next weekend. I've missed you."

"Uh, well, Dylan, that's why I'm calling."

Dylan immediately sensed impending disappointment and regretted his overly enthusiastic and somewhat vulnerable greeting. "What's up?"

"I've met someone, and I don't think it's appropriate that we get together next weekend."

"When did this happen?"

"I didn't want to say anything until I was sure. I met him at the end of the spring semester last year. We talked a few times over the summer, but we started seeing each other after we came back to school in the fall. It really just got serious in the past few weeks. It wouldn't be fair to either of you if you visited this weekend. This isn't easy, but I like and respect you and I owe it to you to be honest about things."

"Well, I appreciate that."

"Dylan, you're such a good guy and so unlike most of the men I've met. I believe this is what's best."

"I really like you too, Penel. It's very disappointing, but I understand, I think."

"Thank you for that. Take care of yourself, Dylan." Before he could say anything further, Penel disconnected the call.

Great, he thought. *What else could possibly go wrong?*

CHAPTER TWENTY

B RITTANY STURM RETURNED TO WORK after another early lunch. She
sat in her small office, two doors down from her boss. She had spent the
morning reading supermarket tabloids and fashion magazines and painting her
fingernails. Her official title was personal assistant to the company's owner, a
position she'd held for approximately six months. She remained in her office
most of the afternoon without hearing from him. This was unusual as he required servicing most every day.

Around four o'clock, the boss buzzed her office. "Get in her now."

Brittany checked her makeup in her office wall mirror and reapplied bright-
red lip gloss. She walked down to Brad Davies's office, avoiding eye contact
with Carmella. She knocked and entered.

He was seated comfortably on the couch, and a black satin gift bag sat on
the table in front of him. "I brought you a little something."

Brittany sashayed over and picked up the bag. "What's this?"

"Open it."

Brittany opened the bag and pulled out a black lace corset with matching
stockings and garter belt. "Excuse me while I go to the restroom and change."

"That won't be necessary. I need you to come over to the house and work
late tonight. We'll be entertaining another guest."

Great, she thought. *He's hired a hooker for a menage a' trois.* "What time
should I be there?"

"Ten. Wear the new outfit and the red high heels I bought you. Nothing
else."

"Brad, for goodness' sake. I have to drive over and it's the middle of November."

"What I mean is wear the outfit underneath an overcoat."

"Right."

Brad handed her an envelope. "Here's your overtime pay. Now get outta here. I'll see you at the house, ten sharp."

Around eight thirty that evening, Brittany awoke from her nap. Her salary allowed her to rent a nice one-bedroom apartment with a garage for her Mustang. She ran a bath and shaved her legs and vaginal area. After toweling off, she blew dry her hair, applied makeup, and put on the outfit as requested. She slipped on six-inch flaming red heels and checked herself in the full-length bedroom mirror. Satisfied, she selected a tan-belted trench coat, buttoned it top to bottom, and cinched the belt snuggly around her waist. She slipped her driver's license and some cash into her coat pocket and grabbed the car keys.

Brittany drove up to the main entrance of the gated Shippen neighborhood complex where Brad Davies lived. She recognized the guard on duty, who in turn, recognized her. "I'm going to the Davies residence."

"Yes, Ms. Sturm."

The gate arm lifted.

Brittany smiled and waved to the guard as she drove through. When she arrived at the house the exterior lights were on, but the interior was otherwise dark. She parked in the driveway and rang the bell. No one answered immediately, so she buzzed the intercom. "Brad, it's me."

"Door's open. Come upstairs to my bedroom and lock the door behind you."

Brittany complied and began the walk up the staircase, her heels clicking loudly against the hardwood steps. She opened the bedroom door and a tall woman with dark features was sprawled out naked on the king-size bed. Brittany stood in the bedroom entrance for a moment and took in the young woman. She had piercing blue eyes and appeared lithe with athletic limbs and well-rounded breasts highlighted by razor sharp nipples. She appeared to be of Mediterranean descent. Brittany felt a tinge of excitement. She sensed a rare opportunity. Not only did she have someone to share the workload, but she could indulge herself with an attractive partner for a change.

Brad emerged from the bathroom wearing a thick terry cloth robe and smoking a pipe, displaying a poor Hugh Hefner imitation. "Brittany, this is Claudia. Please get on the bed and enjoy yourselves. I'm gonna sit here and watch for a while."

Brittany eagerly removed her trench coat, displaying her undergarments. Claudia stared at her, licked her lips, and smiled, rife with mutual anticipation. Brittany moved seductively toward the bed and lay down next to her new friend. Then, a loud crash and all hell broke loose.

A split second later, two dozen men in black body armor emblazoned with POLICE across their backs stormed the master bedroom led by a man carrying a full-length ballistic shield. Spotlights mounted on military-style combat helmets activated, flooding the room with bright light that temporarily blinded the three playmates. Instructions were blared through some type of loudspeaker: "Get down on the ground! On the ground now!"

Brad Davies sat frozen in shock in an overstuffed armchair facing his bed, his right hand firmly wrapped around his manhood. Two of the men threw him to the ground, rolled him onto his belly, and secured his wrists with zip ties and legs with ankle shackles. Two female officers firmly removed the two women from the bed and escorted them into the bathroom where they were covered up and similarly bound with handcuffs and ankle shackles. The man with the shield had a microphone strapped to his helmet and barked out further instructions through his headset. "All clear. All clear."

A short time later, several agents in FBI windbreakers accompanied by the agent in charge, a man dressed in a navy-blue suit, entered the bedroom. The AIC approached Davies and read from a typed sheet of paper. "Brad Davies, you're under arrest for wire fraud, mail fraud, defrauding the elderly, and grand theft." Davies was then read his Miranda warnings.

Davies began to sob uncontrollably. A yellow puddle formed on the hardwood floor around his feet and began to seep into the adjacent antique area rug.

The AIC shouted in the direction of the pathetic sight, "Get yourself together, you pustule."

Davies was then dragged down the stairs and into an awaiting armored vehicle. Neighbors stood outside their homes staring at the scene in utter disgust. This was just the beginning of a bad night for Brad Davies. At the same time, a similar group armed with a search warrant descended upon the offices of OPM Enterprises in downtown Stamford. Computer files, business, accounting, and personnel records, along with other evidence were confiscated and packed up in records storage boxes. All told, the law enforcement task force removed fifty-six boxes of evidence.

Davies was transported to the Stamford Police Station, escorted by a bevy of unmarked government sedans and Connecticut Highway Patrol vehicles, all with lights flashing and sirens blaring. Upon arrival, it was closing in on midnight and a large crowd had gathered at the police headquarters awaiting the convoy. The crowd consisted of key members of a joint task force of the

Stamford Police Department, Connecticut Highway Patrol, and the FBI along with members of television and print media.

Two police officers slowly and deliberately led Davies through the rear doors of the armored vehicle. He clumsily shuffled his feet, ankles restricted by the shackles. Television camera spotlights illuminated the area. The perp walk was interrupted by the ubiquitous AIC. He waited for the cameras to reset and began only after the little red lights came back on. He stated his name, title, and agency and then spelled out his name before initiating his statement.

"Tonight, a major arrest has been made in connection with a massive, nationwide telemarketing fraud campaign originating out of an office building in our own fair city. The perpetrator, Brad Davies, owner of OPM Enterprises, stands before you charged with multiple counts of wire fraud, mail fraud, and grand theft. Perhaps most heinous, a disproportionate number of these charges involve exploitation against the elderly and other members of our most vulnerable citizenry. A major parasite has been removed from society, and I pledge to you he will be prosecuted to the fullest extent of the law."

Just then another man walked up to Brad Davies. The officers stepped aside and allowed the man to shove a thick stack of papers under Davies's armpit. "You've been served."

The AIC then yielded the floor to a distinguished-looking, middle-aged female flanked by two other younger female colleagues. All three were sharply dressed in conservative business suits.

The middle-aged women addressed the media. "My name is Anita Bennett. I'm an attorney with the law firm of Conrad, Bastow, and Bennett. I represent several current and former employees of OPM Enterprises, the company owned and controlled by Brad Davies. Mr. Davies and OPM are defendants in civil lawsuits brought by our clients for sexual harassment, discrimination, and multiple violations of the Civil Rights Act."

The AIC stepped back up. "In a rare joint effort between state and federal law enforcement agencies and private attorneys pursuing concurrent civil actions, we have partnered together to ensure that justice is served on all fronts in this matter. I would be remiss if I failed to mention the brave individual who as of today is a former employee at OPM Enterprises. This individual came forward with the necessary information that culminated in tonight's arrest. A warrant was executed tonight at OPM's offices in downtown Stamford. The raid was successful, and we now believe we have all the evidence necessary to secure convictions. Toward that end, we have frozen all assets of OPM Enterprises as well as the individual accounts and personal assets of Brad Davies. These funds will remain in the protective custody of the federal government until final disposition of all pending criminal and civil charges."

Standing anonymously in the back of the throng of law enforcement and media, Bryan Aranoff watched the impromptu press proceedings bearing a contended air. After his investigation was complete, he had contacted a middle manager who worked out of the OPM data center and confronted him with his investigative findings, including the evidence surreptitiously hacked from OPM's computers. Aranoff had made it clear that OPM was going to be taken down.

Turned out the data manager's disdain for Brad Davies and his business practices carried the day. Realizing this, Aranoff had avoided threatening the man. The data manager confirmed that OPM stole proprietary personal information from credit card recipients and then solicited them to purchase substandard and defective products.

But the jackpot had proved to be the bogus recurring charges, billed in perpetuity by OPM to all credit card holders who had purchased at least one product from its marketing department. Amounts ranging from fifty-nine cents to a $1.90 were billed monthly under nebulous descriptions such as extended warranty fee, personal protection assurance, access fee, bundled services, and credit card franchise fee. Astonishingly, 96 percent of the charges were processed without any challenge or complaint. Davies and OPM were stealing more than a million dollars a year through the billing scam.

Aranoff and Kurt Nesbitt had taken the results of their investigation to their long-established contacts with the FBI and Connecticut State Police. The contacts dated back to their days with NYPD. Both men were aware of the agencies appreciation for receiving tips on high-profile cases. In particular, those which required little in the way of expending further investigative resources. The OPM whistleblower was a key component in that regard.

Bryan Aranoff broke away from the crowd and headed home. He looked forward to a well-deserved nightcap followed by a good night's sleep. Tomorrow he had one final task to complete before his investigation was concluded.

The next morning, Aranoff arrived at his office a little after ten o'clock and kept busy until early afternoon, leaving for a late lunch around one thirty. After lunch he stopped at a newsstand and picked up five copies of the *Stamford Advocate*. As expected, the front-page headline and accompanying story featured last night's activities involving Brad Davies and OPM Enterprises. Aranoff returned to his office and prepared two packages to be delivered by courier. The courier arrived promptly and picked up the packages.

CHAPTER TWENTY-ONE

C HERYL MCDIRT RETURNED HOME FROM work around four thirty. Shortly thereafter, a man knocked on her front door. Dylan was not home yet so she spoke to the man through the locked door. "Who is it?"

"It's Countywide Courier Services, ma'am. I have a delivery for Cheryl McDirt."

Cheryl peered out the front picture window. A plain-white sedan was parked in the street in front of the house. The same business name was painted in black lettering on the car's front door. She cracked the door open slightly and saw a young man wearing a coat and baseball cap embroidered with the same moniker. He also had a company identification badge clipped to his jacket's chest pocket. She opened the door all the way. The man handed her an envelope addressed to her. There was no return address.

"Who is this from?"

The man looked down at his clipboard. "It looks like it's from Malloy Williamson & Associates."

Cheryl recognized the name of the company as the one owned by Alex's father. "Do I need to sign for this?"

"Yes, ma'am. Right here." The man handed Cheryl the clipboard and a pen.

Cheryl signed and thanked the man.

After he left, Cheryl sat down at the kitchen table and opened the envelope. The front page of the *Advocate* headline read, "Local Telemarketing Company Shut Down in Late Night Bust."

Below the headline was a full-size color photo of Brad Davies handcuffed and shackled, wearing only a bathrobe and bedroom slippers and standing in front of the Stamford Police Department. Cheryl read on.

"Late last night a joint task force consisting of local, state, and federal law enforcement agencies arrested Brad Davies, 33, of Stamford on more than 500 counts of criminal charges ranging from wire fraud mail fraud, defrauding the elderly, and grand theft. The charges arose out of telemarketing activities at his Stamford based company, OPM Enterprises. If convicted on all counts, Davies could receive a maximum sentence of what would amount to multiple life terms. Bail this morning was denied and all bank accounts and other assets of both OPM Enterprises and Brad Davies have been frozen. Additionally, at the same time Davies was served with six civil lawsuits filed by the law firm of Conrad, Bastow, and Bennett. The firm represents former female employees of OPM who were allegedly victims of sexual harassment by Davies. Lead attorney Anita Bennett has asked any other victims who may wish to come forward to contact her office."

Cheryl gasped and sat there with her hand over her open mouth. A wave of relief washed over her, and tears of joy streamed down her face.

Just then, Dylan walked through the back door. "Mom, what's the matter?"

"Nothing's the matter, honey. Everything is just fine." She got up and hugged Dylan tightly.

He looked at her suspiciously. "Seriously, are you alright?"

"Yes, dear. I love you, and everything is better than alright."

Dylan looked down at the newspaper lying on the kitchen table. "Why'd you buy the paper today? I bring one home for you every day."

"I didn't buy it, Dylan. Someone gave it to me."

Dylan was convinced his mother was in a good mood, if not acting somewhat peculiar. "Okay, whatever you say. I'm going to clean up and take a shower. What's for dinner?"

"We're going out for dinner. Your choice. Anywhere you want to go."

Now Dylan was really flummoxed. "Are you *sure* you're alright?"

Cheryl hugged Dylan again and held on even longer. "Can't a proud mother take her handsome son out to eat once in a while and show him off to the world?"

Dylan finally gave up. "Well, if you're really serious, then you know I want to go to John's Best Pizza."

"Fine, John's Best it is. Go get ready."

This time Dylan hugged Cheryl. "You know, Mom, sometimes I don't understand you, but don't take it personally. Women tend to confuse me now and then."

"Get used to it, son. That'll never change."

Around the same time, another courier delivered a similar package to Anthony Tomassi at his home in Norwalk. Anthony signed for the package and opened it. The package contained the same copy of the *Advocate*, but this one was accompanied by a note that simply read:

> "As promised, the matter has been handled. I trust it has been resolved to your satisfaction. In the unlikely event that is not the case, please feel free to contact me."

The note was unsigned. Anthony read the front page headline and accompanying article, recognizing the photo of the story's subject. He smiled and shook his head.

CHAPTER TWENTY-TWO

O**VER THE NEXT FEW WEEKS,** Dylan observed a change in his mother's comportment. She appeared in a more felicitously carefree manner than she had in some time. He wondered if something had happened in her personal life, a man perhaps. They had always talked openly about things, but he felt somewhat uncomfortable approaching his mother on the subject. He finally decided to let it be. She appeared happy, and that's all that mattered to him.

Unfortunately, Dylan's mood took a turn for the worse. Stamford's football season ended with a first-round playoff loss to Trumbull. A week later, the University of Connecticut football team lost its final game to end a dismal season with a 2-9 record. The following Monday afternoon when Dylan picked up his newspapers, his eyes were immediately drawn to a small paragraph in the first column at the top fold of page one that read, "UConn Football Coach fired following 2-9 season. Details in Sports C-1."

Dylan tore the top copy out of the bundle and turned to the sports section. The UConn football coach firing was the top story. The article confirmed that head coach Terry Stafford and his entire staff had been dismissed. According to the press release issued by the school's athletic department, an immediate national search for his successor was underway.

Dylan felt an instantaneous pain deep in the pit of his stomach. He pedaled on in a total fog as he began to deliver the newspapers. He tried to think, but his brain failed to form a single definitive thought. He carried on, incognizant of his surroundings, until he heard a loud truck horn that shook him back into the present moment. He hurriedly finished the paper route and stopped at Mrs. Lott's house. When he knocked on the front door, Franklin answered.

"Hello, Franklin. Is Mrs. Lott available?"

"One moment, Mr. Dylan. Let me check for you." Franklin closed the door and returned a few minutes later. "Mrs. Lott will see you now."

Dylan shuffled his feet slowly, his head down and shoulders slumped as he made his way into the sitting room.

Seated on her small couch, Mrs. Lott said, "Dylan, it's good to see you. To what do I owe the pleasure?"

"I wish this was a pleasant visit, but I just received some terrible news."

"Well, sit down and tell me about it."

Dylan explained what happened and how he felt the world had just caved in around him, muscles tensed in his face as he spoke. When he was through, she hesitated and the two sat in silence for several moments.

"Dylan, I understand this comes as a shock to you. This is certainly not good news, but remember, you can only control what's within your purview. What has occurred is not your doing and bears no reflection on you whatsoever. Everyone has limited physical and emotional energy, and you shouldn't expend a great deal worrying about what's happened. Once you get over that, then it will be time to determine a course of action that is within your control. My advice is to go home, hug your mother, and get over the news as soon as you are able. Things will look clearer in a day or so. And remember, you have a lot of people who care about you, present company included. This is the time to lean on those people for support and counsel."

Dylan listened intently and allowed the words to sink in, then finally managed a small smile. "You're right as usual. I want you to know how much I value your friendship and your advice."

The old widow could not help but smile back. "Thank you, Dylan. The feeling is mutual. I am an old woman, but having you as a friend provides me with a great deal of optimism for the future. When you're ready, come back and see me. We'll figure this out."

Dylan got up, walked over to Mrs. Lott, and gently hugged the frail woman. "Thank you. I'm taking your advice and going home."

She smiled as Dylan broke the embrace, then he turned and left.

When Dylan got home, Cheryl was waiting for him. She hugged her son in an inordinately tight manner for the second time in a month. "Dylan, I'm so sorry. Your grandfather just called with the news about the UConn coaching staff. What do you think this means for us?"

"Mom, it's certainly a shock, but there's nothing I can do about it at the moment. In a day or so, things will look clearer and we'll figure it out together."

Cheryl regarded her son with a countenance of admiration and affection. "You really are something. I was a nervous wreck when I heard the news, and here you are all calm, cool, and collected. Do me a favor and call your grandfather. He's more rattled than I am."

"Sure thing, Mom. I need to call Alex too. I'm sure he's heard the news. Heck, he probably knew about it before it hit the papers."

Dylan called his grandfather and carried on a conversation that mimicked the one with his mother, except the latter consisted of an extended version. As soon as he hung up, he called Alex.

"This is crazy. I would've thought Stafford would have gotten another year to turn things back around. I guess all these guys get hired to eventually get fired. I'm real sorry about the razzing I gave you earlier in the season after the Yale game. That may have been Stafford's undoing."

"Forget it. There's nothing I can do about it for now."

"What are you going to do?"

"I'm not sure yet. I'm gonna talk with Coach DaSilva tomorrow and get his input. And I can always reach out to Coach Lundy."

"Good point. That's one advantage you have over all the other recruits who are in limbo right along with you. I doubt anyone else was recruited as a two-sport athlete."

"Well, listen, I better go. I have to keep my mom and grandfather off the ledge. They both took the news pretty hard."

"Sure thing. I'll talk with you later."

As soon as Dylan hung up with Alex, he felt his mood improving. He decided to put things out of his mind as best he could. He would look at it again in the light of day tomorrow.

The next day Dylan went down to Coach DaSilva's office during his study hall period. He saw Dylan approaching through his office window and waived him in.

"Hey, Coach. I'm sure you've heard the news about Coach Stafford."

"Yes, Dylan, have a seat. That's a tough break."

"What do you think I should do?"

"Well, there's not much you can do right now until another coach is hired. I imagine the athletic director will move quickly because it's the heart of recruiting season. And National Signing Day is just two months away. I have a contact in the athletic department. I'll touch base with him in a week or so and try and to get some intel on what's happening up there."

"Thanks, Coach."

"Sure thing, Dylan. Hang in there."

Dylan waited a few days before calling Coach Lundy. The UConn baseball coach was not particularly reassuring. "As we've discussed on multiple occasions, Dylan, here at UConn, football and basketball are the engines that run the athletic department. Until a new head football coach is brought in and hires a staff, there's not much I can do. And once the coach arrives, it's going to be a mad scramble from the moment he sets foot on campus until after signing day. At the appropriate time, I'll go see him and discuss your situation. I do want you to know that nothing's changed on my end. I still want you to be part of the Husky baseball program. Unfortunately, we have limited athletic scholarships and those are long since accounted for."

"I understand, Coach. I appreciate whatever help you can provide."

Dylan hung up the phone thinking he'd done everything he could for the time being. He called Alex.

"What's going on?"

"Not much. I spoke with Coach DaSilva and just got off the phone with Coach Lundy."

"How'd that go?"

Dylan replied, "Not particularly well. Coach Lundy just seems resigned to second class citizenship in the athletic department, like he doesn't have much control over things."

"Dylan, let's be real. He doesn't. College athletics is run by money from a school's football and basketball programs. They bring in most, if not all, of the revenue. It's no different at UConn. It sounds like he still feels the love for you. He's just being realistic about things. And he said he's going to talk to the new football coach when the time comes."

"Yeah, but what am I supposed to do in the meantime?"

"Look, UConn is your number one choice for school, and quite frankly, your only option for playing college sports. You've already been accepted. A lot of kids are still waiting to hear from admissions. If things don't work out, then it'll be time to look at other alternatives."

"I suppose you're right."

"I'm always right. What you need the is comfort and affections of a good woman. Unfortunately, I can't assist you in that department at the moment. And I've learned my lesson about bringing in professional help. What you need is a good laugh. There's this show I just came across on TV. It's on Thursday nights, called *Seinfeld*. It's been on for a few seasons. You should check it out. It's frickin' hilarious. I saw an episode the other day where they had a contest over who could go the longest without pleasuring themself. On television! I couldn't stop laughing."

"Great, a show about guys talking about jerking off. Sounds like your kinda thing."

"First of all, there's a girl involved too. Trust me on this. Give it a try. You'll love it."

"Alright, I gotta go."

"See ya. And remember. You *are* the master of your domain."

"Huh?"

"Nothing. Goodbye."

CHAPTER TWENTY-THREE

T HREE DAYS BEFORE CHRISTMAS, THE University of Connecticut formally announced its new football coach. Skip Tobin, son of legendary retired Nebraska football coach Miles Tobin, was hired to lead the Huskies. Skip Tobin previously worked at college programs in the south, most recently as offensive coordinator for Texas Christian University. Dylan had never heard of Skip Tobin and, upon hearing the news, had no way of contacting Coach DaSilva. School had already let out for the holiday break and was not reopening until the fourth of January. He placed a call to Coach Lundy and got the office answering machine. The message stated that the UConn baseball coach was on vacation until January 3, 1994 and unable to receive any messages left for him before that time.

Dylan called Alex. "Did you hear the news?"

"Skip Tobin? Really? That guy's been riding his father's coattails his entire career. He's an offensive guy having worked his way up from Valdosta State, Florida A&M, Tennessee Chattanooga, and most recently, TCU. No prior head coaching experience at the college level."

"Thanks, Mr. Football History Guy. Tell me something useful."

"Other than that, I don't know much about him. I can tell you that college football is played differently in the south. There's an emerging emphasis on offense toward speed and spreading out the field. Don't get me wrong, they still have the big horses up front and like to run the ball, but the old days of three yards and a cloud of dust are giving way to a more opened-up passing game."

"You think he's going to bring a bunch of new players in?"

"He may eventually. NCAA rules discourage transferring because, in most cases, you're required to sit out a year. But high school players who haven't signed their letters of intent can certainly change schools. It happens all the time."

"Now would be a good time to give me the bright side of things."

"I'm just being real here. My guess is he's putting his staff together, probably already has some of them in place. He'll be looking at reports on all the current players and commits and working the phones over the holidays as much as he can. UConn took over a month to make the hire and that put Tobin at a disadvantage. Which means he may be forced to honor more of the verbal commitments than he otherwise would have if he'd been on the job, say in mid-November. Plus, I doubt he has much of a network of high school coaches and scouts in the northeast. His former schools mostly recruit in the south and west."

"How do you know so much of this stuff?"

"Come on now. I don't spend *all* my time chasing girls."

That managed a laugh on Dylan's part. "Obviously not."

"How about I come over tomorrow. We can go see your grandparents and then hang out on Washington Street and look for girls."

"Sure, why not. My grandparents are always happy to see you and my grandma has started cooking for Christmas. I'll let them know."

"Great. We can watch *Seinfeld* and head out right after that."

"You're still obsessed with this *Seinfeld* show?"

"I'm telling you, give it a try. We'll watch it tomorrow, and I guarantee you'll laugh your ass off."

"Whatever. You know you're not quite right."

"Not that there's anything wrong with that."

Dylan, lacking a reply, simply hung up the phone.

Late Thursday afternoon, Alex showed up at the McDirt house. Dylan had just returned from finishing his paper route and was taking a shower, so Alex hung out in the kitchen and spoke with Cheryl.

"After we go see your parents for dinner, I thought we might hit Washington Street. Any suggestions?"

"Really, Alex? You're asking me for advice on the best place to take my son and corrupt him?"

Alex grasped his heart with both hands. "Mrs. McD, I'm truly hurt. I was just seeking advice on where to take the young lad and expand his cultural horizons."

Cheryl couldn't help but laugh. "You are truly the ultimate charmer."

"It's what I do when I'm not out helping others."

Just then Dylan walked in and observed his mother and best friend engaged in some sort of exchange he wasn't quite sure what to make of. "What's going on here?"

"Nothing, bro. I was just asking your mom if she knew of any libraries open late in Norwalk where you and I could go tonight and get in some light reading."

Dylan rolled his eyes. "Don't worry, Mom. He's in my custody tonight."

"You two are unbelievable. Have fun, but please stay out of trouble."

"Always, Mom." Dylan hugged his mother, followed by Alex, and the two boys were off.

When they arrived at the Tomassi residence, the pungent smell of broiling meat filled the small house.

Dylan went directly into the kitchen and hugged and kissed his grandmother. "Mmm. What's cooking?"

"Broiled lamb chops and mushroom risotto. Dinner should be ready in about fifteen minutes."

While Dylan was in the kitchen, Alex stepped out to the parlor to say hello to Anthony.

Anthony got up from his recliner, pulled Alex close, and lowered his voice. "While Dylan's in the other room, I want to thank you for your assistance on that other matter. I got a note from our mutual friend."

Alex smirked and then winked. "I have no idea what you're talking about. But, in an abundance of caution, you're welcome and don't mention it."

Dylan walked into the room and saw the two men whispering to each other.

"I was just offering Alex a drink. Will you grab me a beer and get you and Alex a refreshment?"

"Sure thing, Grandpa."

Dylan went back to the kitchen and returned with a Rheingold and two Hires Root Beers. He handed his grandfather the beer. "Thank you, Dylan. So what'd you two boys think about the hiring of Skip Tobin?"

Dylan turned to Alex. "Why don't you take this one."

Alex repeated the breakdown he'd given Dylan when the hiring was first announced.

"I suspect you're right, Alex, about Tobin being behind the eight ball. I suppose that may work to Dylan's advantage."

Just then Isabella called everyone to the dinner table. After dinner, the men returned to the parlor while Isabella cleaned up. A short time later she brought in a tray of Christmas cookies for dessert. At nine o'clock, Alex asked Anthony to turn on channel four. "Have you ever watched *Seinfeld*, Mr. Tomassi?"

"Of course. That's the best program on TV since *I Love Lucy*."

Dylan looked at the other two. "Am I the only one who's been living under a rock?"

"Apparently. Now be quiet."

A half hour later, the three men finally stopped laughing.

Alex looked down at his stainless-steel Rolex Submariner. "Well, I guess it's time we be going. The fairer sex is awaiting our arrival."

"You boys have fun."

"Always, Mr. Tomassi."

Dylan and Alex went in the kitchen to say goodbye to Isabella and thank her again for dinner. She was decorating more cookies and making fudge. They piled into Alex's BMW for the short ride to Washington Street. Alex found a parking spot near the Norwalk Yacht Club, which was closed for the winter. They walked the three blocks to the main drag.

The nightclub district was packed. Alex took the lead and beelined for a club called Captain K's. Captain K's was a bar and restaurant located in a two-level structure one block north of Washington on Water Street overlooking Norwalk Harbor. A steak and seafood restaurant occupied the first floor. The bar and nightclub were situated on the upper level with a nice view of the waterfront. The upstairs area served lunch during the day but had live entertainment at night. Admission was limited to ages twenty-one and over after seven o'clock. The entrance to the stairwell and elevator leading to the second floor was manned by two beefy security guards who were checking IDs.

Alex approached the two men with his usual authoritative gait. "Good evening, gentlemen."

The bigger of the two men stepped into Alex's path and folded his arms. "ID please."

Alex reached for his wallet and pulled out one of the two driver's licenses he carried. Both were identical except the one he selected listed his birthday five years earlier than the authentic version. "Of course, sir. Here you are."

The muscle-bound man looked at the license, then at Alex and handed it back to him. "Here you go."

Dylan stood behind Alex, a sheepish look on his face. Once again, Alex took control and motioned the man to step off to the side. He nodded slightly in Dylan's direction and lowered his voice. "Look, this is a little embarrassing for my friend here. We're seniors at U-Ha. He's my roommate from Maine. He had a little incident over the summer in Old Orchard Beach and got busted for a DUI, lost his license." Alex then reached into his pocket, pulled out a twenty-dollar bill, and slipped it into the man's palm before continuing. "I'll vouch for him and assure you that I'm driving tonight. Can we spare him the further indignity, please, kind sir?"

The man looked at Dylan who was clearly bigger and older looking than Alex. He pulled out his stamp pad while Alex held out his right hand. Then Dylan followed suit. The man stepped aside allowing access to the staircase. "Enjoy your evening, gentlemen."

The boys ascended the stairs and looked around. The bar and adjacent area were packed. A cover band was playing dance music from the sixties and seventies on a small stage in front of a parquet dance floor. Clearly, this was an older crowd, with a ratio of two women to every one man.

Alex turned to his friend. "Isn't this great? What'll you have to drink?"

"Whatever you're having."

Alex made his way to the bar and eased in between two bar stools, both of which were occupied by women who appeared to be in their late twenties. He looked left and then right. "Excuse me, ladies. Do you mind if I squeeze in here and order a few drinks?" He then held out a one-hundred-dollar bill between his middle and forefinger and rested his elbow on the bar.

The woman to his right was a blonde with a somewhat weathered appearance but a nice body highlighted by skintight black leather pants and a red turtleneck sweater. Her white lace bra peered through the loosely knitted material. "No problem, but it's gonna cost you."

Alex, not missing a beat, replied, "Let the negotiations begin."

"You can buy me and my friend here a drink."

Alex looked to his left. A curly haired brunette with similar attributes, wearing jeans tucked into knee-high black boots and a low-cut green V-neck sweater, smiled and turned her head, indicating back at Dylan. "Why don't you have your friend join us."

Alex motioned to Dylan. "Done and done. What's your poison, ladies?"

"We're both drinking vodka and cranberry juice."

The bartender came over, and Alex ordered two vodka and cranberries and two Michelob Lights. The drinks arrived promptly. He paid and tipped the bartender generously. Dylan moved in directly behind Alex, knowing from past experience to let him take the lead.

Everyone raised their glasses, and Alex made the introductions. "I'm Paul and this is my colleague and good friend, Steve. Here's to holiday cheers and meeting new friends."

The blonde said, "I'll drink to that."

The brunette said, "You'll drink to anything."

"Stop giving away my secrets. So, Paul and Steve. What is it you two fellas do?"

Alex answered, continuing to spin his yarn, "I own and manage a small hedge fund. My buddy Steve and I work together. How is it you two fine ladies spend your days?"

The blonde continued, "I'm Sue. We're both from the city. I'm a court reporter."

The brunette leaned in. "My name's Arlene. I'm a fashion designer."

Alex sized up the situation. "Ahhh, New Yorkers. Are you ladies football fans?"

Both women shook their heads back and forth in unison.

"Oh, too bad. My friend here played football for the Buffalo Bills. He just retired last year. Played three years before his knee gave out. We went to Boston College together, and I brought him into my business last year."

Sue and Arlene simultaneously reached for Dylan's arm and squeezed his biceps.

Dylan felt his face turning flush.

Alex jumped back in. "What're you ladies up to tonight?"

Sue focused on Alex as she replied, "We're celebrating the holidays. We got a suite at the Marriott Waterside for the night."

Arlene looked at Dylan. "What about you, big fella? You don't say much."

How could I? Alex is making this stuff up as he goes along, Dylan thought before replying, "I'm more the quiet type." He nodded in Alex's direction. "That's why we get along so well."

Alex chimed in. "That's right. He's quiet 'til he gets to know you, then watch out."

Arlene smiled. "Ooh. Then I look forward to getting to know you, Steve. I feel like dancing. Will you dance with me?"

Dylan never had a chance to answer. Arlene got up, grabbed him by the hand, and walked him to the dance floor. The band was playing Donna Summer's disco hit "Hot Stuff." Arlene and Dylan danced until the song ended and the band transitioned to Bruce Springsteen's iconic "Santa Claus is Coming to Town." Arlene indicated she wanted to dance again so Dylan obliged. When the song ended, she grabbed his hand again and led him back to the bar.

As they worked their way through the crowd, Dylan could see Alex was occupying the barstool vacated by Arlene. When he saw them coming back, he dismounted and held the stool out for her. She smiled at Alex. "Thank you. Ever the gentleman."

Alex snuggled close to Sue while Dylan stood behind Arlene. Alex whispered to Sue, "What do you say we take this party back to the Marriott? We can hit the bar there and then you don't have to worry about driving."

"We took the train here."

"Well then, *I* won't have to worry about driving."

"Oh, are you staying at the Marriott too?"

Alex stared deep into her eyes and smiled. "Maybe. We'll see how it goes. Why don't I drive us all over there?"

"Sure thing. Where are you parked?"

Alex continued with his charade. "Over at the yacht club. I'm a member there. It's only a few blocks. We can walk, or I can come pick you up."

"We can all use the fresh air. Let's go."

Dylan and Arlene heard the tail end of the conversation. They all headed toward the exit. Alex and Sue were in the lead, holding hands. Arlene slipped her arm around Dylan's as they trailed behind. When they got to the car, Alex unlocked the passenger side door and held it open. Arlene climbed in the back and Sue got in front. Dylan hopped in behind Alex.

Sue smiled approvingly at Alex. "Nice car."

"Thank you, my dear."

It was a short drive to the hotel. Alex pulled up to the covered front entrance, and a bellman came over and opened the passenger door. He got out and addressed the valet. "We don't have any bags, but could you please park the car." He handed the man a five-dollar bill.

The group walked inside, entered the fairly empty bar, and took a booth.

Sue made eye contact with Arlene. "Would you two gentlemen excuse us? We need to use the powder room."

"Sure, ladies. What would you like to drink?"

Both women spoke at the same time as they turned and headed for the restroom. "Champagne."

When they were out of earshot, Dylan spoke up. "I don't know about this, Alex."

"Which part is confusing you? These two lovely ladies wish to spend the evening with us.

"That part. These woman are probably twice our age."

"Exactly, and twice as experienced. We may learn a thing or two."

"All the same. I'm not comfortable with this."

"Well, I'm more than comfortable. I'm horny. And an older woman is just what the doctor ordered."

"You're always horny."

"What's your point?"

"We need a plan here."

"I've got just the plan. I'm going to rent us a room. You go upstairs. Call your mom and tell her we decided to go to my house and you're staying the night. I already told my folks I was spending the night in Stamford. We'll drink some champagne, and you can keep your options open. You can always go back to the room alone if that's what you decide."

Dylan considered for a moment. "Fair enough."

"I'm going to the front desk to register. I'll be right back."

While Alex was gone, the two women returned. Arlene sat next to Dylan and Sue sat opposite them.

Arlene placed her hand on Dylan's leg. "Where'd Paul go?"

"He'll be right back." Just then Alex returned and handed Dylan the room key. "Here you go."

"Will you excuse me, ladies." Dylan stood and left the bar.

Arlene looked at Alex. "Be honest with me, Paul. Is Steve married?"

Alex bent over in laughter. It took him a moment to compose himself. "Look, Steve is a lot of things. Married isn't one of them. Why do you ask?"

"He just seems like a guy with a heavy conscience or something."

"He's a totally up-front guy. Just like I said, he's shy 'til you get to know him. Truth be told, when he played in the NFL, he had a lot of groupies chasing after him. He got a little cautious, that's all. It carried over after his playing days. Just be gentle with him."

Dylan returned as the champagne arrived at their table. After the champagne was poured and the waitress departed, he looked at the group. "I just called the office and spoke with the answering service. I have to be in early tomorrow to meet with a client. I think I'm gonna head upstairs and call it a night."

Alex looked at the two women. Time for the close. "I'm not ready to call it a night. Are you ladies up to continuing the party in your room?"

"They both looked at each other, smiled, and then looked at Alex. Sue looked at him with piercing eyes. "I don't know, Paul. You think you can handle double duty?"

"Of course. My nickname is ANP."

Arlene looked confused. "A&P, like the supermarket?"

"No ANP. As in All Night Paul."

The women looked at each other approvingly. Arlene then turned to Alex. "Don't worry, Paul. If you need a break, we don't mind entertaining each other. You may even enjoy watching."

"I believe I would." He picked up the champagne bottle. "Shall we, ladies?"

The two women got up, and the three walked arm in arm in the direction of the elevators.

Dylan just sat there frozen like a deer in headlights, staring into space for several minutes before he found himself able to get up and head upstairs to his own room.

Dylan slept soundly and dreamt pleasantly through the night. In the morning he was awoken by knocking on the door. He looked at the bedside digital clock. It read 10:06 a.m. He looked through the peephole. A smiling and disheveled Alex stood outside the door. Dylan opened the door, and Alex walked in.

"And a fine good morning to you. Did you sleep well, Steve, my friend?"

"Actually I did. How was your night?"

"Great. Three consenting adults collaborated on a beautiful adventure."

"Give it a break, Alex. You turned eighteen less than a month ago."

"That's right. It's a good thing you bailed. I couldn't be a party to corrupting a minor."

"For Christ sakes, you're four months older than me."

"Exactly."

Dylan couldn't suppress a laugh. "You're incorrigible."

Alex hugged Dylan and kissed him on the cheek. "And that's why you love me. Come on. Let's check out of here. Breakfast's on me."

They stopped at Duchess, a diner style restaurant on the Old Post Road. Dylan ordered a BLT on wheat, no mayo. Alex ordered the Big D Hungry Man Platter. When the food came, Dylan looked at the mammoth plate of food in front of Alex. Two large pancakes, two sunny side eggs, bacon, sausage, home fries, and toast.

"Really, Alex? The kitchen just called. They're running out of food."

"What? I'm hungry. I worked hard last night satisfying the sexual appetites of two mature women."

"What was their story anyway?"

"They were no different than you or me, really. Well, no different than me anyway. Just a couple of single gals out on the town to blow off some steam and have a good time."

"And they bought all that bullshit you were slinging?"

"Absolutely. And I owe you a big thank you."

"Me? How'd you figure?"

"I think the part of you being a former pro football player really sealed the deal."

"I never said I was a pro football player."

"No, but I think they were impressed nonetheless. Besides, they weren't exactly being honest with me either."

"Yeah, how's that?"

"Arlene said she was a fashion designer. She works in one of those custom T-shirt shops near the Staten Island Ferry terminal, on the other side. Turns out they're both from Staten Island."

"Okay, so she stretched the truth on her job a little. Look at you. Where'd you even come up with that stuff, Paul?"

"I don't know, Steve. It just comes to me."

Dylan finished his BLT and watched with amusement as Alex struggled to finish his enormous breakfast.

When Alex took the last bite of food on his plate, he sat back and rubbed his protruding belly, then looked up proudly at Dylan. "You didn't think I could eat all that did you?"

"Congratulations. Let me know how you feel in a couple of hours."

CHAPTER TWENTY-FOUR

D YLAN RETURNED TO SCHOOL AFTER the Christmas holidays. In the morning of his first day back, he stopped by Coach DaSilva's office. He was on the phone but motioned for Dylan to come in and sit.

Coach DaSilva spoke into the receiver in a somewhat exasperated tone. "This is the second message I've left for him. Tell him again I'm calling on behalf of my player, Dylan McDirt." Coach DaSilva hung up the phone and looked up at Dylan. "That was Coach Tobin's secretary. When I heard the news before Christmas, I sent Tobin a letter and a copy of your highlight video. I also called and left a message a few days later. I haven't heard back from him. I know it was the holidays and all, but I figured the guy needed to hit the road running."

"Thanks, Coach. I really appreciate what you've done for me. I figured I'd wait a day or two and call Coach Lundy."

"The heck with waiting. Call him right now. You can use my office phone. I've got to go up to the gymnasium. Just close the door on the way out."

"Sure thing. Thanks, Coach."

Dylan looked up the number for Coach Lundy in his Day-Timer and dialed the phone. Once again, he got the answering machine. Dylan left a message stating he would call back in the afternoon. After school Dylan returned to Coach DaSilva's office and used the phone to call the UConn baseball coach again. This time he left a message asking Coach Lundy to call him at home that evening.

Dylan did not hear from Coach Lundy that night. Two evenings later as Cheryl and Dylan were finishing dinner, the phone rang.

Dylan answered, "Hello."

"Dylan. Coach Lundy. Do you have time to talk?"

"Of course, Coach. What's up?"

"I got your message on Tuesday and went to speak with Coach Tobin on your behalf. He finally got back to me today and asked me to call you. The football program has decided to pass on you, Dylan. I didn't get much in the way of an explanation except that they decided to go in another direction. New coaching staff, new philosophy, types of players that fit their schemes, that sort of thing. You'll receive a confirming letter from the football program. I do want to reiterate that if you come to UConn as a walk-on, there is a place for you on the baseball team. The University of Connecticut is an excellent school, and you'll receive a top-notch education. I'm sorry about the football scholarship, but I do want you to know you're wanted here as a baseball player."

Dylan felt like he'd been stabbed in the heart. It took him a moment to gain his composure. He swallowed hard. "Coach Lundy, thank you for calling me back. I'm obviously disappointed and have a lot to think about. I do appreciate the invite to the baseball team, but I have other options I have to consider."

"Dylan, I understand. Take the time you need and let me know your decision before signing day next month."

"Yes, Coach. Goodbye."

Dylan hung up the phone, turned, and saw Cheryl standing there staring at him. Tears welled in his eyes, and Cheryl began to cry. They embraced, and Cheryl began crying hysterically. Dylan could feel her body convulsing and knew he had to take control to comfort her.

"Mom, it's gonna be alright. Things will work out. They always do."

Cheryl broke the embrace and looked up at Dylan, tears streaming down her face. Finally she smiled. "I'm so proud of you and the way you handle yourself. You're such a fine young man. I know you're right for those very reasons."

"Let's keep this to ourselves for a few days. I should be getting a letter from the UConn football program shortly. That'll give me some time to think about the best way to move forward before I'm officially declined and everyone finds out."

"You mean we're not going to tell anyone for now? Not even Grandpa and Alex?"

"Especially Grandpa and Alex."

Alex called Dylan the next evening. "What's up, buddy? You hear anything from UConn."

"I spoke with Coach Lundy but nothing official yet."

"That's kind of strange. Makes you wonder how hard Tobin is working at his new job. Anyway, what are we doing this weekend?"

"I'm not sure. My mom wants to do a mother-son thing on Saturday, so maybe we can watch football on Sunday."

"Mother-son thing? What does she have in mind? Is there room for her adopted son?"

"I don't know, Alex. I think it's starting to hit her that I'll be leaving for college soon and she's gonna be by herself."

"Yeah, I can certainly understand that. How about I come by on Sunday, pick you up, and we go over to my house to watch football?"

"Why don't you just come over here. Then you don't have to drive back and forth twice."

"I'm always at your house. Let's mix it up. I don't mind being your personal chauffer."

"Okay fine. We'll be home from church by eleven. Pick me up at eleven thirty, and we can be back at your house and ready for the one o'clock game."

"See you then."

Dylan hung up the phone with a sense of relief. At least he'd put off Alex for a day or so. He grabbed the *Advocate* business section and checked the Apple stock price. His shares were worth about six hundred and fifty dollars. That plus the money he had saved would certainly help pay for college, but it was nowhere near enough to cover four years at the University of Connecticut. Dylan realized it was the first time he had checked on his Apple stock investment. It didn't matter anyway. He'd made a promise to Mrs. Lott that he wouldn't sell the stock and wasn't about to break that promise or even discuss the issue with her.

Dylan got home early Friday evening as Cheryl was in the kitchen preparing dinner. He hugged and kissed his mother and asked her about her day.

"I'm doing okay, Dylan. I spoke with your grandparents, and we're going over there for dinner tomorrow night. I've done some thinking, and we need to discuss how we're going to handle paying for college as a family."

"Did you tell Grandpa about my discussion with Coach Lundy?"

"Not exactly. I just told him that we haven't heard anything for sure, but that we need to start discussing a contingency plan in the event the athletic scholarship doesn't work out."

"That's great, Mom. I put off hanging out with Alex all weekend to avoid the subject coming up. I'm going over there on Sunday, but I told him you and I were doing a mother-son thing tomorrow. Turns out we are, sort of."

Cheryl and Dylan arrived at the Tomassi house early Saturday evening. Isabella was in the kitchen, as usual, putting the finishing touches on dinner.

Cheryl went into the kitchen with Isabella, and they caught up over a glass of Sangiovese.

Anthony and Dylan sat in the living room and talked. Anthony was already working on a Schaefer. Shortly, Dylan went into the kitchen, grabbed another beer for his grandfather and a 7UP for himself.

Anthony looked up at Dylan as he returned with the drinks and smiled. "I guess it'll be a few more years before you and I share a beer together."

"Whatever you say, Grandpa."

The two men talked about the Giants' wild card playoff game against the Vikings before they were called to the table for dinner. Isabella made Linguine alle Pescatore with shrimp, scallops, and calamari in a Diavolo sauce. It was served with Bruschetta Toscana, toasted garlic bread with marinated tomatoes and fresh basil. As they ate, Cheryl brought up the subject of college.

"Dylan and I have been discussing a contingency plan to pay for college in the event the football scholarship doesn't come through."

Anthony chimed in. "That's a sensible idea since we haven't heard from Coach Tobin. He's been on the job for the better part of two weeks and National Signing Day is less than a month away."

Cheryl continued. "We figure the total cost of attending UConn is about seventy-five hundred dollars next year. Unfortunately, most of my paychecks go to covering the mortgage, food, and household expenses. I have some savings in the Teacher's Credit Union, but it's not much."

Dylan spoke up. "I've saved enough to pay for at least the first two years."

Cheryl was aware of this, but his grandparents were surprised. Anthony looked at Dylan with approbation. "I'm proud of you, Dylan. You've worked hard building your paper route all these years, and you've got something to show for it."

"Thanks, Grandpa. You know, I can also look at less expensive options like West Conn or even Norwalk Community College. I could live here, go to NCC, and get a job."

Finally, Isabella weighed in. "Don't get me wrong Dylan, we'd love to have you live with us. It would make your grandfather and me so happy. You could even take the bus to class. But this isn't about us. Living at home or here and going to NCC wouldn't be a true college experience."

Cheryl looked at Dylan. "We can apply for scholarships or financial aid. You would probably qualify for some assistance. Either way, you could start UConn in the fall, pay for the first year out of savings, and go from there. You could work summers and maybe even get a part-time job during school once you get acclimated to college life and the academic workload."

The four of them finished dinner and continued the discussion over espresso and chocolate tiramisu, but no further meaningful options emerged. Afterwards, Isabella and Cheryl cleaned up the kitchen before joining Anthony and Dylan in the parlor. They talked for another two hours before Cheryl and Dylan left.

CHAPTER TWENTY-FIVE

THE NEXT MORNING, ALEX WAS parked on the street outside the McDirt residence when Cheryl and Dylan returned home from church. Dylan got out of Cheryl's VW Bug and approached the BMW driver's window. "You're here early."

"Is that anyway to talk to your taxi driver?"

Dylan laughed. "Come on in. I've got to change and then I'll be ready to go."

Alex waited and spoke with Cheryl in the kitchen. "So what was the big mother-son event that kept me away yesterday, Ms. McD?"

Cheryl looked at Alex. "Are you jealous?"

"Of course. I'm just not sure of who."

Cheryl dismissed Alex's flirtatious comment. "Alex, do you ever turn off the charm?"

"I don't think my off button has worked in years."

"Well, you better see about getting that fixed. It could get you into trouble someday."

"Whoa, now who's being flirtatious?"

Cheryl blushed. "That's not what I meant, and you know it."

Just then Dylan walked into the room and stared at his mother and friend. "Why do I always get a weird feeling when I walk into a room where you two have been talking?"

"I don't know, buddy. Maybe you should see a doctor about that. Let's get going, we don't wanna miss the beginning of the game."

Alex gave Cheryl a hug. Dylan hugged and kissed his mother, and the boys left.

As they were driving, Alex asked, "What are you gonna do about paying for college if your football scholarship doesn't come through?"

Dylan stared at his friend with a look of consternation. "Why are you bringing that up now?"

"I've been doing some thinking. You were obviously high on the former coaching staff's list. The new coaching staff must have a file on you from the previous regime. Yet you haven't heard a thing from Tobin or his staff. I think it's unusual that they haven't reached out to you by now."

"Okay, it's probably not a bad idea to look at other options at this point. Do you have any suggestions?"

"Of course. I'm not just your average cab driver. My dad's home. I've mentioned your situation to him, and he wants to talk with you."

Dylan thought about that. He wasn't particularly close with Jackson Malloy, but, then again, Alex and his dad had a somewhat distant relationship. However, it was axiomatic that Mr. Malloy was a smart and successful businessman and an expert in finance. He had nothing to lose by listening to him.

When they arrived at the Malloy residence, Lillian Malloy was in the living room. Dylan looked at the Columbia walnut grandfather clock before greeting her. "Good morning, Mrs. Malloy."

She glanced at her Cartier Tank wristwatch and smiled affectionately. "Good morning, Dylan. At least for another few minutes."

Alex interjected. "Hey, Mom, where's Dad?"

"He should be in his study."

Alex led Dylan to the study where the door was ajar and knocked.

Seated at his large desk, Jackson Malloy looked up and removed his reading glasses. "Boys, please come in."

Dylan followed Alex into the large room and looked around. The walls were oak paneled, and the ceiling was finished in matching coffered wood. There were built-in bookshelves on one side. The rear wall had two floor-to-ceiling windows on either side of a matching credenza, which provided views of the swimming pool and expansive grounds. There were two cognac leather chairs in front of the desk. The boys were seated.

After appropriate greetings and small talk, Alex dove in. "I told my dad about your situation and the need to come up with an alternate college financing plan."

Jackson Malloy took over. "Dylan, have you thought about how you'll pay for college in the absence of an athletic scholarship?"

"To be honest, I really just started to. I never thought about it until the coaching staff was fired."

"Alex told me you're a saver, and that's a good thing. He also told me you own some stock. Tell me about that?"

Dylan fired off a baleful look in Alex's direction, regretting having told him about the stock and his promise to Esther Lott.

"Yes, sir. I own some Apple stock. But I have no plans to sell it."

"How much stock do you own?"

"A little over two thousand shares."

"Do you know what it's worth?"

"Yes, sir, I checked the price the other day. Probably around six hundred and fifty dollars."

"Well, that's hardly enough to pay for college, but I do have an offer for you. My firm regularly researches stocks, and we're very bullish on Apple. We believe the company's research and development department is working on some exciting and innovative ideas. We also have great confidence in the management team, particularly its CEO, Steve Jobs. I understand you're not in a position to sell the stock. Quite frankly, I wouldn't advise you to do so anyway under the circumstances. How much do you figure it would cost to attend UConn for four years?"

Dylan considered for a moment. "All together for four years, probably thirty to forty thousand dollars."

"My firm handles all types of financial transactions. I've looked into your situation, and I'm prepared to give you forty thousand dollars in exchange for the stock."

Dylan sat there incredulously. It took him a moment to gather himself. "Mr. Malloy, thank you very much for your generous offer. The situation with the stock is complicated. I have some questions."

"I'd be surprised if you didn't."

"First, how can you give me forty thousand dollars for something that's currently worth less than a thousand? And second, there is, how shall I put it, an encumbrance on the stock."

"Tell me about this encumbrance first."

Dylan succinctly explained the situation with Esther Lott and the promise he'd made to not sell the stock.

Jackson Malloy seemed to anticipate the issue. "I understand the promise you made. Please understand that, technically speaking, you would not be selling it. Think of it as a more sophisticated version of a loan, similar to a pawn shop transaction. The stock would remain in your name with an assignment to my firm. The firm would have the right to future ownership of the stock in the event of non-repayment. That would be the case regardless of the stock's performance. You would own the stock until you finished college. At that time, we would take possession of the stock in exchange for complete forgiveness of the loan."

Again there was a somewhat prolonged silence before Dylan spoke. He looked over at Alex who sat there reticently. He dismissed Alex's unusual deference as a dynamic of the father-son relationship. "Why would the firm do this?"

"As I mentioned, we handle all types of sophisticated financial transactions for our clientele. In the interest of complete disclosure, I wouldn't offer this specific deal except for your personal situation and your relationship with my son. Notwithstanding, as I mentioned, we're bullish on this young company and can afford to wait and hold onto the stock long term."

Dylan decided he needed to bring the discussion to a conclusion. "Mr. Malloy, I really appreciate your generous offer. I have a lot to think about. Can I get back to you?"

"Absolutely, Dylan. Take all the time you need. As I mentioned, this is a unique situation and, in your case, we're not bound by any time constraints."

Dylan stood to leave, and Alex followed his lead. "Thanks again, sir. I think it's about time for the Giants game to start."

"Sure thing. You boys enjoy yourselves. Alex, your mother and I are headed to the club for lunch."

Dylan and Alex went to the theater room to watch the game. The Giants won, which temporarily improved Dylan's mood.

CHAPTER TWENTY-SIX

T HE FOLLOWING WEEK, DYLAN RECEIVED the anticipated letter from the University of Connecticut Athletic Department. He opened the letter.

Dear Mr. McDirt:

Thank you for your interest in our football program. This shall confirm that we are unable to offer you an athletic scholarship. We wish you the best in your future endeavors.

Sincerely,

Butch Gillespie

UConn Assistant Head Football Coach and Director of Recruiting

Dylan was surprisingly calm and unemotional after he read the letter. The next day he finished his paper route and parked his bicycle next to the front porch of Esther Lott's home. He knocked on the door and the ubiquitous Franklin answered. Dylan wondered if the man ever took a day off.

"Hello, Franklin. Here's today's paper. Is Mrs. Lott available to speak with me?"

"Good afternoon, Mr. Dylan. I'll check for you."

Franklin took the newspaper and retreated into the large house, closing the door behind him.

Dylan waited for a few minutes until Franklin returned.

"This way, Mr. Dylan. Mrs. Lott is in the sitting room."

Dylan went in and sat across from her. As usual she was meticulously dressed and well-coiffed. "Thank you for seeing me today, Mrs. Lott."

"Come now, Dylan. We're old friends. You always brighten my day when you visit."

"You're very kind. I have a problem, and I need your advice."

Mrs. Lott sat back on the couch and adjusted her impeccable sitting posture. "Please tell me what's on your mind."

"I heard back from the University of Connecticut. The new football coach is not going to honor my scholarship."

"I'm so sorry, Dylan. Have you thought about your options for school without the scholarship?"

"Well, I've been admitted to UConn, which I can't afford. I could apply to Western Connecticut in Danbury where my mom went. I'm sure I could get in, and it's less expensive. Or I can live with my grandparents and go to Norwalk Community College. That would be the least expensive alternative."

"How much money do you have in savings?"

"I have about eighteen thousand dollars in my savings account, and I figure I'll be able to save another two to three thousand before I start school in the fall."

Mrs. Lott paused while she did some math in her head. "My, you are quite the saver, Dylan."

"Yes, ma'am. I don't drive. A car is a big expense for a teenager, so I'm able to save about two-thirds of what I earn."

"That's very admirable. Do you know what it costs to attend UConn each year?"

"Yes. Tuition, fees, books, and room and board alone are about seventy-five hundred next year. And that'll probably go up before I graduate."

"What about the other schools you mentioned?"

"I haven't looked into the specifics yet, but obviously less."

"Let's put the financial aspect aside for a moment. Where would you like to attend college?"

"I've always wanted to go to UConn. It has a good reputation, and they have a great business school."

"Any other reasons you want to attend UConn?"

"I feel I would get a more well-rounded college experience there. Better than West Conn and definitely better than Norwalk Community College."

"And how important is the college experience to you?"

"I haven't really thought about it much since playing football was taken out of the equation."

"Let's talk about that for a moment. Is playing baseball still an option?"

"The baseball coach has offered me a position on the team, so yes, it's an option."

"Is it an option you are considering?"

"I haven't thought about it since my scholarship offer disappeared."

"So originally, UConn was going to provide you with a scholarship where you would have all expenses paid in exchange for playing football and baseball. Do I have that right?"

"Yes."

"And now the offer has changed whereby you can play baseball but not football and you must pay every cent of your college expenses out of your own pocket?"

"Right."

"What about other college experiences. Do you plan on joining a fraternity?"

Dylan thought for a brief moment. "No, I don't think so. I don't know everything about Greek life, but it doesn't sound like it's for me. I'm a little unique when it comes to socialization."

Mrs. Lott couldn't help herself and failed to suppress a smile. "You don't say."

Dylan looked at her defensively. "What? So I'm a little unconventional in that regard."

She continued. "Let's make a few assumptions. UConn is your choice of college, and a good one in your case, I might add. You're not going to participate in intercollegiate athletics, and you're not interested in joining a fraternity. That brings me to the logical conclusion that getting a good education at the best possible value is your major priority. Is that fair?"

Dylan followed along and pondered for a moment. "For purposes of this discussion, that's fair."

"Assuming further, you attend UConn for four years, you're looking at a total of thirty-five to forty thousand dollars, allowing for additional related expenses and increased costs."

"Okay."

"Now understand that young people go to college for any number of reasons. A student athlete's priorities are different from a frat boy and both of their priorities differ from a pre-med student."

"I'm following you."

"So if you decide that your major priority is getting a finance or economics degree from a fine public institution like the University of Connecticut at the least possible expense, then you should formulate a plan to meet that objective."

"Assuming that is my objective, do you have any suggestions on a plan?"

Mrs. Lott smiled and leaned forward. Dylan reflexively leaned in. "Here's what I would do. The first thing is to prepare a budget. You'll have about twenty thousand dollars in savings. I recommend spending half of that on school. You don't want to spend it all because a young man needs some money to start his life after graduation. Normally, I wouldn't recommend borrowing money. But in this case, you're investing in yourself, which I must say is a blue-chip investment." She paused to let all that sink in before continuing. "Student loans are available with deferred payments, meaning you don't have to begin paying them back until after graduation. I would advise you to borrow a maximum of twenty-five hundred dollars per year. Those will be your two main sources of funds. Now how can you reduce expenses? Two ways. Finish school early and find other ways to cover costs without paying out of pocket."

Dylan looked at her quizzically. "How can I do that?"

Living in a dormitory is less glamorous than sharing an apartment off campus, but it's also less expensive. Your costs are fixed, and you don't have to pay rent while you're away for the summer. Have you heard of RAs?"

"No what's that?"

"An RA is a resident assistant. Each dormitory has students who work as RAs, live in the dorm, and sort of manage and advise students and keep an eye on things. Typically, they get free room and board and sometimes even a small stipend. You won't be eligible your freshman year, but if you look into it during your first semester, you'll have a foot up on other applicants for the following year."

"That sounds like a good deal. What else?"

"Say you come home during the summers. You can work and earn money while you live at home for free. You can also take classes at UConn's satellite campus in Stamford. If you take three classes each summer between your first and second years and take an extra class each semester in Storrs, you could graduate in three years. You wouldn't have as much of a social life but college is all about time management. And you've already perfected that during high school. You'd further reduce your expenses twenty-five percent by finishing in three years. By my calculation, the ten-thousand-dollar contribution from your savings and the seventy-five hundred in student loans should cover the total cost of your degree."

Dylan stared at her in amazement. "How do you know so much?"

"I've been around a long time. And I'm gonna be right here waiting when you come by and show me that UConn sheepskin."

"I really appreciate all your advice. Every time I come over here, I always leave feeling better than when I arrived. And that's not just when I'm dumping my problems on you."

"Dylan, the feeling is mutual."

As Dylan stood, he observed Mrs. Lott rising from the couch as well. He hugged her gently and held on for a moment. "Thank you again for your friendship."

As he turned to leave, he saw tears welling up in the old woman's eyes.

CHAPTER TWENTY-SEVEN

Dylan's last semester of high school flew by. In the final game of the baseball season, a win over Wilton at home on senior day, he stood in right field after the last out was recorded and basked in the moment. His high school athletic career had come to an end and the significance was not lost on him. Sports had been a big part of his life dating as far back as he could remember.

During the summer, Dylan completed the transition of his paper route to Ricky Peck, now twelve-years-old. On Dylan's last day, the boys' final stop was at 216 Travis Avenue. Dylan knocked on the door, and Franklin directed the two boys to the greenhouse where Esther Lott was busy with her rose bushes. Dylan introduced Ricky, and the encounter was brief.

Esther Lott was uncharacteristically aloof. After pleasantries were exchanged, she instructed Ricky to leave the paper in the cedar box on the side of the porch each day. Payment would be left in the box each Friday. And with that she wished the boys good day and turned back to her flowers.

Dylan spent the balance of the summer working with his grandfather doing masonry work. On weekends, he continued to work with Cheryl at the Rockrimmon. Anthony was a perfectionist, so Dylan's duties were limited to hauling blocks, mixing mortar, and other gopher-related tasks. Anthony was hard on Dylan but also overpaid him for his work.

In mid-August, Cheryl and Dylan, along with his grandparents, piled into Anthony's loaded-down Plymouth Satellite and drove to Storrs. They helped Dylan move his belongings into the dorm, then shared a final dinner and departed with a tearful goodbye.

Dylan executed his college plan fastidiously as he had discussed with Esther Lott. Midway through his first semester, he was hired as a resident assistant, a position he held for his final two years. He returned home during the summers, took classes at UConn Stamford, and worked with both Anthony and Cheryl.

After his first semester, Dylan got a job at a Friendly's restaurant. He held the job for two years. In his final semester, he landed a prestigious internship at Liberty Bank working in the investment department. It was a paid position and afforded him nine academic credits.

Alex attended Yale University in New Haven, about sixty-five miles south of the University of Connecticut. The boys spoke regularly, although they rarely saw each other during the school year. However, the two friends remained inseparable during summers and holidays. Each time they got together it was as if they'd just seen each other the day before.

During Christmas time of Dylan's third and final year at UConn, Alex suggested they take a trip to Florida during spring break. Dylan agreed, and the two friends flew to Fort Lauderdale where they spent days on the beach and nights on the city's famous strip. Dylan had never flown in an airplane or traveled beyond the boundaries of New England and the tristate area. Upon his return home, he found himself enamored with the Florida lifestyle.

Dylan visited Esther Lott each time he returned home to Stamford. She listened assiduously as he related his college experiences and offered advice when solicited. Dylan confided in her about his Florida experience and his consideration of a move to the Sunshine State following graduation. She encouraged the idea and noted that Florida was a growing state with a booming industry in finance and investment.

As planned, Dylan graduated from the University of Connecticut in three years with a degree in finance. He received his degree with honors in a ceremony held in the recently renovated Gampel Pavilion. Cheryl, Alex, Anthony, and Isabella were in attendance. The group, led by Alex, stood and cheered vociferously as Dylan's name was called and he walked across the stage to receive his diploma.

That night the group celebrated with a dinner at Chuck's Steakhouse. The following day Alex and Dylan drove back to Stamford in Alex's new 1997 Toyota Supra Turbo. Dylan spent the following week reviewing his finances and researching cities in Florida. Palm Beach and Miami were clearly the financial hubs with the greatest concentrations of wealth, but banking and investment were major industries throughout the state.

Dylan had completed his education under budget and prepared his financial statement. His assets consisted of his Apple stock, which had soared in value to thirty thousand dollars and $14,420 in cash. Dylan had seventy-five hundred dollars in liabilities in the form of his student loans for a net worth of $36,920. He could certainly afford a move to Florida and time to get settled and look for a job. He made his decision and would talk with Esther Lott before announcing his plans to his family.

CHAPTER TWENTY-EIGHT

DYLAN GRABBED HIS BICYCLE AND rode in the direction of Travis Avenue. Along the way he thought about the old Peugeot ten-speed he'd ridden for over fifteen years. It had been his mode of transportation since elementary school, served him well throughout the duration of his ten-year newspaper delivery career, and was a reliable companion during his time at UConn. Dylan had turned twenty-one in the spring and made a mental note to add obtaining a driver's license to his to-do-list.

Dylan arrived at Esther Lott's house, and Franklin answered the door. He observed that the man never seemed to change. For that matter, neither did Esther Lott. Neither of the two appeared to age. It was as if time stood still at the large house.

"Good afternoon, Franklin. Is she available?"

"Good afternoon, Mr. Dylan. Unfortunately, no. However, I do have a message for you. Mrs. Lott would like you to come back tomorrow at four o'clock." As usual Franklin's formal manner revealed nothing.

Dylan knew better than to ask questions of the factotum. "Okay, Franklin. Please let her know I'll be here."

"Yes, sir. Mrs. Lott requests that you bring your college diploma and Apple stock certificates to the meeting." Franklin closed the door.

Dylan stood there for a moment in a state of bemusement. Finally, he recalled their discussions about her desire to see his sheepskin, as she'd referred to it. He wasn't sure about the stock but gathered that he'd find out soon enough.

The next day Dylan was having lunch alone in the kitchen. Cheryl still had another week of classes at St. Mary's before school let out for the summer. Suddenly he was overcome with feelings of aberrancy. He reflected that for the first time as far back as he could remember, his days were relaxed and void of a demanding schedule.

At the appointed time, Dylan carefully placed his diploma and stock certificates in his backpack and pedaled over to Mrs. Lott's house. Franklin answered the door in an uncharacteristically affable manner. Dylan observed a small smile in the man's countenance.

"Ah, Mr. Dylan, welcome. Please come in. Mrs. Lott is in the sitting room."

Dylan entered the room, and Esther Lott atypically rose from the couch and extended her frail arms. She was impeccably dressed, as usual, in a canary yellow pants suit and white silk blouse. Appropriate colors for a hot June afternoon, Dylan surmised. He walked over and hugged her. She held on tightly for an extra moment before breaking the embrace.

"Please, Dylan, sit down. We have much to discuss."

They were interrupted momentarily while Franklin served coffee and fresh-baked molasses cookies. He carried the items on a silver platter and carefully placed it on the table between them. After pouring two cups of coffee, Franklin handed her a large brown envelope.

"Now, Dylan, please show me that diploma I've been so eagerly waiting to see."

Dylan produced an envelope from his backpack, carefully removed the certificate from between its two pieces of protective cardboard, and delicately handed it over.

Esther Lott held it in her hands at arms' length, seeming to relish the moment. "Well, Dylan, let me first say how proud I am of you. You graduated in three years and with honors."

"Thank you, Mrs. Lott. I owe you a deep debt of gratitude. I sought your advice after my athletic scholarship fell through, and, as usual, your counsel proved extremely valuable."

"Will you do me a favor, Dylan?"

"Sure, I'd anything for you. Just name it."

"You're a newly minted college graduate and an adult now. It would bring me great pleasure if you would henceforth refer to me as Esther."

Dylan smiled. "Sure, Mrs—I mean, Esther. Sorry, we've known each other since I was eight-years-old, so it may take some getting used to."

"I understand. Have you made a decision yet as to where you're going to begin your career?"

"I have. I want to work in the investment world. I learned so much from you, and college reinforced my passion for finance and investment. I've also decided to move to Florida."

"What about your family?"

"I'll return home when I can, holidays and summers, for sure. My grandparents are approaching retirement age, and my grandfather has worked out in the cold winters all these years. My mom is still young and loves teaching. Privately, I'm hoping that when my grandparents visit, they'll fall in love with Florida the way I did. And, as soon as I am financially able, I'm going to move my mother down. She deserves it. She's a great mother."

"That's very admirable of you, Dylan. When do you plan on leaving?"

"I'm getting things in order. I've decided it's time to retire my bicycle. I'm going to get my driver's license before I move. By then I'll make my final decision on where in Florida I'm going to settle. I'll spend some time exploring the area, and if it's not to my liking, I'll check out other cities. It's a large and diverse state."

"Did you bring the Apple stock certificates?"

"Yes, ma'am, I mean Esther." Dylan pulled another envelope from his backpack and produced the certificates.

She glanced at them before addressing Dylan again. "Do you know how much this stock has appreciated since you've owned it?"

"As a matter of fact, yes. I recently prepared a personal financial statement."

"Then you're aware that approximately eighteen months ago, the stock split. You now own over four thousand shares. The stock is currently trading at about fifteen dollars. Your initial five-hundred-sixty-dollar investment has grown to approximately sixty thousand dollars."

Dylan was astonished. "Wow. But don't worry, I'll keep my promise to hold onto it. I have separate savings to fund my move to Florida."

Esther Lott beamed admiringly at her young protégé. "Indeed, Dylan, you have kept your word. And through some trying times, I might add. You've been a good steward with the investment. You're now free to do with the stock what you will. My final request is that you remain the same man of fine character and decency regardless of your wealth and success in life."

Dylan looked at her and nodded affirmatively.

"Now, I have a graduation gift for you." Esther leaned forward and handed Dylan the envelope. "Please open it."

Dylan examined the rich leather envelope secured by a button and string closure. He carefully unbound the string, opened the envelope, and removed a stack of green and manila stock certificates. He looked at the headings. Each one read Berkshire Hathaway. Dylan's jaw dropped, and he remained mute.

Esther Lott stared at him with a tight-lipped smile and patiently waited for Dylan to speak.

"I don't know what to say. You and I have talked about Warren Buffet frequently when discussing investment strategy."

"Yes, we have. I purchased this stock in 1965, shortly after Warren took over the company. I met him in Omaha a few years later at a shareholders meeting. I believed in his vision and continued to invest in Berkshire Hathaway through the 1980s. I've primarily maintained a buy-and-hold strategy on the stock, although I have liquidated a percentage of my holdings in recent years."

Dylan meticulously thumbed through the certificates again, looked upward for a moment, and then stared back at Esther.

She read his mind. "There's five hundred shares."

"Again, I'm not sure what to say. Obviously, thank you, but clearly that's insufficient."

"Dylan, you're most certainly welcome. You are a dear friend, and it brings me tremendous joy to bestow this gift upon you. I trust you are going to do great things in life, and this will simply jump start your journey."

Dylan stood and walked over to the couch. Esther stood, and the two friends embraced. Both briefly broke down in tears before maintaining their respective composures. They sat and talked about the future for another two hours before Dylan rode home as the sun began to set on the horizon.

CHAPTER TWENTY-NINE

DYLAN SLEPT SOUNDLY THAT NIGHT. The next day he called the Connecticut Department of Motor Vehicles in Stamford and made an appointment to take the driver's exam. He also updated his financial statement and typed it out on an old Corona typewriter. When he finished, he stared at the page in disbelief.

JUNE 1997 FINANCIAL STATEMENT

<u>ASSETS</u>

Cash	$14,420
Securities	
Apple stock	$60,000
Berkshire Hathaway stock	$1,690,000
TOTAL ASSETS	$1,764,420

<u>LIABILITIES</u>

Student loan balance	$7,500
TOTAL LIABILITIES	$7,500

<u>NET WORTH</u> $1,756,920

Dylan called his grandparents and invited them to dinner. He told Anthony that he wanted to treat them and his mom that evening and to meet at six o'clock. Next, he called Alex and told him he was leaving for Florida in a month. Alex agreed to drive down with him. When Alex asked what car they'd be taking, Dylan told him he would handle everything. Finally, he asked Alex if he would accompany him to Malloy Williamson to open an investment account. When Alex peppered him with questions, Dylan advised that all would be revealed the following day on the ride over.

Cheryl arrived home from school, and Dylan told her about the dinner plans. He also explained that he had an announcement to make that evening when they were all together. Cheryl inquired further, but all Dylan would say was that it involved his future career plans.

They dined at John's Best Pizza in Norwalk. After dinner, Dylan asked for everyone's attention. His mother and grandparents looked at him curiously.

"I have some things to tell you. I've made the decision to move to Tampa, Florida. I'll be leaving next month."

Cheryl led the instant deluge of questions. "How will you get your belongings to Florida? How will you get around after you arrive? You don't even drive."

Next it was Anthony. "What will you do for work? Do you have a job lined up?"

And finally, Isabella. "You'll have to learn to cook. Will you come by so I can teach you the basics?"

Dylan raised his hand indicating a request for silence. After everyone calmed down, he began again. "Thank you all for your concerns. Alex and I will be driving to Florida. I've made an appointment to take the driver's test, and I'm going to buy a car."

Again the questions started. "How can you afford a car without a job?" "When will we see you again?" "What if you don't like it down there?" "I heard there's nothing in Florida except old people and mosquitos."

Dylan waited patiently for the hysteria to subside. "Maybe it would be best if we treat this like a press conference. I'm going to take some time and explore the area, including the job market. And yes, Grandma, I would be delighted if you gave me some cooking lessons."

Anthony chimed in again. "How are you going to finance this move and this lifestyle you speak of?"

Dylan looked over at his mother. "I've made some good investments and recently received, shall we say, an extraordinary graduation gift."

Dylan described his meeting with Esther Lott the previous day and filled in some details about their relationship. Cheryl was familiar with the old woman as Dylan had mentioned her from time to time. Dylan's grandparents only knew of her in passing.

"Most importantly, I want all three of you to know that I love you very much and I appreciate everything you've done for me. Change is on the horizon, and things will never be the same again. But please understand these changes are for the best and will be good for all of us. You have my word on that."

CHAPTER THIRTY

ANTHONY DYLAN TOMASSI AWOKE EARLY as he did each morning. He put on his swim trunks and went outside to swim laps in his pool. The long infinity pool overlooked Boca Ciega Bay. He had officially changed his name right after graduating from college over twenty years ago but still went by Dylan. Cheryl had gone with him to the Fairfield County courthouse in Norwalk and changed her name at the same time. She was now known as Cheryl Tomassi.

Cheryl was in her sixties, having recently retired from teaching second grade at St. Gregory Catholic School in St. Petersburg. She lived in a condominium on Isla Del Sol and was an avid golfer, sporting an eleven handicap. The condo had been a fiftieth birthday gift from Dylan. She'd lived there for more than ten years. Cheryl's parents had retired to Florida a few years earlier and she'd been lonely in Connecticut.

Dylan was a member of St. Gregory's church and sat on the parish finance committee. When Cheryl moved to Florida, he'd put in a good word and she had the teaching job at the school waiting when she arrived. It wasn't a tough sell. Cheryl was a board-certified Catholic school teacher and had come from a prestigious Catholic Blue Ribbon School in Connecticut.

Cheryl was dating a retired US Coast Guard Rear Admiral. She'd met Rick Landry at the driving range on the Isla Del Sol golf course. Rick had spent the bulk of his career working out of the Coast Guard Academy in New Haven and the two Connecticut Yankees hit it off immediately. He was a widower, standing just under six feet tall with a lean build and ram rod straight posture. Rick adored Cheryl, who had aged well and remained a striking beauty. The two made a handsome couple, and Dylan privately approved of the relationship.

Dylan finished his workout and sat in a lounge chair overlooking the expansive waterway with a view of Treasure Island on the horizon. When Dylan left Connecticut, he had originally moved to Tampa and rented an apartment on

Harbor Island. He took a job as a junior stockbroker with a national brokerage firm headquartered in the Tampa Bay area. The job required building a client list through cold calling and rainmaking. Dylan had proven to be a highly successful salesperson and investment advisor and quickly built a book of business managing a hundred million dollars in client assets within two years.

However, Dylan experienced difficulty with towing the company line. He had started his own business, Lott Investment Advisors and invested his personal assets using the strategies he'd learned from Esther Lott. She was now in her late eighties but still sharp as a whip. She and Dylan still spoke by phone at least once a week.

Dylan had also established DAT Real Estate Holdings, LLC as an umbrella company for his real estate investments. His financial strategy involved a two-prong approach. First, he accumulated assets that provided an income stream. Second, he invested in a portfolio of stocks, bonds, and other securities. The income stream was derived from his real estate ventures. Originally, Dylan had purchased single and multi-family properties but quickly learned that being a landlord proved to be a full-time job. He divested himself of the residential properties and focused on commercial real estate. He currently owned warehouses, light industrial buildings, and mobile home parks. He also financed the construction of convenience stores, beach resort hotels, and boutique waterfront condominium and townhouse projects along Florida's west coast.

During the three years Dylan worked for the brokerage house, he often shared his personal investment ideas with clients. Some prospects were skeptical of the confident young man and questioned his credentials and experience. Once Dylan vetted and qualified a potential client, his closing presentation involved sharing his own personal balance sheet and tax returns. He rarely failed to sign a prospect.

Dylan's clients had adored him and prospered from his advice. Unfortunately, he routinely missed his quotas moving stocks favored by the company's analysts. He also failed to sell his designated share of highly speculative investments. He personally avoided those types of products and was uncomfortable recommending them to clients. These included derivatives, commodities futures, and variable annuities.

After three years, Dylan and the brokerage had parted ways and Dylan went to work full time, managing his personal investments. Lott Investment Advisors had just under two hundred million dollars in assets under management. Based upon its size, Lott Investment Advisors flew under the business community's radar, and Dylan was the company's only client.

Dylan rose from the lounge chair and headed back to the house. He had purchased the seventy-five hundred square foot, five bedroom, eight bath home in 2009 following the collapse of the financial markets and corresponding real estate downturn. The house was built by a high-flying developer who had spared no expense but filed bankruptcy shortly after completing construction. The gated, contemporary, waterfront home was situated on four acres and located on the prestigious brick road section of Park Street in St. Petersburg. Dylan paid less than half of what it cost to build the home.

The grounds were meticulously landscaped with a sweeping paver driveway entry. A two-story grand portico covered a stairwell, which led to the oversized double front door entry that opened into the second-floor living space. The lower level consisted of a six-car garage, fitness center, and covered outdoor living area with a bar and state-of-the-art kitchen. A gourmet chef's kitchen with custom cabinetry, double islands with Calcutta marble countertops, and high-end designer appliances occupied the second level. There was also formal living and dining rooms, an entertainment room, a five hundred bottle climate-controlled wine room, and two offices. The walls and ceilings were finished in custom mill work and the floors in white oak and travertine. The top floor contained the five bedrooms, including the master suite, all with dramatic water views. The master included his and her bathrooms, custom closets, and a wraparound covered balcony. The house also featured its own elevator, generator, and state-of-the-art security system with infrared cameras that covered the entire property. A large dock with electric lifts held a boat and two Kawasaki jet skis. The thirty-six-foot Yellowfin Center Console was powered by dual Mercury 450 outboard motors. Additionally, the property included a pool cabana with guest house and a separate detached four car garage with an upstairs apartment.

Dylan returned to the house, showered, and went down to the kitchen. He mixed strawberries, a banana, and vanilla yogurt with protein powder into the Vitamix blender and poured the concoction into a large Tervis tumbler before heading to his office. Shirley Taylor, his personal assistant, was in her adjacent office paying bills and going over his calendar. She handed Dylan copies of the *Wall Street Journal* and *Tampa Bay Daily Herald*, the newspaper that covered the greater Tampa Bay area. Dylan also read *Investor's Business Daily*, but the publication was now only available online.

"Good morning, Dylan. Remember tomorrow night you have the party at Evan Withrow's. The invitation said formal. I had your dark navy suit dry cleaned. I'll pick it up this afternoon."

Dylan chuckled. Shirley knew him well enough to anticipate he was not going to wear a tuxedo to the event. Shirley was divorced and in her midforties. She had one son, Ronnie, who was studying engineering at the University of South Florida. Dylan first met Shirley when they worked together at the brokerage in Tampa. She lived in St. Petersburg and had commuted to downtown Tampa each day via Interstate 275 and the Howard Frankland Bridge.

Shirley was short with blonde hair, large breasts, and shapely legs. She had initially reminded Dylan of an aging party girl, but he quickly dispelled the thought when he learned that she possessed two highly valued qualities: a strong work ethic and undying loyalty.

When Dylan left the brokerage, he'd offered Shirley a job. The pay raise, better hours, and short commute appealed to her. She also admired Dylan and enjoyed working with him. Her current job duties involved organizing his business and personal lives and overseeing the running of the household.

Dylan's other employee was Aengus Lobo. Aengus was from Cape Verde and had served in the Cape Verde Armed Forces. He had worked as a military police officer for the National Guard. During his military service, Aengus was also trained as a medic. Aengus had worked as the property caretaker when Dylan purchased the house shortly before it went into foreclosure. While Dylan was doing his due diligence, he'd gained an appreciation for its pristine condition and learned that Aengus was responsible. He'd offered him the opportunity to stay on, and Aengus had accepted. He lived in the apartment above the detached garage and was responsible for the grounds, pool, and buildings on the property. Aengus was incredibly talented and could build or repair just about anything. He maintained a small shop in the garage below and also served as Dylan's driver on occasion.

Dylan left Shirley and went into his own office next door. The spacious oak-paneled room and coffered ceiling had custom built-in bookcases and cabinetry and a large window overlooking the waterfront. It was furnished with a large plain desk at one end and comfortable reading chairs and a small couch separated by an antique coffee table at the other. He fired up the two computers on his desk and began reading the newspapers.

A short time later, Shirley stuck her head in the doorway to tell Dylan that Alex was on the phone. Alex had spent seven years at Yale University, the first four as an undergraduate where he had finally settled on a major in history. From there, he'd attended Yale Law. After graduation, he'd gone to work for the prestigious firm of Baker, Callahan & White in New York City. Alex had been there for fifteen years, a partner for the past ten, and managed the financial services department.

Dylan and Alex spoke on the phone almost daily and visited each other at least four times a year. Sometimes they met in a neutral location, usually in a city where Alex had business as Dylan's schedule was more flexible. Alex had maintained his inextinguishable passion for women. He shocked Dylan two years ago when he called to say he was getting married and asked Dylan to be his best man.

Alex had met Anita Van Widenfelt in the Hamptons three summers ago while spending time at his parents' beach house. She was from Putnam, Connecticut and graduated from Bowdoin College where she was a member of the soccer team. Anita was tall with blonde hair and piercing blue eyes. She was slender with the sinewy body of a former college athlete in her late twenties, fifteen years younger than Alex. Anita had been unemployed when she met Alex and, to Dylan's knowledge, never held a job. Nevertheless, Alex had pledged his undying love and swore to mend his philandering ways.

Anita had insisted on a short engagement and a beach wedding. The couple was married the following winter before two hundred family members and friends in a grand affair on the grounds of the Breakers Hotel in Palm Beach. Dylan had stood up for Alex with Cheryl, Anthony, and Isabella in attendance. Shortly thereafter, Anita had announced she was pregnant. The couple's son, Benjamin Jackson Malloy, had been born two months ago. Alex had wanted to name the boy Jackson Alexander IV, but Anita would hear none of it. The child was named after her father. Alex had to settle for the middle name.

Dylan picked up the line. "What's up? How's the wife and kid?"

There was a momentary silence on the other end before Alex spoke. "I wish I knew. Anita took Ben and left. She said she wants a divorce."

Dylan sat in stunned silence for a moment. "What happened?"

"I have no idea. I came home from work last night and the house was empty. I called her cell phone five times with no answer. She finally called back and said she had Ben and wants a divorce. I don't even know where she is. She said I'd be hearing from her lawyers and hung up."

Dylan grimaced before continuing. "Something must've happened. You've only been married a little over a year and you just had a child together. I have to ask you this. Have you been messing around?"

"No. Absolutely not! Not one time since we got engaged."

"What about the bachelor party I threw for you in Vegas? You spent a night with two hookers."

"Well, there was that. But that was my last chance for a threesome. Seriously, other than that, I haven't even so much as flirted with another woman. I don't get it. How could she do this to our son and me?"

"Look, buddy, I've got a commitment tomorrow night. The next day, I'll fly up and we'll figure this out together."

"You're a good friend, Dylan. I don't know what else to do. I haven't even told my parents yet. My mother's going to be crushed. She's so excited to have a grandson. Kari and her husband have the three girls."

"Just sit tight on this 'til I get there. Except you should go down the hallway and speak to the head of your family law division. Get his or her recommendation on hiring the best divorce lawyers in New York. Don't wait on that. It sounds like Anita's already got a head start on you."

"That's good advice. Are you sure you're not the attorney in this relationship?"

Dylan laughed. "It's good to see you're maintaining your sense of humor. I'll call you back when I have my flight information."

The two friends hung up, and Dylan went over to Shirley's office. She was speaking into her headset, so he waited patiently for her to finish the conversation and disconnect the call.

"I need you to book me on a flight to New York the day after tomorrow."

"Got it. When will you be returning?"

"At this point I have no idea."

CHAPTER THIRTY-ONE

E VAN WITHROW LIVED FOUR HOUSES down from Dylan in the largest of the waterfront mansions on Park Street millionaires' row. The total square footage was almost thirteen thousand square feet and included a ballroom large enough to host up to two hundred and fifty guests. Adjacent to the ballroom was a separate commercial kitchen specifically designed to cater affairs on site.

Withrow had done a lot of entertaining over the years. As the publisher emeritus of the *Tampa Bay Daily Herald*, or the *Herald* as it was known locally, most of his parties were thrown in the name of charities or political fundraisers. Tonight's guest of honor was Florida Governor Rocco Philips, or the Italian Stallion as he was often referred to by the Florida media. On occasion when his surname caused his progeny to be questioned, Philips pointed out that his Italian immigrant grandparents were forced to change their name from Philipeano because of the unrelenting prejudice they faced when first settling in New York. He routinely seized on the opportunity to pontificate on the injustices of the world and crusade as the champion of all people, particularly those who faced discrimination, bigotry, or other harm based on race, ethnicity, or sexual orientation.

The strategy had served Philips well. A decade ago, he was twice elected governor of his home state of New York. But Philips was suddenly forced to resign in disgrace midway through his second term. While initially being investigated for taking kickbacks in exchange for the granting of state contracts, another scandal had broken, which proved to be his demise.

A pusillanimous state legislature's perfunctory investigation into the kickback accusations had shown little progress over the course of a year. Suddenly the national "Me Too" movement was launched. Shortly thereafter, no less than two dozen brave women had come forward and told their stories of being sexually harassed and assaulted by the governor. An opportunistic state attorney general with aspirations for the governor's office had launched an independent investigation.

Philips had earned a well-deserved reputation as a chief executive who ruled with a dictatorial style. He had a battery of lawyers, public relations specialists, and other henchmen who protected him. They ran interference on any negative publicity and ruthlessly attacked anyone who crossed him. Following the new fastidious investigation into the women's claims, Philips's inner circle had advised him to resign with the prospect of making a future political comeback. Initially, Philips had adamantly refused, but after several of his female personnel resigned, including his chief of staff, two attorneys, and one public relations executive, he acquiesced.

Philips, an attorney by training and a career politician, had never held a job in the private sector, yet he left office with a nest egg in excess of twenty million dollars. He'd bided his time for the next five years, employed as a rainmaker for a large, statewide New York law firm. A severe downturn in the New York state economy, caused in large part by Philip's tax-and-spend policies, bloated government bureaucracies and increased violent crime, forcing thousands of New Yorkers to flee the state. A large percentage settled in Florida. Whereas in the past most New Yorkers had found their way to the state's east coast, the new wave of transplants was now spread throughout the state with significant numbers in the Panhandle, Orlando, and the Tampa Bay area.

The migration to Florida was not lost on Philips. Polling in the Sunshine State revealed a majority of relocated New Yorkers held a favorable opinion of him. Additionally, a separate poll among other Floridians showed a minimal negativity rating. The prescient Philips moved to Palm Beach, assembled a staff, and began to reinvent himself.

After the popular Florida governor had left office to run for president, Philips ran and won by a razor-thin margin. The results were confirmed following a recount and allegations of fraud and voting improprieties in Broward County. Philips was now halfway through his first term and beginning to ramp up his fundraising efforts.

Evan Withrow had met Dylan about a year ago. Withrow had been out by his front gate checking the mail when Dylan rode by on his bicycle. Dylan often rode his Trek Domane SL 5 down Park Street and over to the nearby Pinellas trail. Withrow had seen Dylan around since he'd moved in some ten years ago, but the two had never met before then. All the mansions were set back deep on their expansive lots, close to the waterfront and surrounded by high walls and mature landscaping. It was not the type of neighborhood where residents dropped by to chat or borrow a power tool. Curious about the handsome young man who lived in the exclusive neighborhood, Withrow had one of the *Herald's* research assistants prepare a dossier on Dylan. Impressed by the findings, he'd made a concerted effort to become more acquainted with his younger neighbor.

CHAPTER THIRTY-TWO

T HE FOLLOWING EVENING DYLAN SHOWERED and donned his bespoke dark navy suit. The suit was narrowly tailored in the contemporary style. He debated about whether to wear a necktie before finally selecting one in red with a microdot design. He reasoned that most of the other attendees would be wearing tuxedos or dinner jackets, so the least he could do was wear a tie. He completed the ensemble with a pair of black Johnson & Murphy cap-toe oxfords.

Dylan called over to Aengus and let him know he was ready to leave. It seemed frivolous to be driven, but the weather forecast was iffy and Dylan didn't want to get caught in one of Florida's infamous pop-up thunderstorms while walking down the street in a suit. Aengus maneuvered the black Cadillac Escalade out of the garage and pulled under the portico. Dylan descended the front stairway, and Aengus held open the rear door. Dylan preferred to sit up front, but he submitted to Aengus' formal manner on such matters.

Aengus waited for the electronic gate to open, exited the driveway, and turned right onto Park Street. Just down the road, a backup of black SUVs and limousines along with a series of expensive automobiles clogged the right-hand lane. Aengus eased in behind the line of traffic.

When they arrived at the gate, two large men in black suits checked Dylan's invitation before waiving them through. Aengus drove down the long driveway and parked in front of the main entrance. Valets were present to park guest cars. A young valet clad in a red jacket with his hair tied in a man bun observed that Aengus was dropping off a guest and retreated. Aengus exited the vehicle and, once again, held the rear door open for Dylan. Dylan descended and reminded Aengus that he would probably walk home later.

"Either way, sir. I'll be available if you decide you want a ride."

Dylan thanked him and made his way to the front door. The entrance was manned by two Pinellas County Sheriff's deputies. A temporary table and metal detector were set up. Guests were required to place cell phones and other metal devices into a tray before walking through.

Dylan passed through security, entered the house, and looked around. The foyer opened into an enormous great room with views of a winding staircase and wraparound balcony on the second floor. The room had a high-gloss, polished travertine floor and was illuminated by a series of crystal chandeliers. Round tables of six were set up throughout the room with a long table in front. A temporary dance floor and bandstand were situated in the middle of the room.

Dylan walked toward the back of the room and observed that the three sets of glass double doors leading to the back yard and pool area were open. He walked outside where guests were mingling while enjoying drinks and hors d'oeuvres. A string quartet played light jazz from the bandstand inside and the music was piped outdoors through a series of clandestine speakers. The sun was beginning to set on the horizon, and the outdoor area was well lit with string lighting. An abundance of candles floated in the large swimming pool.

Dylan accepted a glass of champagne from a passing waiter. He observed at least six additional beefy men in black suits with earpieces and microphones on their jacket sleeves inconspicuously traverse the house and grounds among the guests. After looking around for a while and not recognizing a soul, he went back inside to locate his table.

There were place cards on each table. Dylan started in the back of the room and worked his way forward in search of his seat. Having no luck, he caught the attention of one of the group of young female hostesses. Each was attractive and dressed identically in a short black dress and heels. He handed one of them his invitation and asked for assistance finding his seat. The young woman looked at Dylan, smiled, and asked him to follow her back toward the entrance. Off to the side was a small platform that held the evening's seating chart. The woman took a moment to consult the chart and double checked the invitation before looking back up at Dylan.

"I must say, you don't seem to fit the profile of the typical guest here."

Dylan smiled at the young woman. "Should I take that as a compliment or an insult?"

She batted her eyes before responding, "It is most definitely a compliment. You're younger and far more dashing than most of the guests."

Dylan placed a hand on his chest. "Now I'm really hurt. I'm not younger and more dashing than *all* of the guests?"

The dance continued. "Okay, I'll be completely honest. Much more than all the guests. I especially admire that you're secure enough to dispense with the monkey suit."

Dylan decided it was time to move things along. "You're very kind, and I don't want to get you in trouble. Perhaps you can show me to my seat."

The hostess seemed to want to continue the banter but twitched her shoulders lightly and smiled again. "Follow me."

Dylan fell in step behind her, appreciating the view. He began to feel unsettled as the woman approached the main table just before veering off to the right. She turned and looked at Dylan. "Here you are."

He was surprised. "Are you sure?"

"If you're Dylan Tomassi, I am 100 percent certain," she turned and indicated, "that's your place card on the table."

He thanked her, and she quickly departed. An older couple was seated at the table, drinking what appeared to be martinis. He stood across the table from them and caught the man's eye. "Good evening, I'm Dylan Tomassi."

The man took charge, standing and extending his hand. "Good evening, young man. My name is Kenneth Grossman, and this is my wife, Janet. We're pleased to meet you. We were just enjoying our evening cocktail. Please join us."

Dylan caught the eye of a passing waitress and asked for a glass of red wine. She turned and headed toward one of the bars set up on either side of the room.

Kenneth Grossman waited for the woman to depart. "So, Dylan, you're a wine drinker?"

"Yes, sir."

"I'm somewhat of an oenophile myself. I fancy Italian and French wines, and I'm a certified sommelier in Italian vintages. What are your favorites?"

"I'm a fan of domestic reds. I prefer cabernets from Napa Valley and pinots from Oregon's Willamette region. I'm also fond of several vineyards in Temecula. It's a well-kept secret."

"I've never heard of it. Where is that?"

"It's in southern California, about halfway between San Diego and LA. The weather is cool and dry, ideal for growing grapes and olives."

"I'll have to visit if I find myself in that part of the world. What do you do, Dylan?"

"I'm a private investor."

Kenneth Grossman raised an eyebrow. "Is that so? What do you invest in?"

"I have a diversified portfolio and also own a commercial real estate company. What do you and Mrs. Grossman do?"

"I'm a retired radiologist and former mayor of St. Petersburg. I enjoy sailing and still keep a hand in local politics. Janet is the president of the St. Petersburg Garden Club, and she's also involved with a number of charities."

Dylan observed Janet Grossman's old school deference to her husband. The group was joined by another older couple and a third person who appeared to be their middle-aged daughter. Introductions were made, and Dylan's initial impression was correct. His newest tablemates were Steven and Wendi Weismann and their daughter, Rigina. Dylan had vaguely heard of Steven Weismann, and their subsequent conversation confirmed that he was the founder and president of Florida's largest independent bank. He was also a major philanthropist with buildings named after him at business schools on the campuses of the University of Florida and the University of Tampa. Steven Weismann was also a major player in politics.

A dinner of cast-iron chicken, garlic mashed potatoes, and butternut squash was served. As dinner was concluding, Evan Withrow stood and clanged a spoon against his water glass. The light jazz dinner music terminated, and a hush came over the crowd.

Withrow addressed the group. "Ladies and gentlemen. Thank you for coming. I hope you are all enjoying yourselves. It gives me great pleasure to introduce tonight's guest, the governor of our fair state, the Honorable Rocco Philips."

Rocco Philips was an ethically bankrupt swine, but he possessed two skill sets that proved invaluable to a successful politician: he was a charismatic speaker and voracious fundraiser. In preparation for the evening, Philips's staff ran background investigations on all 237 guests in attendance. According to their social media accounts, a startling 176 had revoked their White privilege in the past sixty days. Philips knew how to play to a crowd. The governor stood, waived to the audience, and waited for the applause to recede before speaking.

"Thank you, Evan, for inviting me tonight and thanks to everyone here for attending. We've begun our journey, undoing all the repulsive policies of my predecessor. Tonight, I humbly stand before you prepared to move forward and reach higher, doing the work of and for the people of our great state. In the near future I will be introducing my new program, the Rainbow Ribbon Coalition. This movement is not a reform but rather a rebirth. For far too long, minority groups and the economically disadvantaged in our state have been ignored by government in favor of big business and the privileged few. And people have suffered the consequences. The Rainbow Ribbon Coalition, or RRC, has four basic tenets. It involves launching new progressive initiatives in the areas of education, criminal justice, social justice, and common prosperity."

A large screen set up behind the governor displayed the RRC logo, a ribbon colored in stripes of brown, red, purple, black, and yellow. He looked back at the logo admiringly before returning to the crowd and continuing.

"The RRC is a public-private joint enterprise set up as a 501(c) 3 nonprofit organization. We need your financial support to launch this groundbreaking initiative. Your contributions will be fully tax deductible and, additionally, you'll be granted permissive use of all RRC logos and intellectual property to display in your businesses and utilize as you see fit. I will be coming around tonight to speak with you individually and answer any questions; but more details on becoming an RRC partner will be announced in the future. With your help, we can continue to do the work necessary to bring equity to the people."

The governor sat down to thunderous applause.

As the enthusiastic crowd noise continued, Dylan looked around the room and couldn't help but notice that all but a few of the guests were White and exactly none appeared to be economically disadvantaged. The vast majority of the minorities in attendance were the hardworking members of the service staff.

As the applause died down, Evan Withrow rose and spoke again. "Coffee and dessert are being served and, of course, the bars will remain open. The governor did not mention this, as he is focused on his new program, so I will. The next election is just two short years away. In addition to supporting the RRC, I ask that you please donate to the Rocco Philips reelection campaign. Please enjoy yourselves and get those check books out. The governor and I will be around to see you shortly."

The music started up again, and Governor Philips and Withrow began making the rounds. They started in the back of the room and worked their way forward. Dylan's table was one of the last that the pair visited. At the conclusion of the interactions, both Grossman and Weismann handed plain-white envelopes to the governor who smoothly transferred them to his inside jacket pocket.

Finally, Evan Withrow glanced around the room before addressing Dylan. "It looks like the party is beginning to break up. I need to man the door for a time and say good night to my guests. Would you mind keeping the governor company in my study. I'll be in to join you as soon as I'm able."

Dylan sat there in stunned silence. He didn't know much about Rocco Philips, but his initial impression was inimical. He had no desire to spend time with the man. Before he had a chance to object, the governor chimed in. "Come, Dylan. This will give us an opportunity to get acquainted."

Just then a Florida Highway Patrol officer and a hostess appeared and escorted the two men to Evan Withrow's office. The office was large and contained a bar, conference table, and separate seating area. The walls were adorned with several large screen televisions and framed front-page copies of historically significant editions of the *Herald*. Dylan noted headlines announcing the surrender of the Nazis ending World War II, the 1969 moon landing, and the 2008 election of Barack Obama as president.

The men were seated across from each other. Dylan occupied a chair while the governor sat on a small couch. The hostess brought over a silver tray with snifters of cognac and conspicuously sat on the couch next to the governor.

Philips handed Dylan a snifter and raised his own. "To new friends."

Dylan raised his glass in a disinterested manner and took a small sip.

Governor Philips took a large gulp, exhaled, and commented, "Ahhh, D'usse XO. Evan keeps this on hand for his most special guests."

Clearly uncomfortable, Dylan looked over at the young hostess who glanced back at him with what was clearly the acknowledgment of a kindred feeling.

Just then the governor moved closer to the young lady. "Dylan, I understand you and I have much in common. We are both the offspring of Italian immigrants and self-made men who come from modest backgrounds. We're also transplants from the same neck of the woods. I have a great vision for our adopted state, and it would be an honor if you agreed to assist me in that endeavor."

"I'm going to be respectfully candid with you, sir. I've never followed, nor been particularly interested, in politics. And I know little to nothing about you except I do vaguely recall that you were formerly the governor of New York."

Philips readjusted himself on the couch and straightened his spine. "I certainly hope you won't hold anything that happened in New York against me. I was the victim of a political witch hunt. Our country's history is replete with men who have persevered in the face of adversity and gone on to accomplish great things. I am a humble public servant who aspires to be next in that long line of success."

Dylan glanced over at the young woman who rolled her eyes. He then looked back squarely at Philips and asked point blank, "What do you want from me?"

"For starters, I'd like to count you among my friends and supporters. Donations to the RRC and my reelection campaign would be a good start."

"As I indicated earlier, I have little interest in politics, so I'm going to have to pass."

"That's very disappointing to hear. Perhaps you should reconsider. There may come a time when you need something from me. Conversely, I wield a lot of power in this state, and you don't want to end up on my bad side."

"You are correct, sir. I have no desire to be on your bad side, nor do I wish to be a supporter of you or any other candidate. The only thing I can promise you is my fair consideration when I cast my vote."

The governor was unaccustomed to such rejection and clearly frustrated. "Very well. I understand that Evan speaks highly of you and wishes to discuss another matter. Perhaps you'll reconsider after conversing with him."

Dylan stood to leave. "I highly doubt it. Good evening to you, sir."

The hostess could barely contain her enthusiasm while watching Dylan's display of hutzpah toward the powerful man. Her mood changed sullenly when the governor turned his attention to her.

"It's been a long evening. Come with me, dear. I need to go upstairs and blow off some steam."

Dylan could see the look of horror in the young woman's eyes and turned to her. "Are you okay? You don't have to do this. Just say so, and I'll take you out of here."

The governor displayed a smug look while he awaited the woman's reply.

Finally, she answered, "No, it's fine. Whatever you need, Governor."

The state trooper stationed outside the door entered the room. "Is everything alright in here, sir?"

Before the governor could answer, Dylan began walking toward the door.

The trooper stood in Dylan's path, waiting for his boss's response.

"Everything's fine, Terry. Mr. Tomassi was just leaving, and the two of us are headed upstairs."

Dylan made a bee line for the front door, running into Evan Withrow. "Dylan, are you leaving so soon? I was hoping to have a word with you."

"It's been a long night, sir. Thank you for your hospitality. Perhaps we can talk another time."

"I would genuinely appreciate that, Dylan."

The two men bid each other a good night. Dylan walked out the front door, down the long driveway, and turned left for the short jaunt home. It was late spring, and the night air was heavy from the humidity. Dylan found himself in an utter state of befuddlement.

CHAPTER THIRTY-THREE

T HE FOLLOWING MORNING, DYLAN PACKED his bags and stopped in to see Shirley in her office. "Good morning. I'm leaving for the airport."

"How come you didn't want me to book you a hotel room?"

"I'll be staying with Alex."

"Aren't you going to cramp his new marital style?"

"Uh, I don't think that's going to be a problem, at least not initially. If anything changes, I'll call you."

"Okay. I'll hold down the fort here. Let me know what's going on once you figure it out."

"Will do."

Dylan called down to Aengus for the trip to Tampa International Airport. Aengus brought the Escalade around front and loaded his bag into the trunk.

Dylan called Alex from the car. "Hey, I'm on my way to the airport. I'll be arriving at La Guardia around three. Do you want me to take a car service to your house?"

Alex lived in Greenwich and commuted into Manhattan each day, primarily because Anita had insisted on living in Connecticut. "No, I drove to the city today. I'll cut out early and pick you up."

Dylan gave Alex his flight information and terminated the call. He thought about last night's encounter with Governor Philips and called Evan Withrow.

"Good morning, Evan. I wanted to call and thank you again for last night. I also thought I should let you know I had a minor imbroglio with your featured guest."

Dylan heard a chuckle on the other end. "Don't worry about it, Dylan. The governor told me about his encounter with you. He was quite impressed actually."

"How so?"

"Please understand, Dylan, that Rocco Philips is a powerful man and an imperious one at that. He's surrounded by yes-men and people who cater to his every whim. Meeting someone with a strong constitution is a refreshing change for him."

"Trust me when I tell you, impressing Rocco Philips was not my intention."

"Nevertheless, you did impress him. And it never hurts to have a friend in the governor's mansion."

"I suppose you're right, but at what price?"

"Dylan, let me be frank. I've checked you out. A man in my position does that as a matter of course prior to associating with someone. That's good advice, I may add. Nevertheless, you're a very successful man and have achieved that success at a relatively young age. You must now consider what type of legacy you wish to leave behind as all of our time on this earth is finite."

"I don't disagree with you."

"Well, let's forget Governor Philips and politics for the moment. I understand you are not politically active. I want to get together with you to discuss your interest in newspapers."

"Newspapers?"

"Yes. I understand you have a fondness for the fourth estate. The newspaper business has a fascinating and storied history and has been a mainstay of our country for centuries. However, the industry has undergone drastic changes over the past two decades. I'm afraid, the present business model is no longer a viable one. Consequently, we are transitioning to a new cutting-edge format, one I'd like to discuss with you in more detail. Would you be agreeable to tour our news operation and plant facilities and discuss the venture in more detail?"

"You are correct, Evan. I delivered newspapers for ten years in Connecticut, right up until I entered college. I still read at least three papers a day, including the *Herald*."

"Well then, I'll call your office and arrange for the tour. I suggest we block off a day as there's much to see and discuss."

"Very good, Evan. Please call my assistant, Shirley, to make the arrangements. I look forward to it."

The two men hung up.

Dylan looked up and saw they were about to exit the Howard Frankland Bridge. "Aengus, I'm going to the Delta terminal. Just drop me at the departure area."

"Yes, sir."

Dylan entered the airport, took the escalator to the tram, and rode out to

Concourse E. He showed his first class ticket at the Delta Sky Club and was admitted to the private lounge. He went over to the bar, ordered a Diet Coke, and sat down in a leather armchair with his copies of the *Herald* and the *Wall Street Journal.* He was immersed in his papers when he was eclipsed by a human shadow. He looked up and saw a tall, stunning female with shoulder-length, brown hair standing over him. She wore black leather pants, a white short-sleeve sweater, and ankle boots. She looked down at him and smiled, revealing perfect dental work.

"Do you mind if I sit here? The club is sort of crowded."

Dylan looked at her and then around the room. There were at least a dozen empty seating sections. He was simultaneously smitten and flummoxed. "Absolutely. I was saving a seat for you."

The woman laughed. "I see you haven't lost your sense of humor."

Dylan gave the woman a puzzled look. "Do we know each other?"

"I think so if you're, Dylan. It's me, Penel Stanhill."

"Penel. Oh my gosh. It's been what? Twenty-five years?" Dylan stood, and the two embraced. He stepped back and looked at her. "You're still as beautiful as I remember."

"You always were charming. And a perfect gentleman. You know, I've thought about you over the years."

Dylan didn't know how to reply. He hadn't thought of Penel since their summer romance a quarter century ago. He managed to recover. "Well, the years certainly have been kind to you. What brings you to Florida?"

"I gave a speech last night to the American Bar Association. I'm an attorney and the president of the ABA Family Law Section."

"No kidding. What happened to your passion for finance?"

"I guess I went through a rebellious streak and decided I wanted to help people who got screwed. I've always had financial security, so I went to law school and then opened a divorce practice. I only accept cases where I feel passionate about seeking justice for the abuses suffered by the clients I take on. I found that approach makes me a better advocate. The next thing I knew, people were knocking down my door. Presently I take on about one out of every half dozen or so cases I review."

"Are you one of these aggrieved persons?"

Penel smiled broadly. "No, I never married. Maybe I've become jaded from the job, but I'm happy. I find the work fulfilling and have a network of close friends. What about you?"

"I enjoy life, and I don't think I'm aggrieved or jaded."

Penel laughed. "Where are you headed?"

"I'm flying into La Guardia. I'm going to visit Alex. I'm sure you remember him."

"Of course. He really stood up for you that night. I'm not surprised the two of you remained friends over the years."

"We've remained best friends. Are you headed back to New York?"

Penel produced her cell phone and pulled up her boarding pass. "Yes. We may be on the same flight."

Dylan looked at her phone. "We are but seated apart in first class. Let me see what I can do about that."

Dylan went up to the Sky Club courtesy desk and explained the situation. The woman clicked some computer keys, frowned, and told Dylan first class was full and she was unable to accommodate his request. He thanked her for trying and called his concierge at American Express. He was a Centurion card holder. A short time later, Dylan and Penel were emailed new boarding passes, now seated together in 2A and 2B.

On the flight to New York, Dylan explained Alex's situation and the purpose for his trip. Penel was initially skeptical. She represented a fair number of male clients, but her recollection of Alex from twenty-five years ago was the root of her pessimism. Finally, they agreed that Dylan would get more information and call her to discuss the matter further over dinner.

After they landed in New York, Dylan and Penel exchanged phone numbers and then parted ways. He texted Alex who had been waiting in the cell phone lot to pick him up. Dylan walked outside, and Alex pulled up in his Maserati Quattroporte.

Dylan placed his suitcase in the trunk and hopped into the front passenger seat. "How goes it?"

"Still no word from Anita. I called her parents, and they told me they didn't want to get involved. I have no idea if she's with them or somewhere else. By the way, thanks so much for coming. You are truly the best."

"What have you done about retaining counsel?"

"I spoke with Heather Birnbaum. She's the head of our family and marital law division. She handled our prenup but felt it was best to retain outside counsel for the divorce. I have an appointment tomorrow with Rochelle Barnett of Gross, Barnett, and Cook."

"You sound resigned that divorce is imminent."

"It's not what I want, but it seems pretty clear Anita does. I still have no idea what went wrong."

"Have you given consideration to the fact that it has nothing to do with you?"

"You're giving me the 'it's her and not me' speech?"

"I'm simply asking if you've considered it. I also have some additional information. Do you remember Penel Stanhill?"

"Why does that name sound familiar?"

"The Rangers game, Madison Square Garden. A lifetime ago."

"Vaguely. What does she have to do with anything?"

"She's the president of the Family Law Division of the American Bar Association and, apparently, a prominent divorce attorney in New York. I ran into her on the flight up here, and she agreed to look into your case. I think you need a team on this."

The two friends talked a while longer about Alex's dilemma before the conversation turned to other topics. Before long they arrived at Alex's house in Old Greenwich, on the waterfront at the end of a quiet residential street overlooking a cove that led to Long Island Sound. A generic white sedan with a light attached to the roof indicating the driver delivered pizzas was parked on the road next to the driveway. Alex pulled the car into the garage and was about to close the door when a short, frumpy man in a white golf shirt bearing food stains walked up the driveway. Alex and Dylan turned and looked at the man.

"Are you Alex Malloy?"

Alex walked into the driveway and addressed the stranger. "Yes, but I didn't order any pizza."

The man kept walking toward Alex, and as he got within arm's distance, pulled paperwork from his back pocket and handed it to him. Alex instinctively accepted the papers.

"You've been served." The man pulled out a cell phone, took a picture of Alex holding the paperwork, and scurried back to his car.

They walked inside, and Alex spread the papers out on the kitchen table. "Irreconcilable differences? It hardly seems like we've known each other long enough for such disdain."

Dylan sighed. This was not going to be easy.

CHAPTER THIRTY-FOUR

THE FOLLOWING MORNING, ALEX AND Dylan drove into Manhattan. Alex went to work in his office, and Dylan borrowed an empty room down the hallway. He called to check in with Shirley before settling in to get some work done. Just before noon, he placed a call to Penel.

She answered right away, "Hello. It's good to hear from you so soon. Have you found out anything else about Alex's situation?"

"Yes, and I plan to spend the rest of the day looking into it further. Can we have dinner tonight?"

"Sure. I live on Fifth Avenue. Will you meet me at Donohue's Steak House at seven? It's close to my apartment."

Dylan knew the place. "You got it. I'll make the reservation and see you then." He hung up and called American Express. He figured the Amex concierge could exert more influence wrangling a same day reservation than Shirley. Next, he walked over to Alex's office. "How about we grab a sandwich at the deli? I'm meeting Penel for dinner tonight to discuss your situation."

"Sounds good."

The pair left the building and walked across the street. Alex had a turkey club, and Dylan opted for pastrami on rye. He had yet to find a good pastrami sandwich in Florida.

"So tell me, before the baby arrived, what did Anita do to fill her days?"

"Your guess is as good as mine. We belong to the Round Hill and Riverside Yacht Clubs. She likes sailing, and we keep a sloop at Riverside. I know she used to meet her girlfriends for lunch at the clubs several times a week."

"What else?"

Alex appeared deep in thought. "Now that I think about it, the only other things she did were work out, shop, and spend time on social media."

Dylan considered the information. From the beginning he'd had deep-rooted iniquitous feelings about social media. His opinions were the result of researching tech companies for investment opportunities. He'd discussed the prospects with Esther Lott, and the pair had agreed major social networking sites produced no real product or service and resulted in myriad negative effects on its users. While acknowledging it could be an effective marketing vehicle to promote a brand or company, Esther felt that big tech worked to trap the vast majority of its users into a web of addiction, exhibitionism, and a fear of missing out. She was concerned the phenomena would eventually create a society of histrionics.

Dylan had invested in Amazon and Netflix early on, and the stocks produced excellent long-term results. He had distinguished the two companies based upon their dynamic management teams and the fact they furnished bona fide products and services to their customers. He'd missed on a few tech investments, notably a position he took in Digital Lightwave, a local Florida start-up. The 2007 recession was brought on, in large part, by the dot-com bubble. For the most part, he'd survived the financial crisis relatively unscathed. Dylan had never used social media.

After lunch, they returned to the office and Dylan called Esther. Their relationship had evolved over the years. Per her request, he had long ago become comfortable calling her Esther. Franklin usually answered the phone during the day, so he was surprised when she answered.

"Hello, Esther. It's Dylan. How are you?"

"Very well, now that I'm speaking with you."

"I'm in Greenwich with Alex, helping him with a problem, and I was hoping to get some input from you." Dylan went on to explain the situation and relayed what information he had about Anita Van Widenfelt Malloy.

Esther listened intently before responding. "You know, Dylan, you can learn a great deal about a person from their social media accounts. It's astounding the amount of valuable information that can be gleaned from accessing those sites. I do it all the time when analyzing a company and their management team."

"I confess I don't know much about it since I'm a nonparticipant. Do you have any suggestions on how I can get the information?"

"How fast do you need it?"

"No hurry. Yesterday."

Esther laughed. "Give me a few hours. I'll see what I can find and email you the results. When will I see you?"

"I'm knee-deep helping Alex at the moment, but I promise I'll come by before I leave."

"I know you will. I look forward to seeing you, as always. You're a true friend, Dylan."

"Thank you." It was the third time he'd heard that in the past two days.

Dylan checked his email just before Alex was wrapping up his workday. He had a message from Esther with an attachment. He opened it and went through a series of screen shots. Anita was quite active on Open Source, Face Chat, and Chirpster, the major social networking sites. Most of the pictures appeared innocuous. There were several recent photos of Anita with the baby and, earlier, selfies of her dressed up in workout clothes and bathing suits. There were also pictures with her girlfriends dining out or partying. Conspicuously absent were any photos of Alex. There weren't any of Anita with other men, excluding her father and brothers, but Dylan didn't expect there would be.

After sorting through the pictures, Dylan got to her posts. They went back further in time, some all the way to her college years. It appeared that Esther had selected ones relevant to the task at hand. There were several criticizing the former Florida governor and current president, also comments supporting the Black Lives Matter and Defund the Police movements. Most significantly were statements posted more than three years earlier, before she'd met Alex. Two jumped out at Dylan.

Looking to pick up a check? hook up with a pro athlete or trust fund boy.

these guys are really dumb and don't use condoms.

It's hunting season ladies. me & my girls headed to NYC this weekend for a payday $$$.

Dylan printed out the posts and headed down to Alex's office. The door was closed, so he waited outside next to Alex's secretary, Gretchen. She was in her late fifties, overweight, and frumpy. Finally, Alex's door opened. A tall, serious-looking woman dressed in a smart business suit exited the office followed by Alex. He made the introductions. "Dylan, this is Rochelle Barnett. She's going to be representing me."

Dylan took her extended hand and shook it. The woman had a firm grip. She made eye contact with Dylan and never broke it. "Good afternoon. I've explained to Alex that he should not discuss his situation with anyone, including you. I expect that you'll be deposed down the line, and I have an obligation to protect my client."

Dylan maintained eye contact but said nothing in reply.

Rochelle Barnett turned and looked back at Alex. "I'll have copies of the paperwork you signed emailed to your office. Good day."

Dylan waited until the attorney had gotten on the elevator and the door closed before speaking. "Intense woman. She should try the decaf."

"She's certainly not the warm and fuzzy type. But she is what I'm looking for in a divorce attorney."

"I can't argue with you there. I was about to leave and meet Penel."

"About that, I don't know that Rochelle is the type who works well with others."

"Fine. Let me run things by her and see what she says. Do you have a copy of your prenuptial agreement?"

Alex thumbed through his black alligator attaché case and produced a thick, full-size envelope that he handed to Dylan. "How are you planning on getting back to the house?"

"I'll play it by ear. I can always take the train."

"If you end up doing that, call me and I'll pick you up at the station. And don't worry about the time. I'll be up."

Dylan took a cab to Lexington Avenue and got out in front of Donohue's. He entered the restaurant, and the maître de led him past the bar and down the narrow dining room to where Penel was seated. She wore a well-tailored, yellow and tan checkered suit with black trim and black sling pumps. Dylan thought it was a smart, sexy look.

She stood and hugged and kissed him lightly on the lips. "It's good to see you again so soon."

"Same here."

A waiter appeared and took their drink orders. Penel ordered an espresso martini. Dylan asked for water and requested a wine list. When the waiter departed, he handed Penel the prenuptial agreement and filled her in on what he'd learned. She carefully perused the extensive document while listening to him. He mentioned that Alex had retained Rochelle Barnett, and Penel took on a look of intensity. "I know her. Not a bad choice. She's tough and a worthy adversary. Not as good as me, of course."

The waiter returned with the martini and wine list and waited a moment while Dylan read it over.

He looked up at Penel. "Is red wine okay?"

She indicated affirmatively, and Dylan ordered a bottle of 2017 Caymus Reserve cabernet. They caught up on personal matters until the waiter returned with the wine. Dylan tasted it, and the waiter poured two glasses. He then took their food orders. Penel selected the broiled half chicken and Dylan the sirloin steak.

After the waiter left, Penel indicated subtly toward an older man seated at the end of the bar, eating dinner alone. "Fun fact. See that guy? He eats dinner here every night. He has an agreement with the owner whereby he's permitted to come in even if the restaurant's closed for a private party, which happens more than you would think, especially around the holidays."

"Interesting. Does he ever miss a day?"

"Never."

During dinner, they talked more about their lives before returning to Alex's dilemma. Dylan showed her the social media posts.

After coffee and dessert were served, Penel turned to the business at hand. "FYI, in addition to New York, I'm licensed to practice law in Connecticut and New Jersey. Here are my initial thoughts based on the preliminary information you've provided. The wedding took place in Florida, but they have a Connecticut marriage license and lived there for the short time they've been married. Therefore, Connecticut law should apply. Connecticut is an equitable distribution state, which means that, generally, marital assets are divided between the parties. Alex's prenup is well-drafted, and his trust and personal assets should be protected from her. I also don't think she'll get any of his retirement benefits, given the length of the marriage and those social media posts. For the same reasons, I don't believe she'll be entitled to alimony. Alex has a good argument that the only marital assets are the funds in any joint accounts they hold, and he could legally spend those down."

Penel let that sink in before continuing. "Now, the wild cards are custody and child support. There are a wide range of factors that play into it, but the court ultimately considers the best interests of the child. It wouldn't hurt Alex to have his family's influence weigh in on the issue. However, he is looking at a significant child support obligation. It's based on his income, which is substantial. Unfortunately, that inures to the ex-spouse's benefit and, thus, the attitude conveyed in those chirps you showed me."

Dylan absorbed all the information and thanked her.

Penel shot him a lecherous look. "I know a way you can thank me properly. How about a night cap at my place?"

Dylan smiled and signaled for the check. He paid the bill, and the pair walked across Lexington Avenue and down East Sixty-Fourth Street to Park Avenue. Penel's apartment was on Park, near the corner of East Sixty-Second Street. They took the elevator up to the top floor, which opened directly into her foyer. They walked in, and Dylan looked around. Everything inside the apartment appeared brand new and it boasted grand views of Central Park.

Penel explained that she had completed a full renovation of the residence in the past year. She sat Dylan down on the living room couch, poured him a brandy, and excused herself. He heard the shower running and waited patiently.

Finally, Penel emerged from her bedroom wearing a lacy, white robe. Dylan could see her black bra and panties through the sheer material. She sat down and kissed him passionately on the mouth, then stood up and seductively removed her robe, giving Dylan a fine view of her body. She worked her way onto the floor and got down on her knees in front of him, unzipped his pants, and took him in her mouth. Before long, he was fully erect.

She took him by the hand and led him into the bedroom. They lay on the bed and explored each other enticingly with their hands and mouths. He then mounted and carefully entered her. They moved in rhythm, slowly at first, getting used to each other's bodies. The speed and intensity increased until they climaxed together. Afterward they remained silent. Dylan held her in his arms, and Penel rested her head on his chest until they fell asleep.

Dylan awoke early to the sound of activity in the bathroom. He located his phone and texted Alex. He let Alex know he was taking the train back to Greenwich and needed to borrow his car. Alex texted back that he was taking the train to work, and Dylan could use the Maserati. They made plans to have dinner that night in Greenwich.

Penel emerged from the bathroom in a terry cloth robe with her hair in a towel. He jumped out of bed and hugged and kissed her. She smiled and told him how much she'd enjoyed last night. He told her the pleasure was all his and then there was a pregnant pause until Penel spoke. "Will I see you again?"

"I'd like that. I'm going to make sure Alex is in a good place and then I'll call you. I do want to see you again before I go back to Florida."

"When are you leaving?"

"No definite plan on that. It depends on Alex."

"I see. I'll wait to hear from you then."

They hugged and kissed again, and Dylan left. He took a cab to Grand Central and caught the next train back to Greenwich. On the way, he called Esther and made arrangements to stop by in the early afternoon.

When Dylan got back to Alex's house, it was still early. He showered and took a midmorning nap. He had slept well with Penel but not as long as he would have liked. Just after noon, Dylan woke up, dressed, and grabbed the keys to Alex's car. He drove to Esther's house and arrived just before one o'clock.

Franklin answered the door. He looked and dressed the same, but Dylan observed the man seemed to be moving a little gingerly.

"Mr. Dylan. Please come in. It's a pleasant day, and Mrs. Lott decided to sit outside."

He led Dylan through the house, past the greenhouse, and down to the riverfront where she sat at a table under the large gazebo. There were matching chairs covered with comfortable cushions and, set out on the table, a tray of finger sandwiches and a pitcher of lemonade.

Esther stood and greeted him with a smile. She looked vibrant and healthy in black capri pants, a tan blouse, and New Balance sneakers. Dylan reflected that she dressed more fashionably now compared with the dowdy attire she wore while he was growing up.

They hugged tightly, and Esther spoke first. "It's so good to see you. I wasn't sure if you'd had lunch, so I had some sandwiches prepared."

Dylan realized then that he hadn't eaten all day. "It's wonderful to see you. I must say, you're looking young and healthy."

"Why thank you. I feel that way. I walk the property almost every day. I've found it's important to keep moving at my age."

"Whatever you're doing is working, so keep it up."

Esther smiled again and sat. Dylan poured lemonade for them both and helped himself to some sandwiches. They caught up on things, Dylan filling her in on Cheryl and his grandparents.

"I'm pleased to hear about your mom. She deserves to be happy. And it's good to hear your grandparents are doing well."

As Dylan finished a sandwich, she pulled out a folder from an oversized leather bag that sat on the chair next to her. She placed it on the table and shuffled through the papers. "I want to talk with you about a new opportunity. I believe climate change regulation is going to have an exponentially increasing effect on business. We're already seeing finance companies, activist investors, and government agencies compelling businesses to enact carbon mitigation programs. Some businesses are even launching carbon emissions accounting systems. As you know, there are several startups in the electric vehicle industry, reminiscent of the automotive industry in the early twentieth century. Of course, only the Big Three ultimately survived."

Dylan took his last bite, wiped his mouth with his cloth napkin and eagerly leaned forward in his chair as she continued. "One company in particular has caught my attention. Paradise Technology is the parent company of the Paradise Automobile Company, or PAC, and the Paradise Energy Company, known as PEC. PAC has developed a line of electric cars and trucks with the lowest price points yet for electric vehicles. But the real game changer is management's investment in a total vertical integration strategy. They've recruited top energy engineers and are in the final testing stages of battery technology that could revolutionize the transportation industry. The batteries have an average standard range of five hundred miles. Most significantly, the company is developing technology that will allow their batteries to be recharged at stations in the time it takes to fill a conventional gas tank."

Dylan was rapt, as always, when Esther discussed investments. "Wow."

"Let's collaborate on this," she slid the folder across the table. "I'd like you to look this over and do your own research. I want to see if I'm missing anything here before I take a position."

"That sounds exciting. I'll get on it and get back to you."

"Good. Now enough about business. You mentioned you wanted to discuss Alex's problem."

Dylan brought her up to date on what had transpired since they last spoke the day before and gave Esther a summary of Penel's evaluation.

"I'm not an attorney, Dylan, but the advice your friend gave you appears sound. I would add this. There's a child involved, and he's going to need a loving and supportive family to raise him. Families come in all types of configurations these days, but I hope Alex keeps that at the forefront as he goes through this process. You should remind him of that. Look at your own situation. Your father left when you were an infant, but your mother and grandparents were there to take care of you."

"I agree with everything you said except for one glaring omission."

"Oh, what's that?"

"You left yourself out when you listed the extraordinary people responsible for my upbringing."

Esther smiled broadly and used her own napkin to dab her watery eyes. When she regained her composure, they spoke for a while longer until Dylan announced he had to go meet Alex. They said their goodbyes, and Dylan headed back to Greenwich.

Dylan and Alex had dinner at the Elm Street Oyster House in downtown Greenwich. They shared an appetizer of raw oysters and washed them down with cold draft beer. For dinner, Alex chose the lobster roll with truffle fries and Dylan had blackened fish tacos. After their meals arrived, they finally got around to talking about the pending divorce proceedings. Dylan gave Alex a summary of Penel's preliminary evaluation. When he was finished, Alex sat silently staring down at his plate.

Finally, Dylan asked, "So any update today?"

"I spoke with Rochelle. She's doing further investigation into Anita's background and working on a reply to the divorce petition. She was impressed with that stuff you sent me this morning from Anita's social media accounts."

"Have you thought about how all of this is going to affect Ben?" Dylan asked.

"Honestly, that's all I've thought about. If Anita doesn't wanna be married to me, that's fine. I can get over that. But I love my son, and I'm bound and determined to stay involved in his life."

"What'd you think about the suggestion of injecting some Malloy family influence into the proceedings?"

"Funny you should ask. I spoke with my dad about it this morning.

"You're a good man, Alex, and I know you're going to be a great father. After all, you're still a child at heart. It takes one to raise one, I suppose."

"Good point. On that subject, I've been thinking, now may be a good time for me to come down to Florida. I could use the comfort of a good woman, and it's a good idea to have a twelve-hundred-mile buffer from here."

Dylan started laughing hysterically. "I see you're ready to move on and jump right back on the horse."

"It has been a couple of days."

After dinner, they headed back to Alex's house and watched the Yankee-Tampa Bay Rays game for a while. The Rays were an expansion team that began play around the time Dylan had relocated to Tampa. He had followed the team since its inception and become impressed with their innovative style of play and on field success, notwithstanding the limited resources of a small market team. It was owned and run by a group of former Wall Street executives who had revolutionized the game through the utilization of the innovative strategies that fueled their success in the financial world.

Dylan went upstairs and sprawled out on the bed with his hands behind his head as he thought about Penel. He had done everything he could for Alex up here and it was time to head home. He decided to call her. "Hi, Penel, did I wake you?"

"No, I've been lying in bed reviewing some client files."

"I spoke with Alex about your suggestions, and he's very appreciative. I've done about everything I can to assist him for the moment, so I'm going to make plans to return home soon. I'd like to see you again before I leave. Will you come and meet me in Greenwich? I'll be staying at the Delamar."

"I'd love to. I can take the train after work. Can you pick me up at the station?"

"Sure. Just text me when you're on the train and I'll be there to meet you. Is there anywhere particular you want to have dinner?"

"Dylan, I'm a city girl. Connecticut is your turf. I'll defer to you on the restaurant."

"I haven't lived here in over twenty years, but don't worry, I'll come up with something."

"Just as long as you promise me dessert."

"That's the best part."

"Sweet dreams." Then she hung up.

Dylan shook his head and smiled to himself.

About eight miles away, Jackson Malloy II was having dinner at the Stanwich Club with Fairfield County Superior Court Chief Judge Lawrence Morgan. As chief judge, Morgan supervised the judicial branch of government in Fairfield County. He did not carry a caseload, but he was responsible for the assignment of judges and control of the dockets. Judge Morgan and Jackson Malloy were old friends and golfing buddies.

The two men enjoyed their dinner alone in a small, private dining room. Jackson Malloy explained his son's predicament to the judge. Judge Morgan assured him that he would personally oversee the assignment of the case in the Family Court Division and have a discussion with the presiding judge. Under Connecticut law, all divorce proceedings were heard before a judge. No jury trials were involved. At the conclusion of dinner, the two men shook hands and left the club separately by a private exit.

CHAPTER THIRTY-FIVE

THE NEXT MORNING, DYLAN WENT downstairs and found Alex sitting at the kitchen island leaning over a large bowl of cereal. He regarded him as he shoveled circular yellow puffs into his mouth from a sea of discolored milk.

Alex looked up from his bowl and gurgled, "What?"

Dylan scowled, "Really? 1985 called. They want their cereal back."

"Hey, I like this stuff, Alex replied defensively."

Dylan ignored the response, took a deep breath and exhaled deeply. "Well, it seems like things have stabilized around here for the moment. If' you're good, I'm gonna move to a hotel and stay one more night with Penel before heading home."

"Absolutely, at least one of us should have female companionship."

"When you do you think you'll be able to get down to Florida?"

"Soon. When I get there, it'll be just like old times, before I met Anita."

"That's what I'm afraid of."

"Don't worry. I'm a responsible parent now."

"Just remember that."

They hung around in the kitchen until Alex left for the city, and then Dylan called Shirley. "Good morning. I need your assistance with some travel plans." He explained what he needed.

Shirley said she'd handle it and email him the details. A short time later he received her message. She'd booked him into a suite at the Delamar and rented him a Range Rover from Enterprise Rent-A-Car's Exotic Collection. He was on a Delta flight that left at noon the next day and could leave the rental car at La Guardia. Aengus would pick him up at the Tampa airport.

Satisfied that everything was in order, he fired up his laptop and started looking into Paradise Technologies. The company's operations were based in Tennessee. He learned that the company's founder and CEO, Gunner Jansen, was a dynamic and polarizing figure. He was equal parts brilliant and eccentric. Jansen was a trained electrical engineer, active on social media, and something of a brand himself. In some ways he reminded Dylan of Elon Musk. He spent a few hours going over the company's financial data and background information on Jansen.

Around lunch time, he packed his bag and called the local Enterprise office to arrange delivery of his car, then looked for a restaurant and settled on a reservation at Applausi Osteria. By midafternoon, he was checked into his hotel suite and decided to take a nap since he anticipated a late night.

Dylan woke up to his phone buzzing around the nightstand. He grabbed it and looked at the screen. It was a text message from Penel stating she would arrive at the Old Greenwich station at 7:10. He shaved, showered, and got dressed in a pair of light gray trousers, a white dress shirt, and brown casual lace up shoes.

It turned out Applausi Osteria was a short walk from the train station, so Dylan parked the car at the restaurant. The train arrived on time, and Penel departed looking smashing in a black, tailored pants suit and heels and carrying a Louis Vuitton overnight bag. They hugged and exchanged a kiss on the platform. Dylan took her bag and led her to the restaurant.

After they were seated, Penel indicated she wanted wine with dinner. Dylan knew she preferred white, so he selected a bottle of Far Niente chardonnay. Penel flashed him a look of approbation. They both enjoyed the wine and relaxed without over imbibing. Penel dined on the Mediterranean Sea bass, and Dylan had the osso buco, a personal favorite. The food was excellent and proved to be an aphrodisiac.

After dinner, Dylan drove them back to the hotel. The top-floor suite had an excellent view of the illuminated Greenwich Harbor. Penal excused herself and went into the bathroom. Dylan could hear the water running in the bathtub. A short while later, she emerged wearing nothing but a white lace-trimmed chemise. Soon they were in bed in each other's arms.

Penel momentarily broke the embrace and looked exuberantly at Dylan. "Do you remember the first time we were together in the Hamptons all those years ago?"

"I recall that evening with great fondness."

Lying on her back, she took him in her hand. "For old times' sake."

He was soon fully aroused and began reciprocating with gentle movements of his fingers to her moaning approval. The intensity increased as they became more familiar with each other. Their bodies conjoined well, and they became more adventurous. After completely satisfying each other, they fell asleep, exhausted, in the spooning position.

They woke up early in the same configuration. Apparently neither one had moved throughout the night. Dylan ordered room service, and they showered together. They ate a light breakfast, and he drove them back to the city. They made good time despite rush hour traffic. They arrived at Penel's office just before nine-thirty. Dylan parked in front of her office building, departed the Range Rover, and retrieved her bag from the rear compartment. He held her door open while Penel exited. The held a long embrace and shared a passionate kiss.

Penel spoke first. "Thank you for another lovely evening. I really enjoyed seeing you after all these years."

"The pleasure was all mine."

After another awkward pause, Penel broke the silence again. "Until next time."

Dylan responded, "Until then." He hopped back in the car and was gone.

On the flight home, he reminisced about the trip and his chance meeting with Penel in the Delta Sky Club in Tampa. He felt good about where things stood with Alex's situation, and he'd had a good time with Penel. However, something was unsettled in the back of his mind. He figured it would eventually sort itself out.

CHAPTER THIRTY-SIX

I N THE EARLY 1980s, A Harvard University graduate student pursuing a doctorate degree in sociology wrote her thesis challenging the conventional wisdom for remedying race-based discrimination. The paper criticized the longstanding policies of expanded constitutional rights, government mandates and the pursuit of legal remedies as well-intentioned failures. The student hypothesized that racism was pervasive and imbedded in every aspect of society, concluding that a radical change in societal thinking at the grassroots level was the transcendent solution to eradicating the systemic phenomenon. The paper outlined a detailed approach for breaking down current societal norms and instituting a vast resocialization process. She labeled the movement "Critical Race Theory."

The concept remained dormant until the early 2000s when the paper resurfaced in academic circles and its doctrine became the basis for graduate-level university courses, chiefly as a law school curriculum offering. It remained an academic theory until two years ago when a book entitled *The Equity Prism* was published. The book embraced the principles outlined in the original thesis, expounded upon the fundamental philosophy, and advocated mainstreaming Critical Race Theory, or CRT as she labeled it, into society as the linchpin for the eradication of racism. The author concurred with the central premise that racism was present in every aspect of life. Consequently, she concluded, skin color was the single most important personal identifier over qualities such as character. The author's justification was based upon the proposition that every societal institution was created by White people in their own interests and at the expense of Black people.

Accordingly, it was mandatory to constantly seek out racism in daily interactions and remedy any issue upon demand based upon the feelings and emotions of the aggrieved. Failure to agree with and rectify each identified concern was labeled as defensive and racist. Any alternative ideology was rejected out of hand, and anyone who disagreed with the movement was also identified as racist. Capitalism was branded an anathema that must be dispensed with in favor of an equitable redistribution of resources. Finally, the author advocated that the educational system was the most viable instrumentality for dissemination of its doctrine and required instruction as part of elementary education curricula. The book trended on social media and the ideology was gradually adopted by a number of school boards and assimilated into their educational systems.

Governor Rocco Philips was in his office conducting a meeting with his inner circle. Present among them were his chief of staff and his younger brother, Fred Philips, a persistent political liability. Every job or business opportunity bestowed upon Fred Philips was courtesy of a favor to Rocco or their late father, a former politician. Fred was a hotheaded malcontent who self-medicated with drugs, alcohol, and women of questionable virtue. He was currently employed as a principal with the Sunshine State Consulting Group.

When Rocco was governor of New York, Fred had worked as a political commentator with the World News Now Network. WNN, as it was known, was a cable channel viewed primarily in airports, gyms, and office lobbies. Prior to Rocco's resignation amid his sexual harassment opprobrium, evidence had been made public that implicated Fred in the governor's alleged kickback-scandal investigation. Rocco had privatized state prisons and public school bus transport in several districts in upstate New York. Fred had served on the board of directors of both the state's largest private prison contractor and the sole private school bus transport company. Corporate disclosures revealed that Fred had received six-figure salaries from both entities notwithstanding that he lacked any experience in corrections, transportation, or management.

News of Fred's involvement in the kickback-scandal investigation had largely been ignored by the media, but then he was fired from WNN following Rocco's resignation. The knockout blow to his television career had come when the state attorney general's investigation revealed Fred was working behind the scenes advising Rocco on discrediting his female accusers while routinely defending him on his nightly broadcasts.

Fred had moved to Palm Beach at the same time as his brother. After Rocco Philips was elected governor, Fred relocated to Tampa. He lived in a high-rise condominium on swanky Bayshore Boulevard and was currently in Tallahassee on business.

The final agenda on the morning meeting was a briefing of significant events over the course of the weekend. A staff report included news of six shootings in Miami, four in Orlando, and two in Tampa. All but one of the victims was Black. Four people were dead and three critically injured. One of the deceased was a six-year-old boy who had been shot through the wall of his apartment while in the bathtub.

The governor nodded, indicating that the meeting was concluded. He motioned for his brother and chief of staff to hold back. After the others had left and the door was closed, the governor began anew, "How are we doing with the RRC fundraising program?"

Fred Philips sat bearing a disinterested mien.

The chief of staff pulled out her laptop and tapped some keys, then finally said, "We're well ahead of schedule. The climate is ripe for the business community to embrace this waive of reform. The 'Silence is Complicity' social media campaign has also been effective."

"Good. Your man from the book publishing company is due, and I want the two of you to sit in on the meeting."

The phone intercom buzzed. "Governor, your eleven o'clock is here."

"Send him in."

A man dressed in a brown pinstripe suit from Haras McFadden Publishing Company walked into the office carrying a large leather briefcase. To that point, the man had dealt with Fred Philips and the chief of staff. He had never spoken with or met the governor. They had negotiated a deal with Haras McFadden to purchase three million copies of *The Equity Prism* for distribution to Florida public schools throughout the state. The representative was there to meet the governor and finalize the agreement. He walked over to the large desk and extended his hand across the other side. "Good morning, Governor. Don Duffy, Haras McFadden. It's a pleasure to meet you, sir."

The governor remained seated and held up a hand with a slight wave that portrayed mixed signals of a greeting and dispensation of a handshake. "Good morning, Mr. Duffy. It's nice to see you. What do you have for us?"

Duffy withdrew his hand, looked over at Fred Philips and the chief of staff, and nodded to them before turning back to the governor. "Your associates and I have had numerous discussions and we're prepared to move forward with the arrangement. But I'll require some confirmation from you."

The governor raised his hand again. "Let me stop you right there. This is a done deal. I have every confidence in these two people." He gestured toward the others in the room. "I was assured that you were coming here merely as a formality. I agreed to make myself available as a courtesy, not to negotiate or modify terms."

"I simply require assurance from you personally that the books will be purchased without return or refund in the event of any blowback from the local school districts."

The chief of staff intervened. "Mr. Duffy, the funds for the textbooks have been allocated in the state budget, which has been approved. The books will be distributed to the school districts. We can't guarantee they'll be utilized, but the districts have no say in the matter of payment as the funds are not coming out of their budgets."

"And what guarantee do we have that the state won't be pressured politically into demanding a refund?"

The chief of staff glanced over at the governor who was growing impatient. Fred Philips appeared as if he was about to fall asleep. She continued. "No one will be able to ascertain the source of the funding. It's buried in the budget under an unrelated Trust Fund Appropriations Bill."

Duffy seemed to accept the explanation and opened his briefcase, revealing a slightly smaller case.

The governor stood. "If you'll excuse me, I have another appointment. Please use my office to conclude your business." He exited his office by a side door.

Duffy opened the smaller briefcase. It was filled with hundred-dollar bills neatly stacked and banded.

Fred Philips snapped to attention and took possession of the case.

The chief of staff cleared her throat. "I believe you have something else for us."

Duffy took two envelopes from the pocket of the larger briefcase and handed them to the woman. "Here are the company's checks payable to the Rainbow Ribbon Coalition and the Re-Elect Rocco Philips Political Action Committee."

Hands were shaken all around, and Don Duffy exited the office carrying the same briefcase he came in with.

The governor reentered his office from the side door, took possession of the briefcase from Fred, and commented to his chief of staff, "Distribution of the books will fulfill the obligation of the RRC's education rebirth mission. Have those checks deposited in the appropriate accounts."

CHAPTER THIRTY-SEVEN

DYLAN AWOKE BEFORE SUNRISE, AND dispensing with his usual morning exercise routine, gathered fishing poles and tackle from the auxiliary garage instead. He lugged the equipment down to the dock, turned on the lights, and returned to the house where he filled a large Yeti fishing cooler with ice from the commercial machine adjacent to the outdoor living space. He iced down a smaller cooler filled with water, Gatorade, and beer, knowing his grandfather enjoyed a couple of brews while out on the water.

Once everything was loaded onto the boat, Dylan activated the electric lift and eased the Yellowfin into the water. He checked the oil and fuel levels and started the twin Mercury engines. He preferred boating on weekdays, when traffic on the intracoastal waterway was lighter. Conversely, weekends on the water reminded him of rush hour traffic on Interstate 95, replete with aggressive driving maneuvers and obscene hand gestures.

Shortly thereafter, Anthony presented himself in the backyard wearing a long-sleeve PFG performance hoodie and a camo-brimmed mesh fishing hat with several lures dangling from the sides.

"Good morning, Dylan. You ready to shove off?"

"Good morning, Grandpa. All set. I was just waiting on you."

They boarded the vessel, and Dylan eased the boat away from the dock and pointed it in the direction of the Treasure Island Bridge. From there he headed south past Isla Del Sol and into the open bay. He idled the engines and drifted just west of the Skyway Bridge. Anthony casted a net and, after several throws, pulled in a haul of threadies and greenbacks. Dylan loaded the baitfish into one of the Yellowfin's baitwells and activated the recirculating live well, then fired up the engines and headed west into the Gulf of Mexico.

Once they were about two miles offshore, Dylan dropped the anchor. They casted six lines and placed the poles in the PVC holders fastened to the stern. Within two hours, the pair had pulled in their limit of kingfish while they caught up with each other.

"How's Grandma doing?" Dylan inquired. "I haven't seen her in a while."

"She's doing fine. We really love living on the Gulf, and your grandmother's become a real beach bum with her long morning walks on the sand and sitting on the porch at night, watching the sunset. If she was a few years younger, I'd get her one of those bikini's that are so popular nowadays."

Dylan looked away and shuttered. "Please, Grandpa, don't you think those things should be reserved for women under thirty?"

Anthony hesitated for a moment. "I suppose you're right. You know, we really owe you a debt of gratitude for helping us get that place."

"Nonsense. I could never repay you and Grandma for everything you've done for me. I learned long ago that you reap what you sow."

Anthony removed his sunglasses and wiped his brow. "You're right again, Dylan."

As they loaded their haul into the cooler and headed home, Dylan told his grandfather about Alex's separation and his recent trip to Connecticut. It was still early when they arrived and Dylan hosed down the boat while Anthony cleaned and gutted the mackerel on a portable table he had set up on the dock. He cut the fish into filets and wrapped them up, leaving half for Dylan and packing the other half into a cooler to take home. Shirley had stopped at Chick-fil-A on her way to work, so the two men sat on the dock and shared a late breakfast of spicy chicken biscuits.

After Anthony left, Dylan showered and got dressed. He had an afternoon appointment with his attorneys. Driscoll Williams was a full-service law firm with offices throughout the state. The firm handled all of Dylan's real estate legal work and the Private Wealth Services department assisted with financial and tax-planning strategies.

Dylan hopped into his Ford F-150 pickup truck for the trip to the Driscoll Williams office in downtown Tampa. Shortly after crossing Tampa Bay and arriving into downtown Tampa, he pulled into the Bank of America building parking garage, took the skywalk to the lobby, and rode the elevator to the thirty-fourth floor. Driscoll Williams occupied the full thirty-fourth and thirty-fifth floors of the prestigious office building.

The receptionist welcomed Dylan warmly and offered him something to drink, which he declined. Shortly Walt Jackman appeared in the lobby. He was a tax attorney and managed the Private Wealth Services department. He led

Dylan to a conference room where they were seated with a gorgeous southwestern view of Davis Island and Tampa Bay.

Jackman opened a thick file and went over Dylan's real estate portfolio, noting that Dylan carried little debt on his holdings and many of his buildings were approaching full depreciation. He recommended consideration of a Section 1031 exchange on one of the warehouses. They also discussed the prospect of selling one of Dylan's mobile home parks to a developer and financing construction of a townhome and single-family housing development on the property. Land in Pinellas County had skyrocketed in value over the past decade. Dylan was concerned about the legal implications arising from the relocation of his tenants. He owned the land and the park's common areas, but the tenants owned their mobile homes and paid Dylan rent for the land underneath them.

Jackman also discussed additional tax-planning strategies. "Dylan, you should make some capital expenditures. The tax laws allow for accelerated depreciation on these assets this year. Have you considered buying a luxury automobile? We can title it in the business's name."

Dylan had always been fascinated with cars. As far back as a boy growing up in Connecticut, he'd always read the car magazines whenever he found himself in a grocery or variety store, yet he'd never indulged in an extravagant motor vehicle purchase. After finally getting a driver's license as a newly minted college graduate, his first car had been a Honda Accord that he'd bought in Connecticut and kept for eleven years. After that, he'd purchased the Ford pickup truck, which he still used as a daily driver. Dylan had bought the Escalade when he moved into the Park Street house, primarily as a second vehicle for those occasions when Aengus used the pickup to haul debris to the landfill or transport supplies for work on the property.

Dylan left the meeting and drove back to St. Petersburg, thinking about a car purchase. He took a detour home, pulled into the Bert Smith European Motors dealership, and drove over to the Porsche building.

Two salesmen observed as the older model Ford pickup parked in the customer area and a youthful-looking man dressed in golf shorts, T-shirt, and running shoes got out. The younger salesman looked at Dylan with a jaundiced eye and indicated to the older, experienced man that he could take this one. The older man, shrewdly, did not object.

Dylan walked around the showroom, admiring the very limited new Porsche inventory in stock. In fact, there were four vehicles. A Miami blue

Macon, a cherry metallic Panamera, and a jet-black Cayenne. But it was the last car that caught Dylan's eye: a metallic silver, loaded 911 Turbo GTS.

The salesman approached, and Dylan inquired about the car. The salesman went over the car's features and offered him a test drive. Dylan told the man it wasn't necessary and asked about the price. The salesman quoted the figure on the window sticker, and after a short exchange, they sat together in an office writing up the deal. Dylan used his American Express card to put down a deposit and made arrangements to come back the following day with a check and pick up the car.

Satisfied with himself, Dylan drove home. He was hungry and went to the refrigerator. Shirley had left for the day, but she had pulled a filet mignon from the freezer and defrosted it. Dylan found the steak in the Sub-Zero refrigerator. He also took out romaine lettuce, anchovies, Caesar dressing, and parmesan cheese. He put all the ingredients on a tray and carried it downstairs. He went outside and fired up the Viking Grill. While the grill was heating up, he mixed a Caesar salad and selected a half bottle of Duckhorn cabernet from the outdoor wine fridge. Once the steak was done, he took the food and wine over to the dining table to enjoy the beautiful sunset while he ate dinner and privately celebrated his new purchase.

CHAPTER THIRTY-EIGHT

THE FOLLOWING MORNING DYLAN WOKE up and drove to Equinox, a luxury fitness center with locations throughout the United States and in major cities in Europe and Canada. The downtown St. Petersburg location had recently opened. Although Dylan had a complete gym in his home, he joined the club because of its wide range of amenities and extensive workout options, including a basketball court. He was also a member of the nearby Vinoy Club, mainly for the dining and the golf course. Cheryl and Rick also liked the course because it was longer and more challenging than the one at Isla Del Sol.

Dylan did a weight-training workout and headed home, then showered and went down to his office. Shirley greeted him with a pile of mail and a stack of checks to sign. He told her about the Porsche and gave her the figure to prepare the check for payment. Shortly, she returned with the check drawn on the DAT business account.

"Don't forget you have the meeting with Evan Withrow tomorrow. He wants you to meet him at nine-thirty at the *Herald* building downtown."

"I remember. Also, can you let Aengus know I'm going to need a ride to the dealership this afternoon to pick up the new car?"

"Sure thing." Shirley headed back to her office, soon returning to Dylan's doorway. "Alex is on the phone."

Dylan picked up. "What's going on?"

The two friends spoke for a while until Alex got around to the reason for his call. "The divorce proceedings are going smoothly. Our case was assigned to Judge Theresa Lopes. At first I was concerned that a female judge wouldn't be good for me, but it's gone surprisingly well. She laid down the law on the first day and referred us to mediation. She all but threatened Anita and her attorneys and told them we better come back with an agreement. She implied that nothing less than fifty-fifty shared custody would be acceptable."

Dylan didn't inquire but couldn't help thinking Jackson Malloy's influence was at play. "That's great, Alex. And it sounds like it'll be good for Ben also."

"I agree. Anita's living in the house, so I've been staying with my parents. When I have him, my mom watches Ben while I'm at work. I think she's really enjoying it. Which brings me to my next point. Anita's going to have Ben for five days starting on Friday. I thought it would be a good time for me to come down for a visit, if that works for you."

"Sure."

"I'm glad you said that. I've already got my plane reservations." Alex gave Dylan his flight information and hung up.

Dylan worked in his office until almost one o'clock, then went downstairs to the kitchen and grabbed a protein bar and a Diet Coke. When he returned to his office, Shirley told him the salesman had called and the car was ready to be picked up. Dylan went outside and walked over to the auxiliary garage in search of Aengus. One of the garage doors was open, but Aengus wasn't around. After a few minutes, he descended the stairs from his apartment.

"Mr. Dylan, I hope you haven't been waiting long. I was cutting grass all morning and wanted to get cleaned up before driving you to the dealership."

"No problem, Aengus. I just got down here."

They walked back toward the house, and Aengus pulled the Escalade out of the garage.

Dylan climbed in the front seat. "Do you know where the Bert Smith dealership is?"

"Yes, sir."

It was about a fifteen-minute drive. When they arrived, Aengus insisted on waiting in the event an issue arose that prevented Dylan from driving the car home. The salesman greeted Dylan and escorted him to the office of the general manager, an overly enthusiastic fellow who warmly welcomed Dylan as a customer. The two men signed all the necessary paperwork before Dylan was handed back to the salesman. The salesman took Dylan over to the car that was parked under a covered area. The Porsche looked even better than the day before when Dylan had first seen it on the showroom floor. The salesman explained that the car had been detailed, then took Dylan through the entire car and strongly encouraged him to take a driving lesson before he left.

"This car has 550 horsepower. It's incredibly responsive, but you have to understand and respect how the PDK transmission works. Over the years, I've seen more than one customer drive one of these 911 Turbos off the lot and wrap it around a tree before making it home."

The two men spent another half hour driving the car. When they returned to the dealership, Aengus was still parked in the customer lot, waiting patiently. Dylan gave him a thumbs up, and Aengus started up the Escalade and left.

On the way home, Dylan called Cheryl. The salesman had synced the Bluetooth system to his phone and informed Dylan the car came with a complimentary one-year subscription to satellite radio.

"Hi, Mom. I was wondering if you could have dinner with me this evening."

"Dylan, your timing is impeccable. Rick's playing cards with his buddies tonight."

"Perfect. I'll pick you up at six-thirty, and we can eat on the Island. Your choice. I also have something to show you."

Dylan headed home and changed clothes, deciding to take the beach route to his mother's condo. When he got to her complex, he stopped at the security gate. Dylan was on the permanent guest-pass list and recognized the guard on duty. However, instead of waiving Dylan through as he usually did, the guard exited his small building and the gate arm remained in the down position. The guard looked inside the shiny silver Porsche.

"May I help you, sir?"

"Pat, it's me, Dylan."

The guard's look went from stern to surprised and, finally, to amiable. "Dylan. I didn't recognize you. It was the car. Nice ride!"

"Thanks, Pat. I just picked it up today. I'm going to surprise my mom."

"You certainly surprised me. Have a good evening." The guard opened the gate and waived him in.

He backed the car into a guest spot, entered the lobby, and rode the elevator to the top floor. The building did not have penthouses, but there were only four larger units on the top floor, compared with eight on all the lower levels. Cheryl's unit was 2800 square feet and had three bedrooms and three bathrooms. The rear balcony had gorgeous views of Tampa Bay and the Skyway Bridge. The front windows overlooked the golf course. After Dylan bought the condo, he'd had it renovated for Cheryl before she moved in.

Cheryl looked tan and youthful in her white golf skirt and yellow top with yellow and white sandals. She hugged and kissed her son. "You look more handsome every time I see you."

"You're just saying that because it's true."

"Aghh. Now you're starting to sound like Alex."

"Speaking of Alex, he'll be here this weekend. I know he wants to see you, so I thought I would have you and Rick and Grandma and Grandpa over to the house on Sunday afternoon."

"That sounds good. I have church on Sunday, so I'll take the day off from golf. Rick will have to get an early tee time."

"Great. I'll call Grandma now while I'm here."

Dylan called Isabella and told her about Sunday. After he finished the call, they headed down the elevator and out to the exterior parking lot. Cheryl's car was parked in the covered lot underneath the condominium building

She turned to Dylan. "I guess you're driving. I hope you brought the Escalade."

"You'll just have to wait and see."

As they walked down the lot, Dylan slipped behind Cheryl and covered her eyes.

"Hey, what are you doing?"

"You'll see." When they got to the Porsche, he pointed Cheryl toward the car and uncovered her eyes.

"Oh my gosh! Dylan, is this yours? It's gorgeous!"

"I just picked it up today. I wanted to surprise you."

"I'm so happy for you. You're such a good son, and you deserve all the success in the world." She started to cry and pulled a tissue from her small purse.

Dylan smiled while Cheryl regained her composure.

When they got in the car, she ran her hand across the dashboard and looked all around. The seats were black leather with gray suede insets. "Can people actually sit in the back?"

"Small people, maybe. Certainly not me."

They drove over the bridge to the island of Tierra Verde. Cheryl chose The Island Grill for dinner. It was a cool spring evening, so they sat outside by the pool. She ordered the island chicken with jerk sauce, and Dylan selected the grilled grouper with black beans and rice. During dinner, mother and son caught up with each other. He asked about Rick and told Cheryl about the fishing trip with Anthony. Eventually, the subject of Alex's divorce came up. Cheryl was deeply concerned about Alex and said she was praying for him. Dylan gave a brief update and assured his mother that Alex and Ben were going to be fine.

After dinner, Dylan dropped Cheryl off at home. She told him again how much she liked the car. He kissed her on the cheek and watched her enter the lobby, then decided to take the highway home. He drove past Eckerd College and onto the entrance ramp. Once he merged onto the four-lane highway, he carefully accelerated. Traffic was light so he opened up the engine and felt the turbo charger kick in, amazed at the sports car's power. He had never driven anything like it and was glad he had accepted the salesman's offer on the driving lesson.

CHAPTER THIRTY-NINE

EARLY THE NEXT MORNING, DYLAN swam laps in the pool before showering and getting dressed. He was unsure about the specifics of the day's itinerary but knew he would be walking through a printing plant. He wore black golf slacks, an ivory button-down shirt, and black Cole Haan dress sneakers. He drove the Escalade to the *Herald's* offices in downtown St. Petersburg and pulled into the small adjacent parking lot.

A security guard approached him on his driver's side. "May I help you? This is a private lot."

Dylan thought, *Is this guy offering me assistance or telling me to get lost?* He gave the guard his name and said he had a meeting with Evan Withrow.

After consulting a clipboard, the guard's demeanor underwent an instant transformation. "Mr. Tomassi. Welcome. Please take any available spot."

Dylan parked the SUV and walked toward the building's main entrance. More than one hundred years old, the *Herald* building was an eight-story structure adjacent to Tropicana Field, home of the Tampa Bay Rays baseball club. Dylan noted that the building appeared neglected and in need of freshening up. A large 'Office Space for Lease' sign was displayed on the grounds.

Dylan walked into an abandoned and sparsely furnished reception area. A sign on the front desk instructed visitors to use the adjacent phone for assistance. He picked up the receiver, and a woman's voice came on the line. He stated his business, and shortly, a casually dressed female appeared and escorted him to the elevator bank and up to the sixth floor. She led him down the hallway to a corner office with a view of the indoor baseball stadium.

Evan Withrow stood and greeted his guest. "Welcome, Dylan. Thank you so much for coming."

Dylan returned the greeting, and the two men shook hands.

Evan said, "I thought we would start with a plant tour, have lunch, and then come back and go through our news and business operations here."

"That sounds fine, sir."

They went back downstairs and outside to the lot where Dylan had parked. Evan selected one of the double-bench electric golf carts that bore the *Herald* logo on either side of the front fenders. It had a license tag and was street legal. They rode west past Tropicana Field, turned left, and continued into the midtown industrial area. The *Herald* printing plant and warehouse operations were just southwest of the baseball stadium. Evan parked the golf cart next to the main entrance in a reserved parking spot.

They entered the massive building and walked through as Evan pointed out and described the high-speed Goss Metro presses, collators, and bundling equipment. There were less people working than Dylan would have expected. However, it was clear that the employees were keenly aware of the publisher emeritus's presence.

The mailing room was located toward the back of the facility. There was a loading dock with large bay doors for shipping and receiving. A railroad track sat adjacent to the loading dock. Massive rolls of newsprint were being unloaded with heavy equipment and transported to large storage racks.

Evan noted that they no longer used flash drying ink and had reduced the use of color as part of a cost-cutting campaign. He also pointed out that the paper was now an inch and half narrower. The size reduction resulted in annual savings of two million dollars in newsprint costs.

Next, Evan escorted Dylan through an impressive data center, which appeared newer than any other section of the building, and he explained, "The data center runs all of our operations here, at the main building, and at our remote offices. In the old days, we used Linotype hot metal for typesetting. It required much more preparation time and, consequently, earlier deadlines. We've been using computer typesetting for decades now."

They continued to walk along the equipment. "This is also the nerve center for formatting and distribution of our online e-paper, which has become popular, but a significant portion of our subscribers still prefer the printed version. We're constantly updating the e-paper's content as breaking news occurs. It also allows us to maintain up-to-date weather and sports information."

As they left the data center, Dylan thought about how his hands were always covered in black ink stain residue after reading the *Herald*. He dwelled upon it further and recalled it had not been a problem back when he had first moved to Tampa.

"Well, you've seen the production facilities. Do you have any questions?"

Dylan, still unsure of the underlying reason for the visit, replied in the negative.

Evan checked his wristwatch. "Very well, let's head to lunch and then we can return to the offices. There's an editorial meeting at two-thirty that I'd like you to sit in on. I believe you'll find it of interest."

They got back into the golf cart and rode east to the St. Petersburg Yacht Club. Located on the waterfront, it was over 110 years old, and membership included the city's gentry. Several people greeted Evan as they entered and were escorted to their table.

They were seated at a small table overlooking the marina. The two men made small talk while menus were distributed and orders taken. After lunch was served, Evan took the opportunity to discuss the reason for the visit.

"Dylan, as I mentioned previously, the newspaper business is undergoing a major transformation. Prior to the emergence of the internet, newspaper advertising revenue was second only to television. Since that time, social media, online news and entertainment sites, smart phone apps, and other electronic technologies have siphoned off a substantial percentage of our ad revenue. Despite exhaustive efforts, no viable business model has emerged to replace the traditional one. Unfortunately, the problem persists and our earnings continue to shrink."

Dylan nodded in affirmation indicating he understood.

"Consequently, we have come to see ourselves as less of a traditional business and more of a local community asset. Something along the lines of a nonprofit entity, I suppose, like the theater or one of our city's fine museums. I've taken it upon myself to invite a select group to participate in assisting us with financing as a portion of their philanthropic endeavors. It is our sanguine expectation that through this funding, we can continue to serve the Tampa Bay community."

Dylan had been listening intently. Several conflicting thoughts entered his mind, but he decided he would sort those out later. In the meantime, he elected to take a polite and noncommittal position. "Well, I must admit I've never delved into the specifics of the newspaper business. But I certainly understand your point."

"I understand, Dylan. And I'm aware this opportunity isn't for everyone. I thought I would present it to you based upon your deep-rooted interest in newspapers and your success in the financial world. You're still a young man, but it's never too early to begin thinking about your legacy and your contribution to society at large."

Dylan forced himself to suppress a smile. The extent of his interest in newspapers consisted of delivering the *Stamford Advocate* as a youth and his habit of reading several daily papers. "I suppose you're right. You've given me something to think about."

"Fair enough. I believe you'll find our newsroom operations more exciting than production. Perhaps we should head back. There is much to see."

Evan signaled for the bill. He signed the check portfolio, and they headed back to the *Herald* building for what would prove to be an interesting afternoon.

Evan and Dylan toured the first-floor advertising, marketing and circulation departments, and the second-floor news operations center. Dylan noticed there was considerable vacant space on both floors. Evan explained that the third, fourth, fifth, seventh, and eighth floors were empty and recently made available for rent and the building was also for sale. The terms of the sale required the new owner to preserve the *Herald* building name and signage and lease back two floors to the newspaper at below market rates.

They went back up to the sixth floor, which held the corporate and administrative offices. Evan took Dylan to what appeared to be the main conference room. A large banner hanging on the wall above an oversized whiteboard drew Dylan's attention. It read, *PIC: PROMOTE – IGNORE – CRITIQUE.*

Dylan was flummoxed but finally, his curiosity caused him to ask, "What's the banner about?"

"That's a good question. As the newspaper business has evolved, so too has journalism. Objective journalism is an incongruous concept. It really only exists in a pure academic sense. Much like law school teaches aspiring lawyers to brief appellate cases, J-school provides a fundamental background in writing. However, both do little to prepare students for practice in the real world."

"I don't understand."

"Dylan, journalists have always written from a biased perspective. Articles are written and submitted to editors for final approval prior to publication. Editors follow the mandate of the institutional voice of a paper's editorial board. From the very beginning, newspaper content reflected the views of its owners and management team. Over time, the opinions reflected on the editorial pages blended with the daily news articles. No one has ever denied it, although the notion of the quintessential objective journalist persists and has, in varying degrees, throughout history."

"What about journalistic standards and ethics?"

"Again, I refer you back to the legal profession. Attorneys, too, have a set of ethics rules they're required to follow. The black letter rules are somewhat ambiguous and subject to interpretation. In both professions, a wide berth is permitted, and only the most egregious cases are brought to light. For example, lawyers can't steal from their clients and journalists can't knowingly and intentionally commit libel. The ethical rules are otherwise opaque."

"If you say so."

Evan belched out a hardy laugh. "Dylan, I've known you long enough now to understand you possess the character of a rugged individualist. And I admire that. I respect you enough to permit you a look behind the curtain, so to speak, as to the inner workings of our business and afford you the opportunity to participate in our endeavor."

Dylan was about to get back to asking about the PIC acronym when a group of mostly men and a few women began filing into the conference room. It was just before two-thirty. Evan introduced Dylan to the group, which represented the Herald's editorial board.

The meeting began and was run by the CEO, Emory Johnson. Dylan and Evan took seats toward the back end of the long conference table, allowing considerable space between them and the board members. Johnson went over some business and administrative matters before turning the meeting over to Lloyd Flickinger, the editor of editorials.

Flickinger connected his laptop to a small black box and a list of text appeared on the white board that read:

Leaked aerial photographs confirm existence of forced labor camps in China's Xinjiang province.

New presidential policy to curb influx of undocumented immigrants crossing US-Mexico border.

Report: Governor Philips brother's consulting company profiting from Rainbow Ribbon Coalition and insurance business.

Study: Requiring voter identification disproportionately disenfranchises minority voters.

Bank of America challenges employees, unveils 'get woke at work' campaign.

Georgia most recent state to pass law banning Critical Race Theory in schools.

Flickinger verbally went down the list as the board unanimously responded in chronological order, "Ignore. Critique. Ignore. Promote. Promote. Critique."

The meeting concluded. The board members left the room and returned to their offices.

Evan looked over at Dylan. "So what did you think?"

Dylan was baffled by what he had seen and heard in the meeting. "I'm not sure. There's a lot to digest, to be honest with you, sir."

"I agree. It's been a long day. Please, take some time to consider my proposal."

A thought suddenly occurred to Dylan. "One thing I would like to know. Who is currently participating in this program?"

"That information is confidential, Dylan, but I can say this. Participants vary from individuals to private companies, public entities, and even sovereign nations. We are in the early stages of exploring such a relationship. If you have an interest in moving forward, I'd be happy to share additional information with you."

"Fair enough, I suppose. Well, as I said, you've given me much to consider. Thank you for the tour. If you don't mind, I can show myself out."

"Certainly."

The two men shook hands, and Dylan walked casually to the elevator.

CHAPTER FORTY

THE NEXT MORNING, DYLAN WORKED out at Equinox. He observed a group of men shooting baskets as he walked by the court on his way to the weight room. One of them called out to him. "Hey, will you join us? We need one more to play full court."

Dylan hadn't played basketball in some time, but he was still in good shape. He looked at the group of mostly younger guys, everyone appearing to be fairly athletic. However, one man stood out. The guy was closer to Dylan's age and looked vaguely familiar. He was shorter but muscular, with thin legs and disproportionately large chest and arms. Dylan thought the man looked like he spent his time in the weight room bench pressing and curling, but not doing much else.

Dylan answered, "Sure, why not."

The young man that had called over to Dylan held out a hand to shake, saying, "I'm Calvin."

Calvin was slightly taller than Dylan, athletic looking with dark skin and a stylish haircut. It was short around the sides and back and faded into twists on top. He was the only Black guy in the group. Calvin indicated to Dylan they would be teammates.

The one other older guy, who looked to be in his forties, was on the opposing team. He came over and introduced himself, extending his right hand to Dylan. "My name's Fred."

Dylan took his hand, and suddenly Fred began pumping his right arm furiously in a sort of primitive intimidation ritual. It initially caught Dylan by surprise, but he squeezed down tightly on Fred's hand and was able to get his own arm under control. The two men ended up in a stare down, hands clamped together and void of arm movement, until Fred finally made an effort to let go. Dylan said nothing.

Once their hands were separated, Fred started hopping around on the balls of his feet, similar to a boxer. He then yelled out. "Alright, let's ball."

Dylan looked over at Calvin. "What's up with that guy?"

"Just Fred being Fred."

The game commenced and was even for the first ten minutes. Fred spent the entire time trash talking or yelling at his teammates. Dylan defended against one of the two opposing players over six feet tall while Calvin covered the other. One of Dylan's other teammates, defended by Fred, drained a long outside shot from the right side. As he retreated down court, the man waived his hand in Fred's direction. When Fred's team set up their half-court offense, he posted the man up and raised his arm to call for the ball. Fred received the ball, threw an elbow to the man's face, and turned and drove to the basket. Dylan left his man and cleanly blocked Fred's shot, deflecting the ball off the backboard and back onto the court.

Fred immediately began screaming in dramatic fashion. "Foul!" Then he took a step toward Dylan.

Dylan held his ground, and Calvin stepped in between them. "That's enough. Cool it, Fred."

Suddenly everyone turned and looked at the young man who had been elbowed in the face. He was bent over at the waist and blood was gushing from his mouth. It began spilling onto the court. One of the other players ran and grabbed an attendant. The attendant rushed over carrying a first aid kit, a towel, and an ice pack.

Finally, the manager showed up. He looked over the scene and addressed the group. "Alright, will someone tell me what happened here."

Fred spoke first. "It was an accident. I think he ran into my elbow." He began rubbing the back of his arm.

None of the other players spoke, so the manager responded, "Well, the game's over. We've got to get his man to a doctor and clean up the court."

Fred replied, "Great. I'm outta here." He made a dash for the exit and was gone.

Dylan looked over at Calvin. "Was that Fred being Fred too?"

"Unfortunately, yes. And he was my ride over here."

"Where do you live?"

"Over on the west side, next to the St. Pete College campus."

"Really? I live near there. I can give you a lift."

Dylan and Calvin checked on the injured man and then left. As they rode home, Dylan asked Calvin, "Are you from St. Pete?"

"No, I'm from St. Paul, actually. I'm a student at St. Pete College."

"Minnesota, really? What brings you to Florida, besides the weather?"

"I play baseball for SPC. It's the main reason I'm here."

Calvin Strother Jr. went on to explain that his father, Calvin Sr. had played in the major leagues for the Twins. The family loved the area and had stayed after he retired. Calvin Jr. was an aspiring pro ball player but wasn't drafted until the twenty-eighth round out of high school. He'd elected to enroll in junior college where he would have the option of reentering the draft the following year.

"How do you know this Fred guy?"

"He sees the girl in one of the apartments next to me. She's also a student and a real looker too. For the life of me, I don't know what she sees in him. I was talking with Fred one day. He's from Tampa and mentioned he's a member at Equinox. I told him I was too. I ran into him this morning, leaving my neighbor's apartment. Said he was going to the gym to play some hoop and asked if I wanted to come along."

Calvin's apartment complex was a neat, one-level structure with six attached units, directly across from the college campus. Dylan dropped him off in the front parking lot.

"Thanks for the ride, Dylan. Maybe I'll see you around at the gym."

"Sure thing."

Dylan drove the short distance to his house, showered, and grabbed a protein bar before heading to his office. When he got there, the morning papers were lying on his desk.

The *Herald* sat on top of the pile and the main headline jumped out at Dylan. "President's Proposed Immigration Policy Will Lockup Children, Separate Them from Parents."

Dylan shook his head in dismay. He was reading through the balance of the papers when an article in the *Wall Street Journal* caught his attention. The article stated that Paradise Technology stock trading was halted and a planned bond issue was canceled indefinitely following recent revelations about its founder and CEO, Gunner Jansen. The investment bank underwriting the bonds canceled the issue over concerns about Jansen's character.

According to the article, a video was released showing Jansen racing his classic 1969 Plymouth Roadrunner on the Paradise Automotive test track. The muscle car, powered by a 6.4-liter Hemi engine and paired with a Holley four-barrel carburetor, ran on leaded racing fuel and got five miles to the gallon.

Environmentalists were outraged and immediately began a protest that trended on Chirpster.

To add to Jansen's dilemma, one of the environmental protesters discovered a nine-year-old chirp where Jansen had posted that he preferred dogs to cats. Triggered feline lovers went on the offensive and joined the protest. The article concluded that these developments could financially cripple the fledgling electric car maker.

Shirley entered the office to tell Dylan that Alex was on the phone.

He picked up, and Alex said, "Just wanted to confirm we're all set for tomorrow?"

"Sure thing. I'll pick you up at the airport."

"Not necessary. I'll rent a car. My firm is in discussions to acquire a law firm with offices in Tampa and Palm Beach. The partners have been looking to establish a presence in Florida for some time. I have a meeting in the Tampa office and then I'll drive over. I should be there by dinner time. I'm really looking forward to kicking back and having some fun. Rochelle is constantly lecturing me about staying on the straight and narrow while the divorce is pending. We have mediation scheduled in a few weeks."

"That's not bad advice, Alex."

"You think I'm coming just to see your pretty face? No one knows me down there. To modify an expression, what happens in Florida stays in Florida."

"Easy, big fella."

"See you soon, partner." Alex hung up.

Dylan sat for a moment before calling Esther. After catching up for a few minutes, he brought up the Gunner Jansen article. "I read about Paradise Technology. What do you think?"

"Dylan, I'm glad you asked. Business should be free from emotion and umbrage. Too many wild cards are emerging from this social reform movement sweeping our nation. Sound investments must be based upon reliable information. There's no accounting for the consequences of a personal attack from some perceived offensive conduct."

"I understand." Dylan mentioned his visit to the *Herald* and meeting with Evan Withrow.

Esther replied, "Traditional media and social media platforms are the primary vehicles in the movement. It's getting increasingly difficult to dig through the hyperbole and this outrage-focused engagement strategy to locate dependable information. Are you considering his proposal?"

"Not really. What do you think?"

"First of all, I agree with Mr. Withrow that the newspaper business model is antiquated. I've heard about this contemporary newspaper funding concept. A significant number of papers have shifted to an agenda-based role rather than publishing reliable news and information. I canceled my subscription to *The New York Times* for that reason. Were you aware that the *Times* receives a hundred thousand dollars per month from the People's Republic of China?"

"No."

"It's true, the *Times* has publicly acknowledged it. But it's hardly a donation. There's clearly a quid pro quo. I went back and researched five major news stories from the past year involving objectively negative information about China. In four of the five, the *Times* failed to cover the issue. In the fifth instance, they came out with both news articles and editorials portraying China in a favorable light. When media outlets ignore a legitimate news event, it creates the illusion it didn't occur or, at the least, minimizes the significance."

Dylan told her about the *Herald's* PIC policy. "It sounds like the *Herald* is doing something similar. Evan basically told me objective journalism is a myth. Their editorial board takes sensitive news stories and either champions, criticizes, or ignores them depending on how the collective editorial body feels about the issue. I guess I never noticed it before, but since that meeting, I'm starting to look at the news differently."

"I'm not surprised they're doing that. It appears to be part of a strategy to keep newspapers relevant. Dylan, I've been meaning to discuss something else with you. After careful deliberation, I've concluded that the social reform movement has contaminated my investment evaluation strategy. Soon we should have a dialogue about alternative approaches in the current climate we find ourselves in. We should also have a conversation about philanthropy. I do agree it's something that deserves your attention."

Dylan sensed fatigue in Esther's voice. "That sounds good. I'll talk with you again soon."

After they hung up, he looked at the clock. It was barely past noon and for some reason, it felt more like midnight. He did some more work in the office before heading upstairs for a nap. In the evening, he ordered a pizza, watched a movie, and turned in early. He anticipated a busy weekend entertaining his houseguest.

CHAPTER FORTY-ONE

D YLAN WORKED THROUGH THE DAY on Friday. Around four o'clock, Shirley came by his office to see if he needed anything before she left for the weekend.

"No, I think we're all good."

"What do you have planned for Alex this weekend?" she asked conversationally.

"My family's coming over on Sunday afternoon. I'm not sure what we'll do tomorrow, and I haven't heard from him yet today. He had a meeting in Tampa and said he'd be here around dinner time."

"Okay. Well, have fun and keep him out of trouble."

Around seven o'clock, Dylan received a text message from Alex, indicating he was leaving Tampa and would be there within the hour.

A little more than an hour later, Alex arrived and buzzed the house from the front entrance. Dylan pressed some buttons on the phone and the gate rolled open. Alex drove down the long driveway, parked his car, and walked into the house looking somewhat disheveled. His black suit was rumpled, sans the necktie. His dress shirt was unbuttoned about a third of the way down.

Dylan took a good look at his friend. "What happened to you? That must've been one hell of a meeting."

"Oh, man you're not gonna believe it. Our meeting ended around three-thirty, so I decided to head over to the Candy Store."

"Huh?"

"You know, Thee Candy Store, the strip club in Tampa."

Dylan shook his head.

"What? I couldn't resist, after all Tampa is the country's strip-club capital. Anyway, I just went in to check it out and I met a girl. She's a college student and lives here in St. Petersburg, actually. She gave me her number and wants to get together."

Dylan laughed and shook his head a second time. "You met a girl in a strip club? What're the chances of that? I'm hungry. You can tell me all about it over dinner."

Dylan wanted to show Alex the new Porsche, so he pulled it out of the garage and drove to the restaurant.

After they parked, Alex closely examined the car and ran a hand along its sleek lines. "I'm proud of you. I see my taste in fine automobiles has finally rubbed off on you."

They dined at O'Bistro. Dylan hadn't eaten much all day, so he opted for the New York strip. Alex was also famished, and he chose the grilled salmon with spinach orzo. They ordered an appetizer of eggplant fries, a house specialty. Alex had a Glenfiddich single malt scotch while Dylan stuck with ice water. They shared a bottle of Picket Fence pinot noir with dinner.

Alex was still talking about the new friend he made earlier in the day. "Normally, I would just blow it off, but I really feel like we made a connection. She's studying psychology and wants to go to law school."

"Alex, let me state the obvious. First, you're still married and going through a divorce. Second, she takes off her clothes for a living."

"That's just to pay for school. She only works the day shift on Fridays when she doesn't have class. Sunni told me the money's great. She makes more in a day than most people make all week."

"Sunni? Sounds like an enterprising young lady."

"She goes by Sunshine professionally."

"What's her real name?"

"I don't know."

"Of course you don't."

Dylan shifted subjects to their families and work. He was curious about the law firm merger. Afterward, they headed back to the house. Dylan told Alex about the family get-together on Sunday. Alex was excited to see everyone. They made plans to take the wave runners out on Saturday morning and see the Lightning playoff game that night. After dinner, they headed back to Dylan's house for the night.

CHAPTER FORTY-TWO

IN AUGUST OF 1992, HURRICANE Andrew struck southeastern Florida. The category-five storm destroyed more than 63,000 homes and damaged another 125,000. The estimated cost of the damage exceeded twenty-seven billion dollars. Post-Andrew, every major Florida insurance company ceased writing homeowners' policies. Customers, many of whom had been paying premiums to the same insurer for decades, received notices of non-renewal. Politicians, regulators, and academics were acutely aware of the adverse economic effect of a lack of readily available and affordable insurance. The limited carriers willing to write policies significantly narrowed standard coverages. Animal liability, sinkhole, and, of course, hurricane wind exposure were excluded from standard policies without separate riders at additional costs. Customers who were able to purchase insurance saw increases of twenty-five to one hundred percent, depending upon their proximity to the coastline.

Over the years, the state of Florida took several measures in an effort to address the problem, including both incentivizing and sanctioning carriers to entice them to write homeowners' policies. The state even established an ill-fated, state-run insurer of last resort. Unfortunately, three decades later, no permanent solution emerged. The resurging problem was threatening to douse a red-hot Florida real estate market.

Rocco Philips, never one to let a good crisis go to waste, seized upon the opportunity. He collaborated with a group of nefarious businessmen who had established Tropical State Reinsurance Group. Tropical State was based in Barbados and entered the Florida market a few years earlier as an ostensible white knight. Tropical State offered policies to retail insurers at relatively affordable rates to cover portions of their exposure for claims caused by hurricane wind damage. The coverage, known as reinsurance, allowed the retail carriers to limit their losses in the event a major hurricane struck Florida.

A year ago, Tropical State was being audited by the Insurance Commissioner's office due to concerns about its financial condition and claims paying abilities. Governor Philips flew in the state jet to the West Indies where he met with Tropical State's principals at their offices and proposed a solution to make the audit problem go away and allow them to continue doing business. To solve the problem, Tropical State would hire Sunshine State Consulting to lobby and otherwise provide services to assist in navigating Florida's regulatory system. An agreement was reached, and, presently, Tropical State was the largest reinsurance underwriter in Florida.

Fred Philips parked his white Porsche Panamera a few blocks from the Tampa Marriott Water Street hotel. He had a meeting with Tropical State's management team, who had flown into town for the occasion. Philips was on edge and needed a pick-me-up. He rolled down the car's front windows and pulled a glass pipe from the glove compartment, placed a white rock into the bowl, and lit it. He inhaled the smoke deeply and held it in his lungs. Shortly, a euphoric feeling overcame him and he felt a burst of energy.

Philips drove up to Marriott front entrance and was greeted by a valet. "Are you checking in, sir?"

"No. I'm here for a meeting. You can park the car for me though."

"As you wish, sir."

Philips entered the hotel and took the elevator to a twenty-first floor luxury suite. He knocked on the door, and a large dark-skinned man answered wearing a yellow golf shirt embroidered with the Tropical State Reinsurance Company logo. The man had massive arms and shoulders and a neck as thick as the width of his head. He led Philips into a room where several men sat in cushioned high-back chairs at a large glass table. After announcing Philips, the large man went into an adjacent room and closed the door. Floor-to-ceiling windows on two sides of the room offered sweeping views of the Port of Tampa on one side and Tampa General Hospital at the foot of Davis Island on the other.

Philips sat down and greeted the one familiar face, the managing partner of Tropical State Reinsurance Company. "Pierre, how are you?"

Pierre Protois replied, "I'm doing well, Fred. And you?"

"I can't complain. My brother sends his regards."

"Please pass on my regards to the governor as well."

"I'll do that. He did ask me to update you on our solution to your issue with the rating companies."

Insurance rating companies, including AM Best, Moody's, and Standard & Poor's regularly posted grades on the financial condition of insurance companies. Tropical State had never been rated, and for good reason. The company's owners regularly siphoned off funds from the premiums it collected and had no intention of paying any significant claims. Furthermore, it did not have the financial ability to do so. Pursuant to the reinsurance contracts, retail carriers were responsible for covering the first portion of a wind damage claim. Tropical State provided the second layer of coverage with exposure only in the event of claims involving significant damage from a catastrophic event. In Tropical State's short history, no major storm had hit Florida. Its plan was to continue to collect premiums and ride out its lucky streak. When a major hurricane did inevitably hit, Tropical State would file bankruptcy and close up shop.

Philips continued in a choppy, hyperactive tone. "The problem's been solved. It's been made known that Tropical State is a private company with no obligation to publicly disclose its finances. After some doing, the rating companies have acquiesced. They are simply not going to issue a rating."

Pierre Protois breathed a subtle sigh of relief but otherwise maintained a poker face. "Well, you've certainly done your job." He gestured to one of the other men seated at the table who then handed over a large black case that had been sitting on the floor. Protois, in turn, handed it to Philips and watched as he placed it on the table, unlatched the two fasteners, and examined the contents of banded hundred-dollar bill stacks. Lying on top was a letter-size manila envelope.

After Philips looked up from the case, Protois explained, "You'll find two checks payable to the Rainbow Ribbon Coalition and the governor's reelection campaign. And again, I commend you on a job well done."

Philips closed the case without a reply. Of course, other than performing the task of bagman, he had absolutely nothing to do with quashing the ratings evaluations. "Well, I believe our business is concluded here. I hope you gentlemen enjoy your time in our fair state. Good day."

Philips left abruptly, briefcase in hand, went down to the hotel lobby, and called Jasmine Carter. Jasmine was a student at St. Petersburg College and a sometime girlfriend of Philips. "Hey, honey, what's up? I'm in the mood to celebrate."

"I'm kind of busy, Fred. What's the occasion?"

"I just concluded a big business deal."

"Oh, do you have a present for me?"

"Two actually. One comes in an envelope. The other's in my pants."

The young woman laughed at the crude reply. "Well, I guess I can make time. Can you come over now?"

"I'm in downtown Tampa. I can probably be there within the hour."

"I'll be waiting."

CHAPTER FORTY-THREE

Dylan woke up Sunday morning a little later than usual. The Lightning game had gone into double overtime before they scored the winning goal against the Boston Bruins. With traffic from the sold-out event at Amelie Arena in downtown Tampa, they didn't get home until well after midnight. The quietness inside the house indicated Alex was still asleep.

Dylan ran down the road to the bakery and picked up some bagels for breakfast along with Chicago hard rolls and frankfurter-style buns. He came home, ate a plain bagel, and checked on the provisions for the cookout. Shirley had prepared Italian beef using boneless chuck roast and placed it in a large, covered baking pan with peppers and onions. It just required heating up. He also had beef bratwurst to cook on the outdoor grill. Isabella was bringing her famous Fettucine Alfredo.

Alex rolled out of bed well after nine o'clock. "Great game last night. I think the Lightning are going to win the Stanley Cup."

"I hope you're right."

Alex munched on a bagel and then said he was going for a swim. After hitting the pool, he sat in a lounge chair talking on his cell phone for a fair amount of time.

Dylan walked outside as he was completing his call. "Who was that?"

"Sunni. I think I woke her up. She seemed concerned about school. The summer session is starting, and she doesn't have the money she needs for tuition."

"I thought you said she cleans up working at the Candy Store."

"She said it's been a little slow. You know she has to pay just to work there. Anyway, we made plans to go to the beach tomorrow."

They went back into the house and Dylan headed to the kitchen to double check everything was ready for the get-together while Alex showered and changed. Once Dylan was satisfied all was in order, he went upstairs to get ready.

Dylan's grandparents arrived first. They greeted Alex warmly. Isabella wanted to come over early and help Dylan. Soon she had commandeered the kitchen and shooed the men away so Alex and Anthony went outside to have a beer and talk. Dylan hung back to keep his grandmother company and help in the unlikely event she required assistance.

"When the two men were alone, Anthony asked, "How's Ben doing? With the divorce and all?"

"He's great. I get him half the time. My mother helps care for him while I'm at work. I get him back on Wednesday, so I'll be flying home Tuesday afternoon."

"You know, Alex, all's fair in love, war, and divorce. I recall the investigator who assisted Cheryl and me with her stalker was top shelf. Perhaps he can help with the divorce if he's still around."

"I appreciate your concern. Trust me, I'm confident everything's going to work out."

Anthony decided to let it go. The subject changed and the two men talked sports.

Isabella and Dylan made their way outside and shortly thereafter, Cheryl and Rick arrived. Appropriate greetings were exchanged all around. Cheryl and Alex embraced, holding her at arm's length a moment longer, he said, "It's so good to see you, Mrs. T. You know, it's strangely pleasant calling you that. And you look amazing, all fit and tan."

Cheryl laughed. "I get it. After all those years of calling me Mrs. McD."

Dylan took charge and accepted drink orders. Cheryl and Isabella drank white wine while the men stuck with beer. Anthony and Rick talked fishing. Rick had a sixteen-foot Boston Whaler with an outboard Yamaha engine. He lived in a condominium complex down the street from Cheryl. He'd purchased the unit, specifically because it came with a boat lift. Rick was a seasoned seaman from his Coast Guard career. He and Anthony regularly fished together.

While they enjoyed their drinks, Cheryl and Isabella peppered Alex with questions about Ben and his divorce. Alex assured them Ben was doing great and that everything would work out fine. Dylan stood by and listened for a time, then excused himself and went back up to the kitchen. He loaded all the food onto a cart, took it down the elevator and wheeled it out into the back yard. He grilled the brats while Isabella heated up the trays of food in the outdoor pizza oven. The sun was over the water, but it was comfortable under the covered living space. Dylan made plans to take Cheryl and Rick to the Vinoy for a round of golf later in the week after Alex left. The conversation was lively, and everyone ate, drank, and laughed. Just after dark, the guests said their goodbyes and departed.

CHAPTER FORTY-FOUR

O N Monday morning, Dylan went down to his gym. After a vigorous workout, he came back upstairs and found Alex in the kitchen drinking coffee. Dylan grabbed a bottled water and joined him.

"What's on the agenda for today?" Dylan asked.

"I'm going to the beach with Sunni."

"Oh yeah, that's right. Sounds really romantic," Dylan replied with a heavy dose of sarcasm.

"Come on. We're just going to the beach. What do you have today?"

"I've got to meet with the manager of one of the mobile home parks and then I have a meeting with a group of developers who are looking to build condos on Indian Rocks Beach."

"When will you be back?"

"In time for dinner. We can go to the Vinoy since it's your last night in town."

"Sounds like a plan."

Dylan went upstairs to shower.

Alex borrowed Dylan's office for a conference call with his firm back in New York to report on Friday's meeting.

Dylan checked in with Shirley before leaving, then stuck his head into his own office and waived to Alex who was still on the phone. "Don't get sunburned, Romeo," he mouthed.

After the phone conference, Alex checked his messages and returned some calls. A little after ten o'clock, he put on a bathing suit and a long-sleeve swim shirt with SPF 50 protection. He slipped on some flip-flops, stopped off to say goodbye to Shirley, and headed out.

Pulling up his phone's navigation system app, he keyed in Sunni's address. The map indicated it was a short four-minute drive. He was surprised by how close she lived to Dylan's exclusive neighborhood. Then again, Florida's relaxed zoning laws created some interesting neighborhood dynamics. It wasn't unusual to see a rundown beach hut with overgrown landscaping directly next door to a sparkling new McMansion with meticulously maintained grounds.

Alex pulled into Sunni's apartment complex and knocked on her door. She answered almost immediately and invited Alex inside. He looked around the apartment. It was an open layout with a modern kitchen at one end and living area closest to the front door. It was a one-bedroom unit. Sunni apparently did not have a roommate.

It was the first time Alex had seen her outside of the club. She looked the same but somewhat softer in a bathing suit and cover up. She was a striking beauty with sharp features and big, brown eyes highlighted with thick lashes. Her mocha skin and long, dark hair contrasted beautifully with the white crochet-trimmed cover up.

Sunni sat down on the couch and looked at Alex.

He remained standing. "Are you ready to go?" he asked.

She furrowed her brow and extended her bottom lip. "I'm still worried about my tuition. I may have to drop out of school."

"How much do you need?"

Without hesitation, she replied, "Five hundred dollars."

Alex reached into his pocket and peeled off five-hundred-dollar bills.

Sunni jumped up off the couch and into his arms, wrapped her arms and legs around him, and let out an enthusiastic yell. "Oh, Alex, you're a lifesaver." She kissed him on the mouth before grabbing the money and running off into her bedroom. She returned a moment later. "Now I'm ready for the beach."

When they got outside, she hopped enthusiastically into the front seat of his rented Mustang GT convertible. "Nice car. Can we put the top down?"

"Sure. Anything you want, sweetheart." Alex undid the two front latches holding the soft top in place against the windshield frame and pressed a button. The top folded down automatically into a space behind the passenger seat. "Do you want me to roll the windows down too?"

"Sure." She grinned, leaned into Alex, and placed her hand on his leg during the short drive to the beach on Treasure Island.

Alex parked the car in the municipal lot. When they got down to the sand, he rented a cabana with two lounge chairs and a small table. They made small talk for a while under the privacy of the cabana.

Sunni indicated she was going to walk down to the water and removed her cover up, revealing a small white bikini. The young woman had a beautiful athletic body with square shoulders that tapered down to a small waist. What appeared to Alex to be a real diamond was set in her naval. The swimsuit concealed her voluptuous breasts without leaving too much to the imagination. The bottom was another story. It barely covered her firm bubble-shaped backside. Alex sat up, removed his sunglasses, and enjoyed the view, watching with great pleasure as she frolicked about in the water before returning to the cabana.

Alex asked her if she wanted something to drink, and she requested a wine cooler. He walked back to the concession stand and purchased her drink and a can of Corona for himself. After they consumed their drinks, it was almost noon. He asked Sunni if she was hungry. She indicated in the affirmative, so they packed up their things and walked over to the BRGR Bar and Grill. The elevated, outdoor seating area offered a beautiful view of the Gulf of Mexico. They ate lunch, and Sunni had two glasses of Moscato. Alex nursed another beer.

After lunch, they drove back to her apartment. As soon as they entered, Sunni took Alex by the hand and led him to the bathroom. They shed their beachwear and showered together, exploring each other's bodies. Sunni had silver bar piercings through her nipples and was completely shaved between her legs. They moved to the bed where she cheerfully accommodated each of Alex's carnal requests.

Afterward, Alex drove back to Dylan's house contentedly fatigued. He went up to his room and took a nap. After waking up, he showered and went down to Dylan's office. Shirley indicated Dylan was on his way home and he used the phone to check in with his office.

Dylan pulled his pickup truck into the driveway, relieved to see Alex's rental car. *He couldn't have gotten into too much trouble,* he thought. Inside, he found Alex in the living room reading the *Wall Street Journal.* "So how was the beach?" he asked.

"Very relaxing. Just what the doctor ordered."

"And how was Sunni?"

"Very fine, thank you."

Dylan decided to leave it at that. "I'm gonna take a shower and change. Then we can head downtown to the Vinoy. Help yourself to a drink at the bar."

"Don't mind if I do." Alex poured himself a Laphroaig and sipped the drink while he waited.

Shortly, Dylan came down dressed and ready to go.

"My flight doesn't leave until midafternoon tomorrow and it's my last night here. Why don't we hit the town and celebrate? We can take an Uber, so we don't have to worry about driving."

Dylan considered for a moment. "Sure, why not."

He called Aengus and arranged for a ride downtown in a half hour. Then he went down to the wine room and selected a bottle of 2015 Chimney Rock cabernet. He opened the bottle and poured two glasses. Handing one to Alex, he raised his. "To the final chapter of a successful trip."

They toasted and enjoyed the wine, and Dylan refilled their glasses. Looking over at Alex, he said, "You know, I've been thinking about starting a charitable organization."

"Really, Dylan? That's very admirable."

"Yeah. A recent opportunity has made me think more about giving back and leaving a legacy."

"You're not sick or dying, are you?"

Dylan laughed. "Of course not. I've been very fortunate. Now it's my turn to help others and do some good in the world."

"I should think about that too. We have a family foundation, and Malloy Williamson donates substantial sums to charity every year. I need to get more involved with that."

"Well, I wanted you to know. I haven't told many people, and I'm planning on keeping it under wraps until I can work out the specifics."

"Good for you. If you need any help or want to talk to my dad, we have a director of charitable giving who oversees the family foundation and corporate philanthropy."

"Thanks, Alex. I'll let you know. I'm making this project a priority."

They finished their wine and went downstairs. Aengus had the Escalade parked out front, and Dylan and Alex climbed into the back. They drove across town, and Aengus pulled into the Vinoy's front entrance. Dylan told him to head home and he would call when they needed to be picked up.

They dined in the Vinoy Club Grill, which was reserved exclusively for club members. The Vinoy's other restaurants and bars were open to hotel guests and the general public. Dylan and Alex both ordered the scallops with risotto and shared a bottle of Austin Hope cabernet.

After dinner, they walked along Beach Drive and people watched. Downtown St. Petersburg was abuzz. It had become more popular than Tampa's entertainment district in Ybor City, offering world-class dining, bars, and a wide selection of breweries, distilleries, and entertainment venues. They turned onto Central Avenue and headed west toward midtown, stopping in for a drink at Mastry's, an iconic bar dating back to the days when the New York Yankees trained in St. Petersburg. They sat at the bar.

Dylan knew the bartender and greeted her by name. She was the owner's girlfriend and a talented artist and photographer. "PW, how are you?"

"I'm fine, Dylan. It's nice to see you. Who's your friend?"

Dylan introduced Alex, and they both ordered Pabst Blue Ribbon. Dylan pointed out some of the memorabilia on the walls and explained that the Yankees biggest stars had hung out at Mastry's back in the day, including Babe Ruth, Mickey Mantle, and Billy Martin.

After they finished their beers, they continued walking down Central Avenue and into midtown. The streets and businesses were filled with people. It appeared that midtown was even busier than downtown. They ended up at Ferg's Sports Bar, which was located across the street from Tropicana Field. The Rays were playing in Chicago, but the bar was packed. All the big screen TVs were tuned to either the Rays or the Lightning playoff game.

Ferg's was a large, multi-level disjointed structure composed of several indoor and outdoor areas. Dylan and Alex found the last two seats at the very end of one of the interior bars and decided to stick with PBR. Alex was sitting in the last chair when a young women tried to squeeze in and grab the bartender's attention. She leaned over Alex, her light brown hair grazing his arm as she looked up at him with her beautiful blue eyes. She had a prominent nose and sported a deep tan, accented by a white, ribbed half-shirt with spaghetti straps, fashionably torn jeans, and sandals.

Alex smiled in her direction and pounced. "Here let me help you." He raised his hand and immediately drew over the female bartender. "Can you please assist my friend here. She appears to be thirsty and in need of hydration."

The bartender laughed and took the women's order. She could spot a generous tipper a mile away and was betting on Alex. The woman placed her order, requesting three drinks Alex had never heard of.

He replied, "Wow, you really are parched!"

The woman chuckled.

"I can't officially represent you as a friend without a proper introduction. I'm Alex."

The woman extended a well-manicured hand, and Alex shook it gingerly, holding on for an extra moment.

"I'm Tiffany. And thanks for helping me. It's mobbed in here. This is the third bar I've tried to order drinks at."

"Well, stick with me and all your problems will be solved."

"Well, aren't you the smooth talker."

"Actually, I'm quite shy and don't get out much. I'm visiting my friend here." He nodded his chin in Dylan's direction. "I'm from Connecticut. He dragged me out tonight. The guy's an insufferable party animal."

Dylan had sat silently during the exchange, alternating his attention between the hockey game while stealing glances at Alex's act. Shortly, three tall glasses of various bright hues garnished with assorted fruits and vegetables appeared.

Alex asked how much and handed the bartender two bills that represented an amount in excess of fifty percent of the charge. "Keep the change." Then he turned back to Tiffany and asked which of the three drinks sitting on the bar was hers.

She pointed to the bright red one with the orange garnish. "That one."

"What's in it?"

"It's called a Firing Squad. It has tequila, lime juice, orange bitters, and strawberry puree."

Alex handed her the drink and picked up the two others. "Let's get these to your friends."

Alex and Tiffany disappeared into the crowd.

Dylan had to fend off two different guys and a woman who attempted to occupy Alex's seat in his absence.

Alex was gone for a while before reappearing with Tiffany and her two friends and made the introductions. "Dylan, this is Katie and Doreen. This is Dylan."

They all exchanged greetings, and Alex offered Tiffany his seat.

Dylan awkwardly asked the other two women if one of them wished to sit. They both declined, but he got up and reluctantly surrendered his seat to Alex.

The group became acquainted, and Dylan spoke politely with the other two women while Alex locked in on Tiffany. Dylan learned that Doreen worked as a mental health counselor and was pursuing a master's degree at the University of South Florida. Katie, who appeared the oldest and least stylish, was married and had an eighteen-month-old son. Her husband was watching the baby so she could enjoy a rare night out with her girlfriends. Dylan wasn't interested romantically in Doreen, so he kept the conversation casual, consciously including Katie in the dialogue.

Alex turned to the bartender and ordered another round. The three women looked at each other before announcing they were going to the restroom. After the women departed, Alex asked Dylan, "You having fun, buddy?"

"Of course. Watching you in action is always quality entertainment."

"I really like Tiffany's look. Plus, she's a court reporter. Every court reporter I've ever been with has been, how shall I say it, *passionate*."

"Alex, has it ever occurred to you that court reporters are attracted to lawyers the way nurses are attracted to doctors?"

"That's a sexist thing to say."

"It's not sexist at all. There are plenty of male and female doctors and lawyers. The same goes for nurses."

"What about court reporters?"

Dylan broke into a victorious grin. "You've got me there, but you also just made my point."

The fresh drinks arrived and shortly thereafter the women returned. Dylan alternated his attention between the hockey game and small talk with Doreen and Katie while Alex and Tiffany continued their tete a' tete. Finally, Katie indicated she needed to get home to her infant son. Looks were exchanged before Tiffany advised her friends that Alex would take her home. The revelation drew a mild grimace from Dylan. After the two women left, Alex ordered another round. Dylan was feeling good from the consistent imbibing, so he didn't object.

The Lightning game had ended earlier. The Rays game, being played in the Midwest, also concluded and the crowd began to thin out. Dylan called Aengus and asked him to pick them up at Ferg's.

Dylan looked over at the newly infatuated couple. "Our ride's on the way."

Alex explained that Tiffany lived in an apartment complex around the corner and he was going to walk her home.

Dylan, privately hoping Alex was going to call it a night, said he would meet him out in front of the bar. Tiffany and Alex promptly departed. Shortly thereafter, Dylan finished his drink and left to wait outside for Aengus.

Surprisingly and to Dylan's relief, Alex showed up before Aengus. He loved him like a brother but keeping tabs on Alex was exhausting.

Alex strolled up. "Is Aengus on his way?"

"Should be here any minute."

"Great. So what'd you think?"

"About what?"

"Tiffany? She's a nice girl."

"She seemed nice. You know, Alex. I'm proud of you for exercising some restraint."

"Whadda ya mean?"

"You know what I mean. You took that young woman home, and by all accounts, appeared to act like a perfect gentleman."

"Don't lose faith in me, buddy. I'm just a little tired. It's been a long day. Don't worry though, I got her number. Never know when I'm going to require the services of a well-qualified court reporter."

Dylan laughed and just then, Aengus pulled up. It was quiet on the ride back home. They were both well lubricated and stared out their respective windows, each lost in his own thoughts.

CHAPTER FORTY-FIVE

A LEX LEFT FOR THE AIRPORT the next day, and Dylan went to his office. He checked his messages and read the papers. The *Herald* had run a front-page article reporting that Florida's largest school board issued a formal declaration that any opposition to its new agenda represented a public crisis. The board enacted measures to combat any comment that ran counter to its position. The article went on to discuss the merits of Critical Race Theory and was optimistic the declaration could serve as a statewide model.

Since his visit to the *Herald* and discussions with Esther, Dylan had begun reading the papers with a more critical eye. It appeared to him that the proposed school board action amounted to censorship and quelled free speech. He put down the local paper and began reading the *Wall Street Journal*, which carried a major article announcing that Paradise Technologies was up for sale. Increasing public pressure had mounted for Gunner Jansen to resign following revelations of his driving habits and preference for canines. In response to the widespread negative publicity, federal regulators had suspended Paradise Energy's application for approval to begin production of its new battery recharging system. The article discussed a prospective sale and the leading candidates to acquire the company. It also included an interview with Jansen.

Jansen stated he was selling the company in lieu of stepping down. He'd developed the revolutionary battery technology and apoplectically refused to transfer it into the hands of others. Accordingly, any sale included Paradise Automotive Company and the assets of Paradise Energy, but he was retaining possession and control of the proprietary battery technology. Jansen didn't squander the opportunity to push back at his critics. He lashed out at the widespread indoctrination of college students and the resultant difficulty in hiring productive workers. He concluded by announcing plans to spend his time writing, painting, and meditating on his 160-acre ranch in Idaho and then signed off with, "Woof, woof!"

Dylan called Esther and waited for her to come on the line, then steered the conversation to the news about Paradise Technologies.

Of course, Esther had heard the announcement. "Dylan, this weaponized outrage is a real threat. Not just to the economy but to society at large. We have to remain optimistic but also take steps to protect our business interests. We must also do our part to contribute to the greater good. My family fled Nazi Germany when I was a young girl. Over time, I came to understand how a totalitarian regime comes into power. Unfortunately, I see significant parallels with the movement unfolding in our country."

"I understand. I've never been politically active, but these outside influences never seemed to affect me personally until recently. I'm starting to think differently about things."

"I, too, am apolitical, although I have always voted because I believe it's an important civic responsibility. Today our country is deeply divided. People historically engaged in debate but, regardless of political affiliation, at the end of the day respected each other and understood basic right from wrong. This conflict has left people acrimonious and closed-minded, spewing vitriol toward everyone who disagrees with them."

"So what do we do?"

"Dylan, I'm an old woman. I've made the decision to dispense with my long-term investment strategy in favor of a more asset-preservation approach. I've reviewed my portfolio and am in the process of systematically selling off a significant amount of stock. I will retain a portion of my core holdings."

"What's your new strategy?"

"I'm moving the proceeds into cash, treasuries, and a series of ETFs that invest in broad market indexes. Institutional investors, supercomputer algorithms, and amateur groups organizing through internet forums are disproportionately affecting the markets. Add to that the consequences of this movement we've been discussing, and all these forces combined with a fragile investor psyche have led me to the decision."

"I understand your decision to liquidate a large chunk of your assets, but what are the advantages of broad-based market indexes?"

"I maintain my faith in the United States and the market economy. Investing in index funds offers an assortment of stocks in a particular sector. For example, the Fortune 500 or Russell 2000. In addition to diversification, index funds are less expensive and enjoy favorable tax treatment. It reduces volatility compared with an individual company's susceptibility to the adverse effects of outside actions. It's frightening to me how a social media mob can bring down a company and destroy its market value."

"I see.

"Please understand, I'm not suggesting you follow my plan. I do think it would be wise for you to suspend individual stock purchases, reduce some of your holdings, and consider index investing. But you are also younger, with a considerably longer time horizon. You also built a successful commercial real estate company. Hard assets remain good investments. You may also want to consider a small position in precious metals."

They talked a little longer about their revised business plans before Dylan changed the subject. "I've thought about what you said regarding philanthropy. I'm going to start a nonprofit organization."

"I'm proud of you, Dylan. Taking meaningful action to contribute to the betterment of society is a noble endeavor. Have you thought about which causes you're going to support?"

Dylan explained his vision as Esther listened intently. When he was finished, Esther commented, "I think that's wonderful. You have some excellent ideas."

CHAPTER FORTY-SIX

T HERE ARE TWO OPTIONS FOR obtaining a liquor license in Florida: purchase one from an existing license holder or apply for a new one through an annual state lottery where one new license is granted per county for every 7,500 increase in population. Typically, about fifty new liquor licenses, referred to as quota licenses, are awarded each year. The lottery system is utilized to fairly distribute the quota licenses into the marketplace. The application fee is one hundred dollars per entry and an individual or business may submit one entry per county. Applications are accepted annually during a specified forty-five-day period. Approximately, 24,000 entries are submitted each year. A quota license awarded through the lottery could be used anywhere in the county where zoning laws allow for the sale and distribution of alcohol. They are a valuable commodity, ranging in value from $450,000 to $600,000. Lottery winners typically turn around and sell their licenses on the secondary market.

While Rocco Philips conducted a staff meeting, an aid reported that a police officer had shot a ninety-five-year-old World War II veteran.

The governor perked up. "What are the details?"

The aid read from his report. "A nursing home resident in Fort Lauderdale began acting unruly over a dispute during a bingo game. The police were called and one of the responding officers shot the man five times with a beanbag gun."

"Was the victim Black?"

"No, sir. The man was White. The police officer was Black though."

"Oh. That'll be all ladies and gentlemen. You're dismissed."

After the room cleared out, the governor met with his chief of staff. Darcie DeLuca was a petite woman with shoulder-length red hair. A graduate of

Vassar, she'd become interested in politics after interning for Senator Hillary Clinton during her first year in office. DeLuca had moved to Florida during the great New York migration.

"I need four liquor licenses to distribute to my constituents in south Florida."

"But, sir, the quota license system's been in place for half a century. This year's licenses are set to be issued next week. How are we going to get around that?"

"Here are the names of the people who need licenses. Go see Dan Rowley now and figure it out. He owes me." Philips had appointed Rowley to secretary of the Florida Department of Business & Professional Regulation last year after his predecessor resigned in what she cited in her letter of resignation were "philosophical differences." In reality, after a business trip with Philips, she'd learned of her fate for rebuffing the governor's crude drunken advances

She furrowed her brow as she gathered up her belongings. "Yes, sir."

Later that afternoon, the chief of staff returned to the governor's office and popped her head in the door. "Just wanted to let you know we figured out a way to have those liquor licenses issued."

The governor looked up, his face void of expression. "Good job. When they're ready, bring them to me."

The quota license lottery was held the following week and forty-nine winner names were released on the DBPR website the next day. Actually, fifty-three licenses were issued. The additional four were not considered quota licenses although they'd been born on the same day as the others. Darcie DeLuca promptly delivered the licenses to Philips.

"Nice work. Were you able to get my brother on the line?"

"I haven't been able to reach him. I'll put him through as soon as I contact him."

Fred Philips drove over to St. Petersburg unannounced to see Jasmine Carter. When she wasn't home, he'd driven over to Thirty-Fourth Street and cruised the strip between Tenth Avenues North and South.

Eventually he found what he was looking for. A thin woman in bike shorts, a tube top, and high-top Converse walking south on the east side of Thirty-Fourth Street attempted to make eye contact with each passing motorist. Heading north, Philips waved to the woman and pulled into a nearby paint store parking lot. She casually walked up to the driver's side of the Porsche Panamera and a conversation ensued.

Soon she was in Philips's car as he drove them to nearby Jamestown Park. On the way, he stopped at a convenience store. When they arrived at the empty park, he pulled behind a building. He and his new friend smoked crack and drank the thirty-two-ounce beers he'd bought at the store. After imbibing, the woman buried her face in Philips's lap. After some time, she lifted up her head, took a big swig of beer, and swallowed hard. She then opened the car door and began walking back in the direction of Thirty-Fourth Street.

Philips had fallen asleep in the car when the buzzing of his phone finally woke him. He checked the screen, seeing that the familiar Tallahassee number had called three times and left a text message. It read "call when U get this, UR bro is pissed."

Fred Philips called the number and was immediately put through to the governor. Rocco Philips sounded unusually terse as he explained to his brother a package was being sent overnight for him to take to Miami. The governor provided the location of the meeting with instructions to deliver the package in exchange for a briefcase with familiar contents, then stated a figure and told him to count it before he handed over the package.

CHAPTER FORTY-SEVEN

D YLAN SPENT THE WEEK REVIEWING his investment portfolio and going over DAT's financial statements. He had called his attorneys office and held a long conversation with Walt Jackman. After discussing his ideas, Dylan requested that Jackman put a plan together.

A week later on a Friday, Dylan traveled to Tampa to meet with his attorneys. Upon entering the lobby of the Driscoll Williams' offices, he was promptly greeted by Walt Jackman.

"Dylan, it's nice to see you. We've made substantial progress on your new project over the course of the week. Come, we have much to discuss." Jackman led Dylan to the familiar conference room.

A woman dressed in a sharp blue pinstripe business suit stood at the front of the room. Tall and attractive, her light brown hair was pulled back and she wore fashionable glasses that highlighted her facial features. Three younger people, two women and a man, sat around the front of the conference table. They appeared to be legal assistants or young attorneys. Coffee, ice water, and small trays of vanilla cruffins and croissants were set out on the table.

Walt Jackman made the introductions. The woman standing was Ann Hefner, a partner and the head of the firm's Nonprofit and Tax-Exempt Organizations department. The two women seated at the table were an associate attorney and a legal secretary. The man was a paralegal. Dylan and Walt sat down, and Ann Hefner began her presentation.

Using a PowerPoint display, she started with an overview of the department and then explained the scope of the various services they provided, from formation of a new nonprofit entity to assistance with navigating ever changing IRS tax and governance issues. A list of current clients appeared on the screen, including prominent names in the fields of education, healthcare, private foundations, religious organizations, and trade and professional associations.

Next, the presentation turned to Dylan's project. A name appeared in bold, blue letters across the screen: The Tomassi Family Charitable Foundation. Dylan was handed a leather-bound booklet, which covered in detail the information being presented.

Ann continued with an overview of the initial IRS filing requirements and the necessary disclosures for maintaining tax-exempt status. Next, she discussed the specific design of the Tomassi Foundation with a proposed budget for funding requirements and administrative expenses, creation of a board of directors, and finally, a mission statement and proposed plan for distributing annual income consistent with the charitable mission.

When Ann concluded, the group looked at Dylan for a reaction.

Dylan leaned forward, his hands folded on the table in front of him. "Thank you. You've done a nice job in a short period of time, and I appreciate your diligence. I'm ready to move forward on this."

Ann looked over and smiled earnestly. "Thank you for your confidence in us. I've taken the liberty of preparing the necessary engagement paperwork. Of course, you certainly may have it reviewed by outside counsel."

Dylan turned to Walt Jackman. "Walt, have you reviewed the paperwork?"

"I have."

"Then I'll sign everything now so we can get started."

Dylan signed the paperwork, then watched as the secretary placed copies of the paperwork and the leather-bound booklet in a separate folder. The formal Tomassi Foundation name was printed across the blue folder in reverse white print. Dylan shook hands with everyone in the room, thanked them, and headed home. He had a lot of work to do.

Dylan arrived back at the house by midafternoon and went down to Shirley's office. "Do you have some time?" he asked from her doorway.

Shirley removed her reading glasses and looked up from her paperwork. "Sure, I was just looking over proposals for the work that needs to be done at the Sundown Mobile Home Park. What's up?"

"Please come down to my office."

Shirley got up and followed Dylan next door. He entered his office and sat on the couch, indicating to Shirley to take one of the chairs across from him.

Dylan asked her, "How's everything going?"

"Everything's fine, Dylan. I should ask you the same question. You've been acting kind of different all week. Like your mind's not in its usual place."

"Actually, I've never been better. It's just occurred to me that I've never given you a formal review."

Shirley burst out laughing. It took her a moment to gather herself before she replied, "I've known you for twenty years and we've worked together the entire time, going back to the brokerage house. If you don't mind my asking, why do you want to conduct a review now?"

"It's time for your vicennial review."

Shirley chuckled again. "Did you just make that word up?"

"Actually no. It's really a word."

"Okay. Whatever's going on with you, I'll play along."

"Do you like working here?"

"I hope you know I do. Let me be frank. You're a wonderful man and a pleasure to work for. Coming over here from the job in Tampa has allowed me to be there more for my son and improved the quality of my life in general."

"I'm glad to hear that. How's Ronnie doing?"

"He's great. He'll graduate from USF next year. I'm so proud of him."

"Has he decided what he wants to do?"

"He's working this summer for an engineering firm that does a lot of forensic work. He seems to like it and thinks they like him. He may get a job offer at the end of the summer."

"That's great. You've done a good job raising him."

"Thank you, Dylan."

"How do you feel about your workload here?"

"Honestly, it's very manageable. I would describe it as consistent but not overwhelming."

"Do you think you could take on more responsibility?"

"Sure I could. But what else would there be for me to do?"

"I'm starting another venture." Dylan sat back and launched into his vision for the Tomassi Family Charitable Foundation. He talked about his childhood growing up without a father and how he wanted to help other young people in ways others had helped him. Then he offered Shirley the position of administrator of the Tomassi Foundation.

Tears welled up in her eyes. She jumped up and hugged Dylan. "I'm so proud of you. It would be an honor to assist you with the foundation."

"It's going to be a lot of extra work. How does a fifty percent raise sound?"

Shirley, already pleasantly surprised, became overwhelmed with emotions that brought more tears.

Dylan went over to the small fridge in his office and got her a bottle of water. When he could see she had regained her composure, he continued. "We'll have to move some figures around because, technically, you'll be receiving two paychecks. One from my businesses and another from the foundation. We'll continue to work from here for now. I'm going to ask my mother, Alex, and Walt Jackman to serve as board members."

Shirley took a sip of her water, and they talked in more detail about the plans for the foundation. After she had finished her water, Dylan excused himself for a moment. He went down to the wine room and returned with a bottle of Krug Grande Cuvee and two flutes. He popped the cork, poured the bubbly, and handed a glass to Shirley.

Raising his glass, Dylan said, "To a successful new venture."

CHAPTER FORTY-EIGHT

THE FED EX PACKAGE ARRIVED the next morning, and Fred Philips called his contact in south Florida and arranged to meet the next day. Not feeling like driving, he booked a same day, round-trip flight from Tampa to Miami International Airport, leaving at nine in the morning and returning by four in the afternoon.

The American Airlines flight to Miami was unremarkable. Upon arrival, he rented a car and drove a half an hour to Peacock Park in Coconut Grove. Parking the car, he looked at his watch. It was close to the lunch hour, but he was about fifteen minutes early.

He called Jasmine Carter. "What're you doing?"

"Nothing, but I have a problem." Jasmine always seemed to have a problem, and it typically involved money.

"What is it this time?"

"My rent is due, and I'm short this month."

Philips knew from previous experience how much this was going to cost him. "I suppose you want me to help you out."

"Would you? You're such a sweetheart." Jasmine often got what she wanted from Philips through dissimulation, but he was too narcissistic to notice.

"It's going to cost you. I'll be flying back from Miami this afternoon and then you and I are going to get together at your place."

"Whatever you say, Fred. See you soon."

Philips hung up the phone as a black Mercedes Maybach GLS 600 pulled into the lot three spaces from his. There were no other cars parked in the immediate area. He had heard about the new Maybach SUV but never seen one.

A slightly built man emerged from the back seat and walked over dressed in standard Miami business attire of tailored tan slacks, a bold-pattern dress shirt, and brown leather shoes sans socks. Philips rolled down his window, and the man walked up to his car, maintaining a short distance. The man appeared harmless, but that was not the case with the driver. The SUV's back windows were blacked out, but Philips could see through the front. The view of the driver from the chest up presented an image of a large and imposing figure.

The man said authoritatively, "Fred Philips."

"That's me."

"I believe you have a package for me."

"And I believe you have something for me."

The man turned and gestured to the driver who disembarked from the vehicle with a large, brown case. Philips's initial impression of the man was confirmed. He had strikingly pasty skin, a crew cut, no neck, and broad, muscular shoulders that melded into his chest. The man was wearing a guayabera shirt, and the sleeves were bursting at their seams. Philips could not tell whether it was concealing a handgun and wondered how the man remained so pale in the unyielding Miami sun.

The pale gorilla handed the briefcase to the other man who in turn handed it to Philips.

Philips accepted the briefcase. "My instructions were to count it."

"Certainly." The man waited patiently while Philips opened the case filled with banded stacks of hundred-dollar bills.

Philips thumbed through the stacks and counted down and across, doing some basic math in his head. He closed the case and set it on the passenger seat, reasoning that the guy wouldn't be foolish enough to shortchange his brother.

Philips handed the man an envelope from inside the Fed Ex package.

The man accepted the envelope without bothering to check the contents. "Pleasure doing business with you. Give my regards to the governor." He then turned and walked back to the SUV.

The pale gorilla held the rear door open for the man before firing up the ignition and driving off.

Fred Philips watched as they left and was smitten with the vehicle. He made a mental note to check one out. His return flight was on time, and he had no problem getting the case through security at the Miami Airport. There was no legal limit on how much cash a person could carry on a domestic flight, and Philips had a story ready in the event TSA inquired. They did not.

After he landed in Tampa, he called Jasmine. "I'm on my way. Do you have any booze in the house?"

"No."

"Okay. I gotta make a stop. I'll be there in an hour or so depending on traffic."

When Philips retrieved his car from the airport short term parking lot, he opened the brown case and pulled a handful of one-hundred-dollar bills from a stack, then locked the case in the trunk of his car. He left the airport and headed to St. Petersburg. Traffic moved surprisingly well along southbound Interstate 275 except for a short bottle neck near the Park Boulevard intersection. He stopped along the way and picked up a bottle of Hennessy. He arrived at Jasmine's apartment carrying the bottle of liquor and his laptop computer.

Jasmine greeted him warmly. "Do you have my rent money? I want to get that out of the way so we can enjoy ourselves. You know how I worry about those things."

I know how obsessed you are with asking for money, Philips thought as he peeled off several bills from the stack he'd borrowed from the briefcase and handed them to her.

Jasmine excused herself and went into another room, then returned shortly with a sudden change in demeanor.

Philips sat down at the kitchen table and fired up his crack pipe. Jasmine poured herself a glass of the cognac Philips had brought and sipped as she waited for him to finish imbibing. After the drug had taken its desired effect, he led her to the bedroom. "Take off your clothes and lie on the bed."

Jasmine complied and began to undress while Philips set up his laptop on an adjacent dresser and activated the camera. She spread her naked body across the bed, leaning on her right arm and facing the camera, smiling while Philips adjusted the angle.

"What's with the computer?"

"You and I are gonna make a movie." Philips undressed and joined her on the bed. He posed for the camera in a bizarre series of flexing positions before turning his attention to Jasmine. He executed the multiple roles of director, producer, and costar, and his female costar was adept at taking direction.

After the production was complete, Philips went back into the kitchen and watched the movie while consuming multiple glasses of Hennessy. He outwardly expressed his pleasure with the quality of the feature film. Eventually, he staggered over to the couch, laid down, and was soon in a catatonic state.

Jasmine paced about quietly, fretting over the video. She was uncomfortable performing sex acts on tape and certainly didn't want the movie distributed. He had promised her it was just for his personal use, but his assurances failed to instill confidence in her.

She knew she couldn't delete the video. Philips would be livid, and she had learned from prior experience that he had a volatile temperament. After agonizing over the matter for some time, she slipped the laptop into an empty kitchen drawer. He could be absent minded, and when he woke up from his drug and alcohol induced stupor, there was a good chance he would leave the computer behind. After that, she would swear he had taken it with him when he left. He would then embark on an unsuccessful wild-goose chase and the problem would be solved.

CHAPTER FORTY-NINE

T HE FOLLOWING WEEK, DYLAN CALLED his mother and made a dinner date to share "some exciting news." Next, he called Walt Jackman and invited him to serve on the board. Finally, he typed a letter to Evan Withrow.

Dear Evan,

Thank you for the tour of the *Herald's* operations. After much consideration, I must respectfully decline to accept the offer you extended. However, I want you to know that our meeting caused me to do much soul searching and I am pleased to announce that I have recently established the Tomassi Family Charitable Foundation. I am aware of your impressive history supporting several charities which benefit disadvantaged youth and I hope that we may be able to collaborate on such an endeavor in the future.

Your friend and neighbor,

Dylan Tomassi

Dylan called Alex and told him about what had transpired with the foundation they had discussed on prior occasions. He asked Alex to serve on the board of directors, and he readily accepted. Dylan indicated he planned to travel up to Connecticut on foundation business in the near future. Alex shared the news that his firm had purchased the Florida law firm he had met with on his recent trip. They had agreement in principle and the details were being worked out. Scheduled to close next month, Alex would be spending more time in Florida assisting with the transition.

Dylan congratulated Alex and asked about Ben and the divorce proceedings.

"Ben is doing well," Alex replied. "The temporary joint-custody agreement is working out nicely. Anita and I have put our differences aside, at least as it pertains to Ben. Mediation is scheduled for next month."

"That's good news. I still have some stuff to get settled down here with the foundation. I'll let you know as soon as I have the dates for my trip up north."

They hung up.

Dylan thought about calling Penel but decided to hold off until his trip was scheduled. The next evening, he met Cheryl for dinner at the Vinoy and after they were seated in the Grill, he broke the news to her. "Mom, I've made the decision to start a charitable foundation. It's still in the early stages, but the focus is going to be on helping underprivileged kids. I've got my lawyers working on getting everything set up."

"Dylan, that's wonderful. I'm so proud of you. What made you decide to do this now?"

"Another opportunity came up and caused me to do some thinking. I've been very fortunate and decided it was time to start giving back. And I'd like you to serve on the board of directors."

"Oh, Dylan, I would be honored. And if you find you need more help with things day-to-day, I'd be happy to assist you with that."

"I appreciate that, Mom. There's going to be a lot of work to do, especially to get things up and running. Shirley has already agreed to serve as the administrator. I expect to hire several additional people and put together a volunteer staff."

Dinner was served, and they spent another two hours discussing the details.

Ann Hefner and her team managed the legal work required to get the foundation up and running, keeping Dylan regularly posted on their progress. Walt Jackman agreed to serve on the board, and he and Dylan established a tax-favorable plan to transfer assets from Dylan's business and personal accounts to fund the foundation.

Shirley became engrossed in her new administrator role. She set up a computer program to handle the foundation's various business functions and opened new bank accounts, ordered stationary, and launched the foundation website.

Over the next several weeks, Dylan was engrossed with investigating projects consistent with the foundation's mission. He had very specific ideas in mind and embarked upon a detailed plan to bring his vision to fruition. Having grown up in a single-parent household where money was a constant concern, he understood the importance of having devoted and loving surrogates in his life to help him develop good habits and avoid potentially destructive distractions. He also firmly believed that competitive athletics provided invaluable life lessons in responsibility, teamwork, and time management. He planned to establish a youth center in St. Petersburg as the foundation's centerpiece. The facility would be geographically located to serve underprivileged and minority youth from the city's southside. The physical requirements for the proposed center included a property with a main building, indoor athletic center, and outdoor athletic fields. The center would provide after school tutoring, athletic activities, and access to a state-of-the-art entertainment venue with the primary goal of providing children a safe setting where they could study, engage in recreational activities, and develop productive habits away from negative influences on the tough city streets. The center's staff, comprised of employees and volunteers, would serve as mentors. The facility would also function as the headquarters for organized athletic programs, fielding teams in basketball, volleyball, baseball, and softball that would compete in regional and state tournaments.

Dylan was familiar with a property located in midtown, south of Tropicana Field, that was currently enclosed with an eight-foot chain link fence topped with razor wire. The facility included three buildings in various stages of decay and two unidentifiable athletic fields engulfed in weeds. It had once been owned and operated by the city as a park and recreation center before being sold to a developer more than a decade ago. After the developer defaulted on the loans, the banks had repossessed the property and let it sit in its current state of disrepair since that time.

Dylan had instructed Walt Jackman to locate the current owners and research any encumbrances on the property. After approaching the owners, Walt advised Dylan they were willing to sell, and Dylan authorized him to begin negotiations and leverage the nonprofit foundation's mission to negotiate the best deal. In the meantime, he received permission to enter the property with his architect and contractor to evaluate the facilities and obtain estimates on the renovation costs.

Feeling his parochial school education had provided him with a solid academic background and instilled a strong moral code, Dylan's second phase involved providing academic scholarships. He scheduled a meeting with Monsignor Scully, the head of St. Gregory's parish. He knew Dylan from the time he served on the parish finance committee and also knew Cheryl and was familiar with their family background. They discussed the proposed scholarship idea, and Dylan requested a tour of the school with an opportunity to audit several classes. He had studied the recent, trending radical change to school curriculum and dogma and believed that a race-obsessed doctrine perpetrated divisiveness. It casted shame, vitiated relationships, and created a culture of victimization. He wanted assurance that the St. Gregory school program was consistent with the foundation's mission and not caught up in that trend.

While spending time in the classroom and meeting with teachers and administrators, Dylan reviewed textbooks and observed in action the school's fundamental principles that emphasized reading, writing, and math skills while teaching individual responsibility, integrity, and respect for others. Courses discussed major issues in an objective and respectful manner. Dark periods in United States' history, including slavery and segregation, the stock market crash and Great Depression, the bombing of Japan and internment camps during World War II, and 9/11, were openly discussed. Healthy discourse was encouraged. Students were never chastised for asking questions or challenging alternative points of view.

After completing his due diligence, Dylan reconvened with Monsignor Scully and presented his plan to set up an endowment that would provide full scholarships for underprivileged children. Initially, two scholarships would be granted for transfer students in each class from first through eighth grades. Thereafter, two additional scholarships would be awarded each year to new incoming kindergarten and first-grade students. The scholarships would be renewable annually provided the students met academic standards and adhered to the school's code of conduct.

Monsignor Scully was most appreciative and readily accepted the plan, saying, "Dylan, this is a fine example of the Christian spirit needed in the world today."

Dylan agreed to present his proposal to the St. Gregory finance committee for final approval at the next meeting.

Dylan heard back from Walt Jackman. The bank had accepted his most recent offer on the property and the firm's real estate department was drawing up the contract. Due diligence on the property would be considerable. In addition to environmental studies, variance and zoning reviews, and a traffic analysis, historical and archaeological studies were required. The Tampa Bay area had recently experienced issues where several old burial grounds had been discovered underneath properties being redeveloped.

Dylan hired commercial contractor, Kellogg CCS, to oversee the renovations. Dylan and their president, Gregg Thomas, had a long history of working together on resort hotel and retail building projects. Dylan instructed him to move forward with the final architectural plans for the center.

Next, he contacted St. Mary School in Stamford. It had been more than thirty years since he had graduated from there and more than twenty since Cheryl had left her teaching job. Dylan looked up the principal's name on the school website. According to her bio, Rebecca O'Brien held undergraduate and master's degrees from Boston College and had served in the role for the past ten years. Notably, she had spearheaded the development project that raised the funds for renovation of the old school building and construction of a new addition that had been completed four years ago. After introducing himself to Principal O'Brien, he stated he was an alumnus and explained that his mother had taught there for more than twenty years. He told her about the foundation and that he wished to visit the school in person to discuss a donation. She described the school's recent construction project and the state-of-the-art technological changes designed to enhance the student learning experience. Rebecca O'Brien possessed an engaging personality, and she insisted that Dylan call her Becky. He could see why she was an effective fundraiser. He made plans to meet with her and tour the school the following week.

Dylan asked Shirley to book his flight to New York and reserve a suite at the Greenwich Delamar. Satisfied with the progress of the foundation's work in Florida after a frenetic month, he planned to spend four days in Connecticut. He'd fly up on Monday, visit St. Mary's on Tuesday, and after taking care of foundation business, he would have two days to visit with Alex and Esther and see Penel.

After completing his travel plans, Dylan tried Penel's cell phone, which went straight to voicemail. Next, he called her office and the woman who answered the phone advised she was in a client conference and offered to take a message.

On the Friday morning before his trip, he decided to work out at Equinox. Passing through the gymnasium on his way to the weight room, he heard a ruckus break out on the basketball court and looked over at the half-court game in progress. He saw the same muscle-bound oaf who had caused a brouhaha the last time and heard the guy whining and complaining incessantly about being fouled while the others stood around silently shaking their heads.

Moving on, Dylan completed his workout and headed home. As he was driving west on First Avenue North, he observed a white Porsche Panamera weaving recklessly through the three lanes of traffic. He caught up to the Panamera at a red light at the Thirty-Fourth Street intersection and pulled up next to the driver's side but couldn't see inside due to the dark tinted windows. When the light changed, the Panamera found itself boxed in by slow-moving traffic. Dylan arrived at the next red light at Forty-Ninth Street well ahead of the Porsche. Looking in his rearview mirror, he saw a white sports car bearing down on him. There was no way it was going to be able to stop without crashing into the rear of his SUV. At the last minute, the Panamera swerved right, drove onto the shoulder, and ran through the light just missing several cars that had entered the intersection from Forty-Ninth Street.

Dylan got home, showered, and went to the kitchen. He mixed crushed ice, almond milk, vanilla yogurt, a banana, and chocolate protein powder in the blender, then poured the concoction into a large cup and walked down to his office. Since starting the foundation, his workload had increased dramatically. He studied some investment opportunities, moved some funds around, reviewed a pile of paperwork from DAT, and signed a stack of checks.

Shirley buzzed his desk phone to let him know Penel was on the phone, and he picked up.

"Hi, Dylan. I'm sorry it took me so long to get back to you. I've been swamped at work."

He recalled Penel describing her strict criteria for accepting cases and had been under the impression that the selective process resulted in a manageable workload.

She continued. "I have back-to-back trials scheduled, which rarely happens. Most of my cases settle."

"I understand." He explained the reason for his call, telling her about the foundation and his trip the following week to meet with a potential donee and extended an invitation for them to get together.

She responded somewhat tepidly, "Wow, Dylan, that's a very admirable thing you're doing. I'm slammed right now at work. Can we play it by ear?"

"Certainly. I'll be arriving on Monday and leaving Thursday. Why don't you see how things go with your trials? If you get some free time, call and let me know. I can rearrange my schedule around yours."

"Dylan, you're such a sweetheart. Thanks for understanding." She disconnected the call before he could say another word.

Fred Philips arrived at Jasmine Carter's apartment around midmorning. She had just gotten out of bed and was in the shower. He joined her. They spent time under the water soaping and massaging each other, paying particular attention to specific areas of their respective anatomies. Afterward, they got dressed and Jasmine packed a duffel bag.

"You're giving me a ride to work, right?" she asked.

"No problem. I'm on my way home. By the way, Jaz, have you seen my laptop? I may have left it here."

She looked at him innocently. "It's not here. I specifically remember you took it with you when you left the last time."

Philips didn't reply and nothing else was said on the subject.

CHAPTER FIFTY

S INCE LEAVING FLORIDA FOR THE White House, the president of the
United States had become disgusted with the downward spiral of his
beloved home state. The progress made by his administration during his two
terms as governor in the areas of education, election reform, and economic
opportunity were being emasculated by the current administration. Increased
violent crime was rampant in the major cities, and the state was mired in an
economic downturn with record unemployment, particularly among minority
groups. Tourism had plummeted after multiple incidents of vacationers being
robbed and murdered in Orlando and south Florida. Several state employees
and elected officials had contacted the president with their concerns, so he'd
asked the FBI deputy director, a trusted colleague, to monitor the situation and
provide him with periodic updates. The president held a closed-door meeting in
the Oval Office with the deputy director of the FBI.

He reported to the president, "We're concerned about the legitimacy of the
Rainbow Ribbon Coalition. It's set up as a 501(c)3 and has raised millions of
dollars from individual and business donors. It appears to be a shell company
that does nothing more than hand out paraphernalia and promote a public
awareness campaign. We've been unable to identify any specific projects or
major expenditures funded through the organization. The distribution of that
textbook to the school boards we thought may have been financed by the RRC
turned out to be a dead end."

"Do you have evidence of any improprieties that amount to a federal
crime?"

"We have our suspicions, but nothing substantial enough to take to the attorney general at this time."

"Stay on it then and keep me advised of any significant developments."

"Yes, sir."

After Dylan's flight arrived at LaGuardia airport at midafternoon on Monday, he rented a car and drove to Greenwich. It was prior to the rush hour so he made good time. After checking in to his suite at the Delamar, he called Alex who told him he had Ben with him for an extra day because Anita claimed she had some sort of emergency. Dylan didn't want to disturb their father-and-son time together, so he spent the afternoon and evening at his hotel. He ordered room service and read a book before turning in.

In the morning, Dylan drove to St. Mary School and met with Becca O'Brien. Things at the school had changed dramatically since he'd moved to Florida. The school was set back on a twelve-acre plot in a wooded section of suburban Stamford, and in Dylan's time, the church had been separately located downtown. About ten years ago, the Diocese of Bridgeport had sold the downtown church property and used the proceeds to build a new church on vacant land in front of the school building.

Dylan arrived at the school offices, located in the front of the remodeled building, announced himself, and was buzzed in. He was about to have a seat in the lobby when Becca O'Brien came out and greeted him warmly. She was a pleasant-looking woman in a navy-blue dress and black heels, appearing to be around Dylan's age.

Becca took Dylan through the old school building first. Classes were in session, so they spoke in the hallways before standing silently in the back of each classroom they entered. When the pair initially walked in, students and teachers looked over before promptly focusing back on their studies. Schools in Florida were already out for the summer break. This was the last full week of school for St. Mary, and there was no evidence of summer fever.

Dylan noticed that the classrooms were larger and more modern than back in his day. He also observed that the school uniforms had changed. In his days, boys wore blue pants, dress shirts, and blue ties, and girls wore plaid jumpers over Peter Pan collar blouses. Students had been required to wear dress shoes except when participating in physical education classes or at recess. Today, boys wore khaki pants and blue polo shirts embroidered with the St. Mary School logo, and girls wore the same shirts and a choice of khakis or a skirt. All the students now wore sneakers or casual rubber-soled shoes.

Becca explained that renovation of the existing building first involved expanding the square footage. Internal walls were removed so that the new, larger classrooms occupied two of the old ones and the administrative offices underwent a makeover. The cramped teachers' lounge was gone, replaced by individual offices where teachers could meet with students individually or in small groups. All classrooms were wired to provide state-of-the-art technology, including high-speed internet and smart boards, and every room had separate boys' and girls' restrooms. Each student was issued an iPad, onto which was downloaded the school calendar, textbooks, and class assignments. Homework and other projects were input into the iPad and submitted electronically.

The additional classrooms in the new building were set up similarly to the renovated, old section. The architect had done a nice job of designing the exteriors so that the two structures blended seamlessly. The new building also included a large center with a full industrial kitchen that served as a cafeteria during school days and could also be used as an auditorium.

Finally, Becca took Dylan over to the gymnasium. It remained in the same condition as back in Dylan's day. The entire space was covered in a gleaming hardwood floor marked with basketball lines. Backboards and hoops extended from the steel rafters at either end. A raised stage with a dark-blue curtain pulled across the front sat at the opposite end. On one side was a small locker room with two shower stalls. Basketball was a highly popular and competitive sport among Fairfield County parochial schools, and St. Mary also had a longstanding reputation for putting on an annual student musical production that rivaled a Broadway quality play.

Finally, they went outside to the back of the property. The entire rear section was surrounded by woods beyond two full-size basketball courts and a tennis court on the asphalt portion and a multipurpose ball field and separate field for soccer, lacrosse, and field hockey at the extreme back of the property, both well-manicured.

After the tour, Becca escorted Dylan back to her office. Her desk was in the back of the room with two chairs situated in front. Off to one side was a conference table and chairs with a smart board on the wall. A series of windows on the other side provided a view of the church.

Becca sat behind her desk and explained that the school had recently undergone recertification and its blue-ribbon, exemplary status had been renewed by the US Department of Education. Dylan asked questions about the curriculum and textbooks, privately noting that there had appeared to be a fair number of students of color. He inquired about the current tuition and the number of children who received financial aid.

Becca patiently answered all his questions, then went on to discuss the national trend of shuttering Catholic schools and proudly stated that St. Mary was at ninety-eight percent capacity with a waiting list for several grades. She explained that a US Conference of Catholic Bishops mandate required all schools to be financially independent. Tuition covered approximately sixty percent of the total costs, and the difference was made up from the school endowment and annual fundraising efforts.

"The school buildings are very impressive. I noticed the gym is the same as when I was a student," Dylan noted.

Becca pointed to a framed blueprint on the wall. "We have the plans to build a new field house complete with a basketball court, retractable spectator seating, and two locker rooms. Also included is a separate wing with a theater to include modern backstage operations, and stadium-style seating. It'll be used for theater productions and student assemblies. We ran out of money and had to cut something out because the diocese doesn't allow us to borrow money to fund construction projects."

"May I have a copy of the school's annual budget and the estimate for construction of the new field house?"

Becca leaned back in her chair with her hands loosely gripped around the end of the armrests. "Dylan, I appreciate you coming to visit and your interest in our school. Alumni as well as parents of existing students provide the vast majority of the funds required to keep us operating in a fiscally healthy manner. I'd be happy to provide the information. However, before we proceed, I'll need some additional information from you as well."

"I understand." Dylan took a thick folder from his bag and placed it on her side of the desk. It contained literature about the foundation's mission, copies of its financial statements including a balance sheet and first year budget, computer images of the proposed St. Petersburg youth center, and a summary of the bequests to St. Gregory School. "These are for your records. I understand that the foundation was recently launched, so I took the liberty of bringing my personal financial statements. You may review them, but I'm unable to leave copies." He handed over a second folder, which held his personal financial statement and personal and business tax returns for the past three years and copies of balance sheets for Lott Investment Advisors and DAT Real Estate Holdings.

Becca leaned over her desk and reviewed the files while Dylan sat patiently and looked around the room, eventually settling on the view outside her office windows. She finally returned the second folder to him, her face void of any expression that betrayed her thoughts. She spun around in her chair and pulled some papers from the credenza. "Here are the documents you requested."

Dylan flipped through them. "Thank you for providing these. Would you also provide me a list of the textbooks used in all of the classes?"

"I could have that put together from our computer files and have it emailed to you by the end of the day."

"That would be fine. I'm going to meet with the foundation's board when I return to Florida. Then I'll be back in touch with you."

After they said their goodbyes and thanked each other again for the respective opportunities, Dylan returned to his hotel and called Alex about plans for that evening. They agreed to go back to the Elm Street Oyster House because Dylan had really enjoyed the place on his last visit. He collapsed on the bed and fell asleep.

An hour and a half later, Dylan woke to his phone buzzing on the nightstand. He reached for the phone, looked at the screen, and then answered, "Hello, Penel."

"Dylan, how are you? How was your trip?" she replied with a noticeable difference in the tone of her voice.

"I'm fine. I had a productive meeting today. How are you doing?"

"I couldn't be better. I felt tremendous pressure with those two trials set for the same time. One was continued yesterday, and the second just settled. I suddenly have an open calendar."

"Maybe I can help you with that. How about spending tomorrow afternoon and evening with me?"

"That would be wonderful. Where are you staying?"

"I'm at the Greenwich Delamar."

"What would you like to do?"

Dylan thought quickly. "It's supposed to be a nice day tomorrow. Why don't you come up here? We can take a boat ride on Long Island Sound and have dinner. Stay the night, and I'll drive you back Thursday on my way to the airport."

"That sounds perfect. I'll take the train and be there tomorrow around lunchtime."

"Perfect. Text me when you're on the way. I'll meet you at the station."

They hung up, and Dylan contacted the hotel concierge. The concierge arranged a boat rental to be delivered to the hotel marina by noon the following day. Dylan also arranged for a cooler of drinks and snacks for the trip and then tipped the young concierge generously.

After making the arrangements, he jumped in the shower, suddenly finding himself in a contented mood.

CHAPTER FIFTY-ONE

O N Monday morning, the Florida governor received his daily briefing. Two days earlier, a twenty-three-year-old Black man had been shot by a security guard during an attempted robbery at a high-end jewelry store in Delray Beach. The guard was an off-duty Palm Beach County Sheriff's deputy working private security, and the young man had walked into the store and pulled a Browning 9 mm from his waistband. He was to be charged with armed robbery but died the next morning at Delray Medical Center. The story had not received much press coverage, and there had been no public reaction.

Upon hearing the news, the governor perked up. He demanded information on the deceased man's family and ordered up the state jet for a flight to the Palm Beach Airport. He had his press secretary alert all major state and national news outlets of a press conference scheduled for the following afternoon at the Black Lives Matter offices in Palm Beach County.

The following day, a large crowd gathered. Throngs of newspaper and television outlets crammed into the front section reserved for media. Many in the diverse crowd held signs supporting BLM and the Rainbow Ribbon Coalition. Others carried signs or wore shirts bearing "Rocco-sexual" and "Italian Stallion."

The governor delivered one of his patented, fiery speeches that began by calling out the systemic oppression suffered by Black people at the hands of law enforcement. He expressed his empathy, comparing the discrimination suffered by his immigrant ancestors, and called for a national rejuvenation on action against widespread police corruption and violence toward people of color. After working the crowd into a frenzy, he challenged people to revoke their White privilege and support his criminal justice reforms by donating to the Rainbow Ribbon Coalition. Two large screens on either side of the dais set up to broadcast the speech displayed the RRC website. The governor concluded to a now raucous crowd, "This is my truth! If you're not with me, then you're a racist!"

The governor's security detail whisked him out a side door, and his motorcade made a bee line for the airport. The story of the police shooting of a Black man in Florida was all over the state and national news. That evening, there were video images of riots and looting throughout Palm Beach County and all major Florida cities. Donations to the Rainbow Ribbon Coalition set a single-day record.

Dylan woke up the next morning and worked out in the hotel fitness center. The previous evening, he and Alex had enjoyed another good dinner at the Elm Street Oyster House. During dinner, Alex had informed Dylan that he was due back in Tampa on Monday for meetings at the new law firm. He was flying in on Friday afternoon to spend the weekend at Dylan's house before moving to a Tampa hotel on Monday.

After his work out, Dylan went back to his room and showered and dressed in a stylish orange and white swimsuit, long-sleeve white swim shirt, and water shoes he'd purchased in the hotel gift shop. He had not planned on going out on the water when he packed. He ate a protein bar while he read the newspapers on his iPad. The *Herald* front-page headline grabbed his attention. "Police Shoot and Kill Black Man, Sparking Mostly Peaceful Protests." The article discussed how the shooting at a Delray Beach jewelry store was the most recent example of systemic police racism and proliferated the growing distrust between law enforcement and the Black community. It went on to laud the prompt response from the governor. Conspicuously absent in the story were any details about the actual shooting.

A national business paper also covered the story. The writer took an antithetical approach, laying out the facts of the attempted armed robbery and included a comment from the young man's mother. The woman tearfully discussed her son's mental health issues and violent past and asked the community for peace and to pray for her family. She encouraged people to engage in meaningful discussions on racial issues. The writer concluded by raising the question of whether the governor's conduct amounted to race-baiting.

The article turned out to be an outlier. The vast majority of news outlets that covered the story omitted the mother's comments. The prevalent theme was the emergence of Governor Rocco Philips as a rising star on the national political scene.

After he finished reading the papers, Dylan called Shirley. They discussed business that required his immediate attention. At the conclusion of the call, he dialed Esther's number and told her he was in town for a few days on foundation business and apologized for not being able to stop by and see her.

They talked for a while on a variety of subjects before Esther brought up the protests in Florida. "It's all over the news. There were images of people destroying police cars, starting fires, and looting businesses. What was it like in St. Petersburg?"

"I'm not sure. I've been up here the last few days. I did see the video of protesters interrupting people dining on Beach Drive. One protester sat right down at an elderly couple's outdoor table and ate their food."

"I didn't see that. What did the couple do?"

"The old guy just ordered another drink. The woman was pretty upset though."

"You know, Dylan, just last weekend in Chicago, sixty-five people were shot. Almost all the victims were Black and several were children."

"I wasn't aware of that."

"Most people aren't because it wasn't widely reported."

"I don't understand. These protests are in support of saving Black lives."

"The difference seems to be in who the perpetrators are. Most of the Chicago victims were shot by other Black people. None were shot by police."

"I have a hard time understanding this movement. The whole approach appears divisive. What's the purpose of categorizing people based on the color of their skin and either shaming or victimizing them? When I was growing up, sports were a big part of my life. My teammates were Black, White, and Hispanic, but we never saw color and it never defined who we were. We were out to compete and win as a unit. If you got close with certain teammates, it was because of their personality and character. And if you had a problem with someone, it was for the same reasons."

"I understand that, Dylan. Unfortunately, sports seem to be politicized by race today as much as any other segment of society."

"Well, I believe the solution lies with young people. Underprivileged children should learn that poverty is as much a state of mind as anything. I grew up in a household where money was scarce, but we never felt or acted poor. There are plenty of opportunities for people who are willing to work hard, regardless of their background. That's why all the foundation programs will provide opportunities for the underprivileged. And I expect that a sizable portion of the scholarships will be awarded to children of color."

"That's a very good thing you're doing, Dylan. You can't change the world by yourself, but it's a good start. And you're setting an excellent example."

After he hung up with Esther just before noon, Dylan walked down to the marina to check on the boat. It was a warm, sunny day. He introduced himself to the dockmaster, who then led him to a gleaming blue and white, nineteen-foot Sea Ray bow rider. The craft was powered by a single Mercury outboard. The dockmaster took him through the boat and handed him the keys. Dylan signed some papers and handed the man a twenty-dollar bill.

He went back to the concierge desk and checked on the provisions. There were two soft-sided coolers. One contained water, Gatorade, and small bottles of champagne for Penel. Dylan did not drink while operating a boat. A separate cooler bag held cheese, crackers, and assorted cut fruit, along with plastic champagne glasses, paper plates, and napkins. He took the two coolers and a stack of hotel beach towels down to the boat and loaded them into the large rear storage compartment. As soon as he was finished, he received a text from Penel. Her train was fifteen minutes out.

Dylan worked his way to the valet and requested his car. It was a five-minute drive from the hotel to the train station, and he arrived shortly before Penel. He walked over to the platform and waited for the inbound train from Grand Central Station. Departing passenger traffic was light on the afternoon weekday. Penel emerged carrying the same large Louis Vuitton shoulder bag she'd brought with her on the last trip.

As soon as she saw Dylan, she ran over, dropped her bag, and jumped into his arms. She hugged and kissed him. "It's so good to see you. It's been too long."

Dylan held her at arm's length and gave her the once over. She was wearing a multi-blue-striped cover-up dress, and a royal blue bikini peeked out from underneath. "It's nice to see you too. You appear a lot more relaxed than when we spoke last week."

"You're very perceptive. I get real wound up while preparing for trial."

"Perhaps I can help you relieve some of that built up tension."

"I'm counting on it."

Dylan grabbed her bag and hoisted it over his left shoulder, then held Penel's hand with his right. He led her to the parking lot and popped the trunk on the white Audi A6 rental. Shirley usually rented comfortable American sedans for Dylan, so he figured her recent selections had something to do with

Penel. They drove back to the hotel and left her bag with the bellman, requesting that he deliver it to their suite. Then they headed down to the marina.

Dylan helped Penel aboard and showed her around. She sat on one of the built-in seats in the bow while he started the engine and navigated the boat out of Greenwich Harbor. Once they were out on Long Island Sound, he pushed the throttle forward and opened up the 150-horsepower engine. They cruised a comfortable distance from the shore, keeping the coastline in sight. She shed her coverall and sprawled out in her bikini, taking in the sun.

Dylan found a secluded spot with no other boats in sight, cut the engine, and dropped the anchor. He went aft to the stern and jumped off the swim platform and into the cool water. It was early summer, and the water temperature was invigorating. Penel joined him, and they swam for a while before climbing back aboard.

Dylan opened the storage compartment and produced the two coolers. He poured Penel champagne in a plastic glass and got himself a bottled water. She spread out the snacks, and they ate lightly. Afterward, she cleaned up while he pulled up and stored the anchor. He started the engine, and they cruised slowly back in the direction of Greenwich Harbor. On the way back, she sat in the seat next to Dylan and they talked. The new foundation dominated the conversation. She was interested and asked a lot of questions.

They got back to the marina in late afternoon. A crew member immediately took their line and assisted Dylan with docking and tying down the boat. They gathered up their belongings and headed back to their suite. He showered first while Penel unpacked. Next it was her turn. She took a garment bag and a case containing cosmetics and toiletries and commandeered the bathroom.

While she was getting ready, Dylan called down to L'Escale and booked a table in the hotel restaurant. He dressed in tan slacks, a white dress shirt, and tan loafers. After considerable time, she emerged from the bathroom looking stunning with her hair down and her color enhanced by the day's sun. She wore an off-the-shoulders, purple-knit dress with tan high heels. Dylan could hardly contain himself.

They went down to the restaurant, and the maître d' led them to their table. As they walked through the dining room, other patrons turned to sneak a glimpse of the tall, handsome couple. They were seated at an indoor table overlooking the harbor.

Penel looked at the drink menu and settled on a Treasure of the Sierra Madre, a house specialty consisting of rum, amaro, and orange bitters. Dylan stuck with ice water and requested a wine menu. Deferring to Penel's taste, he ordered a bottle of Sequoia Grove chardonnay. They shared a mixed salad with a port wine glaze, and both selected the salmon for dinner. Skipping dessert, they took a short walk along the harbor. They held hands and began kissing lightly. Dylan led her back to the hotel and up to their room where they attacked each other ravenously as soon as the door closed behind them. To his surprise, Penel was not wearing underwear. She was more adventurous than ever, constantly changing positions and offering herself in ways Dylan had not previously experienced. They exhausted themselves, took a short break, and started in again.

They finally fell asleep in each other's arms. They woke up early and engaged in a final encore before showering together and packing. A continental breakfast was brought up to their room.

The conversation flowed smoothly on the ride back to New York. To Dylan's delight, Penel discussed plans to visit him in Florida, brought up the foundation, and looked forward to seeing the progress of the new youth center. As Dylan dropped Penel off at her office and drove toward LaGuardia, he felt a sense of déjà vu. This time he found himself feeling carefree and content.

On Friday morning, Dylan slept later than usual and then spent the day working in his office. Alex's flight was due into Tampa midafternoon, but Dylan wasn't sure of his plans. He expected Alex would call when he was on his way.

CHAPTER FIFTY-TWO

Alex's flight landed in Tampa early. He took the tram to the rental car agency and picked up a black Cadillac CT5, then made the short drive over to the Candy Store. He walked in and sat at the bar with a view of the main stage, ordered a beer, and watched the girls dance for a while. When the occasional dancer approached, he tipped her a dollar bill and politely dismissed her.

A short while later, someone approached Alex from behind and put her arms around him. He turned around. "Sunni. It's nice to see you."

"How are you, sweetheart?"

"I'm well."

Just then the attractive female bartender appeared and asked him, "Would you like another beer, Alex?"

"Sure. And whatever Sunni's having."

Sunni ordered a Moscato and focused her attention on Alex while the bartender served the drinks. "I have to make the rounds, but my shift ends in an hour."

"How about dinner?"

"Sure, but I don't have anything appropriate with me to wear."

"Don't worry about that. I'll take care of everything."

"Okay. I'll circle back when I'm ready to make my exit."

Alex spent the next hour making plans. He texted Dylan and told him he'd be late. Next, he called the Tampa Renaissance Hotel and reserved a room. Finally, he called the Capitol Grill and made a dinner reservation for nine o'clock. He switched to coffee and watched the dancers. Other than seeing Sunni take her turn on stage, he paid no mind to what she was doing.

Finally, Sunni made her way back over to Alex and told him she was ready to leave, then explained the club rules. Dancers were not allowed to leave with customers. He had to go outside and wait. She would gather her things and leave out a back entrance. She instructed him where to park, and he provided a description of his car.

About ten minutes later, Sunni appeared in the parking lot, carrying a large shoulder bag. She had changed into yoga pants, a tank top, and tennis shoes. She put her bag in the back seat and hopped in the front. They drove over to International Plaza, and Alex took her shopping. They visited Gucci, Nieman Marcus, and Lululemon. He bought her several pairs of fashionable leggings, a handbag, and some lingerie. For dinner, she picked out a metallic sleeveless jumpsuit and black heels. The shoes were fashionable but more conventional than her work-related footwear.

After they finished shopping, the pair headed over to the adjacent Renaissance Hotel and checked into their room. Sunni took a shower, then emerged naked from the bathroom and serviced Alex orally. Afterward, she got dressed and ready for dinner. They walked over to the Capitol Grill and enjoyed a steak and champagne dinner.

After dinner, they returned to the hotel and Sunni offered herself up again. Alex graciously declined. They gathered up the shopping bags and headed to the car. Traffic was light on the ride over to St. Petersburg, and it was close to midnight when they arrived at Sunni's apartment. On the drive home, Alex invited her to go boating and she enthusiastically accepted. When they arrived at the apartment, he helped her inside with the bags. They hugged, and Alex left and drove over to Dylan's house.

Dylan had fallen asleep watching the Rays game. The baseball team was out on a west coast swing. When Alex buzzed, he checked the security cameras and saw a car parked at his front gate. He opened the gate and waited for Alex to get to the house.

"How goes it, buddy?"

"Fine. What've you been up to this evening?"

"I've been with Sunni. I invited her to go out on the boat tomorrow. I hope that's okay."

"Of course you were, and of course you did. It's late. We'll figure it out in the morning."

CHAPTER FIFTY-THREE

F RED PHILIPS SHOWED UP AT Jasmine Carter's apartment in the evening and knocked on the door. There was no answer. He tried her cell phone, and again, no answer. Finally, he texted her, "I'm here waiting where RU?"

He went back to his car to wait. He had backed into the parking spot, so he had a view of her front door. He rolled down the car windows and fired up his glass pipe. After the drug took its effect, Philips was too antsy to sit and wait any longer. He walked the few short blocks to a dive bar popular with locals and tourists.

The bar was packed and the Friday night crowd lively. A local band played tropical-themed music featuring the Beach Boys, Jimmy Buffet, and Bertie Higgins. Philips joined in the festivities and drank Hennessy before switching to beer, talking with a few women, and buying a round of drinks. One woman recognized him from his past television career but was ultimately turned off by his arrogance and crass behavior.

Two hours later, Philips staggered back in the direction of his car. As he approached Jasmine's apartment complex, he squinted in the direction of her unit. A man was just leaving. Philips watched as the man got in his car and drove off. Livid, Philips knocked sharply on the door.

Jasmine answered, "Fred, what're you doing here? You're wasted. Go home." She tried to close the door, but Philips forced his way in.

"You *bitch*!" He slapped her across the face and lunged at her.

"You asshole!" Jasmine swung her open right hand in the direction of his face. Her long fingernails pierced the skin, leaving three parallel lines across his left cheek.

Even in his intoxicated state, Philips sensed a warm, painful feeling across the side of his face. With rage pulsating through his veins, he tackled Jasmine and landed on top of her. He punched her repeatedly about the head and face before wrapping his hands around her neck. At one point, Philips lifted her off the ground, threw her down, and pummeled her until the screams ceased and her body lay motionless. He abruptly left the apartment and drove down to the beach where he passed out in a parking lot.

Philips woke up behind the wheel of his car about a half an hour after sunrise. His head was throbbing, and the left side of his face stung. He looked in the mirror and saw the swollen, red marks covered in dry blood.

He drove back to his Bayshore Boulevard apartment, cleaned himself up, and paced around, trying to piece together the previous night's events. Finally, he did what he had always done after screwing up. He called his brother.

Alex woke up in the morning and went downstairs but did not see or hear Dylan. He poured himself a cup of coffee and sat down in the kitchen to read the weekend edition of the *Wall Street Journal.* Eventually Dylan arrived from downstairs wearing athletic gear and drenched in sweat. He grabbed a bottle of water and joined him.

"What've you been up to?" Alex asked.

"Working out in the gym. You should try it sometime."

"Are you kidding me. I'm in great shape."

"You've always been naturally thin, but age has a way of creeping up on you, my friend."

"Hey, the last time I was here, Sunni and I went to the beach. I didn't hear any complaints about my body."

Dylan rolled his eyes. "Well then, forget everything I just said."

"Speaking of Sunni, I get the impression you're not crazy about my bringing her over here."

"First, you are correct. I'm definitely not crazy about you bringing a stripper over to my house. Second, boat traffic is crazy on summer weekends. That's why I usually take the boat out during the week."

"Hey, she's not a stripper. She's a student who's working her way through college. Besides, she seemed excited when I invited her to go boating."

Dylan thought for a moment. "Here's what we're gonna do. I'm swamped with work from being gone all week. Plus, I've gotta go down to the foundation property and meet with the contractor on some site-development stuff. You can have your friend over. Use the pool house and take the wave runners out. No boating, and do not bring her in the house."

"You sound like my mother."

Dylan laughed. "I do, don't I?" He headed off to the shower, leaving Alex in the kitchen.

Alex got ready and called Sunni but got no answer. *Probably still sleeping and has her phone on silent,* he thought. Around eleven o'clock, he decided to drive over to her apartment.

When he knocked on the door, there was no answer. *Strange,* he thought. College students (and strippers) had a reputation for sleeping late. He knocked a second time, a little louder. Still no answer. He tried the door. The knob turned, and he cracked the door open enough to call out, "Sunni?"

Still no answer.

Finally, Alex opened the door and walked in. The macabre scene shocked his every sense of being.

CHAPTER FIFTY-FOUR

ON Saturday at noon, Governor Rocco Philips entertained a Florida State law school student who was working as an intern at the capitol building. The perky blonde had caught Philip's attention, and a member of his security unit had escorted her up to the governor's mansion. Philips always had a penchant for young women. He'd married a twenty-two-year-old woman when he was thirty-three and divorced her five years later after the couple had two children together.

Just as the intern had finished her assignment, there was a knock on the door.

The governor zipped up his trousers while the young woman pulled her sundress back on. "Just a minute." Then shortly, "Come in, and it better be important."

An aide accompanied by the police officer standing guard at the door burst in. The aide said breathlessly, "Your brother's on the phone. It's an emergency."

The governor said to the officer, "Please take Ms. Wilcox home." Then he picked up the nearest phone. The operator came on and patched Fred Philips through.

"What is it that's so important?"

"I may have *really* screwed up."

What else is new, the governor thought. "Fred, you're gonna have to be more specific."

"I stopped by my girl's place last night and we got into an argument. It got pretty heated."

"So?"

"So, it turned physical, and I may have really hurt her."

The governor cut him off. "That's enough. Call me back on the other line."

The other line involved the use of prepaid, disposal phones the brothers used to discuss matters the governor did not wish to come through state phone lines. After the call was reconnected on the throwaways, Fred Philips contin-ued. "I left her apartment last night, and I'm not sure she was conscious."

"Whaddya mean you're not sure?"

"I was pretty wasted."

"Jesus Christ, Fred. What time did you leave her?"

"I don't know, but it was late."

The governor looked at his watch. It was just past one o'clock. "Give me the address." He jotted down the address and asked, "Where are you now?"

"I'm at home."

"Stay there. Don't leave, and do not speak to anyone. Do you understand?"

Fred Philips whimpered, "Yes."

Rocco Philips called a member of his special crisis team. This team was off the books and funded through one of the governor's campaign accounts. "It's me. We have a situation in St. Petersburg. How soon can you get a team over there to survey the damage?"

"I have a man in Tampa who can run recon. He can be there in an hour."

"Send him now and get back to me." He gave him the address.

An hour later, the man called back and said, "It's not good."

CHAPTER FIFTY-FIVE

I T TOOK A FEW MOMENTS for the initial shock to wear off. The entire time, Alex stood frozen in place. He had to think. Sunni was sprawled out on the floor. Her hair partially covered her face, but it was clear she had bruising about her head and neck. Her body appeared cold and swollen. She was barefoot but still wearing the silver jumper he had bought her. There were traces of blood on the carpet. She wasn't moving and did not appear to be breathing.

Alex put his lawyer's hat on. He couldn't touch her. He had left Sunni around midnight and barely been in her apartment. There was probably none of his DNA in her body or inside the home, but he couldn't be certain. His fingerprints were on the front door, at the least.

There were several people who could place them together yesterday afternoon and last night. The strip club, the mall, the hotel, and the restaurant. Sunni was clearly not her real name. On the few occasions they'd been together, the focus was on having fun. Neither asked too much about the other's personal life and they both respected the boundaries.

Fuck it, he decided. He had to admit this looked bad, but he hadn't done anything wrong and he had to help the poor girl. He dialed 911, knowing full well everything he said was being recorded.

"911, what's your emergency?"

"I just arrived to pick up a friend. There was no answer when I knocked, so I walked in. She's lying on the floor, unconscious. She appears to be dead."

Alex provided his name and Sunni's address and apartment number, was advised assistance was on the way and directed to stay on the line before he was transferred to a homicide detective. He repeated what he'd told the operator, and the female detective instructed him to stay put and not touch anything. He stepped outside and waited.

Within minutes, the apartment complex was swarmed with emergency vehicles, lights flashing and sirens blaring. A pleasant-looking Hispanic woman dressed in khaki pants and a green St. Petersburg Police Department polo shirt approached Alex. She had a badge and holstered gun attached to her belt and wore a serious demeanor. Another male detective stood beside her.

"Alex Malloy?"

He nodded in the affirmative.

"I'm Detective Katrina Cardenas-Santos, deputy chief investigator of homicide with the St. Petersburg Police Department. This is Detective Lew McIntyre." She paused while a group of uniformed and un-uniformed personal waited at the front door for directions. "I need to go inside. Please wait here. I'll be back to speak with you when I'm able. Detective McIntyre will take some information from you." She turned toward the apartment and led the others inside.

Detective McIntyre was a large man with broad shoulders, wearing black cargo pants, military-style black boots, and the ubiquitous green polo shirt. Alex noticed a gun on his belt and a bulge around his left ankle. He removed a small pad and a pen from his side pants pocket and said, "I'll need your full name and address."

Alex provided the information.

"What brings you to Florida?"

"Business."

"On a Saturday?"

"I'm an attorney. I'm a partner in the New York firm of Baker, Callahan & White. We're in the process of acquiring a Florida law firm headquartered in Tampa. I'm here to assist with the transition." He thought the fact that he was an attorney would carry some weight with the stone-faced detective. No such luck.

"Is the law firm open on Saturday?"

"The office is technically closed, but most of the lawyers and some staff do work Saturdays. It's especially busy now, keeping up with the regular workload in addition to the work associated with the merger."

"I thought you said it was an acquisition. That infers a sale and purchase."

Here we go, Alex reflected privately. *These people are going to parse every word I say and then others will take turns repeating the same questions.* "It's a complicated transaction. From a legal standpoint, it's both an acquisition and a merger."

"Are you suggesting I'm not sophisticated enough to understand that?"

More private thoughts. *Oh, boy. This guy must be the bad cop. Makes sense. The deputy chief detective probably plays the good cop role. In another setting, I might have asked her out. I wonder if she's into role playing.* He finally snapped himself out of it. "No, sir. Since you raised the issue, I'm simply explaining that my use of the two terms to describe the pending deal are legally consistent."

"Stay here. Do not leave the scene." The detective turned and walked toward the house.

The detective spoke to a uniformed officer standing guard at the door and motioned toward Alex.

Alex stood alone with his thoughts. He had been in tight situations before and prided himself on always rising to the occasion. This was no different. He wasn't on his home turf, but he certainly had assets at his disposal. And besides, as bad as it may have looked to law enforcement seeking a quick resolution, he hadn't done anything wrong. He had been generous with Sunni and treated her with respect. He suddenly began to feel sad. The poor young girl had had her whole life ahead of her.

Alex looked around at the gathering crowd. Two uniformed officers strung yellow police tape around a significant section outside Sunni's apartment. In addition to an EMS wagon, there were several marked St. Petersburg Police cars, three unmarked ones, lights still flashing from the grill and rear windows, and a white sedan marked 'St. Petersburg Police Forensics' on the sides.

Eventually Detective Cardenas-Santos emerged from the apartment and walked toward Alex, shedding blue surgical gloves as she approached. "Mr. Malloy, we're going to be here for a while. I'm going to need to interview you in more detail after we're finished here. I understand you live in Connecticut and are down here on business. You must remain in St. Petersburg until such time as we complete our preliminary investigation. I'll need a local address where you'll be staying."

Alex thought about that for a moment, then provided Dylan's address. Under the circumstances, he would be staying with him indefinitely. He made a mental note to cancel his Tampa hotel reservation for the following week.

"You're free to go. For now." She handed him a card. "Here's my business card. My office will be contacting you to schedule the interview."

"Thank you, Detective." She turned and walked back into the apartment.

Alex watched her, thinking the posterior view was a pleasant one. As she approached the front door, he noticed the uniformed officer looking at him and shaking his head.

Alex made a phone call on the short drive back to Dylan's house.

Dylan answered, "What's up?"

"Where are you?"

"I'm at the youth center property."

"How much longer are you going to be?"

"I'm not sure. Why?"

Not wanting to say much over the phone, Alex replied, "I'll come down there. What's the address?"

Alex pulled the rented Cadillac over, took down the address, and keyed it into his cell phone app rather than mess with the car's navigation system. The app directed him on the twelve-minute drive to the address.

The large property was fenced-in, but two adjacent gates were swung open. He saw Dylan's pickup truck and another fancier truck parked side by side. Alex pulled next to the two pickups and got out. He saw Dylan and another man exit one of the buildings. As Alex approached them, he remained locked in on lawyer mode. He had to be careful as to what he said in front of this stranger.

Dylan spoke first. "Alex, this is Gregg Thomas. Gregg is the contractor on the project." The two men shook hands.

"It's nice to meet you, Gregg. Dylan, when you have a moment, I have to speak with you in private."

Dylan looked back at Gregg who took the cue.

"I need to get some photos and measurements on the building," Gregg said and then turned and walked back to the structure from which he had emerged.

Alex took several steps in the opposite direction, and Dylan instinctively followed.

"Okay, Alex, what's going on?"

Alex gave Dylan a detailed recap of the events from the time he arrived at Sunni's up to the time he left the scene.

"Jesus, Alex. Now you're a suspect in a murder?"

"No. At most I'm a person of interest. Here's the thing. I'm innocent, but I'm also a seasoned enough attorney to know that doesn't always matter. I have several things going against me, optics aside. First, I'm in foreign territory here with no connections whatsoever. If I was back home, I could speak to someone with a friendly ear and get this straightened out. Second, and more importantly, not a word of this can get back to my family, my law firm, and most of all, Anita and her legal team. This needs to be resolved without any word of my involvement with this young woman getting out."

"Oh, is that all?"

"Not the best time for humor, Dylan."

"Fair enough." Dylan stood quietly for a moment. "I have some thoughts.

Head back to the house. I need to speak with Gregg, then I'll be right behind you."

On his way back to the house, Dylan called Walt Jackman on his cell. Walt picked up right away, notwithstanding it was the weekend. Dylan explained the situation and emphasized the sensitive nature of Alex's name being associated with the investigation.

"Our criminal division is really limited to white collar defense. However, the department is run by Charles Shelnutt who is a former federal prosecutor and has handled a number of high-profile homicide cases. I'll call Charles and get back to you."

Charles Shelnutt was indeed a well-known defense attorney. Prior to joining Driscoll Williams, he had defended the harbor pilot whose cargo ship collided with a span of the Skyway Bridge, causing the bridge to collapse and resulting in the deaths of twenty-eight people; the St. Petersburg physician who crashed his speed boat into another vessel, killing four teens; and the Tampa dance instructor who killed two young brothers in a hit-and-run motor vehicle accident. In each case, he had won an acquittal or negotiated an extremely favorable settlement.

Dylan was home for about fifteen minutes when Walt called back. Alex had been standing outside on the second-floor balcony, leaning on the railing and staring out over the water.

Walt got right to the point. "I spoke with Charles. He called a colleague over in St. Pete. The lawyer's name is Byron Wells. He's a former lead homicide prosecutor for the Sixth Judicial Circuit. He knows the lay of the land over there and is well respected by law enforcement. He's also friends with Grant Adams, the state attorney, and has a good relationship with his office. They're going to jointly represent Alex. All three of us can be at your house within the hour."

Dylan thanked Walt and hung up, then told Alex, who seemed to relax a little. The three attorneys arrived separately at Dylan's house within fifteen minutes of each other. Aengus greeted each man and escorted him to Dylan's office.

After all introductions were made, Charles began. "Byron and I are going to act as co-counsel. We spoke on the way over and have begun to strategize. Since this is Byron's backyard, I'm going to let him take the lead."

Byron stood and spoke in an authoritative voice, commensurate with his physical appearance. Dressed in fashionable slacks, dress sneakers, and a golf shirt, he was clearly a man who commanded a room. He requested that Dylan leave the office, succinctly explaining the basics of attorney-client privilege in anticipation that he would be deposed, or at least interviewed at some point. Dylan left and went down to the kitchen to wait.

Byron asked Alex to take them through the chronology from his initial contact with Sunni after he got to town, through the discovery of her body and his subsequent actions. Alex stated the salient facts. Charles typed notes into a small laptop. Byron wrote nothing down. Instead, he listened attentively and asked some follow-up questions as Alex spoke. When he was finished, Byron inquired further, "How many other times had you been with Sunni?"

"Once. Well twice, technically."

"When was that?"

"I met her three weeks ago yesterday at the Candy Store. I spent the following Monday with her at the beach and then we went back to her apartment." Alex once again took the attorneys through the events of their prior interactions.

Byron noted, "Thank you, Alex. I appreciate interviewing a lawyer-client. None of the usual rambling or going off in a tangent. I do have a few additional questions."

After Alex furnished the balance of the information, Byron continued. "I'm going to send our joint letter of representation to St. Pete PD, to Detective Cardenas-Santos's attention. I anticipate she'll request a time to interview you, and I'll set that up. I'm satisfied with your recollection of the events. It's unlikely your fingerprints or DNA were left in the apartment from the prior visit. Same with DNA on the body from the previous evening, but we can't be certain. Stick with the details you provided to us. The last thing we want is for you to deny your sexual interactions or your presence in the apartment on the first encounter and have them discover physical evidence to the contrary."

Alex acknowledged his understanding of the instructions, then advised the attorneys of his concerns regarding his pending divorce and his role in the merger with the Florida law firm. He emphasized that his name could not be publicly linked with the case.

Byron cautiously assured him, "I have a good working relationship with the lead detective. I'm also friends with the state attorney. I'll leverage our cooperation to obtain a commitment on that. A lot will depend on how quickly the investigation proceeds and how soon the police are able to make an arrest."

The group discussed some other matters and contact information was exchanged. Finally, the meeting broke up and the attorneys left. Dylan escorted the group to the door and thanked everyone for their prompt response.

After the attorneys left, Dylan asked Alex for the address of Sunni's apartment. He provided the information, and Dylan left alone in his pickup. He drove slowly by the apartment complex and took in the scene. Two police cars were parked out front. Caution tape surrounded one of the units, and a uniformed officer was stationed outside the door.

Too much activity. I'll check back later.

Dylan and Alex spent the balance of the weekend around the house. They talked and ordered take out. Alex did some reminiscing about their time growing up in Connecticut, and Dylan joined in. He figured talking about the old days would take Alex's mind off things.

On Sunday, Alex accompanied Dylan to church, a rarity. After church, Dylan dropped Alex off at the house and told him he was going to run an errand.

Dylan drove back to Sunni's apartment complex. The yellow police tape was still present, but there were no police officers on the premises. He knocked on one of the other apartment doors. A tall, lanky-looking kid wearing a St. Pete College baseball T-shirt and ball cap answered, "Yeah?"

"Is Calvin around?"

"Sure, just a minute."

Calvin appeared at the door. "Hey, Dylan, what's up?"

"I haven't seen you around the gym in a while. I was driving by and saw the police tape, thought I'd stop to check and see if everything was okay."

"I'm fine, but it's been crazy around here." He told Dylan about the discovery of his neighbor's dead body inside her apartment.

"Have you spoken with the police?"

"Not yet. My roommate, who you just met, said they knocked on all the apartments yesterday and questioned everyone about Jasmine. That's the girl's name."

"Yeah, I heard something about that. By any chance, was Jasmine the girlfriend of that guy we played basketball with at Equinox that time?"

Calvin looked at Dylan quizzically. "Yeah, what about it?"

"I just remember you telling me he saw a girl in your apartment complex when we were talking on the way home."

"You think he had something to do with this?"

"I have no idea. Anyway, thanks for the information. I'm glad you're alright. I'll see you around."

"Yeah sure, Dylan."

On the way home, Dylan called Walt and told him about his conversation with Calvin Strother, Jr. and about the familiar-looking man from Equinox that knew Sunni/Jasmine. He requested that Walt immediately pass the information on to Alex's attorneys and have them look into it. Dylan drove home and decided not to discuss it with Alex. In the afternoon, Byron called Alex to inform him they had an appointment to meet with Detective Cardenas-Santos on Monday at one thirty.

CHAPTER FIFTY-SIX

O N MONDAY MORNING, ALEX LEFT early for work in Tampa. Dylan reminded him of the foundation board meeting that evening at eight o'clock. Alex promised he'd be there, even if he had to continue his police interview.

Alex was in meetings and on the phone with his New York office all morning. At lunchtime, he advised his colleagues he had to leave for the afternoon to attend to some personal business. He drove back to St. Petersburg and parked his car at the new police headquarters building in midtown. When he entered the lobby, Byron was already there waiting for him. He had prepared Alex for the interview the previous evening and told him that it would just be the two of them attending. He explained this was not the time to display a show of force in numbers. Rather, their objective was to present an air of cooperation.

Detective Katrina Cardenas-Santos presented herself in the lobby wearing a blue paisley business dress and heels. Her hair was pulled back, and she wore light makeup. She greeted Byron, and the two shook hands. She did not offer Alex her hand. The detective scanned her badge, unlocking a heavy door just off the lobby, then led the two men to a room a few steps down the hallway. It resembled more of a conference room where depositions were conducted than an interrogation room. There was a rectangle-shaped conference table covered with beveled glass and cushioned executive chairs. This was for Byron's comfort rather than his, Alex surmised.

Byron sat with Alex on one side of the table, and the detective sat opposite them. Alex looked around briefly, noticing a camera mounted on the wall opposite of him. Brad had advised Alex earlier that the interview would be recorded. None of the walls contained a mirror, so he figured no one else was observing.

The detective produced a laptop and three-ring binder from her briefcase, flipped on the computer, opened the binder, and located the page she was looking for. While she did that, Alex took a deep breath. The detective turned in her chair, held up a remote control, and pointed it at the camera. The camera rotated on its mount and a red light came on.

Detective Cardenas-Santos read from the binder, initiating the preliminary colloquy. She stated the date, time, and location of the interview and the names of the three participants. She read Alex a summary of his constitutional rights, asked if he voluntarily agreed to answer questions, and confirmed Byron was his legal representative. Then she began the questioning.

Alex drifted into a zone. He cleared everything from his mind and locked in on the detective, making eye contact the entire time. He never hurried his answers and avoided any evasiveness, even when discussing the details of how he'd met Sunni and the extent of their sexual relationship. The first time she mentioned the name Jasmine Carter, Alex said he did not know her by that name. Thereafter, the detective referred to her simply as the victim.

The questioning continued at a steady pace for two hours before Detective Cardenas-Santos indicated they were taking a break. She turned off the camera and left the room. Byron wrote on his note pad and showed it to Alex. It read, "don't say anything about the case."

Alex nodded, stood and stretched his legs, looking at his watch. It read 3:54 p.m. He explained he had to attend a board meeting at the Vinoy at eight.

Byron assured him that the interview would be concluded by then.

The detective returned to the conference room a short time later carrying three bottles of water. She handed one each to Byron and Alex. The camera was turned back on, and the questioning continued for just shy of another two hours. At the conclusion of the interview, the detective stated, "Thank you, Mr. Malloy. I have no further questions. The time is now 6:01 p.m."

Byron and Detective Cardenas-Santos shook hands. She then turned to Alex and extended her hand. "Thank you again, Mr. Malloy, for coming in." She led the two men to the door.

Alex followed Byron out to the lobby.

After they exited the building, Byron suggested to Alex that they meet at his office downtown on an upper floor of one of the city's glass towers, a five-minute drive from the Vinoy. Byron provided the address, then got into a blue Maserati Gran Turismo coupe and Alex followed him down Central Avenue where they turned into a parking garage. Byron pulled his car into a reserved spot and sat inside for about ten minutes. Alex found a nearby visitor's spot and waited in his rental car for Byron to exit the Maserati.

When they got up to the office, Byron offered Alex a drink and he asked for a scotch. Byron walked over to a handsome walnut hutch situated on one side of his office and pulled up on the rolling door, which revealed a series of liquor bottles and mixers. Adjacent to the hutch was an ice machine concealed behind a matching wooden door. He poured each of them a Dewar's.

The two men sat in armchairs across from each other separated by a coffee table. Byron set his glass down. "You did very well, Alex. Your answers were consistent with everything we discussed. I spoke with Detective Cardenas-Santos on the way over here. There's been significant progress in their investigation, and the police are chasing down a promising lead. In the meantime, their official position remains that investigation is in its infancy and they have no suspects. I've been told there are good reasons for taking that approach. I've also been assured that your name will not be released in conjunction with the investigation. Eventually, after an arrest is made, however, you will have to be identified as a witness."

"I understand. And thank you, Byron, for your efforts in that regard."

"You're still required to remain in town for the time being, but an arrest could be made within the week."

"That's no problem. I planned on being here for work all week anyway."

The men finished their drinks and talked about other things lawyers talked about when they got together. At seven-thirty, Alex left the office. It was a clear night, and the temperature and humidity had dropped to tolerable levels. He elected to leave his car in the garage and walk to the Vinoy.

During their conversation, Byron avoided telling Alex about his involvement with the break in the case. Yesterday afternoon, he had been connected to a conference call with Charles Shelnutt and Walt Jackman. They explained what Dylan had told Walt about Calvin Strother, Jr. and the familiar-looking man from Equinox who was dating Jasmine Carter. Byron had called Katrina Cardenas-Santos on her cell phone a short time later. The detective and her team worked through the night and into Monday afternoon chasing down information on the lead.

The investigation had uncovered DNA material under several of Jasmine's fingernails. They caught a break when they located a match in the Florida DNA database. Under Florida law, each person arrested and booked into a jail or other state correctional facility is required to submit fingerprint and DNA samples at the time of booking.

The lead suspect in Jasmine Carter's murder had been arrested two years earlier in Tampa, charged with driving under the influence, and processed into the Orient Road jail. Two days later, the charges had mysteriously been dropped when the Tampa state attorney filed an Announcement of No Information without comment. However, the man's booking records had never been redacted.

291

CHAPTER FIFTY-SEVEN

LEX ARRIVED AT THE VINOY and joined the board meeting in one of the small conference rooms on the hotel's main floor. A side table held a platter of Cuban finger sandwiches and a plate of brownies and assorted cookies. There were also pitchers of water, iced tea, and coffee. Besides Dylan and Alex, Walt Jackman, Cheryl, and Shirley were present. Everyone had a bite to eat and engaged in small talk until Dylan called the meeting to order.

Shirley began by reading the minutes from the previous meeting. Next, Dylan provided the group with a summary of the donations to St. Gregory School and a progress report on the youth center. Shirley took notes as Dylan spoke. Finally, he gave a presentation on the proposed gifts to St. Mary School to fund the fieldhouse and establish an endowment for purposes of providing four annual scholarships for underprivileged students. Each board member signaled their approval.

At the conclusion of the meeting, Shirley handed out quarterly compensation checks. The checks to Walt and Alex covered their expenses. Cheryl's compensation was larger because, in addition to birthing Dylan, she was tasked with performing additional duties for the foundation.

Rocco Philips met after hours in the governor's mansion with Darcie DeLuca and the point person on his crisis team. He asked for an update on the St. Petersburg homicide investigation.

The man swallowed hard before stating, "St. Pete PD has really closed ranks on this one. They're playing it close to the vest. The official word is that they've just begun their investigation and don't have much to go on at this point."

"Did you get anything on the crime scene evidence?"

"Nothing has been leaked, and unfortunately, we don't have a contact inside St. Pete PD at this time." The man did not want to break the news to the governor that he was not held in high regard by law enforcement agencies these days.

"Do you think it's possible Fred sanitized the scene before he left?"

"It's unlikely. When we spoke with him, he said he'd been drinking before things got physical. Our best bet is shielding him from providing a DNA sample. We're also not sure anyone can link him to the girl. Apparently, she had several other boyfriends. Mostly he met with her at her apartment in St. Pete."

The governor looked over at his chief of staff. "What do you think?"

"I think we should have a contingency plan."

"Do you have something in mind?"

"Yes, but you're not going to like it."

The governor addressed the crisis team leader. "Do you have Fred under control?"

"Yes. We've got a guy staying with him at his condo. The guy brings him food, drugs, booze, and women, so Fred's content staying home for the time being."

"Good. That's all for now. Keep poking around St. Pete PD and keep me updated." After the man left, the governor looked at his chief of staff. "You wanna tell me about this contingency plan that I'm not gonna like?"

Darcie DeLuca outlined the plan.

When she was finished, he sat for a moment in thought, rubbed his temples, and then looked up at the ceiling. "Father, please forgive me if it comes to this."

CHAPTER FIFTY-EIGHT

THE FOLLOWING MORNING, DYLAN SAT in his office reading the papers. The *Herald* front-page headline read "Kindergarteners to Select Gender as Part of New Curriculum."

Buried inside the paper was a small follow-up article on the Jasmine Carter homicide. The article included a short statement from the lead investigator, Detective Katrina Cardenas-Santos. The detective was quoted as saying, "Our investigation has just begun. We are committed to finding the person or persons responsible, but we currently have no substantial leads and no suspect has been identified. Unfortunately, I have nothing else to report at this time." Conspicuously absent from the statement was the usual appeal to contact Crime Stoppers of Pinellas County with any information about the incident.

Next, he called Becca O'Brien. Greetings were exchanged, and she was her usual congenial self. He informed her that the foundation would be funding the balance needed for construction of the fieldhouse and theater as planned. Additionally, an endowment would be established to grant four annual scholarships to be awarded to underprivileged students.

After discussing details about the gifts, Rebecca thanked Dylan and offered him the opportunity to name the fieldhouse. Without hesitation, Dylan told her he had one in mind: the Cheryl Tomassi Fieldhouse. He also requested that the adjacent theater be named the Esther Lott Theater.

On the opposite side of the bay, Fred Philips grew more and more antsy. He asked the man who had been acting as his babysitter the past several days how long he was going to be holed up.

"As long as the governor says so," the babysitter replied.

Philips sighed, then went into to the bathroom and splashed cold water on his face. He looked at his image in the mirror. His teeth were yellow and in the early stages of decay, symptoms of his smoking habit. His face was sickly pallor, contrasted with the three raw lines across his left cheek that showed early signs of keloid scarring.

Philips walked outside onto the wrap around balcony, which offered a beautiful view of the bay, Davis Island and, to the northeast, the city skyline. He had every creature comfort available at his disposal but still felt trapped in his own home. He fired up his crack pipe and enjoyed a smoke, then ordered up a hooker and the man called the number for a high-end escort service. The selection was somewhat limited for early afternoon appointments. Philips requested a full-figured blonde. The agency was sending a woman, but she had to stop at a wig store on the way over.

The FBI deputy director arrived at the Oval Office for an appointment with the president. "Good afternoon, Mr. President. I have some information on the Florida matter. Fred Philips is a suspect in a homicide case in St. Petersburg. As part of the investigation, a laptop computer was discovered at the crime scene. The laptop apparently belongs to Philips and is currently in the possession of the St. Petersburg Police Department. I'm going down to Florida personally to look into the matter."

"Please keep me updated on any developments."

"Yes, sir."

CHAPTER FIFTY-NINE

I N THE WEE HOURS OF Thursday morning, a large group of law enforcement agents gathered at the Hillsborough County Sheriff Operations Center in Ybor City. The group included members of the St. Petersburg and Tampa Police Departments, Hillsborough County Sheriff's Office, and the Florida Department of Law Enforcement. The task force had been assembled the day before, for purposes of executing an arrest warrant.

A convoy left the operations center led by a Hillsborough County Sheriff Office armored SWAT vehicle. The vehicles drove within the speed limit, no sirens or flashing lights. When the motorcade arrived at its destination, a portion of northbound Bayshore Boulevard was blocked off by Tampa Police Department vehicles. Other vehicles were positioned on Julia and South Carter Streets. Officers armed with AR15 rifles and outfitted in black tactical gear, helmets, and night vision goggles entered the lobby of a luxury residential building. The leader presented a document to one of the two doormen manning the front desk and instructed them to step away from the desk. Two officers stayed with the doormen to make certain no phone calls were made.

The balance of the team took elevators and stairs to their destination two floors below the penthouse level. Officers were positioned in teams of two at each of the stairwell exits. A large group of officers gathered outside the unit number designated on the arrest warrant. A Blackhawk Entry Ram was used to breach the door. Then it was game on.

The officers entered the condominium unit shouting commands to get on the ground. A large man dressed in slacks and a guayabera shirt was asleep on the couch, a Glock 9 mm handgun sitting on the table in front of him. He was quickly detained. Officers entered and cleared each room until they reached the master bedroom. Fred Philips, who had been fast asleep, stirred and looked up shortly before being smothered by three officers. Wearing pajamas, he was easily subdued, handcuffed, and leg shackled.

The task-force leader observed a glass pipe on the nightstand with a yellowish residue inside the bowl. It was seized, placed in an evidence bag, and marked. After observing the left side of Philips face, the leader ordered Philips to be photographed. He was read the charges from the warrant followed by his Miranda warning. Within an hour, there was no sign of a police operation on Bayshore Boulevard and Fredrick Philips was in the Pinellas County Jail, charged with second-degree murder.

Less than an hour later, word of the arrest reached the governor's mansion. The governor arranged to have an attorney visit his brother, giving him explicit instructions to advise Fred not to mention the governor's name or any of his business under any circumstances.

The attorney found Fred Philips in an isolation cell, lying on the bed in the fetal position. The lawyer explained that he was sent to represent him. He also relayed the governor's instructions and explained that continued representation was contingent upon his compliance with the orders. Between sniffles, Philips acknowledged his understanding.

Darcie DeLuca received an early morning call instructing her to cancel the governor's morning agenda and report to his office immediately. She was also told to round up his personal attorney and public relations team for a meeting ASAP.

Darcie arrived in the governor's office in less than an hour, finding him on the phone and drinking coffee when she walked in. He motioned for her to sit while he completed the call, then hung up the phone and directed his attention to the chief of staff. "That was a contact in Tampa. A raid was executed on Fred's condo early this morning. His apartment was searched, and he was arrested and transported to St. Petersburg. He's been charged with second-degree murder. We're going to have to be proactive on this."

"What evidence do the police have? They had to have something substantial to get a judge to sign off on a warrant."

"We don't know that yet. The attorney will file for disclosure this morning. All my guy knows is that the only significant evidence taken from his condo was a handgun and a glass pipe that probably contained crack."

"That's good. Nothing to come back on you."

The governor looked at her sternly. "Nothing to come back on *us*."

"Right."

"We need to be ready to execute alternative plans on a moment's notice. The crisis team meeting is in an hour."

"Here's my recommendation. Until we know what evidence the police have, you'll stay out of the public eye. I checked your calendar and there's nothing for several days that requires a public appearance. In the meantime, I'll have your communications director issue a short statement that your thoughts and prayers go out to the deceased and her family, you were shocked to hear of your brother's arrest, you will have no further comment at this time, yada yada. Next, we'll identify an alternate suspect and blame Fred's arrest on a vindictive police department looking to get back at you through your family for standing up for the rights of minorities and fighting against racial injustice and police brutality. Fred's attorneys will weave this into a central theme of his defense. Finally, if all else fails, you deliver 'the speech,' " she explained, although she knew the governor did not relish publicly portraying his brother as a self-destructive drug addict and womanizer with a history of mental health issues who rebuffed repeated attempts by the governor to assist with straightening out his life. The speech, featuring crocodile tears, would conclude with the introduction of a new fundraising campaign to establish an arm of the Rainbow Ribbon Coalition dedicated to treating mental illness and substance abuse.

The governor closed his eyes, looked up, and exhaled slowly. Then he gave DeLuca the look. "This is going to be a long day, and I don't have time to get an intern up here. I need to relieve some tension."

She knew the drill. Although she was the governor's top aide and confidante, no one was above being victimized by his predatory demands. She removed her blouse and lace bra, exposing her perfect breasts. Per their routine, she went to work in a specific manner on an intimate section of the governor's anatomy.

As they were concluding the act, the governor's secretary buzzed the office. "Everyone is here for your first meeting."

"Give me a few moments," he said breathlessly. He finished, pulled up his pants, and straightened himself up while his chief of staff cleaned up and did the same.

Fred Philips had been booked into the Pinellas County Jail early enough to make the roster for that Thursday morning's first-appearance hearings. Philips was seated in the large courtroom separate from a dozen other defendants. The Pinellas County Criminal Complex technically carried a Clearwater address but was geographically located in the middle of the county. In addition to comprising the court system for all criminal and traffic cases, the complex also housed the offices of the state attorney and public defender. The Pinellas County Jail and a sheriff's substation were located on an adjacent property.

Except for Philips, all the detainees in the first appearance room were dressed in orange jumpsuits. He was dressed in red, the designation for high-risk inmates segregated in a maximum-security unit. The designation was reserved for notoriously violent defendants or the occasional celebrity or other public figure.

Grant Adams entered the courtroom along with the duty prosecutor. It was rare for the state attorney himself to show up at first appearance.

The judge greeted Adams warmly. "To what do we owe the honor, Mr. Adams."

"An arrest was made early this morning in the murder of a young St. Petersburg woman. I'm going to be handling the case personally."

"I see. Well then, let's start with that case."

"It's the case of State of Florida versus Fredrick Philips, Your Honor."

The judge pressed some buttons on his computer until the filed appeared on his screen. He perused the file and then looked up with a raised eyebrow. Aware of Fred Philips from his days as a political commentator on WNN, the judge advised him of the charges against him and noted for the record that he was represented by counsel. His attorney immediately requested that bail be set.

The judge turned and looked at Grant Adams. "What says the state?"

"Your Honor, the defendant in this case is charged with the brutal murder of a young woman. We have substantial evidence linking him to the crime. The state believes that Mr. Philips is a man of some means, or at least, access to means. In addition to being a flight risk, we believe he has substance-abuse issues and poses a violent risk to others."

The judge looked back at Philips attorney. "What does the defense have to say?"

"Your Honor, if bail is set, Mr. Philips will forfeit his passport and agree to home confinement."

Before the judge could make a ruling, Adams spoke up again. "May the state respond?"

"Certainly."

"Mr. Philips is not a resident of Pinellas County. He lives in a luxury high-rise condominium in Tampa. Our law enforcement personnel would have no jurisdiction over him. We respectfully request that bail be denied."

"Bail is denied. Anything else from the defense?"

"Yes, Your Honor. The defense moves for an *ore tenus* motion requesting expedited disclosure of the state's evidence to date, including any DNA profiles, autopsy reports, and preliminary witness and exhibit lists."

The judge looked at Adams for a reply.

"The state has no objection, Your Honor."

"How much time does the state need?"

"We'll have it to the defense by the close of business tomorrow."

"Very good. This hearing is concluded. You gentlemen are excused." The judge looked at the clerk, who then called the next case.

Adams and Philips's attorney left the courtroom. Philips, handcuffed and shackled at the ankles, was escorted back to the jail by three detention deputies.

That same morning Alex drove over to Tampa and was at the office working diligently on the merger. His mind had cleared following his meeting at Byron Wells's office on Monday evening. He found was he was able to relax and return to his regular routine. He and Dylan had dinner together each night, and he checked on Ben each evening. For the past three days, the two friends' discussions had not included a word about the pending murder investigation.

Around ten thirty, Alex received a call on his cell phone from Byron who informed him that an arrest had been made and Fred Philips, the brother of Florida's governor, had been charged with the murder of Jasmine Carter. He provided a summary of the evidence against Philips and shared his impression that a media frenzy was on the horizon.

Well acquainted with the Philips brothers from their time in New York, Alex replied, "I have to say, I'm pleased that an arrest was made, but I'm concerned this is going to end up a shitstorm with me in the middle of it, and without an umbrella. My name is now going to be associated with what will probably turn out to be the latest version of the trial of the century."

"I spoke with the state attorney before I called you. The judge granted a motion for expedited discovery. Your name will be disclosed on the preliminary witness list, which will be filed and served by tomorrow. However, your name will appear with the Esquire designation, care of my office address, and listed among each of the attorneys who have touched the file or weighed in on the smallest of matters up to this point in the investigation. I understand the names of no less than fifteen lawyers from the state attorney's office will also be disclosed."

"Isn't it unusual to list attorneys as witnesses?"

"Yes, and if any of them are deposed, they'll claim work product privilege. It's legal subterfuge, designed to bury your name and spare you any publicity in the case."

"How did you manage that?"

"That's why you hired me."

Alex felt that familiar secure feeling he had always known while operating back home. "I appreciate everything you've done for me, Brad."

"Don't mention it, Alex. I'm expensive, and I make sure I earn my fees."

"Speaking of that, please send me your bill. I haven't even paid you a retainer."

"It's all been taken care of." He hung up the phone.

Alex stood there for a moment, alone in deep reflection. He finally shook his head and grinned widely before saying to no one in particular, "Dylan."

That evening, Dylan and Alex had dinner at Ville Gallace, Dylan's favorite Italian eatery. The restaurant was in Indian Rocks Beach, directly across the street from the beachfront condominium where Anthony and Isabella lived. They shared appetizers of fried calamari and gnocchi, along with a bottle of Masi Amarone. For the main course, Alex ordered chicken parmigiana and Dylan the veal chop with risotto special. They split a second bottle of Amarone with dinner. Afterward, they both enjoyed a cognac. Dylan was glad he'd had Aengus drive them to the restaurant.

During dinner, Alex told Dylan about the details of the developments in the murder case, including the arrest of Fred Philips. As Alex recounted the details, a lightbulb went off in Dylan's head. Alex's news confirmed it was the oaf from the gym who had been charged with the murder. Dylan had rarely watched World News Now, but that's where he knew of Philips from and why he looked familiar. Alex also told him about the collaborative effort to shield him from any publicity in connection with the case.

"Well, old boy, you landed on your feet again, as usual."

"Thanks to you, Dylan. You're a true friend."

"I have no idea what you're talking about."

"If you say so. I'm flying back tomorrow afternoon, as scheduled. I have Ben for the weekend, and I'm looking forward to spending some time with him. Quite frankly, it's going to feel great to be home and away from here. I need a break from Florida."

Just then, the proprietor, a tall, dark-haired man dressed in all black, approached their table. "Dylan, it's nice to see you. How are your mother and grandparents?"

"They're doing fine, I'll bring them in soon. Luigi, this is my friend Alex. He's visiting from Connecticut."

"Nice to see you, Alex."

"Luigi, can you have the waiter bring the check please?"

"It's already been taken care of, Dylan." He shifted his eyes and nodded slightly toward Alex, who looked around the room bearing an innocent expression.

"Thanks, again. Everything was wonderful, as usual."

"Take care, Dylan. You too, Alex."

The two men departed the restaurant and climbed into the back of the Escalade for the ride back to Dylan's house.

Earlier that afternoon FBI Deputy Director Clint Landis's executive jet landed at the St. Pete-Clearwater International Airport. A portable staircase was rolled out to the plane's main door, and Landis emerged, where he was met by two of his Clearwater based agents. The three men got into a government sedan parked on the tarmac and drove directly to the St. Petersburg Police headquarters. There they were met by Detective Cardenas-Santos and St. Petersburg Police Chief Leroy Thompson. Hands were shaken all around. The G-men were escorted to a conference room adjacent to the chief's office. A laptop computer sat on the table in an evidence bag. A separate computer was connected to the smart board at the front of the room, a flash drive plugged into its side.

Detective Cardenas-Santos operated the computer, projecting an itemized list onto the whiteboard.

Chief Thompson summarized how the laptop, which appeared to belong to Fred Philips, was found hidden in the back of a closet in Jasmine Carter's apartment. Then, using an electronic presentation pointer, he turned his attention to the display on the board. The list showed the computer files by name with a brief description of the subject matter. The chief went through the listings in enough detail to give the FBI agents an overview of what was found. After discussing the items cataloged on the screen, he continued. "We've had our forensics people comb through every file. There are also several, uh, home movies starring Fred Philips and a host of different females, including the victim. The film featuring Philips and the deceased is the only thing relevant to our case. We've made a copy of that. We're turning the laptop over to your office and not retaining any other copies. You may also take the flash drive. I'll just need a receipt for everything."

Deputy Director Landis had leaned forward, listening intently, his right elbow on the table and his chin resting on his hand. After the chief was finished he adjusted himself in his seat, leaned back and sat up straight. "We appreciate your cooperation on this, Chief Thompson. And let me congratulate you and Detective Cardonas-Santos and your team on an excellent job investigating this case. On behalf of the FBI and the White House, I also appreciate your department's discretion in keeping news of the laptop discovery from public disclosure."

It was, in fact, unusual for such cooperation between state and federal law enforcement agencies. Historically, the FBI and local police departments did not play nice together. However, this case proved to be an anomaly for several reasons. First, other than the movie featuring Philips and Jasmine Carter, none of the other computer records were germane to the murder investigation. Second, although there was a plethora of other evidence cogitable of illicit activity, none of it appeared to involve crimes committed within the jurisdiction of the St. Petersburg Police Department or Pinellas County Sheriff. Chief Thompson saw no point in dedicating considerable resources to an investigation that would ultimately be turned over to the Florida Department of Law Enforcement or the federal authorities anyway. Finally, most law enforcement agencies had come to share a similar disdain for the Philips brothers and their anti-law enforcement rhetoric, in some cases, dating back to Fred Philips's time as a WNN political commentator.

After the meeting concluded, Deputy Director Landis was driven back to the airport. He boarded his jet and was back in Washington in time for a late dinner at his regular Georgetown restaurant.

CHAPTER SIXTY

L ATE FRIDAY AFTERNOON, THE GOVERNOR met with the point man on his crisis team. The man briefed him on the information that had been disclosed by the state to Fred Philips's lawyer.

"Is there anyone on the witness list we can use for our scapegoat media campaign?"

"There doesn't appear to be. Most of the names were associated with law enforcement, including a long list of attorneys. No lay witnesses or other people that the woman associated with were disclosed. It's early on though, so that could change."

"What about our independent investigation?"

"We canvased the area. It appears the woman had visitors now and then, but no one that could be identified in any meaningful way. Also, the apartment complex has no surveillance cameras."

"How's Fred doing? Does he understand I can't communicate with him while he's incarcerated?"

"His lawyer explained it to him. We think he may be dealing with drug and alcohol withdrawal. Otherwise, he seems to be holding up okay."

"Has his attorney been reminding him not to mention my name or my office under any circumstances?"

"Every time the attorney meets with him in person."

"Good. That'll be all."

As soon as the man left his office, the governor texted his press secretary and authorized her to release a previously prepared statement in time for the evening news. The statement read:

"Governor Philips is saddened to hear about the death of the young woman in St. Petersburg. His thoughts and prayers go out to her and her family. The governor is likewise shocked and saddened to hear about the arrest of his brother, Fredrick Philips, in connection with her death. He asks that the public reserve judgment until all the facts come out. Out of respect for all involved, he will have no further comment at this time to avoid any appearance of interference with the legal process."

News of Fred Philips's arrest on a murder charge dominated the statewide evening news channels and was also covered by the national networks. Old video footage and photos of Philips from his time at the World News Now Network accompanied the stories. There was not much coverage on the details of his relationship with the Florida governor beyond the sibling connection.

By the weekend, word started to spread on Chirpster and other social media sites that a laptop computer belonging to Fred Philips had surfaced. A few of the local press outlets contacted the St. Petersburg Police Department for a comment on the matter. Early the following week, the police spokeswoman issued a statement:

"To date, all relevant evidence gathered in our investigation pertaining to the murder of Jasmine Carter has been turned over to both the State Attorney's Office and the defendant's attorney. No laptop was included, and we will have no further comment on the matter."

Some national news outlets, including a cable news channel and several websites, ran with the story of the mysterious laptop. They reported that an unnamed reliable source had confirmed the laptop contained video files of Fred Philips using drugs and engaging in sex acts with various women, some of whom appeared to be prostitutes. There was also speculation that the computer contained files with information about Sunshine State Consulting, a company of which Fred Philips was a principal. The reports suggested there was evidence of financial improprieties involving Sunshine State Consulting and the governor's office.

The Chirpster universe was outraged and characterized the news as an apocryphal story. The overwhelming majority of chirps supported a conspiracy theory that no laptop existed and the governor's political enemies were taking advantage of an unfortunate family tragedy to attack him personally. Most newspapers and electronic media ignored that story angle entirely. Eventually, the Chirpster Policy Enforcement Program banned all chirps that disclosed or otherwise discussed content alleged to have been contained on a computer belonging to Fred Philips. Chirpster issued a statement defending the decision under its policy prohibiting deceptive or false statements designed to mislead or confuse others or cause harm to a specific person or group of people.

The governor's crisis team continued monitoring the laptop situation closely. The team's contacts at the Florida Department of Law Enforcement reported that they had no knowledge of the existence of a laptop belonging to Fred Philips. All attempts seeking information from the St. Petersburg Police Department circled back to the department spokeswoman who referred to her earlier public statement.

Fred Philips had become increasingly agitated since his attorney asked about the laptop. The sex video he had made with Jasmine Carter certainly wasn't going to help him beat the murder charge. Anything else on the computer was of no consequence, and he was beginning to feel the governor and his attorney were preoccupied with collateral issues and no longer acting in his best interests.

Since his arrest a week earlier, members of the media had been stopping by the jail intermittently requesting to visit Philips. He was under strict instructions from his attorney not to speak with reporters but decided granting an interview would help sway public opinion in his favor. After all, he was a former television personality and knew how to play to an audience.

As luck would have it, a young field reporter and her cameraman signed the visitor log at the Pinellas County Jail about the same time Philips had his change of heart. A detention deputy made the slow walk to the restricted area where Philips was housed in a separate cell and yet again asked if he wished to speak with a reporter who had requested a visit. Anticipating the same "no," he'd been getting, the guard started to turn away and leave again as quickly as he told Philips there was a reporter there asking for him.

"Is it a TV reporter?"

The guard stopped and turned his head toward Philips. "I didn't ask, but she has a cameraman with her."

"It's a female?"

"I just said that."

"Anyone I know?"

"How the hell should I know?"

"Anyone *you* know?"

"Look, do you want to see the woman or not? I don't have all day."

"Yeah, send her back."

The deputy perked up, probably thinking his boring routine day was about to get interesting. "Give me a few. I'll set her up in the interview room and be back to get you."

A short time later, Philips was escorted to a conference room where a young reporter sat at one side of a conference table, staring at her iPad. Her cameraman had set up his lighting and the camera was directed at an empty chair on the opposite side of the table. After Philips was seated, the deputy removed his leg shackles and chained his ankles to steel rings mounted in the concrete floor. Philips rested his cuffed hands on the table.

The deputy turned to the reporter, "We can remove the handcuffs for the interview if you're going to record it, it's up to you."

The woman excitedly replied, "Yes, please."

"My partner will remain in the room, off camera. I'll be stationed outside the door. There's a panic button on the side of the table in front of you. Just push the button in the event of an emergency." He then unlocked and removed Philips's handcuffs, stepped outside, and closed the door.

The reporter introduced herself and the cameraman to Philips and thanked him for agreeing to see her. She went over some preliminary information and then asked Philips if he was voluntarily consenting to answer her questions on camera. He indicated in the affirmative but warned her he would not answer any questions about the pending charge against him. The reporter nodded slightly and turned toward her cameraman. The red light on the camera illuminated, and they began.

"Good afternoon. My name is Natalie Hall. I'm a reporter with Bay News 9. Would you please state your name and then spell it?"

"Fredrick Philips. F-R-E-D-R-I-C-K P-H-I-L-I-P-S. I go by Fred."

The reporter asked a series of preliminary questions, and Philips answered in a calm and relaxed manner, utilizing his old authoritative, on-camera voice.

Suddenly, she pounced. "Did you know Jasmine Carter?"

"I've been advised by my attorneys not to answer that."

"Had you ever met Jasmine Carter?"

"I've been advised by my attorneys not to answer that."

"Were you in St. Petersburg on the night of her murder?"

"I've been advised not to answer that. But as I stated earlier, I live in Tampa."

Philips observed the reporter hesitate and look down at her small screen before continuing. "How have you been treated since you've been incarcerated?"

"Fine, I guess. I have some complaints about the food though. And my bed at home is more comfortable than the one I sleep on here."

"Do you use drugs?"

"Not since I got here." He cackled at his own joke.

"There have been news reports that a laptop computer belonging to you has been found and the contents of the files have been discussed at length. Have you heard about that?"

"Yes."

"Is that laptop yours?"

"It could be?"

"Some of the reports discuss videos of you engaging in sex acts with several women."

"Several women in separate videos or several women all at once?" More laughing at his own answer.

"Let me ask the question another way. The reports about the laptop speculate that it contains images of you using drugs and engaging in sex acts. If these images are confirmed, could this be your laptop?"

"It could be. But I may also be a victim of theft or possibly hacking."

"Have you had an opportunity to speak with your brother, Governor Rocco Philips?"

At the mention of the governor, he twitched and his cheeks turned flush. "Look, this isn't the way I wanted it. I can handle things. I'm not dumb like everyone says I am. I want respect!" Philips pounded his fist sharply on the table. "The interview's over! Take me back to my cell!"

The door buzzed opened, and the other deputy entered the room. He handcuffed Philips and released the ankle shackles from the floor mounts. The two deputies escorted him back to his cell.

The Fred Philips interview was the lead story on the six o'clock news. Following the broadcast, Bay News 9 was flooded with requests for permission to replay the interview. By ten o'clock that evening, it was being shown throughout the state and in many parts of the country. The national news story portrayed the former media personality as a tragic figure in a continued downward spiral who had never measured up to his accomplished older brother.

Rocco Philips was alone in bed when he saw the interview on television. He called Darcie DeLuca. She had already seen it. The governor told her to schedule a press conference for the next day. It was time to do the one thing he had hoped to avoid, but he would take the opportunity to capitalize on it.

CHAPTER SIXTY-ONE

AT TWO-THIRTY THE FOLLOWING AFTERNOON, the governor held his press conference on the capitol lawn. In addition to the regular Tallahassee news reporters, a throng of national news media along with a large crowd of supporters had gathered. The governor stood at a portable podium between display screens and banks of speakers erected to broadcast the speech.

Governor Philips stated, "I stand before you with a heavy heart. This is a very difficult time for my family. I will never be able to accept that my brother is capable of what he has been accused of. I was there the day he was born, and I watched him grow up. He has had his ups and downs, as we all have. I was there to celebrate his successes, and I was there to lift him up when he failed. I will say this, drug and alcohol addiction are diseases. I've done all I can to help my brother, but he continues to battle his personal demons. Please pray for my family and for my dear brother, Fred. I will have no comment about his case pending the outcome of the legal proceedings."

He asked the family of Jasmine Carter to accept his condolences, then spoke of the violence and injustice women and minorities faced. He quickly moved on to the issues of drug abuse and the number of Floridians who died each year from overdoses caused by illegal drugs flooding city streets and rural towns. Finally, he discussed the mental health crisis gripping the state and nation and cited the number of Floridians living with serious mental health issues, pointing out that seventy percent had no access to treatment. He concluded that a vast majority of people in the thralls of drug abuse and mental illness ended up in the criminal justice system, many charged with violent crimes. He then paused for effect, allowing a single tear to fall from his left eye and roll expertly down his cheek without moving to wipe it away. Then he began his pitch.

"We have made great progress with our Rainbow Ribbon Coalition movement. We have brought awareness to the issues of education, criminal justice, social justice, and common prosperity. Issues that, for far too long, have been ignored. Ignored by the elite and the powerful who have run our beloved, yet beleaguered, state. Today I stand before you to say that together, we have begun to do great work, but it's just a beginning. We can and will take on more. We will battle these common enemies of drug abuse and mental illness. And together we will climb to the top of the mountain and declare victory!"

The crowd's applause and shouts quickly became deafening. The ubiquitous RRC signs, banners, and T-shirts were scattered throughout the crowd. A chant of "Italian Stallion" began to gain momentum.

Rocco Philips let it carry on for a moment before raising his hands, requesting silence. "Thank you. Thank you. You're very kind, and I truly appreciate your support. But what's really needed is action. Action in the form of financial support. Support to fund drug counseling and education, drug treatment centers, and mental health wellness and treatment. Our state has a long history of falling short in these crucial areas. It's clear the state cannot tackle these problems on its own. It takes all of us working together. Real sacrifice from each and every one of us."

The RRC fundraising website and a number appeared on the screens with the following message: "You can donate by going to the website or texting DON82RRC."

The lively crowd began a new chant. "Rocc-o-sexual, Rocc-o-sexual, Rocc-o-sexual!" Heads dropped to look at cell phones as fingers worked at light speed to text their donations of five, ten, twenty, fifty, one hundred, two hundred-fifty, or other dollar amounts.

As the crowd's frenzy continued, Governor Philips left the stage without an opportunity for the press to ask questions. He and his chief of staff got into a nearby waiting black Chevy Suburban for the short ride to the governor's mansion.

Staring straight ahead, Philips asked DeLuca, "How do you think it went?"

"It sounded like we were throwing Fred under the proverbial bus, but I think the fundraising tie-in was well received. Our spotters reported a large number of people in the crowd texting donations."

"We needed to begin distancing ourselves from Fred in the event he goes completely off the rails. That babbling interview he gave yesterday was a real cause for concern. What are your thoughts about this laptop matter?"

"We've been unable to confirm the existence of any laptop. I've had Fred's condo searched, and no computers were found. I'm not even sure he used one. I never saw him with a laptop when he was in Tallahassee."

"Me neither. What would he need one for? He never did any actual work that required one. I'm headed home to unwind and enjoy a few stiff drinks. Care to join me?"

Darcie DeLuca thought quickly. "Thank you, sir, but I think I'll head back to the office and monitor the donations. I'll have a report on your desk first thing in the morning."

"Good idea. We need to strike while the iron's hot."

It was a short drive to the mansion. When they reached the residence, the police officer handling the governor's security opened his car door. The governor instructed the driver to take Darcie DeLuca back to her office. As the officer escorted Philips to his front door, he asked him to take his cruiser and go pick up the blonde intern. "It's well before five so she should still be in her office. I'll be in the study."

The officer understood the instructions. "Yes, sir."

CHAPTER SIXTY-TWO

P ROGRESS CONTINUED ON THE YOUTH center. The preliminary site-development work had begun and plans for renovation of the buildings finalized. The plans had been submitted to the St. Petersburg Building Department for approval and permits had been issued in less than a week.

Dylan called Alex. "How's everything going?"

"Great. I'm enjoying spending time with Ben. He said 'dada' last night. It was awesome."

"I read somewhere that babies always say dada before they say mama. Has something to do with dada being easier for them to pronounce in their early development."

"Thanks a lot, Dr. Spock. Did it ever occur to you that Ben likes me better?"

"Or maybe it's that. Definitely one of the two. What's happening with the divorce proceedings?"

"Mediation is scheduled again for next week. My lawyers are optimistic that we may be able to hammer out a final agreement."

"That's good news. I imagine it'll be nice to have that done and over so you can put it behind you and move on."

"You're not kidding. I haven't even looked at a woman up here."

"Come on now, Alex. You expect me to believe that?"

"Okay, so I look all the time. But I don't touch or even approach women. The only person I'd gotten involved with since the separation was Sunni, I mean Jasmine. And look how that turned out."

"Poor girl. You know that wasn't your fault."

"What's going on with that case anyway?"

"It's in the news constantly down here." Dylan gave him a summary of Fred Philips interview and the governor's press conference.

"I heard about that. You believe that guy, taking advantage of this girl's death and his brother's arrest to raise money? What a piece of work. At least he's not in New York anymore. He did enough damage up here. The state's never recovered from his administration."

"And now he's back in office down here, creating the same problems. How do these people keep getting elected?"

"I just said it. By raising money. That and spreading fear and divisiveness."

"Will you be coming back down here for work anytime soon?"

"I've been making excuses and sending other people. I got a lot done before I left, and I'm handling most of the work by phone and Zoom now. Do you think you'll be coming up here anytime soon?"

"I'm not planning on it. I'm busy with work and the foundation."

"How are things with Penel?"

"We talk now and then, but we both have our own lives, 1200 miles apart. She mentions coming down to visit."

"What you need is a local girl to keep you company in between."

Dylan laughed. "That's more your style than mine, Alex."

"You have more women in your life than I do."

"I see one woman on an extremely part-time basis, and you see none. That's really uplifting, Alex. Thanks a lot."

"I'm surprised you're not married."

"Okay, Alex, I gotta go." He hung up.

Dylan spent the rest of the day working in his office. He thought about calling Esther but decided against it. He had not spoken with her much since Jasmine Carter's death, having decided he didn't want to tell her about Alex's involvement.

Privately, he was proud of the way he'd assisted Alex in his time of need. Growing up, Alex and Esther had always helped him. In his younger years, he would have run straight to Esther for advice. He concluded that it was probably her plan all along that he start to figure things out for himself.

CHAPTER SIXTY-THREE

EXCERPTS FROM THE GOVERNOR'S PRESS conference were included in all the papers and news reports broadcast throughout the state. Soon, word of the governor's comments about his brother spread around the Pinellas County Jail. Deputies began referring to Fred Philips as Fredo. Other inmates yelled out the name as Philips passed by. He continued to sink deeper into despair.

Two days after the governor's press conference, just before five o'clock in the morning, a detention deputy at the Pinellas County Jail was making his rounds in the maximum-security unit. When the deputy got to Philips's cell, he found him lying on the concrete floor in his underwear, a torn red pants leg wrapped around his neck. The deputy sounded an emergency alarm, entered the cell, and checked for a pulse and heartbeat. Philips was unresponsive.

Fred Philips was transported by ambulance to Bayfront Hospital and pronounced dead of an apparent suicide at 7:02 a.m. His attorney and brother were notified by the Pinellas County Sheriff's Office. Rocco Philips was at home, alone, when he received the news.

Upon being told of his brother's death, a strange calm overcame him. Rocco Philips was an undiagnosed psychopath, but even he was confused by his complete lack of emotion. He sat silently with his own thoughts as the early morning wore on and his cell phone constantly buzzed with phone calls and text messages. He ignored them all. Word of Fred Philips's suicide was all over the news.

Philips loved his brother but had been sincere when he'd stated publicly that he'd done all he could to help him. Fred was a lost soul. It was a polite way of saying he was a perpetual fuck up. The bottom line was that Fred had possessed information that could prove harmful to him. He had begun to worry his brother was losing it and, thus, Fred had posed a serious threat. That threat was now extinguished.

Philips never forgave his advisors for convincing him to resign from office when he was governor of New York. He'd vowed to never let that happen again. He was, after all, the Italian Stallion. He'd climbed his way back and was now poised to soar even higher on the national stage.

He continued to evaluate possible threats. The conjecture about Fred's missing laptop was just that, a bunch of contrived hype designed to defame him and his family. He had the best investigators and intel money could buy, and no was able to confirm the existence of the reputed laptop. The media had been helpful in dispelling the rumors. Polls conducted by the governor's office concluded that a majority of the public believed there was nothing to it.

The only other person left who could bring him down was Darcie DeLuca. Notwithstanding his public image, among his repulsive traits, Rocco Philips was a misogynist and a homophobe. Darcie had explained her personal preferences to Philips several years ago, when he'd harassed her for the first time. The information only seemed to arouse Philips, and he pursued her more vigorously. Ultimately, Darcie, a laser-focused career woman, was able to convince him she was more valuable as a trusted aide. After some negotiation, they'd agreed to limit her duties to manual stimulation and he had stuck to the arrangement. She had been with him since his reemergence in Florida politics and proven over time to be a loyal soldier and valued advisor. Further, she was complicit in his schemes and had almost as much to lose as he did. Philips finally concluded she wouldn't be a problem.

Satisfied that everything was in its proper place, Philips decided it was time to plan his mourning tour and strategize on how to leverage his brother's death most effectively. Potential political and financial windfalls awaited him, provided the right plan was put into place. He called Darcie. She was smart and cunning, and she also gave a good hand job.

Darcie DeLuca was on her back in bed when her cell phone rang. Her girlfriend's face was buried between her legs. She glanced at the phone but was about to climax and decided not to answer. She would call back shortly and tell the governor she'd been in the shower.

Later that morning, Dylan was in his office when Shirley knocked on the door and told him, "Hey, did you hear that the governor's brother who was charged with murder killed himself in jail?"

Dylan looked up at Shirley. He'd never told her directly about Alex's involvement with the case, but he hadn't intentionally kept it from her either. She was his trusted employee and confidante. He simply had not asked her to do anything in connection with the assistance he rendered to Alex, so he wasn't sure how much she knew.

"Really? That case keeps getting stranger."

"You're not kidding. You may want to call Alex. I'm sure he'd like to know." Shirley smiled, winked at Dylan, and returned to her office.

Dylan shook his head and smiled to himself, appreciating the fact that Shirley was so perceptive. He called Alex on his cell phone. "Did you hear the news?"

"What news? I've been in meetings all morning."

"Fred Philips is dead. Apparently, he killed himself in jail."

"Wow. That case just keeps getting weirder by the day."

"No kidding. The good news for you is that should put an end to the criminal case. The focus now will be on his death and what happened in the jail. Any minute chance of your involvement in the case coming to light just vanished forever."

"Yeah, I suppose you're right. Justice has been served and then some. It's not like the guy was facing the death penalty. Thanks for letting me know. I've got to get back to work."

"Sure thing. I knew you'd want to hear the news."

As soon as it hit the news, Fred Philips's death began trending on Chirpster. Discussions ranged from suicide to death by law enforcement designed to look like suicide. The governor's office issued a statement through his spokesperson.

> "Governor Philips was shocked and saddened to hear about the death of his beloved younger brother, Fred Philips. He is too brokenhearted at this time to speak personally about the tragedy. We ask that the public respect the governor's privacy as he undergoes the grieving process, and the governor wishes to reiterate the urgent need for additional funding for mental illness and suicide prevention."

The Rainbow Ribbon Coalition fundraising information was displayed across the crawl on all television stations broadcasting the statement.

Mainstream media reported the preliminary cause of death as suicide, pending an autopsy. Coverage also speculated on alternate theories. A common theme emerged that featured varying degrees of law enforcement complicity. The articles discussed the governor's criminal justice reform movement and his anti-law enforcement rhetoric as possible motives.

News of Fred Philips's death had legs for several days before the media finally moved on to something else. After delegating the responsibility for his brother's funeral arrangements, the governor took the opportunity to leave Tallahassee for Little Palm Island in the Florida Keys, a longtime vacation sanctuary for the rich and famous. Access was limited by boat or seaplane and a premium placed on that level of privacy. A day later, the blonde intern from Florida State College of Law arrived and kept the governor company for two days. She left a day before the governor departed.

CHAPTER SIXTY-FOUR

DYLAN WAS BUSIER THAN EVER working on the foundation. In addition to his involvement with the renovation and construction of the youth center, he was busy getting the St. Gregory scholarship program off the ground. The foundation was awarding sixteen initial scholarships for the upcoming school year, and Dylan was actively involved in the selection process.

In addition to its website and marketing program, the foundation promoted the scholarship opportunities in several other ways. Over the past decade, St. Gregory had experienced a significant shift in the demographic makeup of its congregation. There'd been a considerable increase in minority membership. Additionally, low-income households comprised a larger portion of the parish than in the past. Accordingly, current active parishioners proved to be a good starting point from which to draw qualified applicants.

However, most members of the congregation lived near St. Gregory, and Dylan desired a wider geographic applicant pool. After much research and due diligence, he partnered with a private nonprofit organization called Great Beginnings based on the city's southside. They provided Pre-K and Kindergarten for predominantly minority and poor students, and the program was loosely modeled after the Pinellas County Fundamental School Program. There was a strict student code of conduct that emphasized respect and accountability. Students wore uniforms and parental involvement was required. Most students in the Great Beginnings program applied for admission to the county's Fundamental schools but the demand for seats was great and exponentially exceeded supply. A lottery system was utilized and about ten percent of all applicants were awarded a spot.

Great Beginnings also offered after school programs for elementary and middle school students, providing after school snacks, tutoring, and access to a state-of-the-art library, as well as opportunities to participate in sports and other physical activities. Students were required to change into uniforms that resembled physical education clothing, everything provided to them at no cost.

Each St. Gregory scholarship prospect was required to complete an application and furnish a handwritten essay on the topic of what education means to them and why they wish to attend St. Gregory. School transcripts and three personal written references were also required. Finally, one parent or legal guardian had to complete a separate application. The parental application included questions on the parent's background, the reasons they wanted their child to attend St. Gregory, and their current involvement level with their child's academic and extracurricular activities.

Dylan understood that some parents faced personal issues and hardship themselves, but he also felt strongly that a child's best chances for success occurred when parents were actively involved in the child's life. He couldn't help everyone, and he wanted to select candidates with the best potential for success. The scholarship program was not a babysitting service or a place to park a child and expect the school to singlehandedly furnish an education.

Given the late start in launching the program, a higher-than-expected number of applications were submitted. In Pinellas County, most school choices were made months prior to the announcement of the foundation scholarship program. Shirley and Cheryl performed the initial application reviews. Students submitting incomplete information were notified of the omissions with a strict deadline for curing the defects. Once the initial applications were reviewed and complete, Dylan and Cheryl met with Father Scully and the school principal, Dawn Reedy, to evaluate each one. The list was eventually pared down to a group of finalists. Finalists and a parent or legal guardian underwent personal interviews conducted with Dylan, Father Scully, and Ms. Reedy. The winners were presented to the foundation board for final approval.

More than half of the scholarships had been awarded to minority students. Although race had not been an identifying factor in the application and selection process, the objective of seeking candidates outside of the parish boundaries was to draw a more diverse candidate pool, and Dylan was pleased with the results.

A luncheon was held at the Vinoy honoring the scholarship winners, and family members were invited to celebrate the students' achievement. Father Scully and Dawn Reedy addressed the group, and Dylan also gave a speech.

Dylan's central theme focused on poverty as a state of mind and education as the key to success. Not just formal education but a genuine intellectual curiosity. He told the story of a young boy who grew up poor without a dad because his father abandoned him and his mom when the boy was an infant. He talked about drugs, gangs, crime, and the other distractions the young man faced growing up and the special people in the boy's life and how they made a difference in keeping him on track. He talked about the young man's successes, accomplished through hard work and discipline. He also spoke of his setbacks, including how the young man's athletic scholarship offer was withdrawn just prior to beginning college. He told the group the young man enjoyed success in life through the grace of God and the lessons he learned from all the people who loved and cared for him. In conclusion, Dylan said, "That man is here today, and I'd like to introduce him. He's the one who has been standing before you."

After the ceremony, Dylan went home and told Alex about it. When they were through discussing the award luncheon, Dylan asked about the divorce.

"It's all finalized. We'll have fifty-fifty shared custody of Ben. That's the most important thing to me. Anita got the house and a financial settlement as outlined in the prenup agreement. Nothing else. The child support award was calculated per state guidelines, and I'm fine with it. I want Ben to have a similar quality of life growing up when he's with Anita."

"That all sounds like good news, Dylan."

"It is all good. I know, go ahead and say it. I landed on my feet once again."

"I wasn't going to say that."

"Then my next guess is you're going to lecture me on getting involved with another woman?"

"Nope, wrong again. You don't go looking for love, it finds you. In my opinion, going out and searching for love only leads to problems."

"You've become so wise and mature. I don't know if I can hang out with you anymore."

"Don't worry about it, Alex. You possess enough immaturity for the both of us."

"Roger that. Now that I'm officially a free man, it may be time for me to head back to Florida soon. You know any girls you can introduce me to?"

Dylan laughed. "If I knew any nice girls, the last thing I'd do is introduce them to you."

"I didn't say anything about introducing me to *nice* girls."

CHAPTER SIXTY-FIVE

Autopsies in Pinellas County were performed by the Office of the District Six Medical Examiner and the reports typically took thirty to sixty days. The investigation of Fred Philips's death was handled by the Florida Department of Law Enforcement and the report was completed, reviewed, and released in five days.

Exactly one week later, Fred Philips's funeral was held at Sacred Heart Church in downtown Tampa. The governor sat quietly in the front row with his sister and their family. He wore dark glasses and did not speak during the service. A small private reception was held at the Tampa Club before the governor flew back to Tallahassee.

Approximately a week later, the governor was back in his office. His official schedule was full, portraying a public image that he was back doing the people's work. Darcie DeLuca was in his office going over some matters on his schedule when his secretary buzzed his office.

"There's a call on the line. You may want to pick this up," she said over the speakerphone.

"Who is it?"

The secretary hesitated. "It's the deputy director of the FBI."

"What the hell does he want? I've never met the man."

"He said it's a courtesy call that requires your immediate attention."

The governor picked up the receiver and pressed the blinking line. "Governor Philips."

"Governor, this is Clint Landis, Deputy Director of the FBI. I have a federal warrant for your arrest. This is a courtesy call, sir. My team is about five minutes out from the capitol building. In deference to your office, I'm notifying you for purposes of escorting you out of the building and into federal custody quietly and without fanfare."

"Sir, I am the governor of the great state of Florida. I have never heard of you. I have no way of verifying your identity or the veracity of this phone call. I would expect a law enforcement officer of the standing you claim to hold to act in a more dignified manner and extend some professional courtesy. If you are who you claim to be, then you should know the name of my personal attorney. I suggest you call him." He slammed down the phone.

Darcie DeLuca sat motionless, her heart pounding against her chest as she listened intently to the half of the conversation she could hear.

The governor held his head in his hands and rubbed his temples. "That was some clown claiming to be a deputy director of the FBI with a federal warrant for my arrest."

"On what charges?"

"He didn't say. He just said he was calling as a courtesy to negotiate my surrender in the next five minutes."

"Do you think it's legitimate?"

"How the hell should I know? If I jumped every time some nut threatened me, I wouldn't have time to do anything else."

"Why don't I go back to my office and make some calls? See what I can find out?"

"Good idea."

Darcie DeLuca rose from her chair and walked out of the office in as calm a manner as she could muster. She had prepared for this day in the event it really was the FBI calling and had two contingency plans. One involved fleeing the country with her girlfriend and leaving everything behind. Her girlfriend was good in bed, but that was far from the only skill set Darcie valued.

Darcie's girlfriend was a self-employed charter pilot who flew her own leased Citation CJ4 out of the Tallahassee airport. Her clientele consisted of business executives, celebrities, and high net worth individuals. She and Darcie had a signal in the event Darcie was forced to flee. Upon receiving the sign, her girlfriend would drop everything and head to the airport, perform her preflight check, and have the plane ready as soon as possible. She would file an initial flight plan for another location in Florida. Once they were in the air, she would refile for a predetermined island in the Caribbean, chosen for its lack of an extradition treaty with the United States.

Darcie DeLuca sat in her office and thought for a moment. The governor appeared not to take the phone call seriously, but she couldn't be sure. She decided not to run. She would wait and see what happened. The second plan only took a matter of seconds to execute. She called a contact at the Capitol Police, which was under the direction of FDLE and the agency responsible for furnishing the governor's security detail. It took a moment for the man to come on the line. "Hi, Lenny. Darcie DeLuca."

On the other end, silence.

"Lenny are you there?"

Finally, a voice replied, "Yeah, I'm here."

"Listen, I'm calling because the governor just received a phone call from a man claiming to be a deputy director of the FBI and said he had a federal warrant for his arrest. The governor asked me to investigate the validity of the call. Do you know anything about it?"

More silence.

Uh oh. "Lenny, talk to me goddammit."

"I wish I had something to tell you. Excuse me I have to take another call." He hung up.

Shit. This is *the real deal.*

Darcie pulled out a small, non-government issued portable computer from her oversized handbag and typed some letters and numbers into the keyboard. She remotely tapped into the governor's computer and accessed one of his private bank accounts, then set up an external wire transfer and keyed in an eight-figure sum. Next, she typed in the information for an untraceable offshore account and hit Send. Staring at the screen, she tapped her fingers on the desk as the little circle rotated and an empty horizontal bar filled with green color. When the message Transaction Complete appeared, she exhaled sharply and looked out the window. Several unmarked black sedans were pulling up to the entrance of the Capitol Tower building. She watched as the cars came to a stop and almost a dozen men departed and headed for the building. She placed her computer back in her bag and calmly left her office. She took the elevator to the lobby and held her breath while the doors opened.

Darcie stood and looked around as several people walked through the lobby. An unusual number of Capitol Police officers were stationed at the doors, but they were not preventing anyone from coming or going. She glanced at the officers, not recognizing anyone. She began to walk confidently toward the exit, her bag on her right shoulder. Pulling out her phone, she looked down at it, appearing preoccupied and disinterested in her surroundings. No one stopped her, and she continued to the parking lot where she got into her car and drove away.

As Clint Landis led a group of FBI agents and Capital Police officers into the building, Governor Philips sat at his desk and buzzed Darcie to ask if she'd found anything out about the earlier phone call. She didn't answer, so he turned his attention to other matters and forgot about it.

A few minutes later his secretary buzzed his phone.

He answered, "What is it?"

She whispered into the phone, "I just got a text from a secretary downstairs. Something's going on. A bunch of FBI guys are on the elevator. She's not sure what they're doing. I thought you'd want to know."

Rocco Philips dropped the phone and sprang into action. He quickly ran through the alternatives in his mind. Arrest and prison, not an option. Neither was leaving elected office again. The people had elected him, and this was where he belonged. He decided, given the circumstances, that martyrdom was the best choice. For the most part, the media had always protected him. They'd proven to be a trusted ally during his political comeback. He expected they would portray him as a hero who'd died at the hands of a violent, overbearing federal law enforcement agency. That would be his legacy.

Philips opened a desk drawer and removed a Ruger handgun. The compact nine-millimeter pistol held fifteen rounds. He checked the magazine and racked the slide, flipped off the safety and then sat calmly in his chair and waited.

About sixty seconds later, there was banging on his office door. "Rocco Philips. FBI. We have a federal warrant for your arrest."

No answer.

"Governor, I'm not going to announce again. Open the door."

Again, no answer.

Deputy Director Clint Landis motioned for the other team members to take positions on either side of the door. He tried the handle, and the door was unlocked. As he turned the handle, gunfire originating from inside the office pelleted the door and walls, splintering wood in all directions.

Landis felt a warm sensation in the upper portion of his left arm. He ignored it, kicked in the door, and led the group into the office.

Philips stood unloading the balance of the magazine in their direction.

Several agents and officers returned fire. Philips fell slouched over, landing face-first on his desk.

An alarm sounded, indicating to the occupants of the Capitol Tower that they should exit immediately per evacuation procedures. Within another minute, the alarm was turned off and a message was broadcast, instructing everyone to remain in their offices until further notice.

The Capitol Tower was descended upon by additional law enforcement, fire, and emergency medical personnel. The scene was processed by an investigation team with the Florida Department of Law Enforcement. FBI Deputy Director Clinton Landis was transported to Tallahassee Memorial Hospital where he was treated and released for a gunshot wound to his left arm. Governor Rocco Philips was pronounced dead at the scene.

CHAPTER SIXTY-SIX

A MEDIA FRENZY DESCENDED UPON TALLAHASSEE. News of the shootout between Governor Rocco Philips and the FBI, resulting in the death of the Florida governor, dominated the news as the lead story on virtually every broadcast and in newspapers across the country. Despite the tragic, straightforward facts of the incident, the narratives were split among the divisive, well-defined ideological and political lines.

The FBI and Florida Department of Law Enforcement issued a joint statement that a laptop computer belonging to the late Fredrick Philips was in the possession of law enforcement. At the time of the laptop discovery, a federal investigation into corruption involving Rocco Philips's office had already been underway. Evidence gathered from the laptop had been crucial to sealing the case. The statement continued.

"A federal warrant had been issued and the FBI was at the Capitol building to arrest Rocco Philips on charges of wire fraud and tax evasion related to the Rainbow Ribbon Coalition project. Philips had been notified of the arrest in advance as a courtesy, and rather than submit peacefully and answer to the charges, he elected to ambush the FBI agents and Florida Department of Law Enforcement officers when they arrived. One FBI agent was struck by a bullet fired from Philips's gun and received a nonlife threatening injury. He is expected to make a full recovery."

The statement also outlined a summary of the evidence taken from the laptop and included details of Fred Philips complicity in his brother's illegal activities through his company, Sunshine State Consulting. Calendars, emails, text messages, and financial records confirmed that the Rainbow Ribbon Coalition was nothing more than a shell organization that spent little to none of the funds it collected on its stated objectives. It was merely a conduit for soliciting donations for nonexistent projects designed to enrich the Philips brothers.

Finally, the discovery of the laptop had launched a separate investigation by the Florida Department of Law Enforcement on state charges involving theft, fraud, embezzlement, and misappropriation of government resources. Although the criminal investigation was now suspended due to the death of the former governor, the state would continue its investigation for purposes of identifying donors to the Rainbow Ribbon Coalition and furnishing refunds from the recovered assets.

The front-page headline of the *Tampa Bay Daily Herald* read, "Insurrection at the Capital Building." The article portrayed the FBI investigation as the latest example of overreaching, heavy-handed federalism and described a botched arrest operation resulting in the needless death of Florida's governor. The reporter characterized the events as one of the most egregious attacks on state sovereignty in US history.

That same evening, Florida Lieutenant Governor Michelle Chen was sworn in as governor by the chief justice of the Florida Supreme Court. Governor Chen had not been part of Rocco Philips's inner circle and was rarely present in any of his meetings. Chen installed her own chief of staff into Darcie DeLuca's office and made no attempt to contact her to assist with the transition.

Darcie DeLuca laid low for several days following the incident. Her phone message and automated email reply stated that she was shocked and traumatized by the recent events and unable to respond while she sought treatment for her condition. Meanwhile, she spent several days in bed, watching Netflix and entertaining her girlfriend. She had been somewhat surprised when law enforcement did not attempt to contact her as part of their investigation following Philips's death.

After several days in seclusion, she scheduled her own press conference and read from a prepared statement she had written herself. "This had been a difficult time for me. I have been traumatized by the recent events involving the disclosure of alleged wrongdoing by my former boss, the late governor. However, I have managed to reach deep into my soul and tap my inner strength. The death of Rocco Philips and the realization that he can no longer hurt me has given me the courage to stand before you today. While I had no knowledge of any wrongdoing involving Governor Philips and his brother, I have suffered great indignities. As a gay woman, I was the enhanced victim of abuse at his hand for a very long time. I was verbally and physically abused. Rocco Philips forced me to perform sex acts on him. I sympathize with any woman who is the subject of such abuse. But I ask you to imagine the utter humiliation of forcing someone to engage in sex acts the victim finds inherently repulsive. I do not believe I will ever be able to get over the emotional trauma and mental anguish I have suffered. Consequently, I have made the difficult decision to leave politics and vanish from the public eye. Please pray for me that I may begin the healing process and one day experience inner peace."

It took several days for daily updates of the tragic events at the Florida capitol to taper off. A few days after the media moved on to the next story and the nation turned its collective attention elsewhere, Dylan and Cheryl flew to New York. They were scheduled to appear at St. Mary School for the groundbreaking ceremony signifying the commencement of construction on the Cheryl Tomassi Fieldhouse and Esther Lott Theater. After the frenzy getting the St. Gregory School scholarships awarded before the new school year, the decision had been made to defer the inaugural St. Mary scholarship program until the following year.

Dylan spent time with Alex, who was celebrating his divorce. He'd purchased an Audi R8 Panther Edition coupe and a Breitling chronograph gold and steel watch and begun dating a former model currently enrolled in medical school at New York University.

Alex's new house in Greenwich included a nursery for Ben and servants' quarters for a live-in nanny. The interview process for the nanny position came down to two finalists, a fifty-four-year-old spinster who'd previously cared for an old money New York family and a twenty-three-year-old blonde from Sweden with no previous experience. Alex hired the spinster.

The president of the United States awarded FBI Deputy Director Clint Landis the Public Safety Office Medal of Valor for the bravery he displayed in limiting the loss of life during former Florida Governor Rocco Philips's ambush on law enforcement officers.

Following Darcie DeLuca's heartfelt statement, twenty-six women came forward to tell their stories of the loathsome abuses they'd suffered at the hands of Rocco Philips. A prominent Tallahassee law firm that had earned its reputation taking on the tobacco and pharmaceutical industries filed suit on behalf of the women against the estate of Rocco Philips.

The Florida Department of Law Enforcement announced that a fund had been established for purposes of refunding donations made to the bogus

Rainbow Ribbon Coalition. A website was set up for purposes of registering and filing claims. The procedures were spelled out, including an explanation of the formula to be applied for determining payouts once the filing deadline was reached. The announcement also stated a figure that represented the amount of money recovered to date. An addendum stated that efforts remained underway to recover the balance of the missing donation money and described how Philips had managed to transfer ten million dollars to an offshore account minutes before he'd opened fire on law enforcement. The FDLE was working with the FBI and CIA to track down the missing funds, but they were stymied by the sophistication of the complex web of anonymous, offshore bank accounts the funds had passed through.

Dylan and Cheryl stayed in suites at the Greenwich Delamar. In the late morning on the day following their arrival, Dylan asked Cheryl if she would take a ride with him. They got into their rental car and drove to Stamford. Dylan drove down Cold Springs Road and parked the car across the street from their old house. They both sat quietly in the car for a moment until Dylan got out. He stood next to the car and snapped a picture of the house with his phone. It appeared much smaller than he remembered, although all the neighborhood trees had grown significantly and seemed to dwarf the homes. Cheryl got out of the car, stood next to Dylan, and put her arm around his shoulder as she stared at the old house.

As they stood there, a small freckle-faced boy with a huge toothy grin ran from around the back of the house with his mother in tow. The boy pushed a small bicycle with butterfly handlebars, a banana seat, and training wheels. When they reached the street, they both waved to Dylan and his mom. The two watched as the boy rode down the street, the back tire wobbling between the training wheels as his mom jogged along holding onto the back of the seat. The little boy shrieked with joy as his mother encouraged him.

As they watched the scene unfold, Dylan looked at his mother. "You know, time really does fly by."

Cheryl gazed back at him. "Truer words have never been spoken."

On the way back, they stopped at John's Best Pizza for lunch. Later that afternoon Dylan left the hotel and drove over to Esther's house. When he arrived, he stood in the driveway and fixated on the large gray house. In all the years they had known each other, they had never been together anywhere except at her home. He went to the back of the car, opened the trunk, and removed a large, slim package wrapped in brown mailing paper. Franklin answered the door in his usual manner and led him down to the riverfront where Esther was seated at a table on the deck. She appeared chipper and was smartly dressed in tan culottes, a light sweater, and tennis shoes. As Dylan approached, she rose from her chair, took a few steps toward him, and embraced him tightly.

They each inquired about the other and then the conversation turned toward the plans for the new buildings at St. Mary. Dylan described them in detail. "It's a large fieldhouse with a gymnasium and separate theater. The gym will have three parallel courts that can be converted into a single main court with expandable seating that closes into the walls. The school basketball and volleyball teams will play their games on the main court, but it can be converted to the multiple-court configuration for practices, PE classes, and recreational activities. There's also two fully equipped locker rooms. The theater has a full modern stage with state-of-the-art lighting, sound, and backstage operations. There's stadium-style seating for three hundred people."

"Dylan, that sounds wonderful."

"There's one other thing." He picked up the package and placed in on the table. "This is for you."

She looked at the large parcel. "What's this?"

"Open it."

She stood and tore at the corners. It was flat but somewhat bulky, so Dylan stood next to her and held it up off the table while she unwrapped it. She pulled the packing paper down from the top and revealed a framed artist's rendering of the new fieldhouse and theater. The large signs above the structures read Cheryl Tomassi Fieldhouse and Esther Lott Theater.

She put both hands up to her mouth and inhaled deeply. "Oh, Dylan, I don't know what to say."

"When I was given the opportunity to name the facilities, it took me only a matter of seconds to decide."

She looked at him with moistened eyes, hugged him again, then looked back at him. "Thank you, I love you so much."

"I love you too. There is one thing I want you to do for me?"

"What's that?"

"I want you to come with me to the grand opening."

"I wouldn't miss it for the world."

Penel came to Connecticut and stayed with Dylan. She met Cheryl, and they all attended the groundbreaking ceremony together and then flew back to Florida. Penal was looking forward to her long-awaited visit, spending more time with Dylan, and eager to see the progress on the St. Petersburg Youth Center she'd heard so much about.

The day after they returned to Florida, Dylan woke up early as he did each morning. He looked over and Penel was still asleep in his bed. He slipped out and went downstairs. Shirley was not in her office yet, but Aengus had brought up the morning papers. However, only the *Wall Street Journal* was on the table. The *Tampa Bay Daily Herald* was missing.

Dylan grabbed a bottle of water from the fridge, pulled up a stool at the kitchen island, and began flipping through *The Journal* when a headline in the Business & Finance section caught his eye. It read, "Florida Newspaper Group Announces Massive Cuts, Layoffs." The article announced that due to protracted decreases in circulation and advertising revenue, the *Tampa Bay Daily Herald* had laid off sixty percent of its workforce and ceased publication of its printed newspaper, effective immediately. The entire production staff had been eliminated, the printing plant shuttered, and the building and equipment put up for sale. The news operation had not been spared from the cuts. Layoffs ranged from national and international correspondents to local reporters. Going forward, the paper would rely on the wire services and reduce local news coverage, including the elimination of high school sports reporting. An online version of the paper would remain available, but the subscription rate was increasing by twenty-five percent.

A NOTE TO READERS

I hope you enjoyed reading *PAPERBOY* as much as I enjoyed writing it for you. Be sure to visit your favorite online retailer and leave a quick review. It only takes a few moments and will mean the world to this writer.

I am always happy to hear from you. The best way to contact me is through my website at authordanromanello.com. You can also sign up for my free newsletter, *Uncommon Sense*, and receive information on author news and commentary, upcoming events, and future books.

Be sure to grab your copy of the next book in the Dylan Tomassi series, *BLINDSIDED JUSTICE*, at your favorite retailer.

BLINDSIDED JUSTICE

(A Dylan Tomassi Novel, Book 2)

Having grown up poor, Dylan is now a successful private investor, wealthy beyond his wildest dreams and living an idyllic lifestyle on Florida's gulf coast. Cognizant of his humble beginnings, he is committed to paying it forward as he prepares for the opening of his charitable foundation's crown jewel.

But crime is raging out of control following the election of an opportunistic carpetbagger and Dylan and those closest to him become victims of a broken system that places them in grave danger. He utilizes his considerable resources to protect those he holds dear, but everyone and everything are not what they appear to be.

An exhilarating action thriller, *BLINDSIDED JUSTICE* drops you in the middle of an epic battle between justice and subversion.

ABOUT THE AUTHOR

DAN ROMANELLO began his career working for a large Florida newspaper before attending law school at the University of Florida. After serving as an assistant state attorney, he entered private practice where he spent more than 20 years as a civil trial lawyer litigating cases in courtrooms throughout Florida. He retired from the active practice of law in 2017 and, before writing *PAPERBOY,* spent the last four years coaching college athletics. He lives in St. Petersburg, Florida.

Like and Follow this author at:

https://www.facebook.com/thedanromanello

https://twitter.com/TheDanRomanello

www.ingramcontent.com/pod-product-compliance
Lightning Source LLC
Chambersburg PA
CBHW021134310726
48971CB00002B/316